THE
DARKEST
STAR

THE
DARKEST
STAR

Jennifer L. Armentrout

TOR TEEN

A TOM DOHERTY ASSOCIATES BOOK

New York

THE DARKEST STAR

Copyright © 2018 by Jennifer L. Armentrout

All rights reserved.

A Tor Teen Book
Published by Tom Doherty Associates
175 Fifth Avenue
New York, NY 10010

www.tor-forge.com

Tor® is a registered trademark of Macmillan Publishing Group, LLC.

The Library of Congress Cataloging-in-Publication
Data is available upon request.

ISBN 978-1-250-17573-1 (hardcover)
ISBN 978-1-250-31467-3 (international, sold outside
the U.S., subject to rights availability)
ISBN 978-1-250-17572-4 (ebook)

Our books may be purchased in bulk for promotional, educational, or business use. Please contact your local bookseller or the Macmillan Corporate and Premium Sales Department at 1-800-221-7945, extension 5442, or by email at MacmillanSpecialMarkets@macmillan.com.

First Edition: October 2018

Printed in the United States of America

0 9 8 7 6 5 4 3

For all the fans of the Lux
series who wanted more.
I love you, guys.

ACKNOWLEDGMENTS

None of this would be possible if it weren't for you, the reader. Without your support, Luc's story would never have ended up in your hands. Thank you from the bottom of my heart and I hope his story is worthy of your support.

Thank you to my agent, Kevan Lyon, who is simply amazing, and a huge thanks to Taryn Fagerness, my foreign rights agent, who gets my books into as many countries as possible. These two women are my dream team. Seriously.

The Darkest Star was a team effort and the Origin series found its home at Tor Teen and with my amazing editor, Melissa Frain, who I think wanted to see a story about Luc just as badly as some of the readers did. Thank you, Melissa and the amazing team at Tor, for believing in this story and supporting it.

Jen Fisher. Girl. You helped me fix this book, and come up with, you know, a plot. So thank you.

Thank you to my assistant and friend, Stephanie Brown, for always being there and finding me as much llama-orientated stuff as humanly possible. Writing books can be a very solitary experience, so I cannot thank my family and friends enough—Andrea Joan, Hannah McBride, Laura Kaye, Sarah Maas, Stacey Morgan, K. A. Tucker, Jay Crownover, Cora Carmack, Drew, and many, many more.

THE
DARKEST
STAR

I

If Mom ever found out I was sitting outside of Foretoken, she
would kill me. Like, legit hide-my-body-in-a-deep-dark-grave
kind of kill me. And my mom totally had the means to do so.

When she went from Momma baking brownies in the kitchen
to *Colonel* Sylvia Dasher, she put the fear of God and then some
in me.

But knowing just how much trouble I'd be in if I got caught
obviously hadn't stopped me, because here I was, sitting in Heidi's
car, applying yet another coat of lipstick with a shaky hand. Shoving the lipstick wand back into its tube, I watched fat raindrops
bomb the windshield. My heart threw itself against my ribs as if it
were determined to punch its way out.

I couldn't believe I was here.

I'd rather be home, finding random things in my house to take
pictures of and posting them on Instagram. Like those new gray-
and-white vintage candleholders Mom had bought. They'd look
amazing paired with the pale blue and pink pillows I had in my
bedroom.

From the driver's seat, Heidi Stein sighed heavily. "You're
second-guessing this."

"Nuh-uh." I eyed my final results in the little mirror in the
visor. My lips were so red, it looked like I'd French-kissed an
overripe strawberry.

Nice.

And my brown eyes were way too big for my roundish, freck-
led face. I looked scared, like I was about to walk naked into class
twenty minutes late.

"Yeah, you are, Evie. I can see it etched into the five hundred coats of lipstick you just applied."

Wincing, I glanced over at her. Heidi looked completely at ease in her strapless black dress and dark eye makeup. She had that cat-eye thing down, something I couldn't re-create without looking like an abused raccoon. Heidi had done an amazing job on my eyes before we'd left her house, though, giving them a smoky, mysterious look. I thought I actually looked pretty good. Well, except for the whole looking-scared part, but . . .

"Is the red lipstick too much?" I asked. "Do I look bad?"

"I'd be into you if I liked blondes." She grinned when I rolled my eyes. "Are you sure you want to do this?"

I peeked out the window at the dark, windowless building squeezed in between a closed boutique shop and a cigar store. My breath hitched in my throat.

FORETOKEN was written in black paint above the red double doors. I squinted. On second thought, the name of the club looked like it had been spray-painted on the gray cement. Classy.

Everyone who went to Centennial High knew of Foretoken, a club that was packed every night, even on Sundays, and was notorious for allowing outrageously fake IDs to slide by.

And Heidi and I were most definitely seventeen and 100 percent in possession of some fake-as-hell driver's licenses that no one in their right mind would believe were real.

"Because I'm worried you're not going to have fun." Heidi poked my arm, drawing my attention. "Like you'll get freaked out and call Zoe. And you know you can't call April to come get you either. That girl is not allowed within a ten-block radius of this place."

I drew in a shallow breath that felt like it went nowhere. "I'll have fun. I swear. It's just . . . I've never done this before."

"Done what? Gone somewhere you weren't supposed to? Because I know that's not true." She held up a finger, and the nail looked like it had been dipped in black ink. "You have no problem breaking and entering when it comes to climbing around abandoned buildings to take pictures."

"That's different." I dropped the lipstick into my little wristlet. "You sure these IDs are going to work?"

She shot me a bland look. "Do you know how many times I've been here and had no problems? Yes, you do. You're stalling."

I was totally stalling.

Looking out the window again, I could barely suppress the shiver tiptoeing down my spine. Puddles were forming in the vacant street and there was no one on the sidewalks. It was like once the sun went down and Foretoken unlocked its doors, the streets emptied of everyone who exhibited an ounce of common sense.

Foretoken also had the reputation for something entirely different than allowing fake IDs.

Aliens were known to hang out here.

Like legit extraterrestrial beings that had come from trillions of light-years away. They called themselves the Luxen, and they looked like us—well, a better version of most of us. Their bone structure was often perfect, their skin airbrush-smooth, and their eye colors were shades that we humans couldn't achieve without contacts.

And not all of them had come in peace.

Four years ago, we'd been invaded, totally Hollywood movie–level invaded, and we'd almost lost the war—almost lost the entire planet to them. I'd never forget the statistic that had dominated the news once the TVs starting broadcasting again: 3 percent of the world's population. That was 220 million people lost in the war, and my father had been one of them.

But over the last four years, the Luxen who hadn't been on Team Kill All the Humans and had helped fight their own kind had been slowly integrated into our world—into our schools and jobs, government and military. They were everywhere now. I'd met plenty of them, so I didn't know why coming here freaked me out so much.

But Foretoken wasn't school or an office building, where the Luxen were typically outnumbered and heavily monitored. I had a sinking suspicion that humans were the minority beyond those red doors.

Heidi poked my arm again. "If you don't want to do this, we don't have to."

I twisted in the seat toward her. One look at Heidi's face told me that she was being genuine. She would turn the car on and we'd go back to her place if that were what I wanted. Probably end the night gorging ourselves on those cupcakes her mom had picked up from the bakery. We'd watch really bad romantic comedies until we passed out from a ridiculously high caloric intake, and that sounded . . . lovely.

But I didn't want to bail on her.

Coming here meant a lot to Heidi. She could be herself without worrying about people getting all up in her business about who she was dancing with or checking out, whether it be a boy or another girl.

There was a reason why the Luxen were comfortable coming here. Foretoken was welcoming to everyone, no matter their sexuality, gender, race, or . . . *species*. They weren't a human-only establishment, which was rare nowadays when it came to privately owned businesses.

Tonight was special, though. There was this girl Heidi had been talking to, and she wanted me to meet her. And I wanted to meet her, so I needed to stop acting like a dork who'd never been to a club before.

I could totally do this.

Smiling at Heidi, I poked her back. "No. I'm fine. I'm just being stupid."

She stared at me a moment, cautious. "You sure?"

"Yes." I nodded for extra emphasis. "Let's do this."

Another moment passed and then Heidi broke out in a wide smile. She leaned over, throwing her arms around me. "You're the best." She squeezed me tight, causing me to giggle. "Seriously."

"I know." I patted her arm. "I put the *awe* in *awesome*."

She snort-laughed in my ear. "You are so weird."

"I told you I am." I untangled myself from her hug and then reached for the car door before I could chicken out. "Ready?"

"Yep," she chirped.

I climbed out and immediately shrieked as cold rain hit the bare skin of my arms. I slammed the door shut and then darted across the dark street, my hands forming the weakest shield ever over my hair. I'd spent way too much time curling the long strands into waves for the rain to ruin it.

Water splashed over my heels, and when I hopped up on the sidewalk, I was surprised I hadn't slipped and fallen face-first into the asphalt.

Heidi was right behind me, laughing as she rushed under the awning, shaking the mist of rain from her pin-straight crimson hair.

"Holy crap, this rain is cold," I gasped. It felt more like the rain that fell in October than in early September.

"My makeup isn't running down my face like I'm some chick about to be killed in a horror movie, is it?" she asked, reaching for the door.

Laughing, I tugged on the hem of my strappy blue dress I normally wore leggings under. One wrong move and everyone would see the skull design on my undies. "No. Everything is where it should be."

"Perfect." She pulled on the massive red door with a grunt.

Violet light spilled outside, along with the heavy thump of music. A small entryway appeared, leading to another door, this one a deep purple, but between that door and us was a man sitting on a stool.

A gigantic man.

A huge bald man wearing jean overalls and absolutely nothing else under them. Studs glinted from piercings all over his face—his eyebrows, under his eye, and his lips. A bolt went straight through his septum.

My eyes widened. Oh my word. . . .

"Hey, Mr. Clyde." Heidi grinned, completely unfazed.

"Yo." He looked from her to me. His head cocked to the side as his eyes narrowed slightly. That couldn't be good. "IDs."

I didn't dare smile as I pulled my ID out of the little card slot on my wristlet. If I did smile, I would totally look like I was seventeen and close to peeing myself. So I didn't even blink.

Clyde glanced at the IDs and then nodded toward the purple door. I peeked at Heidi, and she winked.

For real?

That was all he was going to do?

Some of the tension leaked out of my neck and shoulders as I shoved my ID back into its slot. Well, that was exceptionally easy. I should do this more often.

"Thanks!" Heidi patted Clyde's big, bulky shoulder as she went for the door.

I was still standing in front of him, like an idiot. "Th-thank you."

Clyde raised a brow as he pinned me with a look that had me quickly wishing I'd just kept my mouth shut.

Heidi reached back, grabbed my hand, and yanked me forward as she opened the second door. I turned, and every one of my senses was immediately overwhelmed by, well, *everything*.

The thump of heavy drums poured from speakers, coming from every corner of a large room. The tempo was fast, the lyrics a blur as white light burst from the ceiling, shining over the dance floor for a few seconds before tossing it back into shadowy darkness.

People were everywhere, sitting at high, round tables and lounging on oversized couches and chairs under alcoves. The center of the floor was a mess of twisting, churning bodies, arms up and hair flying. Overlooking the throng of dancers was a raised stage shaped like a horseshoe. Rapidly flickering bulbs lit the edge of the stage, and dancers up there urged on the crowd below with their shouts and their hips.

"This place is pretty wild, isn't it?" Heidi curled her arm around mine.

My wide gaze bounced from person to person as the scent of perfume and cologne mingled. "Yeah."

"I so want to get on that stage." Heidi grinned when my eyes widened. "That is my goal for the night."

"Well, it's always good to have goals," I replied dryly. "But can't you just walk up there?"

Her brows lifted and she laughed. "No. You have to be *invited* up there."

"By who? God?"

She snorted. "Something like that—" She squeaked suddenly. "There she is."

"Where?" Eager to see this girl, I scanned the crowd.

Heidi stepped into my side and slowly turned so our bodies were angled toward one of the large shadowy recesses behind the tables. *"There."*

Soft candlelight lit the alcove, casting a glow over the area. I doubted candles were safe in a bar, but what did I know? More oversized chairs flanked a gold-trimmed, crushed red velvet couch that looked like an antique. Two of the chairs were occupied. I could see only profiles. One was a blond guy staring down at his phone. His jaw was clenched like he was trying to snap a walnut shell in two with his teeth.

Across from him was another guy with a shockingly blue Mohawk—like, Smurf blue. His head was thrown back, and even though I couldn't hear him, I could tell he was letting out a laugh of the deep-belly variety. My gaze shifted to his left.

I saw her then.

Good Lord, the girl was gorgeous.

Easily a head taller than Heidi and I, she had the most awesome haircut *ever*. Her dark hair was buzzed on one side and shoulder length on the other, showing off the sculpted angles of her face. I was so jealous of that haircut, because I didn't have the courage or the face to pull something like that off. She looked a little bored as she eyed the dance floor. I started to turn back to Heidi, but then a tall figure cut in front of the girl and sat on the couch.

It was a man with sandy-blond hair cropped close to the skull. The haircut reminded me of what you saw from guys in the military. From what I could see of his profile, he appeared to be older than we were. Maybe in his midtwenties? A little older? He didn't exactly look happy. His mouth was moving a mile a minute. My gaze shifted to who he'd sat down next to.

My lips parted on a soft inhale.

The reaction was startling and embarrassing. I sort of wanted to smack myself, but in my defense, the guy was stunning, the kind of beauty that almost didn't seem real at first.

Messy brown hair toppled over his forehead in waves and curls. Even from where I was standing, I could tell that his face knew no bad angle, the kind of face that needed no filter. Impossibly high and broad cheekbones were paired with a carved, square jaw. His mouth really was a work of art, full and tipped up on one corner, forming a rather impressive smirk as he eyed the man who'd sat next to him. I was too far to away to see his eyes, but I imagined they were just as striking as the rest of him.

But the allure went beyond the physical.

Power and authority radiated from him, sending an odd shiver curling down my spine. Nothing about what he was wearing stood out—just dark jeans and a gray shirt with something written on it. Maybe it was the way he was sitting, thighs spread and one arm tossed over the back of the couch. Everything about the lazy sprawl looked arrogant and somehow misleading. He appeared as if he were seconds away from taking a nap even as the man beside him became more animated, but there was the distinct impression in the way his fingers tapped along the gold trim that said he could spring into action at any given second.

"Do you see her?" Heidi asked, startling me.

Goodness, did I forget Heidi was there or something? I had, which meant I needed to get a grip. Dude was hot, but come on. I was here for Heidi.

I dragged my gaze from the guy and then nodded. None of these people, except for the blond guy and the one who'd just sat down, looked old enough to be anywhere near this club. Then again, neither did we. "Is that her?"

"Yes. That's Emery." She squeezed my arm. "What do you think?"

"She's really pretty." I glanced over at Heidi. "Are you going to go over and talk to her?"

"I don't know. I think I'm going to let her come to me."

"Seriously?"

Heidi nodded as she sucked her bottom lip between her teeth. "The last three times, I approached her. I think I'm going to let her find her way to me this time. Like, to see if it's just a one-sided interest or not, you know?"

My brows rose as I stared at my friend. Heidi was not shy or patient, nor did she get nervous. That could only mean one thing. I clasped my hands together. "You're really into her, aren't you?"

"I like her," Heidi said after a moment. A small grin appeared. "I just want to make sure she likes me." She lifted a shoulder. "We've talked a little and danced, but she hasn't asked for my number or asked to meet up outside of here."

"Have you asked for hers?"

"No."

"Will you?"

"Hoping she'll make that move." Heidi exhaled loudly. "I'm being stupid. I should just ask for hers and get it over with."

"You're not being stupid. I would be doing the same thing, but I think you should at least ask for her number tonight. *That* should be your goal."

"True," she replied, forehead creasing. "But that stage . . ."

"Stop with the stage." I laughed.

The truth was, I wasn't the best person to be dispensing relationship advice. I'd only ever been in one somewhat serious relationship, and Brandon and I had lasted a whopping three months, ending right before summer.

I broke up with him over text.

Yep.

I was that person.

As awful as it was to admit to even myself, I'd only gone out with Brandon because all my friends had been coupling off and, well, peer pressure was a bitch and I wanted to feel whatever it was they kept going on and on about every time they posted online or in their snaps. I wanted to be . . . I wanted to know what that felt like. I wanted to fall in love.

And all I did was fall into boredom.

I drew in a shallow breath as my gaze found its way back to the couch, the one with the guy with the messy bronze hair. He looked about my age. Maybe a year or two older. Instinct told me that anything to do with him would not be boring. "Who . . . who is that?"

Heidi seemed to know who I was talking about without my pointing him out. "His name is Luc."

"Just Luc?"

"Yep."

"No last name?"

She laughed as she spun me around, away from them. "Never heard his last name. He's just Luc, but you see the blond guy who appears as friendly as a rabid porcupine?"

"The one looking at his phone?" I smiled, because that felt like a good description of the guy.

She started walking around the dance floor, pulling me with her. "He's a Luxen."

"Oh." I resisted the urge to look over my shoulder to see if he was wearing a metal band around his wrist. I hadn't noticed it when I saw the phone in his hands.

The band was known as a Disabler, a form of technology that neutralized the Luxen's otherworldly talents, which were derived by what the Luxen called the Source. *The Source.* Still sounded completely made-up, but it was real and it was deadly dangerous. If they attempted to go all Luxen on someone, the Disabler stopped them by releasing shocks equivalent to being hit by a Taser. While that wasn't pleasant for anyone, it was particularly painful and debilitating to the Luxen.

Not to mention, all public spaces were designed to immediately quell any incidents that might arise with the Luxen. The shiny reddish-black metal above every door and the specks in the ceilings of most establishments were some kind of aerosol weapons that had no effect on humans.

Luxen?

Whatever mist it dispensed supposedly caused extreme pain. I'd never seen it happen—thankfully—but my mom had. She'd told me it was one of the worst things she'd ever witnessed.

I doubted Foretoken had such a weapon installed.

Because I was nosy, I asked, "Is Luc a Luxen?"

"Probably. Never been close enough to him to tell for sure, but I'm guessing he is." Their eye color was usually a dead giveaway, as was the Disabler. All registered Luxen were required to wear them.

We stopped near the stage, and Heidi slipped her arm free. "But the guy with the blue hair? He's definitely human. I think his name is Kent or Ken."

"Cool," I murmured, curling an arm over my stomach. My wristlet dangled. "What about Emery?"

Heidi looked over my shoulder at Emery. Relations of the fun and naughty kind between humans and Luxen were illegal. No one could stop a Luxen and a human from getting together, but the two couldn't marry and they faced hefty fines if their relationship was reported.

"She's human," Heidi answered.

I honestly couldn't care less if a Luxen and human wanted to engage in a little bow-chicka-wow-wow. Not like it impacted me on any level, nor was it any of my business, but relief still swept through me. I was happy that Heidi wasn't trying to get involved with someone she'd have to hide her relationship with while also risking paying thousands of dollars or going to jail if she couldn't. Heidi would be eighteen soon. The responsibility to pay such a ridiculous fine wouldn't fall on her family.

I glanced up at the stage again, spotting the girl dancing closest to us. "Wow. She's beautiful."

Heidi followed my stare and nodded. The girl was older with a head full of shimmery blond hair. She spun and twisted, her body snakelike in its movements.

Arms in the air, hands clasped together, the girl whirled, and her skin was . . . it was fading and blurring around the edges, almost like she was disappearing right in front of us.

Luxen.

The girl was definitely on the away team. Luxen had this wild ability to assimilate our DNA and look like this, like humans, but that wasn't their true appearance. When they were in their real form, they glowed like a high-watt lightbulb. I'd never seen what was under all the bright light, but my mom told me they had skin that was nearly translucent. Kind of like a jellyfish's.

Heidi cast a grin over at me. "I'm going to dance. You coming?"

I hesitated as I looked at the teeming throng. I did love to dance . . . in the privacy of my bedroom, where I could look like a double-jointed Muppet. "I'm going to grab a water first."

She pointed a finger at me. "You better join me."

Maybe I would, but just not now. As I backed up, I watched her disappear onto the mass of twisting bodies, and then I wheeled around and moved along the edge of the stage. I made my way to the bar, squeezing between two occupied stools. The bartender was down at the other end of the bar, and I had no idea how to get his attention. Should I lift my hand and wave it around like I was hailing a cab? I didn't think so. That would look stupid. How about the three-finger Hunger Games salute? I'd just seen the movies on TV last weekend. A marathon of all four movies had been playing, so I felt like I could pull it off. *I volunteer for a glass of water.*

Luckily, the bartender was slowly making his way to where I stood. I opened my wristlet and tapped on the screen of my phone. There was a missed text from Zoe. A call from April and—

An odd feeling started at the nape of my neck. It was like a breath with no air. It traveled down my spine, raising the tiny hairs all over my body. It felt like . . .

It felt like someone was standing right behind me.

I zipped up my tiny purse and then glanced over my shoulder, half expecting to come face-to-face with someone, but no one was there. At least not creepily close or anything. I scanned the crowd. There were so many people, but no one seemed to be paying any attention to me. The feeling, though, it only increased.

I swallowed hard as my gaze tracked over to that alcove.

The guy who'd sat down was gone, but the big guy in overalls—Mr. Clyde—was inside. He was leaning over that old-looking couch, speaking to Luc, and Luc was—*oh God*—he was staring straight at me. Anxiety burst open, spreading through my system like a noxious weed.

Did Clyde realize we had fake IDs?

Okay. Wait a second. He had to have known from the moment we came in that we had fake IDs, and even if he now had a problem with the IDs, why would he report that to Luc? I was being ridiculously paranoid—

"Yo. Need a drink?"

Twisting back to the bar, I nodded nervously. Bartender was a Luxen. Those bright green eyes were definitely not in the human color wheel. My gaze dipped. The silver band was tight around his wrist. "Just a, um, a water."

"Coming up." He grabbed a plastic cup, filling it up with water he poured from a bottle, and then shoved a clear straw into it. "No charge."

"Thanks." I took the cup and then slowly turned back around. What to do? What to do?

Sipping my drink, I ambled around the stage and stopped by a pillar that looked like a unicorn had puked glitter all over it. I stretched up on the tips of my toes and scanned the crowd until I found Heidi.

A wide smile broke out across my face. She wasn't alone. Emery had come to her, and she was eyeing Heidi like I eyed tacos on most days.

That was what I wanted at some point in my life, for someone to look at me like I looked at tacos.

Heidi's back was to me, her shoulders swaying as Emery's arm swept around Heidi's waist. I so wasn't going to bust up their little dance party. I would wait until they were done. Meanwhile, I was going to do my best not to think about how I looked lurking by the edge of the dance floor. I knew I probably looked pretty dumb. Maybe even a little creepy. I took another drink. Wasn't like standing here all night was a viable—

"Evie?"

I turned at the sound of a vaguely familiar voice. Shock splashed through me. A girl from school stood behind me. We had had class together last year. English. "Colleen?"

She smiled as she tilted her head. The tops of her cheekbones glittered. She had the smoky eye thing going on, just like me. "What in the world are you doing here?"

I lifted a shoulder. "Just hanging out. You?"

"With some friends." Her brows knitted as she tucked several strands of blond hair behind her ear. "I didn't know you hung out here."

"Um, this is my first time." I took a sip of water as I glanced over my shoulder. I didn't know Colleen all that well, so I had no idea if this was something she did every weekend or if this was her first time here too. "Do you come here a lot?"

"Sometimes." She smoothed a hand over the skirt of her dress. It was a slightly lighter blue than mine, and strapless. "I didn't know you liked to come—" Her head jerked toward the dance floor, and her flushed cheeks deepened in color. I thought maybe someone had called her name. "I've got to go. You'll be here for a while?"

I nodded, having no idea how long I'd be here.

"Cool." She started backing up, grinning. "We should chat later. Okay?"

"Okay." I wiggled my fingers at her and watched as she turned, slipping past the churning bodies along the edge of the dance floor. I knew that people from school came here, but I guess I hadn't been expecting to see anyone, which was stupid—

A hand landed on my shoulder. Startled, I jumped and water splashed over my hands and hit the front of my dress. Wrenching forward, I pulled away from the grip and spun around, prepared to throat-punch whoever had grabbed me, like my mom had taught me. I froze, my stomach dropping as I found myself staring into the studded face of Mr. Clyde.

Oh, this couldn't be good.

"Hi?" I said weakly.

"You need to come with me." The hand on my shoulder grew heavier. "Now."

2

My stomach hollowed as I glanced at the sparkly pillar like it could be of some help. "Uh, why?"

His dark gaze met mine, and all I could focus on was the tiny diamond under his eye. That had to be such a painful piercing. He didn't speak as he gripped my arm with a meaty hand and wheeled me around. Panic blossomed as I looked at the dance floor, unable to see Heidi or Emery in the crush of dancers.

Heart pounding in my chest, I held on to my water as Clyde led me away from my pretty pillar. My cheeks caught fire as a few people at the tables stared. An older girl smirked and shook her head as she lifted a glass of amber-colored liquor to her mouth.

This was *so* embarrassing.

I was about to be thrown out. Just my luck. Which meant I was going to have to text Zoe or someone to come get me, because I was not going to ruin Heidi's night. Not when Emery had approached her. I was going—

Clyde wasn't leading me to the front of the club.

He suddenly cut to the left, dragging me along with him. My heart dropped all the way to my pinched toes when I realized where he was taking me. The shadowy alcove—to the couch.

Sitting in the same lazy sprawl as before, still tapping those long, tapered fingers, was Luc. His lips tilted up at the corners.

Shock stole my breath. Normally I would be relatively excited about chatting with an extraordinarily hot guy—especially with a guy who, *wow*, had such thick black lashes—but everything about this was wrong.

I was not the kind of girl who got randomly picked out in a club and then escorted by someone who looked they belonged in the WWE for a one-on-one with the resident hottie. I wasn't knocking myself. I was just the embodiment of the Triple A.

Average life.

Average face.

Average body.

And what was happening right now was *not* average.

"What is going . . . ?" I trailed off as Clyde steered me past the blond Luxen, who was *still* staring down at his phone, toward one end of the couch. The hand left my arm and then landed on my shoulder once more.

"Sit," Luc said, and that one word was spoken in the kind of voice that probably left a trail of really bad decisions in its wake.

I sat.

Not that I had much choice. Clyde sat me down and then lumbered off, bumping and moving people out of the way like a human bulldozer.

Pulse pounding erratically, I stared in the direction Clyde had gone in, but I was completely aware of the boy sitting about a foot from me. My hand was shaking, and when I inhaled deeply, I caught the scent of pine and soap over the bitter tang of alcohol. Was that coming from him? The pine and soap scent? If so, he smelled amazing.

Was . . . was I really *smelling* him?

What was wrong with me?

"You can stare in Clyde's direction all you want, but no amount of wishful thinking is going to bring him back," Luc advised. "Though, if you're wishing for that and it works, then you're made of awesome dark magic."

I had no idea how to respond to that. My brain had emptied of all words. The plastic cup crinkled under my fingers as the music halted for a brief second. Several people on the dance floor stopped, their chests rising and falling heavily. Then a thick, steady tempo of drums picked up, and the people on the dance floor just lost it.

My eyes widened as fists pumped the air and the dancers on the stage dropped to their knees, slamming their palms against the floor. Shouts grew louder and louder, a rising crescendo that matched the drums. Voices rose, chanting out lyrics that made goose bumps explode all over my arms.

Safe from pain and truth and choice . . .

A shiver broke out across my skin. Something about this—the song, the chants and cheers—was familiar. The weird feeling of déjà vu rose as I frowned. I didn't recognize this song, but that wiggling sensation was still dominating the back of my brain.

"Like the song?" he asked.

Slowly, I turned my head toward him. His smile was a wolf's smile, leaving me wholly unnerved. I lifted my gaze. The breath I'd taken punched out of my lungs.

The smile faded from his lips, and he stared at me like . . . I don't know. There was an almost surprised pinch to his striking features, but his . . .

His eyes.

I'd never seen eyes like his. They were amethyst in color, a vibrant, polished purple, and the black lines around his pupils were irregular, fuzzy even. They were utterly beautiful eyes, but . . .

Heidi's suspicion was correct. "You're a Luxen."

The blond staring at his phone snorted.

Luc tilted his head to the side as the odd look washed away from his face. "I'm not a Luxen."

Yeah, I was calling total BS on that. Humans did not have eyes like that unless they were wearing contacts. My gaze shot to the hand that rested on his thigh. There was a leather cuff around his wrist with some kind of weird stone in the middle of it. An oval gem that was a kaleidoscope of milky colors. What he wore was not a Disabler used to keep a Luxen from killing half of the people in this club in less than ten seconds.

"Are you a human wearing freaky contacts then?"

"Nope." He raised a shoulder in a halfhearted shrug. Why would he deny being a Luxen? Before I could ask that question, he spoke again. "Are you enjoying yourself tonight?"

"Uh, yeah . . . I . . . think so."

He bit down on his plump lower lip, drawing my attention.

Goodness, those were totally kissable lips. Not that I was thinking about kissing him or anything; it was just a pure, clinical observation that anybody in my situation would make.

"You don't sound very convincing. You actually look like you would rather be anyplace but here," he continued, those heavy lashes lowering once more. "So, what are you doing here?"

His question jolted me.

"Your friend comes here a lot. She fits in. Has fun. You have never come here." Those lashes lifted and his odd eyes latched on to mine. "And I would know if you had been here before."

I stiffened. How in the world did he know this was my first time here? There had to be at least a hundred people here, and all of them blended together.

"You stand by the dance floor all by yourself. You don't have fun and . . ." His stare dropped, coasting over the front of my dress. Without looking, I knew he was staring at the water stain. "You don't fit in here."

Okay. Wow. That was blunt, and I finally found my voice. "This is my first time here—"

"I already knew that." He paused. "Obviously. Because I just said that."

Irritation chipped away at the unease and confusion. Luxen or not, I didn't know who in the hell this guy thought he was. He was rude, and I was not going to sit here and let someone talk to me like that. "I'm sorry. Who are you again?"

That half smile spread an inch. "My name is Luc."

Was his name supposed to hold the answers to the universe? "And?"

"And I want to know why you're here."

Frustration pricked at my skin. "Are you like the official club greeter or something?"

"Something like that." He kicked a booted foot up onto the square glass table in front of him as he leaned toward me. The distance between us evaporated. His eyes met and held mine. "I'm going to be blunt with you."

I barked out a harsh laugh. "You haven't been blunt already?"

He ignored that comment and didn't look away, not once. "You shouldn't be here. Like, of all the places for *you* to be, this is the last place. Isn't that right, Grayson?"

"Beyond right," answered the blond Luxen.

Warmth burst open in my chest, burning up my throat. Sucking in a sharp breath, I willed my face to remain emotionless even though what he said stung for reasons it shouldn't. It didn't matter if he was human or not or that I'd never seen this guy before and probably would never see him again once I walked out of this stupid club. Having someone tell you that you didn't fit in didn't feel good. Ever.

No way was I letting him, a complete stranger—an *alien*—get the better of me. At the end of the day, he was a jerk-face, and I wasn't going to allow him to hurt my feelings. Absolutely no way.

Holding his gaze, I summoned a little of my mom—scary mom. "I didn't realize I needed your permission to be here, *Luc*."

"Well," he drawled, his broad shoulders tensing, "now you do."

I drew back. "Are you serious?" A shocked laugh escaped me. "You don't own this place. You're just some—" I cut myself off before I said something incredibly ignorant. "You're just some guy."

Tipping his head back, he chuckled deeply. "Now, I know that's not what you were about to say or what you're really thinking." His fingers tapped along the back of the couch, and I wanted to reach over and smack my hand down on them. "Tell me what I really am. I *cannot* wait to hear it."

"Whatever." I glanced over at the dance floor, unable to see Heidi, since it appeared the crowd had tripled all of a sudden. Dammit. "I came here to hang out with my friend. That's all I'm doing. It has nothing to do with you."

"Everything has to do with me."

I blinked once and then twice, waiting for him to laugh, but when he didn't, I realized I'd officially met the most arrogant being on this planet.

"By the way, you're not hanging out with your friend. Like I pointed out earlier, you were standing by the dance floor . . . just standing there, all by yourself." His eerie eyes tracked over my face with such intensity that the tips of my ears started to burn. "Is that what you normally do when you hang out with your friend? Stand by yourself, drinking water?"

My mouth moved, but there were no words. He was absolutely the most antagonistic thing I'd ever met.

The one side of his lips tipped up even farther. "You're not even old enough to be in here."

I was willing to bet he wasn't either. "I'm old enough."

"Really?"

"Your big burly friend checked my ID and let me in. Ask him."

Luc's chest rose deeply. The breadth of his shoulders stretched the worn gray cotton. His shirt read NO DRAMA LLAMA. That shirt was a lie. This boy was all about the drama llama. "Let me see your ID."

I scowled. "No."

"Why not?"

"Because you're some rando dude in a club. I'm not going to show you my ID."

That gaze slid back to mine. Challenge was etched into every striking feature. "Or maybe you don't want to show me your ID because it proves you're not twenty-one."

I said nothing.

One eyebrow rose. "Or is it because you think I'm a Luxen?"

"Now *that* sounds like the real issue," Grayson chimed in, and my gaze darted to him. He'd finally put his phone down. Unfortunately. "That's probably also why she's not comfortable. I bet she's one of those people."

"Those people?" I repeated.

Grayson's ultra-blue eyes met mine. "The kind scared of the Luxen."

I shook my head as the music and the club seemed to fade into the background. It was then when I realized no one, not a single person in here, approached this area. Everyone gave this alcove a wide berth.

Luc made a noise under his breath. "Does being around Luxen like this, out of the public eye, bother you? Scare you?"

"No. It doesn't." That wasn't exactly true, because come on, I wasn't part of the Hate All Luxen train roaring through every city and small town, but they were scary. You had to have absolutely no common sense if you didn't fear them a little. They'd killed millions of people. Maybe these two guys hadn't, but they weren't wearing Disablers. They could kill me before I even saw it coming.

But the urge to prove that I didn't care if they were Luxen or not rode me hard. My ID wasn't real. It didn't have my address or real name on it. Showing it to him wouldn't endanger me. I sat my drink down on the table and pulled the ID out of the thin slot.

"Here you go," I chirped, forcing as much brightness into my voice as possible.

Luc lifted his hand off the back of the couch and took the card. His fingers brushed over mine in the process. Static crackled, sending a tiny jolt up my arm. Gasping, I pulled my arm back.

His smile kicked up a notch, and my stomach pitched. Had he done that purpose? Shocked me? His lashes lowered. "Nola Peters?"

"Yes. That's my name." That was so not my name. It was a combination of two cities I'd never visited—New Orleans and St. Petersburg.

"It says you're twenty-two." He lowered his hand as he looked at me. "You're not twenty-two. I bet you're barely seventeen."

I inhaled deeply through my nose. I was not "barely" seventeen. In six months I'd be eighteen. "You know, you don't look like you're twenty-one."

"Looks can be deceiving." He moved the card over his fingers, flipping it back and forth. "I have a baby face."

"Doubtful."

"I like to think I'm going to age gracefully. People will think I've found the fountain of youth."

"Okay," I said, drawing the word out. "Look, it hasn't been nice talking to you, so I have to go. I need to find my friend—"

"Your friend is busy, you know, having fun." His grin spread into a cheeky smile that would've been endearing if I didn't want to straight up punch him in the face. "Unlike you. You are *not* having fun."

"You're right. I'm not." My eyes narrowed, and I resisted the near primal urge to pick up my water and throw it on him. "I was actually trying to be polite—"

"Quaint," he murmured.

Oh my God, this guy was going to make my head spin right off my shoulders. "But truth time? I really don't want to spend another minute in your presence." I started to get up. "You're a dick and I don't know you. I don't want to get to know you. Peace out, home skillet."

"But I know who you are." He paused. "I know who you really are, Evelyn."

3

He knew my name. Not my fake ID name, but my real name. It felt like the entire building was moving even though nothing had. My spine turned to steel as an icy sensation drenched my skin. I stared at him for several moments. "How do you know my name?"

He looked up at me through his lashes as he moved both arms to the back of the couch. "I know a lot of things."

"Okay. You just took creepy to a creeptastic level of unknown proportions." It was time to find Heidi and get the hell out of here.

Luc chuckled again, and the sound would've been nice, attractive even, coming from anyone else. "I've been told that a time or two in my life."

"Why am I not surprised? Don't answer that question," I said when he opened his mouth. "Can I have my ID back?"

He shifted suddenly, dropping his feet to the floor. Without warning, our faces were inches apart. As close as we were, it was hard not to get a little lost in the beauty of his features. And as close as we were, it was also hard not to get really freaked out. "What if I told you a truth? Would you tell me one in return?"

I clamped my mouth shut so hard, my jaw ached.

"You were right earlier. I'm not twenty-one," he said, the gleam in his eyes now dancing. "I'm eighteen." There was a short pause. "*Almost* nineteen. My birthday is December twenty-fourth. I'm a Christmas miracle. Now it's your turn."

"You're creepy," I replied. "That's a truth I will tell."

Luc was silent for a moment and then he laughed—laughed long and hard, surprising me. "Now, that is not how you play this game, *Evie.*"

I sucked in another sharp breath.

Suddenly the overhead lights came on, flooding the entire club in a harsh white glare. I squinted, momentarily confused. The music cut off, causing shouts of dismay. Those on the stage froze. People on the dance floor slowed and then stopped, exchanging bewildered looks as they panted.

"Damn." Luc sighed. "This is going to be inconvenient."

Someone darted past the alcove, heading toward the bar area. Forgetting about the stupid ID, I twisted in my seat and watched the guy disappear down a narrow hall.

"Hell." Luc shot to his feet as fast as a strike of lightning. And holy canola oil, he was *tall,* and if I had been standing, he would have towered over my five-foot-five-inch frame. "Here we go again." Sounding bored, he looked to Grayson. "You know what to do. Move them out."

Grayson slipped his phone into his pocket and stood. Then he was gone, moving so fast he was nothing but a blur. If he'd been wearing a Disabler, he wouldn't have been able to move like that.

"You're coming with me," Luc announced.

"What?" I squeaked. "I'm not going anywhere with you. Like, I wouldn't even walk from here to the dance floor with you."

"Well, that's kind of offensive, but we're about to be raided and not in the fun way."

There was a fun way of getting raided?

Luc reached down, wrapping his hand around mine. A charge of static passed through me again, duller than before. He pulled me the rest of the way up. "And hey, you're underage. Don't think you want to get busted, right?"

I didn't, but that didn't mean I was going anywhere with him. "I need to find Heidi. She's—"

"She's with Emery." Luc pulled me around the low glass table. "She'll be fine."

"And I'm supposed to trust you?"

He looked over his shoulder at me. "I didn't ask you to trust me."

That was about as reassuring as a loaded gun pointed at my head, but the door up front burst open and the RAC—Retinal Alien Check—drones entered the club.

A shudder rocked me.

I hated those drones.

They hovered about five feet off the floor, all black with the exception of a white light in the center of the top. RAC drones became a thing about two years ago. There was something about Luxen pupils that the RAC registered as nonhuman. Mom once tried to explain the science behind it, but I'd checked out when she'd gotten to the part about rods and cones doing something with infrared light. All I knew was that it picked up on alien DNA.

And if they were here, that meant they were searching for unregistered Luxen—aliens like Luc and Grayson, ones without Disablers.

Those drones weren't here alone. Pouring into the group like a horde of white insects were the Alien Response Task Force—ART—officers, and they were decked out to take care of business. Dressed in all white, their faces shielded by shiny helmets. Two had normal-looking assault rifles. Another two carried the heavier, thicker version—a rifle that was an electronic pulse weapon. One hit with that and a Luxen was done for.

Luc pulled me between the couch and a chair, tugging me toward the bar. I started to dig my feet in, because I'd rather be busted being underage in a club than get caught with a potentially unregistered alien.

That wasn't a fine.

That was immediate jail time for harboring and abetting and a ton of other fancy criminal words. I tried to pull my hand free as Luc started dragging me along. "Let go!"

"Everyone, down!" one of the officers shouted.

Chaos erupted.

People ran in every direction, scattering like roaches when the lights were flipped on. Bodies crashed into me. I yelped as my heels slipped on the wet floor. I lost my footing. Fear exploded like buckshot, shooting out darts of panic. I started to fall.

"Oh no, you don't." Luc's grip on my hand tightened, and he yanked me up. One heel came off my foot and then the other as he dashed behind the bar, pulling me along with him.

My bare feet slipped in pools of liquid I didn't even want to think about. A guy vaulted over the bar, landing in a crouch. Another came over, slipping on the spilled drinks. He went down, smacking into the floor, immediately followed by yet another person falling right behind him.

Everything was happening too fast.

A rapid firing—*pop, pop, pop*—commenced. Screams rose over the commotion, and my heart leapt in my throat as I tried to see over the stage. What was happening? I couldn't see, and I had no idea where Heidi was in this mess.

Luc dipped down, sliding under the bar and blocking people from entering. I followed as several bottles flew off the wall. Glass and liquid exploded, flying everywhere.

"Such a damn mess," Luc muttered, his jaw locked in disgust.

The mess was the last thing I was worried about as we suddenly raced down a dark hallway, blowing past others who were scrambling to get out of the way. Cutting to the right, he pushed open a door.

A black void enveloped us as the door swung shut behind me. Terror rose as I threw up my free hand. "I can't—I can't see anything."

"You're fine."

Luc charged ahead, walking at a fast clip I struggled to keep up with. There was a distinctive smell of laundry detergent. He reached another door and we slipped through it just as the door behind us exploded open.

"Stop!" a man yelled.

My heart was going to launch itself out of my chest. We darted into a dimly lit hallway. Luc twisted suddenly, grabbing me around the waist. I shrieked as he lifted me up.

"You're too slow," he complained.

Luc picked up speed, moving so fast the hall was nothing but a blur of hair and walls. He hung a sharp left and then I was sliding off him, down his side. I staggered back as he placed a hand on what appeared to be just a wall. A second later a door appeared, sliding open.

"What the . . . ?" I stared in shock. There were hidden rooms here? Why would they have hidden rooms? Only serial killers had hidden rooms!

Luc shushed me—he actually *shushed* me as he yanked me forward. I skidded into the dark room. He let go, and I stumbled, bumping into the wall. I whipped around. This wasn't a room. It was the size of a closet! Barely big enough for one person, and he was sliding the hidden door to the right until the tiny sliver of light disappeared, pitching us into darkness.

Holy crapola . . .

I pressed against the wall. My pulse pounded so fast, it felt like an ocean roaring in my ears as I strained to see anything in the small space. There was nothing but darkness and Luc.

And Luc was practically on top of me.

His back was against my front, and no amount of trying to climb into the wall was going to help me put space between us. The piney scent from earlier was definitely coming from him. It was all I could smell. How in the world did I end up here? What series of really bad life choices had I made that led me to this very moment?

I could be at home, snapping pretty pictures with my phone or separating knee-high socks from the crew-cut ones—

Something slammed out in the hallway. I jumped, knocking into Luc. I reached out, my hands landing on his back. He shifted suddenly, and every muscle in my body locked up. My hands were suddenly flattened against his chest, and that wasn't just a chest. Those were pecs—pecs as hard as the wall behind me.

I started to yank my hands away, but even in the complete darkness, he caught them, keeping them right where they were. I started to protest, but whatever I was about to say died on the tip of my tongue as I felt his breath skate over my forehead.

We were close, way too close.

"They have to be back here," a disgruntled voice boomed from the hall. Static crackled over a radio. "I've checked the other rooms."

My breath caught. What would happen if they came in here? Would they shoot first and ask questions later?

A heartbeat passed, and then the hair around my ear stirred as Luc whispered, "I hope you're not claustrophobic."

I turned my head, tensing as my nose grazed his cheek. "It's a little late for that."

"True." He shifted again, and I felt his leg brush mine. I shivered. "We just need to play it cool in here for a little bit and then they'll be gone."

A little bit? We'd already been in here for far too long, but I could hear the guy out there, pacing back and forth. "Does this happen often?"

"About once a week."

"Lovely," I muttered, and I thought maybe he chuckled under his breath. I was going to smack Heidi for coming here, to a club that got raided once a week. "What are you guys doing here to get raided?"

"Why do you think we have to be doing something?"

"Because you're getting *raided*," I whispered-yelled back.

Luc's fingers moved, and I felt his thumb smooth over mine, sending another acute shiver through me. "Do you really think they need a reason to come in here, search for people? To hurt people?"

I knew who "they" were without asking. The ART Force answered to our government. "Are you registered?"

"I already told you." His breath now coasted over my cheek. "I'm not a Luxen." There was another pause. "You . . . you smell."

"Excuse me?"

"You smell like . . . peaches."

"It's my lotion." I closed my hands into fists as frustration mingled with fear and something . . . something *heavy*. "I don't want to talk to you anymore."

"Good." There was a pause. "I can think of a lot more interesting things to do in a tiny, dark space that would pass the time."

My muscles locked up. "You try something and you will regret it."

Now I heard him chuckle quietly. "Calm down."

"Don't tell me to calm down," I snapped, so furious I wanted nothing more than to scream. "I'm not who those men are looking for. I have no reason to stay quiet."

"Oh, you do." His thumb glided over my palm.

"Stop that."

"Stop what?" His low voice dripped innocence as his thumb dragged over the center of my hand again.

"That." With my heart thumping, I tried again to free my hands. "And come to think of it, how do you—"

The shrill ring of a phone silenced me.

Where was that—*Oh no.*

It was my phone, ringing from my wristlet.

"Well, that's truly inconvenient timing." Luc sighed, dropping my hands.

I felt around until I was able to open the wristlet and pull my phone out. I quickly silenced it, but it was too late.

A shout from the hallway sent a bolt of fear through me as I felt . . .

Luc's cool hand suddenly curve around the nape of my neck. What the—

His nose suddenly touched mine and when he spoke, I could *feel* his words on my lips. "When I open this door, you're going to run to your left. There's a bathroom. Inside said bathroom is a window you can climb out of. Do it fast."

A fist or a boot slammed into the hidden door.

"Are you kidding me?" I demanded, in disbelief. "We could've just run outside through the bathroom?"

He slid his hand off my neck. "But then we wouldn't have had these precious moments alone."

My mouth dropped open. "You are—"

Luc *kissed* me.

One moment I was a heartbeat away from cursing him out with an impressive display of f-bombs, and then his mouth was just *there,* on mine. His head tilted just the slightest. I drew in a startled breath and my fingers spasmed. The phone slipped out of my hand, thudding softly on the floor. Just the tip of his tongue touched mine, sending little shivers of pleasure and bitter panic through me, and then he shifted his head, slightly pulling back.

"A Luxen didn't kiss you, Evie." His lips brushed mine. "But neither did a human."

"What?" I said breathlessly, my heart lodged somewhere in my throat.

Luc's hand slipped off my neck, and I fell back against the wall. He pivoted. "Get ready."

My thoughts were completely scattered. Oh God, I wasn't ready for this. "But—"

Luc slid the hidden door open. The light from outside was blinding, and it took a terse second for my eyes to adjust. The first thing I saw was one of those EMP guns pointed directly at Luc. He stepped forward, throwing his hand out.

He caught the officer in the chest, grabbing a fistful of white material. Lifting the man up off his feet, Luc tossed the officer across the hall. The man slammed into the wall, cracking the plaster. He fell forward onto the floor, out cold.

"Holy crap." I stared down at the prone man. That kind of strength . . .

Static crackled from a radio hooked to the man's chest, and a voice echoed from it. Backup was coming.

"Go," Luc ordered, his pupils constricting and churning with inner white light, a sure sign that a Luxen was about to slip into their true form. "I'll see you later."

4

Heidi flopped onto her back, sprawling across the center of her bed. "That was *wild*. We so need to go again."

Sitting on the floor of her bedroom, I stared up at her. "No. No, we do not need to go again. Ever. Again."

She laughed, and I shook my head as I dragged my hands down my freshly scrubbed face. Climbing through that bathroom window in a dress and dropping down into an alley had not left me in pristine condition. The first thing I'd done when we got back to Heidi's place was shower, rinsing off the grime from the bottom of my feet. I'd also smelled like I'd robbed a liquor store and then rolled around in all the alcohol I'd stolen.

It had been Heidi calling me while Luc and I were hiding in our own Room of Requirement. She'd gotten outside somehow and was panicked, but she had been smart and gone straight to her car, where I found her waiting for me.

"We were almost busted. Could you imagine what my mom would've done? She would've flipped," I said from behind my hands. "Not only that, I was so worried you'd been trampled to death or something."

"Girl, I freaked out too. I had no idea where you were until Emery said you were with Luc."

Ugh.

If I never heard his name again, I'd die happy. Not only was he an unbelievable jerk, he had kissed me—actually kissed me.

A Luxen didn't kiss you, Evie. But neither did a human.

What was that supposed to mean? There were only Luxen and humans. Unless he considered himself in a league of his own, which wouldn't be surprising. After just a short time with him, I knew there were very few beings in this universe who had an ego as massive as his.

"I cannot believe you were hiding with him in a hall closet or whatever," she went on. On the drive back to her place, I'd filled her in on most of what had happened. "I can't believe you didn't take advantage of that."

I made a face against my hands. I hadn't told Heidi that Luc had kissed me. I probably wouldn't even tell Zoe, because both she and Heidi would have questions, tons of questions. Ones I couldn't answer, because when he'd kissed me, I . . . I didn't even know what I felt. Panic? Yes. Pleasure? Oh God, yes, I'd felt that, too, and that made no sense. I was not attracted to any guy, no matter their species, if they were a jerk who thought they could just randomly kiss someone.

Besides, it hadn't even felt like a real kiss, and I had been *really* kissed before. Brandon and I had kissed. A lot. What had gone down in that hidden room was barely a kiss—

Why was I even thinking about this? There were so many more important things to focus on, like, for example, the fact that we both could be sitting in jail at the moment.

"Luc is hot, Evie." Apparently, Heidi hadn't gotten the memo to move the conversation along.

"He's a legit alien," I muttered.

"So? From what I hear, they have all the working parts necessary. Not that I know from personal experience, but that's what I've heard."

"Glad to hear that they have the working parts." That was a phrase I'd never thought I'd ever say in my entire life. I didn't want to think about Luc and his working parts. "And side note, the last time I checked, you don't know anything about working parts."

She giggled. "Just because I'm still part of the purity parade doesn't mean I haven't done a lot of research or used the internet for nefarious purposes."

I smiled as I dropped my hands. "He was a jerk, Heidi. If he talked to you like he did me, you would've punched him in the face."

"Was he really that bad?" She threw up her hands, extending her middle fingers. "Like on the scale of one"—she wiggled the middle finger on her left hand—"to ten middle fingers, how bad was he really?"

"Fifty." I paused. "Fifty times a million middle fingers."

She laughed as she rolled onto her belly. "Then I probably would've punched him in the nuts."

"Exactly."

"That's a shame." She sighed. "When someone has the physical thing working out for them, it really sucks when the inner part is as ugly as a skinless rat."

Skinless rat? Ew. "It was so weird. He was just so rude. He kept demanding to know why I was there, like I had the audacity to walk into that stupid club." On a roll now, I wanted to start punching things. "Who is he? I mean, obviously, he's an alien named Luc, but . . ."

Heidi sat up, dangling her pajama-clad legs over the edge of the bed. Her hair was twisted up in a messy bun that had flopped to one side. "But what?"

Pressing my lips together, I shook my head. There was something else I hadn't told her. "He . . . he knew my name, Heidi."

Her eyes widened. "What?"

I nodded. "How is that possible? He said he knew who I was and he knew that I'd never been there before." Uneasy, I folded my arms over my waist. "That's really freaky, right?"

"Yeah, it is." She slipped off the bed and came to her knees in front of me. "I don't know if I said something to Emery when I was there before. It's possible I mentioned your name to her. I mean, I know I've talked about you."

"That . . . that would make sense." Relief seeped into me. That made so much sense, but . . . but why would Emery be talking to Luc about me?

"It has to be that. There really is no other way he would've known you. He doesn't go to our school. None of them do."

Exhaling roughly, I nodded again. I didn't want to think about Luc anymore. "Promise me you won't go back there."

Her gaze drifted over my shoulder. "Well . . ."

"Heidi!" Leaning forward, I smacked her arm. "The place gets raided for unregistered aliens. Those ART officers had the kind of guns that also kill humans. That place is not safe."

Heidi let out a heavy, loud breath. "That's never happened before."

"Luc said it happens, like, once a week," I told her. "And even if he was just being dumb, once is still enough. So many bad things could've happened tonight."

Biting down on her lip, she sat back on her butt. "I know. You're right." She peeked up at me through her lashes. "But guess what?"

"What?" I wasn't sure if I believed her or not when it came to her going back to that club.

A small smile appeared. "I got Emery's phone number."

"Really?" Seeing the excitement on her pretty face was a nice distraction from what had happened. "Well, if you have her number, there really *is* no reason for you ever to step foot in that club again."

"Right." Her smile spread. "She was so excited to meet you tonight. I was super-bummed that you didn't get the chance."

"Me too, but if you got her number, then maybe that will lead to hanging out, and I can third wheel it?"

"There's no better third wheel than you."

My nose wrinkled. "Thanks? I guess."

Heidi snuck downstairs after that and stole the box of cupcakes. We gorged ourselves on the chocolate-goodness-topped-with-peanut-butter-frosting heaven while she gave me all the details on Emery. Heidi fell asleep pretty quickly, but what felt like hours passed before I could relax enough to even stop staring at the glow-in-the-dark stars dangling from the ceiling above Heidi's bed.

Tonight was wild and it was scary and it could've ended so badly. That knowledge was hard to shake, to let go. Heidi could've been hurt. I could've been hurt. The dangers we all faced after the invasion hadn't really gone away. They'd just *changed*.

As soon as my thoughts started to drift, they found their way to Luc. Heidi had to be right. She must've mentioned me before and somehow I came up in random conversation with Emery, and Luc had capitalized on that.

But I still couldn't figure out why he'd lie about being a Luxen.

It didn't matter, though, because I was never going back to Foretoken and no matter what he'd said to me, I was never going to see him again.

Thank the Lord and baby Jesus—

Oh my God.

Sitting straight up in bed, my eyes went wide as I cursed. *My phone*. Where was my phone? I threw the covers off and scampered from the bed. I found my clutch near my book bag. I grabbed it, peeled it open, and felt around, confirming what I already knew.

I'd left my phone in that damn club.

I clenched the steering wheel as I stared at the red doors of Foretoken. Part of me had expected to find it roped off with police tape since it had been raided just last night.

But it wasn't.

"You don't have to go in with me," I said. It was about thirty minutes after I'd left Heidi's house, and cars streamed up and down the street outside of the club. In the daylight, it didn't look so intimidating. Kind of. "You can just stay here and if I don't come out in, like, ten minutes—"

"Call the police?" James Davis laughed as I looked at him. "I'm not going to call the police and tell them my underage friend just walked into a club looking for her missing phone and hasn't come back out yet. I'm going in with you."

Relief left me feeling dizzy. I really hadn't wanted to go back in there by myself, and honestly, I should've known that James wouldn't let me go in there alone.

As corny as it sounded, James was the epitome of the boy next door, and he got away with so much because of it. Brown hair, warm brown eyes, and as big and cuddly as a teddy bear, all he had to do was flash those dimples, and parents around the world just opened the door for him. Even my mom. She didn't have any problem with James hanging out in my bedroom with the door closed.

But because he was big and often unintentionally intimidating, I recruited him this morning by showing up at his house and promising him breakfast afterward. James was always swayed by food.

My knuckles were starting to ache. "I need to get my phone back. Mom will kill me if I lost it. Do you know how much that thing costs?"

"Your mom will kill you for being here."

"True, but she's never going to find out, especially if I get my phone back," I reasoned. "If you lost your phone here, what would you do?"

"I wouldn't be here to lose my phone, but whatever." He turned to the window. The Baltimore Orioles baseball cap he almost always wore shielded the upper half of his face. "I know why you asked me to do this and not Zoe."

"Because you gave me a fake ID that enabled me to be a complete idiot and come here in the first place?"

He snorted. "Uh, no."

"Because you think Zoe would've smacked me upside the head if I asked her?" When he nodded, I smiled. "Then you're right. I knew you'd go with me and you wouldn't smack me."

At least I had a plan. Not the greatest, but someone had to be there during the day. Well, unless everyone got arrested, but hopefully someone was there, and I was prepared to beg and plead to be allowed to check out the room I'd dropped my phone in.

"You think anyone is going to answer?" he asked.

I exhaled loudly, let go of the steering wheel, and turned off the car. I hadn't told him about the raid last night, which probably made me a bad person. "I don't even know if anyone is in there." Truth was, after the raid, Luc and everyone could've cleared out. "You sure you want to come in?"

He slowly turned his head toward me. "I know what kind of place this is, so if I stay behind in this car, I'm pretty sure I'm violating some kind of friend code."

"Probably," I agreed, and reached over, tweaking the bill of his cap.

He opened the passenger door. "What's the worst that could happen?"

I lifted my brows. There was, like, a metric crap ton of things that could happen, but I didn't point that out. I grabbed my purse off the backseat and then climbed out of the car to join James. Once there was a break in traffic, we hurried across the street, narrowly avoiding getting run over by a speeding taxi that seemed to come out of nowhere.

I hopped up on the curb and stepped around a man dropping coins into a parking meter. Without warning, my heart started thumping heavily against my ribs as I walked under the awning.

A tremor coursed down my arm as I stopped a good foot in front of the doors, the red paint reminding me of fresh blood. Being here felt . . . It felt *final* somehow, like once I walked through these doors again, there was no going back. I didn't even fully understand that sensation or where it truly came from. It was overdramatic, because all I was doing was coming back to get my stupid phone, but the feeling of dread was filling my pores and seeping through my skin.

Instinct roared to the surface, forcing me to take a step back, and my shoulder bumped into James's chest. Something primal inside me demanded I turn around and get the hell out of there.

Tiny hairs all over my body rose. Air hitched in my throat and pressed down on my chest. The tips of my fingers started to tingle.

Fear.

I was feeling *fear*.

The dark and cold kind that rose from a deep well. I could taste it in the back of my mouth. *Bitter.* The last time I'd felt this kind of bone-chilling fear that bordered on panic was . . . It had to have been during the invasion. Those moments were vague and a blur, but it would've been that kind of fear.

Mr. Mercier, high school counselor extraordinaire, would say what I was feeling right now was just a symptom of living through the invasion. Post-traumatic stress. That was what I kept telling myself as a shiver curled its way down my spine.

The feeling didn't go away.

Get away, whispered a voice that sounded like mine. It came from the recesses of my mind, an inherent, elemental part of me that I wasn't even sure I recognized.

I had no idea why I felt this way or why, with every second, the sensation of going *too far* increased. My heart rate skyrocketed into cardiac arrest territory. I opened my mouth, but I couldn't get my tongue to work.

James reached around me for the handle, but the door swung open before he could even touch the tarnished metal, and I knew right then.

It was too late.

5

The bouncer named Clyde blocked the entryway, one muscular arm bracing the door open, the other lifted to the top of the door, showing off a bicep that was about the size of a tree trunk. A gray shirt stretched across his broad chest and shoulders. Was that unicorn on his shirt spewing . . . *rainbows out of its mouth*?

Yep.

That was definitely a unicorn shooting rainbows out of its mouth.

The razor-edge panic and biting fear receded as quickly as it had swept over me. Gone so fast, it was like it had been a figment of my imagination.

"Whoa," James murmured, dropping his hand to his side.

Maybe I should've warned him about Clyde.

Sunlight glinted off the numerous piercings in Clyde's face as I snapped out of whatever stupor I was in. "I don't know if you remember—"

"I remember you," he said, and I was sure that wasn't a good thing. He fixed his gaze on James. "But I don't remember you."

James was apparently struck silent.

"We're not here to, um, go clubbing or whatever," I tried again. "I was here last night." I winced. "You already know that. I lost my phone."

Clyde turned that huge bald head toward me. "And you came here because . . . ?"

I thought it was pretty obvious, but I went ahead and explained. "I lost my phone when I was with . . . Luc."

"Luc?" murmured James.

I'd also left out the part about Luc when I'd talked to James.

Clyde didn't blink. Not once. "So you're here to see Luc?"

"Not necessarily." I really didn't want to see him. "We were in a room last night, and I just need to check out that room for my phone."

"You were in a room with some dude named Luc?" James repeated. Then he said under his breath with a grin, "You hussy."

I ignored him.

One pierced brow rose. "Are you here to see Luc or not?"

Every muscle in my body tensed. For some reason, I didn't want to say that I was, but if that was the only way I was going to be able to get into the club, I would. I gritted out, "Yes."

Saying nothing, Clyde stepped back as he held the door open. Relief smacked into me. He was letting us in. I exchanged a quick look with James as a horn blew from a car passing by. I stepped forward. James didn't. I grabbed his arm and pulled him through, squeezing past Clyde. The door swung close behind us, shutting out the sunlight and sealing us inside. I let go of James's arm.

I ignored the bubbling nervousness as Clyde shuffled around us in the small space. He opened the door to the club. I hesitated for a moment and then followed him. What I saw was nothing like last night. The lights over the dance floor were on, pressing the shadows back to the bar and the alcoves. Most of the chairs were off the floor, placed upside down on the round tables. Only a few tables remained set. There were two people at the bar, but they stood half in the shadows, and I couldn't make out who they were.

Gone was the scent of overpowering perfume and bitter liquor. The place smelled like someone had recently scrubbed down every surface with a lemony disinfectant.

There were no signs of the raid. All the bottles behind the bar had been replaced. It was as if it hadn't happened.

"I can just go look in the room. I remember—"

"Sit." Clyde gestured at one of the tables that had the chairs down, and kept walking, disappearing past the bar and into a narrow hall to the right, one I hadn't been down before.

James dropped onto a stool. "That is the biggest dude I've ever seen in real life."

"Right?" Too nervous to sit, I stood behind the stool.

Dragging the bill of his cap around so it was on backward, he then lowered his hand to the smooth surface of the table as he looked around the club. "Interesting place."

I eyed the hall Clyde had gone down. Was he going to find my phone or, God forbid, find Luc? My stomach knotted. I really didn't want to see Luc again.

"So, you told me you came here last night with Heidi," James said, cocking his head to the side. "But you didn't tell me about being in some random room with some random guy."

My cheeks heated. "It's not like that. At all. It's, well, it's a long story."

"We have time—wait. Hold that thought." James leaned in, squinting as he stared across the club. "Don't we go to school with him?"

"Who?"

He jerked his chin toward the bar, and I turned. The two people who'd been standing there had moved farther into the light, and I immediately recognized one of them. The dark-haired Luxen. His name was Connor. No idea what his last name was. Surprise flickered through me. "Yeah. We do."

"Wonder what he's doing here?"

Before I could answer, Grayson appeared from across the club, walking from where the shadows clung to the walls as if he had been conjured out of thin air. I stiffened, wondering if the Luxen had that kind of ability and we just didn't know about it.

"Oh hell," James muttered, apparently realizing in that moment that Grayson was a Luxen and wasn't wearing a Disabler.

A smirk tipped up the corner of Grayson's mouth as he stopped in front of our table. He passed a dismissive glance over James, and then those ultra-bright blue eyes landed on me. "I'm told that you're looking for your phone?"

"Yes. It's a slim black—"

"I know what a phone looks like," he replied. "I don't have it."

"Okay." I didn't think he did. "I just need to check a room. I dropped it in there and—"

"You can't check the room."

Irritation swelled. "Why not?"

He simply shook his head.

"Look, I'm not trying to be a pain, but I really just need to find my phone. That's all. So, if you'd—"

"Your phone isn't in that room," he cut me off.

I frowned. "How would you know?"

"Because I know what room you're talking about, and there's no phone in there."

"But—"

"I do know where your phone is." Grayson focused on James like I imagined a lion did when it spotted a limping three-legged gazelle. "Do you like horror movies?" he asked James, pulling what appeared to be a Blow Pop out of the pocket of his jeans.

James looked over at me nervously. "Yeah, uh, I guess so?"

The Luxen's smile was like a razor as he unwrapped the lollipop. It was green—sour apple. "My favorite is an older movie. *Hostel*. There's this young, witless guy who basically stumbles into a den of freaks who take great pleasure in torturing and murdering people." He shoved the Blow Pop into his mouth and spoke around the thin white stick. "Have you seen that one?"

James lifted his brows. "I've . . . Yeah, I've seen it."

"You kind of remind me of that guy. You know. The young, witless one."

Well, that was super-creepy.

Grayson's gaze slid to mine. "Luc has your phone. It's his new treasured possession."

Dammit. "Can you get it from Luc?"

"Nope."

The urge to scream hit me hard. I had no other choice. "Then I want to see Luc."

He tilted his head to the side. "Luc is unavailable."

"Then make him available." My hand tightened around the edge of the table.

Grayson's smirk turned into a full-blown smile. "Obviously, you don't know Luc if you think I can simply make him available."

"I don't care if I know him or not; I'm not leaving here without my phone."

James looked a little pale. "Maybe we can buy you a new one."

Buy me a new phone? With what? Monopoly money? I didn't even have any of that.

"That would be wise," Grayson commented.

"No." I glanced down the hall Clyde had disappeared into. "If you won't go get Luc, then I will."

The older Luxen tilted his head to the side. "Is that so?"

"Evie," James said. "I really think we should leave."

Grayson smile reminded me of barbwire. "For once, I actually agree with a *human*."

This was ridiculous. All I was asking for was my phone, not the secrets to the alien race. Angry, I twisted toward James. "Stay here. I'll be right back."

"Stop," Grayson called out flatly. "Don't." There was a pause. "Definitely don't take the door at the end, on your right, to the stairwell."

I halted.

"Or go onto the second floor," he continued in the same monotone voice. "Luc would be *very* unhappy about that."

What in the world? I looked over my shoulder at him and saw that he was now sitting across from a very, very uncomfortable-looking James. I had no idea why he'd possibly tell me where Luc would be if Luc was so unavailable, but it didn't matter.

I hurried down the hall, passing several doors. Two led to bathrooms, and another one had an EMPLOYEES ONLY plaque on the door, but half the words had Xs over them, leaving the word *ploy* behind, which was . . . notably odd.

Really odd.

I scanned the narrow hall and found the door to the staircase.

I threw it open and started up the flight of steps, not giving myself time to think about what I was doing. And maybe that was stupid.

Or maybe it was brave.

I could see my mom doing something like this. Definitely my dad, and they *were* brave. Obviously. So maybe sometimes it took a little stupidity to be brave.

Rounding the landing to the second floor, I entered the dimly lit hallway and saw several windowless doors. It kind of reminded me of an apartment building. Except, there were no peepholes.

Sighing in frustration, I bit down on my lower lip. Luc could be in any number of these rooms and there were a lot. I was literally going to have to check each one. Or I could just start screaming his name until he came out.

I walked down the hall, my steps slowing when I heard what sounded like whispers coming from the right. I stopped and saw that one of the doors was cracked open.

I went to it, placing my hand on the cool surface. Pushing it all the way open, I stepped inside and saw *nothing*. The room inside was pitch black, as if heavy curtains had been hung, blocking out all possible light.

"Hello?" I called out.

Thump.

I jumped as something moved or fell over in the room. Scanning the darkness, I tried to see something—anything—but it was useless. My ears strained to hear another sound, but there was nothing. It was quite possibly a good time to get the hell out of this room.

I took a step back.

Air stirred around me, lifting the hair around my face. My breath caught as instinct flared to life. I so wasn't alone in this room. I moved to get the hell out—

A hand gripped my arm, jerking me forward. A scream rose, abruptly cut off as I was shoved. Hard. My back hit the wall, knocking the breath out of me and shooting pain up my spine, where it exploded along the base of my skull.

Before I could move or make a sound, the same hand—a cold hand—closed around my throat, tight enough just to let the tiniest bit of air wheeze in. My hands flailed until I found it—*his* arm in the darkness. Digging my fingers in, I tried to pry the hand away from my throat as adrenaline pumped through my veins. My heart slammed against my ribs as bitter tendrils of panic burrowed deep into my stomach.

Oh God. Oh God—

I *felt* him lean in. I *felt* his breath ghost over my cheek as I was lifted up onto my toes. I *felt* his words all the way to the marrow. "You shouldn't be here."

6

Who are you?" the man demanded.

I opened my mouth to respond, but since he was half strangling me, I couldn't get a single word out.

"Why are you here?" he demanded, and his grip tightened. My feet left the floor, forcing out a raspy gasp. Fear dug in with razor-sharp claws.

In the darkness, two bright white pinpricks of light appeared, casting a luminous glow. Pupils. They were *pupils*. This man was so not human. My fingernails scraped over his skin. Oh God, I was going to be choked to death all over a damn phone—

The door swung open. "Let go of her *now*."

At the sound of the familiar voice, the hand around my throat disappeared. I fell forward, throwing my arms out into the empty space around me. A scream built in my throat—

An arm circled my waist. For a second I was hanging in the air, arms and legs flailing by a steely arm. Without warning, I was suddenly upright, on my feet, my back pressed against a very solid chest—*Luc's* chest. I inhaled sharply, surrounded by that all-too-familiar woodsy scent of his.

This wasn't any better than being choked.

I jerked forward, but the arm around my waist was like a steel band. I made it about an inch and then was hauled back.

"Stay still," Luc warned directly into my ear.

Every muscle in my body locked up. About to inform him he could not tell me what to do, I winced as light suddenly flooded the room. My vision adjusted, and I saw an older man—an older *Luxen*—standing a few feet in front of us.

And then I saw what—who—was behind him.

There was a woman holding a small child, maybe a toddler. The little girl with curly pigtails had her face buried in the woman's shoulder. Her tiny body was trembling so badly, she was shaking the woman cradling her. Real primitive fear was etched into the beautiful woman's face as she stared at us with wide, terror-filled eyes.

Luc was as still as a statue behind me. "Explain yourself."

"You told me we were safe here," the Luxen male said, nostrils flared. "You swore that to us."

Shocked that this adult Luxen would answer to Luc's somewhat arrogant demand, let alone listen to him, I was struck silent.

"You are safe here," Luc replied.

"She walked into this room. A *human*." His hands opened and closed at his sides. "What was I supposed to think?"

"You should've thought, *Wow, she's an idiot and therefore harmless*," Luc retorted, and my mouth dropped open. "Throwing her against a wall wasn't exactly necessary."

Did he seriously just call me an idiot?

The Luxen male's lips thinned and then he shocked me even more by saying, "I'm sorry. It won't happen again."

I felt Luc nod behind me and then he said, "And *this*"—his arm tightened even more, and a tiny squeak escaped me—"won't happen again."

The male didn't respond, nor did he take his eyes off us as he backed up, keeping himself firmly planted between us and the others.

Understanding flared to life, and I probably would've seen it earlier if I hadn't been so wrapped up in almost being *choked to death*.

The Luxen was protecting the woman and child from—*from me*. I was so dumbfounded by the realization, I didn't protest when Luc removed his arm from my waist and then wrapped his fingers around mine, pulling me out of the room. The door closed behind us, but I swore no one had touched it.

Once we were in the hall, I tried to tug my hand free. "You called me an idiot in there."

"And I'm wrong?" He kept walking, the muscles along his back tense. "Because I really don't think so."

"Yeah, you're as wrong as—"

Luc spun, and without any warning, I was once again pressed against a wall. He towered over me, keeping our joined hands between us. When he spoke, his voice was incredibly soft. "When I said I'd be seeing you again, I hadn't meant today. Not that I'm complaining, but I'm kind of busy. But I guess you missed me already?"

Missed him? Ha. No. My throat dried as I stared up and into those odd amethyst eyes. The color seemed to . . . churn restlessly. "I didn't plan on coming here—"

"But you're here."

"Yes. I have a reason, a good one—"

"There are no good reasons for you to be here today."

"I'm looking—"

"For me?" His brows lifted, disappearing into the wavy locks of brown hair. He stepped in, and I imagined I could feel the heat coming off his body. Maybe it wasn't my imagination, because he was close enough that if I shifted one way or another, my legs would brush his.

"Do you have to talk to me like you have no idea what personal space is?" I demanded. "And *no,* I'm not here for you."

"I don't have to talk to you like this, but I want to. I like it." One side of his lips kicked up when my eyes narrowed. "And *yes,* I have a sinking suspicion that you are here, in fact, for me."

My jaw locked down. "I need to find my cell phone—"

"And you thought you'd find it in a room full of Luxen?"

If he interrupted me one more time, I was going to scream my throat raw. "It would be nice if I could finish a sentence. Then I would be able to tell you why I'm here."

He tilted his head to the side, staring at me like he'd been hanging around for an hour. "I'm waiting."

I pulled on my hand again. He held on. "Who were they?" I demanded. "Those Luxen in there?"

"That's why you're here? To ask about them?"

It wasn't, and their presence wasn't any of my business, but it didn't take a rocket scientist to know that they were hiding in here. I thought about last night's raid. The ART officers were looking for unregistered aliens. Luc had them here.

Hell, he obviously was one.

And apparently, the ART officers weren't very good at their jobs, because Luc, and what I was guessing was a family, were still here.

Luc's gaze dropped to my mouth, and I drew in an unsteady breath. A muscle flexed along his jaw. "How did you even get up here? I told Clyde to send you away."

"Grayson . . ." I stilled.

Wait. Had Grayson set me up? He told me to come up here; he had to know that family was hidden in one of the rooms.

Luc's gaze lifted to mine. "Grayson sent you up here?"

"Kind of," I gritted out, holding his stare. "Can you back off?"

There was a moment of silence. "I feel like we're having déjà vu."

"Probably because you have no respect for personal space."

His lips pursed. "Sounds about right."

I stared at him.

Luc dropped my hand and took a step back. His gaze flickered over my face. "Are you okay? Did he hurt you?"

His question sort of surprised me. "No. He didn't hurt me."

"He was choking you."

"Yeah, he was doing that, but I'm . . . I'm okay."

He watched me a moment, shook his head, and then pivoted. He started stalking down the hall, and it was then that I realized he was carrying something in his other hand. A cloth—a washcloth.

I peeled myself off the wall and hurried after him. "I need—"

"Your phone," he interrupted. "I know."

"Okay." I struggled to keep up. His long-legged pace was impressive . . . and annoying. "Can I have it?"

"No."

"What? Why not?"

"You don't need it."

"I need it—I totally need my phone. It belongs to me."

Luc kept walking, and I just—I just lost it.

Leftover adrenaline from being thrown against a wall mingled with the frustration burning at my skin like a swarm of fire ants. Snapping forward, I grabbed his arm and stopped him. In the distant part of my mind I knew that he had allowed me to do that. That if he had wanted to keep walking, he would've and then simply dragged me behind him. But I didn't care that he could throw me down the hall with a flick of his wrist if he wanted to.

"I'm not leaving here until I have my phone."

A smile played at his mouth as he glanced down at my hand and then back up. "Really?"

"Why are you being so difficult? Just give me my phone and you'll never have to see me again."

His thick lashes lowered, shielding his eyes as he reached down and pried my fingers off his arm. He did so gently, as if he were well aware of his strength and thought my fingers could snap like dried twigs. "But what if I want to see you again?"

I swallowed as my eyes narrowed. "But I don't want to see your face ever again."

The almost teasing smile began to fade. "Well, that's rude."

The irritation gave way to reckless fury. "If you don't give me my damn phone right now, I will call the police." I glanced down at the leather cuff he wore before meeting his gaze head-on. I hated saying what I did next, because I would never do what I was about to threaten, but I was willing to say just about anything to get my phone so I could leave and forget all about Luc and this damn place. "I doubt the Luxen back in that room would want that to happen, would they?"

Luc's eyes widened slightly as he faced me. A measure of surprise splashed across his striking features, parting his full lips. "Are you actually threatening me?"

I had the common sense to recognize I was treading on thin ice with lead boots. Like the kind of thin ice that was already cracking under my feet. "It's not a threat." I managed to keep my voice level. "It's a warning."

"That's the same thing, *Evie*." Luc stepped toward me, the pupils of his eyes seeming to expand. "It's a threat."

The air stalled in my lungs and my body moved without thought. I took a step back, but he came forward once more. I kept going until I was against a damn wall again.

"No one has even the tiniest inclination to threaten me," he said, the pupils of his eyes starting to turn white. An icy chill ran down my spine. "Because they know better."

My chest rose sharply.

"They especially know better than to threaten what I'm trying to do here." His chin dipped, and he was right back in my space, eye to eye. Several seconds passed, and the stupidest, absolute dumbest thoughts occurred. I thought about that meaningless kiss that wasn't even a kiss—about how those full lips had felt.

How they were soft yet hard, and I—

What in the world was wrong with me? Had I hit my head and damaged my brain earlier? The answer was yes, a resounding *yes*.

"Dammit," he growled, and then he did the strangest thing—stranger than me thinking about kissing him, which was next-level bizarre.

He dropped his forehead to mine as he breathed in deeply. "Peaches. I am really beginning to have a thing for peaches."

I tensed as my eyes widened. What was happening? And why was I standing here? At this point I probably shouldn't even be trusted to own a phone. "It's j-just lotion."

A breath shuddered through Luc. "You were never supposed to be here. Do you understand that? That was the *deal*."

My heart lurched in my chest. "What are you talking about?"

The tips of his fingers brushed my cheek, and my entire body jolted as if I'd touched a live wire. He pulled back. A stark intensity filled his stare, and I thought maybe his gaze dropped again, to my mouth. He tilted his head to the side, almost like he was lining up his mouth with mine, and whispered, "The deal was I would stay away . . ." He paused, the brilliant light of his pupils increasing. "If *you* stayed away."

"What?" I said breathlessly.

Tension filled the air, popping and sparking around us. Static cracked, and the overhead lights flickered, dimming briefly before roaring back to life, becoming ultra bright.

I sucked in a sharp gasp.

Luc smiled.

Just a few feet away, the door at the end of the hall opened. The lights in the hall returned to normal. The acute pressure and edginess seeped slowly out of the hall, but my pulse was pounding so fast, I felt like I'd run up five flights of stairs. I broke eye contact with Luc and saw the blue-haired guy standing in the doorway. His name was Ken or Kent.

He checked out Luc and then me. "I was wondering what was taking so long."

Luc took a step back, but even though I wasn't looking at him, I could feel the intensity of his stare still focused on me. "What's up, Kent?"

"He's getting worse," he replied.

Swearing under his breath, Luc stalked off. For a moment I didn't move—I *couldn't*. I was stuck to the wall. What had just happened there? And what deal was he talking about? None of that made sense.

And none of that mattered.

All I needed—all I wanted—was my phone and then to be out of here.

I sprung off the wall, hurrying to catch up to Luc as Kent stepped aside. He held the door open. I half expected both of them to shut the door in my face, but Kent just arched a reddish-brown brow at me as Luc prowled into the room.

It wasn't empty.

There was a guy standing in the corner, and it took me a moment to recognize him. I'd seen him last night with Luc. It was the guy with the military haircut who had sat down next to Luc.

He turned toward me, and the first thing I noticed was his eyes. They were just like Luc's. An extraordinarily violet color, and those eyes widened. "What the—"

"Don't," Luc warned.

The man twisted toward him. "Don't what?"

"You know exactly what I'm telling you not to do." Luc kept his back to the man as he sat down on the edge of what appeared to be a narrow bed.

I had no idea what was going on as the stranger faced me once more. "I have so many questions," he said, looking at me in a way that made me feel like I was under a microscope.

Kent snorted. "Don't we all?"

"She is no one you need to worry about, Archer."

Archer? What kind of name was that?

"Huh," Archer murmured, and then gave a little shake of his head. "Anyway, you think it's wise that she's here? Now?"

"No," Luc replied.

My brows shot up, and I opened my mouth to speak, but Luc leaned back, and I got an eyeful of who was lying on the bed. Gasping, my hand flew to my mouth. "Oh my God . . ."

A man lay on his back. At least, I was guessing it was a man. His brown hair was matted, coated in sweat and . . . and blood. His face was a mess of angry, purplish bruises. Eyes swollen shut, lips puffy and torn. The man's chest barely moved.

"What . . . what happened to him?" I asked.

Luc's gaze drifted to me and he sighed. When he spoke, he sounded way older than eighteen. "Good question. I'm not quite sure." He folded the washcloth in half. "I was about to find out, but I was interrupted."

Me. He was talking about me.

Archer crossed his arms. "I found him like that, outside by the dumpsters in the alley."

A shiver danced over my shoulders. I knew what dumpsters he was talking about. The window I climbed out last night emptied right into the alley beside those dumpsters.

"I don't know who he is," Archer continued, glancing over at me. A strange look crossed his handsome face. "Or what he was doing out there."

"That's Chas." Kent sat in a small, metal chair. "He . . . helps out around here."

It was like Luc forgot I existed as he leaned over the man,

carefully dabbing the washcloth along the man's forehead. The man named Chas shuddered, and the very edges of his body blurred. His bloody skin lost some of the color, becoming . . . translucent. Another gasp parted my lips as I lowered my hand.

The man was a Luxen, a very badly injured Luxen.

I saw the bluish veins in Chas's still arms for only a brief second before his human form took hold again. I saw no sign of a Disabler. Based on only the injuries I could see, I had a feeling that if he were human, he wouldn't be breathing.

"When was the last time you saw him?" Luc asked.

"Last night." Kent rubbed the heel of his palm along his chest. "After the raid."

Archer's jaw locked. "You think the ART officers did this?"

My stomach tumbled at the thought. The man looked like he was near death. Why would the officers do that?

"No," answered Luc. "If it were them, they would've taken Chas into custody. They wouldn't have left him lying out there."

"Had to be another Luxen to get the upper hand on Chas." Kent glanced over at Archer. "Especially considering those types of injuries. Chas knows how to defend himself."

Feeling like I shouldn't be here for this conversation, that I was hearing things I shouldn't, I started to back up. I only made it about a foot.

"Stay put, Evie," Luc said softly, and I stopped, wondering if he had eyes in back of his head. "Just for a few more moments."

I stopped, not even sure why. I wanted my phone, but I could wait out in the hallway until he was done in here. I glanced around the room. "Shouldn't . . . shouldn't he be in a hospital?"

"A hospital isn't going to help him," Luc answered, his voice stoic, and I wondered if that was because Chas might be unregistered.

Archer was staring at me again, his expression curious. I folded my arms over my chest and looked away. "So, Evie," he said, and I tensed. "How do you know Luc?"

"I don't know him," I said, and Luc's shoulders stiffened.

"That's interesting," Archer began. "I wonder if—" A phone rang from his pocket and he pulled it out, a soft smile forming on his lips as he answered. "Hey, babe. Give me a sec, okay?" He lowered the phone as he pushed away from where he was standing, starting for the door. "It's Dee," he said to Luc's back. "I'll tell her you said hi."

Luc didn't respond, and that seemed normal to Archer, because he walked out of the room, glancing in my direction. The man on the bed moaned again as a shudder rocked his entire body.

"You've got to let go," Luc said to Chas as his arm moved, blocking his face. "It's the only way you're going to heal. You're safe here. Just let go."

I bit down on my lip as Luc leaned back, turning the cloth over. I saw streaks of red staining it. Luc was cleaning his face, wiping away the streaks of blood.

The man's body shook once more and then I saw him change into his true form. Part of me thought I should look away, but I couldn't as a flickering white light encased Chas's entire body. Within seconds, the human façade slipped away. My lips parted, but there were no words as I took in the luminous skin and the intricate veins appearing beneath it. This was the first time I'd seen beyond the light of a Luxen, and it was . . . it was strangely beautiful. Mom had been right, in a way. Their skin was like a jellyfish's.

Luc twisted, facing me. "You brought someone with you?"

I frowned, unable to take my eyes off Chas. He'd stopped moaning and appeared to have settled down. Or he'd passed out. "Yes. He's downstairs."

"Boyfriend?" he asked.

I shook my head.

"Figured. If he was a boyfriend, you'd need a new one. Well, he's obviously not a good friend either if he didn't insist on coming up here with you."

My spine stiffened. "I can take care of myself, thank you very much."

"Did I suggest you couldn't?" Luc folded up the stained cloth and tossed it to the left without looking. It landed in a small trash can as he turned back to Chas. "Take care of the *friend* downstairs, Kent," he said. "Make sure he gets home safely but fully understands that he was never here."

I almost stopped breathing. "Wait. James rode with me."

Kent stood, sending a half smile in my direction as he walked past me, toward the door.

Luc dropped his hands to his thighs, his back still to me. "James might've ridden with you, but you are not leaving with him." There was a pause that felt like an eternity. "Actually, you're not leaving at all."

Every part of my being stilled. There was no way I'd heard him right. No way at all. "You . . . can't be serious."

Slowly, Luc rose and turned to me. "Oh, I'm as serious as heart attack. Cliché saying, I know, but you came here and you've seen things you shouldn't have. Multiple things. Things I don't want you repeating, especially to that mother of yours."

I gasped. Why was he bringing her up? Did he know her?

That wolfish grin returned, turning the almost angelic beauty of his face to something darker, crueler. "Then you threaten me and what I'm doing here, and if you haven't quite figured it out yet, that really doesn't sit well with me. But most important?" Drawing his bottom lip between his lips through his teeth, he inched closer. "You broke the deal. You're not leaving."

7

Aw, hell no.

Fear pinged around inside me, but anger was like battery acid in my veins. Luc was out of his freaking mind.

"I don't think so," I said, backing up toward the door. "You can't keep me here."

"Really?" He tilted his head to the side. "Is that a challenge? Because I love challenges. I find them a fun way to pass the time."

Finding my phone *was* my top priority, and I would do some insane level of stupid to get it back, but *this* was going too far.

"It's not a challenge." I backed into the hallway, discovering it was empty. No Archer. No Kent. The only exit was at the end of the hall, feeling like a mile away. "It's a statement."

Luc smiled, and it was so misleading. It was the kind of smile a predator showed off as it sized up its next meal.

Not wanting to take my eyes off him until the very last second, I headed to the right. My plan was pretty much to run—run as fast as I ever had in my entire life. I lost sight of Luc. Pressure clamped down on my chest.

I spun around and took off, arms pumping at my sides as my flats slipped over the carpeted floor. I didn't even make it to the halfway point when something rushed past me, blowing my hair around my face. Inherently I knew it was Luc. The Luxen were fast, mind-bendingly so.

And I was correct.

Luc appeared in front of me.

I shrieked as I slid to a halt, almost losing my balance but catching myself at the last moment. Breathing heavily, I straightened. "That's not fair."

"Never said it would be." He came forward. "There's no place in here for you to run. This building, all of it, belongs to me."

"That's impossible. You're only eighteen. You can't own this building or a club."

"Nothing is impossible . . . when you're me."

"Wow. You're so special." Dismay rose as I looked behind me. I was trapped. There was no stairwell behind me, only rooms, and I knew I wasn't going to get past Luc.

Luc prowled forward, and I panicked. With my heart in my throat, I darted to the left and grabbed a handle. The door opened about an inch, but then slammed shut as if a gale-force wind had pushed it. Fear and anger swirled inside me as I whirled around.

Luc arched a brow. "Not sure where you think you're going."

I rushed to the left, a scream of frustration building inside me. "You need to let me leave."

"But I thought you weren't leaving until you got what you wanted," he mocked. "Your phone."

"You're not going to help me." I pressed against the wall, inching sideways toward the stairwell. "You're—you're trying to kidnap me."

"Hmm." He turned slowly so he was facing me. "I wouldn't say I'm trying to kidnap you. I would say that I'm actively offering you a place to stay for an undetermined amount of time."

My jaw hit the floor. "That's just a really nice way of saying you're kidnapping me!"

"You say kidnap; I say offering you an all-inclusive vacation."

"I don't want an all-inclusive vacation!"

"Well, it's a break-it-you-buy-it kind of thing."

"I didn't break anything," I seethed, putting a decent amount of distance between us. "If I don't go home—"

"People will come looking for you." He rolled his eyes. "Blah, blah. This sounds like a boring version of *Taken,* and how do you make—"

Launching off the wall, I took off running. Part of me knew it was pointless, and it was. A rage-filled scream erupted from me as Luc suddenly appeared in front of me.

I didn't get a chance to turn around. He shot forward and dipped low. I screeched as he scooped me up, tossing me over his shoulder like I was nothing more than a sack of potatoes.

"Put me down!" I shouted, my chest smacking off his back as he turned.

"I really don't feel like chasing you around, so sorry, that's not happening."

"Oh my God." Completely forgetting what he was, I pounded my fists into his back. "Put me down, you son of a—"

"Ouch." He bounced, causing my stomach to come down on his shoulder. "Hitting is not nice."

I guessed he was also going to have a problem with kicking as I swung my knee into his stomach.

"Jesus," he said, and grunted, clamping his arm over the backs of my legs. "You do realize I could easily pitch you out of a window, right?"

"Then do it," I spat back, digging my elbow into him. "I'd like to see you try explaining my splattered body on the sidewalk to the authorities."

Luc snorted. "That sounded really dramatic."

Fury burned my skin as he prowled down the hall. "My mother—"

"Your mother isn't going to do anything. You know why?" Luc shifted swiftly, and for a second I thought I was going to slide right off his shoulder. "Because your mother knows better."

I hit him again. "Let me go, Luc."

He stopped, and I felt his cheek press into my hip. "If I do, do you promise not to run off?"

My face wrinkled. "Yes."

"You're a liar, liar." The door in front of him opened. "The moment I put you down, you're going to run. Probably end up hurting yourself."

Groaning, I jabbed my fist into his lower back and was rewarded with another grunt. "I'm going to hurt you!"

Luc chuckled.

He actually *chuckled* as he walked into a room.

I swore to God and the Holy Ghost, I was going to ninja kick him in the face.

Luc stopped in the dark room, and I was suddenly sliding down him—down his entire front. The contact was like a brush burn, frying out my nerve endings. The moment my feet hit the floor, I swayed unsteadily as I reached out, finding nothing around me but him. I kept moving until the backs of my thighs hit something soft, and I plopped down.

The overhead light flipped on, and my wild gaze darted around. It was a small windowless room with narrow beds pushed against the wall. It reminded me of a cell. Panic took root in my chest and blossomed.

This isn't happening.

His expression was as hard and cold as a sheet of ice. "Stay," Luc ordered, backing up.

Stay? Like a dog?

I sprung up from the narrow bed and darted to the side. Luc's sigh could've rattled the walls as he snagged me with one arm like I was an errant child running amuck in the frozen food section of a grocery store.

Tucking me against his side, he walked me back to the bed and deposited me there. "We can keep doing this all day if you want." He let go, folding his arms across his chest. "But I really hope you don't, because I have things to do. I'm kind of a busy guy."

"Then let me go," I reasoned, clenching the edge of the mattress. "And you can get back to being the busiest guy in the world."

He arched a brow. "If I let you go, I have a feeling I'm going to be even busier."

I started to stand, but Luc lifted his arm. My hair blew back from my face. I sucked in a sharp breath as I tried to straighten out, but it was like there was hands on my shoulders, pushing me back down. Within a heartbeat, I was on my butt and I wasn't getting back up.

Luc wasn't even touching me.

No one was.

He was just standing there, staring down at me with a raised brow. He even lowered his hand, but I couldn't . . . I couldn't stand up. A shiver danced over me as my heartbeat stuttered.

Holy crap.

I stared at him with wide eyes. *This* was how powerful he was, and it was terrifying.

And it was also infuriating.

I didn't like to be told what to do or forced to do anything, and I sure as hell didn't like feeling afraid.

Sweat broke out across my forehead as I fought the unseen weight bearing down on me. Arms trembling, I managed to lift my hands from the mattress as fury poured through me.

Luc closed his eyes, brows pinching as his shoulders tensed. It was almost like he was in pain—like he was the one struggling to stand. "You're still so incredibly stubborn."

"You . . . don't know me," I gritted out.

He didn't respond, and I honestly didn't care what he was talking about at the moment. I couldn't move any farther against the force pushing on me. Desperation trickled in. I would wear myself out in minutes, getting nowhere while he just stood there, and then what? He was going to keep me here, against my will?

"You're hurting me!" I shouted even though it wasn't true. I didn't feel any pain.

Luc moved so fast, I couldn't track him. In a second he was crouched in front of me, eye to eye. The pressure was gone, but before I could move, he clasped my cheeks in an oddly gentle grasp.

His stare met and latched on to mine. His pupils were black against the purple, the irises fuzzy. "I could do a lot of things. I *have* done a lot of things, and sometimes, I do hurt people," he said quietly, softly. "But I could never hurt you."

I didn't want to believe him, because it didn't make sense. He could easily hurt me, but he sounded so incredibly genuine. Like he was speaking the only truth he knew. I couldn't look away, even though I wanted to. An odd sensation washed over me. A sense of . . . a sense of *awareness* seeped in. Luc inhaled sharply as his eyes took on a hooded quality, as if he were suddenly half asleep. My heart stuttered and then sped up.

"Luc," a male's voice came from the door.

A muscle flexed along Luc's jaw. "You couldn't have worse timing."

"I like to think I have the best timing," was the reply. "But obviously, I'm interrupting."

"And you're still standing there because?" Luc's eyes closed.

"Because I'm nosy." There was a pause. "And I have nothing better to do at the moment."

Luc swore under his breath, and his hands left my cheeks in a slow, dragging way that caused my skin to tingle. He rose, and I saw the tall man who stood in the doorway.

He was . . . Wow, he was gorgeous.

The stranger's hair was dark and wavy, brushing his temples. His eyes were the color of polished emeralds, bright and shiny. The eyes were a dead giveaway. Luxen. But so was his chiseled, sculpted face, because it was almost too perfect, like Luc's. As if there were no flaws to be found in how he was pieced together, and all humans had flaws.

This guy appeared to be college aged, maybe a little older, and he seemed familiar, but I would've remembered him. I know I would've. No one could forget the name that belonged to a face like that.

"What are you doing, anyway? Archer and I—" The man's dark brows lowered and then his eyes shot wide open. "Holy shi—"

"Don't." Luc turned to the man. "Don't say what I know you're going to say."

The corners of my lips turned down. Archer had had the same reaction to me. Was it so shocking that I was human?

The Luxen snapped his mouth shut and blinked. "Now I know why you don't visit anymore. Never call to chat with us. You've been keeping secrets, Luc."

"You know why I don't come, Daemon."

A shadow crossed over the man's face and then smoothed out, disappearing. "True."

Luc exhaled heavily. "Don't you have something you should be doing right now?"

"I do," Daemon replied. "I'm here for the . . ." Those stunning eyes glanced off me. "Just getting things ready for the . . . package, but I heard a ruckus. Thought I'd check it out."

"A *ruckus*?" Luc repeated. "Have you been watching TV from the fifties?"

"Well, you know how deprived Archer is. He's on this *Happy Days* kick recently. Freaking annoying as hell. Every time we get out of the city, he's watching it on the damn tablet. Then we get back, Kat wants a damn breakdown of every episode. It's driving me insane."

"Good to know." Luc sounded impatient. "Would love to chat more about Archer's TV obsessions, but I'm kind of busy right now."

"Yeah, you're busy with . . . ?"

"Evie," Luc said. "This is Evie."

Daemon's brows lifted. "Evie." That eerie gaze settled on me again. "Hi, Evie."

I had no idea what was going on, but I was no longer frozen by super-special Luxen power or my own stupidity. I lurched to my feet and blurted out, "He's trying to kidnap me."

"Is that so?" The brilliant green gaze slid to Luc. "I didn't know you were into that kind of stuff. Freaky."

Luc rolled his eyes.

"I'm being serious." I took a step forward and then stopped when Luc shifted toward me. "See! If I walk toward that door, he's not going to let me leave."

"Well, Luc, you know that's illegal, right?"

"No shit."

"It's totally illegal, but he's trying to say he's offering me a vacation—an all-exclusive vacation! In other words, he's trying to kidnap me."

Daemon drifted into the room. "And why is he doing that?"

"Seriously. You do have things to do, Daemon. Go do them."

The man pouted—actually plumped out his lips and pouted. "But this is really more interesting."

"He took my phone and won't give it back."

Daemon cocked his head to the side. "I wasn't expecting that."

"No. You don't understand. I left my phone here last night and I came back to get it, because you know how expensive those things are," I tried again, my heart thumping.

"Uh-huh," Daemon murmured.

"That's all, and everything has completely gotten out of hand. He sent my friend home with some blue-haired dude who looks a little serial killer-ish. I've seen a guy who I'm pretty sure is half dead," I rushed on. "I've been picked up, carried around, and *choked*. And all I want is my damn phone and I've yet to see it—"

"I have your phone." Luc reached around, patting his back pocket. "I was going to give it back you."

Slowly, I turned to him. I couldn't think of anything to say as I stared at him for what felt like an eternity. "You've had my phone in your pocket this whole time?"

Luc lifted a hand, knocking a wavy tumble of hair off his forehead. A second later it fell back in place. "I have."

"In your back pocket?"

"Yes."

My mouth dropped open. "And why haven't you just given it to me?"

His lips pursed. "I was planning to, but then I got distracted when you almost got yourself choked to death."

"That wasn't my fault!" I shouted.

"We're going to have to disagree on that."

"Then why didn't you give it to me afterward?" I demanded.

A smirk formed. "Well, I was just messing with you then."

"Oh my God." I shook my head, glancing over at Daemon. "Are you hearing this?"

He held up his hand. "I'm just an innocent, enraptured viewer of this."

A lot of help he was.

"But then you threatened to call the police and run your mouth," Luc added, the smirk fading. Daemon's gaze seemed to sharpen. "And that changed everything."

I stepped toward him, hands shaking. "I wouldn't have threatened you if you had just given me the stupid cell phone!"

"I have to say, Luc, that sounds reasonable." Daemon leaned against the wall, idly crossing his arms. "You could just—"

"I didn't ask for your opinion." Luc turned to him. "And why are you still standing there?"

Daemon lifted a shoulder. "This is so much more entertaining than hanging around Archer and Grayson."

Violet eyes narrowed. "Daemon, if you don't leave, I'm going to help you leave."

"Damn," Daemon drawled. "Someone's in a bad mood." He backed up, a look of amusement settling into his features. "Talk to you later, *Evie*."

Wait. He was leaving me? Here? With the guy I just said was trying to kidnap me? What was wrong with these people? "But—"

Daemon pivoted and was gone in the blink of an eye. I was left here, with Luc. Drawing in a deep breath, I faced him once more. "I wasn't really going to call the police. I wouldn't do that."

Luc pulled his gaze away from the now empty doorway. "Then why did you threaten that?" He moved toward me, stopping when I stiffened. "Do you know how serious that is?"

"I just need my phone back. That's all. I wasn't going to breathe a word of this to anyone. I swear."

His jaw worked as he stared at me. A moment passed. "You know what the big problem is here?"

I glanced around the otherwise empty room. "You trying to kidnap me?"

"No," he replied. "You know nothing about anything, and that makes you so incredibly dangerous."

I glared at him. "That makes no sense."

"It makes perfect sense." He leaned against the bare white wall. "There are things you have no clue about—things that a lot of people have died to keep secret. What's stopping you from running back to your friends—to the guy you brought with you?"

"What would I tell them?" I threw up my hands, exasperated with him—with *everything*. "I'm not going to tell anyone about . . .

about those Luxen. Just please give me my phone and I will be gone from your life. Forever."

An odd look flickered across Luc's face, and then he reached around, pulling something out of his pocket. He opened his hand, and in his palm was my phone. My phone! "Here it is."

I almost fell over in a rush to snatch my phone, but I held back, staring at him warily. "So, I . . . I can have my phone and leave?"

Luc nodded.

Drawing in a shallow breath, I extended my hand and he dropped the phone in my palm. I started to pull my hand back, but he closed his fingers around mine.

A slight shock of electricity traveled from his hand up my arm as he tugged me forward, into his side. Luc lowered his head to my ear. "You speak a word about what you saw today to anyone, you'll be endangering innocent people—friends, family, strangers," he whispered. "I won't hurt you. Ever. The rest won't be so lucky."

I was still in shock as I drove home. Part of me couldn't believe I'd walked out of that club and was in my car, but Luc had given me back my phone and hadn't stopped me from leaving.

The first thing I did when I got in my car was call James. He was fine and had just been dropped off at his house. Of course, he had a thousand questions, but I made him promise that he wouldn't tell anyone about the trip to Foretoken.

I knew I'd never see Luc again, but I didn't want to tempt it by either of us blabbing anything to anyone.

But what had Luc meant about the deal? About him staying away if I stayed away? That made utterly no sense. I didn't know him. Last night was the first time I'd ever seen him.

"I doesn't matter," I said out loud. And it didn't, because obviously there was something very weird and wrong with Luc, and whatever he'd meant by that was irrelevant.

I just wanted to forget about this weekend, and I would. Heidi had reassured me that she wouldn't step foot in Foretoken again, and I was convinced that I wouldn't immediately blab the truth about last night and today to Mom the moment I saw her and she gave me that look.

That *Colonel* Sylvia Dasher look.

Luckily, I knew Mom was going to be at work and probably wouldn't be home until late tonight. I had all day to not succumb to that look and confess every dumb thing I'd done in the last twenty-four hours.

I couldn't remember if Dad had ever mastered that look or not. Mom had always handled the discipline. Then again, I didn't remember much about my dad anymore and that was *sad*.

My hands tightened on the steering wheel. This car, an older Lexus, sometimes felt like the only thing I had left of Dad's. I didn't look like him. I took after Mom, so when I looked in the mirror I didn't see him, and with each passing year, it was getting harder to remember what he looked like.

My dad—Sergeant Jason Dasher—had died in the war against the Luxen. His service to our country, to mankind had been posthumously awarded.

He'd been given the Medal of Honor.

The thing was, when I thought about Dad, it wasn't just hard to see him, but also to *hear* him. Before the war, he hadn't been home often. His job had him all over the States, but now I wished there had been more time, more memories to fall back on. Something more than a car, because when I thought about Dad, I had trouble piecing his face together in my memories and there weren't any photos. All of that had been left in the house we discarded during the invasion.

But I still had my mom. Not a lot of people could say that after the war, and she was a damn good mom.

So much had been lost, but Columbia was one of those cities that had been lucky. For the most part, it was virtually untouched by the invasion. Only some of the buildings had been damaged, mostly due to random fires that broke out, and I heard that there'd been riots here, but there had been riots everywhere.

Mom and I hadn't been so lucky. We'd originally lived outside of Hagerstown, another city in Maryland, and nearly all the cities along the I-81 corridor had been damaged during combat. There'd been ground fighting and airstrikes.

And there were other cities that had had it so much worse.

Some had been completely overrun by the Luxen, and those cities where the Luxen had rapidly assimilated the DNA of humans, basically replacing them, had been total losses. Alexandria. Houston. Los Angeles and Chicago. Nonnuclear electromagnetic pulse bombs had been dropped on those cities, effectively killing every Luxen while also rendering *every* piece of technology useless.

The newly formed Department of Restoration said that it would take decades to repair those cities, now referred to as zones. They were walled wastelands, empty of life and power. No one lived there. No one went there.

It was hard not to think of them when I looked in the rearview mirror and saw the skyscrapers stretching into the sky like steel fingers. It was hard to not think of those days and weeks after the invasion.

It was even harder for me to really process how it only had been four years and everything was almost normal. Mom had gone back to work at the United States Army Medical Research and Material Compound at Fort Detrick in Frederick the moment it was okay to return to the area. Around two years ago, movies had started getting made again and TV stations stopped showing reruns. New episodes of my favorite shows started airing with some new cast members, and one day, life was just back to the way it was before.

At school, we'd just started meeting with college advisors on Tuesday. I was planning to apply to the University of Maryland next fall and would hopefully get into their nursing program, because even though I loved taking pictures, I knew I wasn't good enough to make a career out of that. Though, after my reaction to the guy Luc was helping, I wondered if nursing was the right fit for me.

Anyway, life was happening again.

Some days it was like everyone made a conscious decision to

move on from the war and all the death, from the knowledge we weren't alone in this universe or on this planet. The world had exhausted itself on fear, and then said, *Nope, no more.*

Maybe that was for the better, because how could we keep living if all we feared was what the next second or minute would bring?

I didn't have an answer for that.

My phone rang, pulling me out of my thoughts. I glanced at the screen and saw April's name pop up. Did I want to answer the phone? It felt like it was too early to deal with her. Immediately, guilt churned. I hit the accept call button on the steering wheel. "Hey!"

"What are you doing right now?" she asked, her voice carrying through the speakers.

"Um . . . driving past Walkers." My stomach grumbled. I could practically taste the greasy amazingness. "I really would love a burger right now."

"It's, like, eleven in the morning."

"So? There is no bad time for a hamburger."

"Well, maybe add some bacon and eggs to it, and you could call it breakfast."

My stomach rumbled even louder. "God, now I'm really hungry."

"You're always hungry," she commented. "Better keep an eye on that. Metabolism slows down as you get older."

Rolling my eyes, I then scowled. "Thanks for the info, Dr. April."

"You're welcome," she chirped back.

I stopped at a red light. "What are you doing?"

"Nothing really, but have you been online today?"

"No." I tapped my fingers along the wheel. "Am I missing drama?"

"There is always drama online, no matter the time or day, whether it's a holiday or an apocalypse," she replied dryly. "But yeah, there's drama online. Except it's the real deal. Oh wait. Is Heidi with you?"

"No. I'm heading home. Does this have to do with her?" Knowing April, if something horrible was circulating about Heidi online, April's first call would be to everyone and anyone other than Heidi. Wasn't anything personal. She'd do the same thing to any of us.

Sometimes I wondered why I was friends with April, but she was like two different people. There were times when she was the sweetest person, and then there was this other side of her that could be downright nasty. Then again, we weren't exactly that close. She usually only called me when she had something she wanted to gossip about or needed a favor. Like now.

"It has nothing to do with Heidi," she replied.

The light flipped green and I hit the gas pedal. "What's going on?"

"You know Colleen Shultz, right? She was in our English class last year."

As I slowed down to approach yet another stoplight, my stomach tumbled. Holy crap, I'd forgotten all about seeing Colleen at the club last night. "Yeah. What about her?"

"She's missing."

"What?" I slammed on the brakes, causing the seat belt to choke me. My gaze flew to the rearview mirror. Thank God no one was behind me. "What do you mean?"

"Supposedly she went out last night with some friends and they got separated. Doesn't sound like a big deal, right?"

My grip tightened on the steering wheel. "Right."

"Once everyone found each other later, Colleen never showed up. They went looking for her and ended up finding her purse and her *shoes* in this alley. Like you and I both know, that isn't a good sign." April's voice heightened with excitement, because apparently there was nothing more exciting than a missing classmate. "But here's the scandalicious part of it. Colleen was at that club last night. You know the one where supposedly all the aliens hang out? She was at Foretoken."

8

Colleen's disappearance was all I could think about the rest of the day, shoving aside everything that had happened with Luc and my stupid phone.

I knew why Colleen had gotten separated from her friends. Obviously. It must've happened during the raid, and I was pretty sure I knew what alley April was talking about. The same one I'd nearly face-planted into after scrambling out of the window. I hadn't seen a purse or shoes, but I also hadn't been paying attention to anything other than getting away from that club and finding Heidi.

April had insisted that Colleen's friends had gone to her house and her parents hadn't seen or heard from her either. It may be too soon to say she was truly missing, but no one knew where she was and April had been right about one thing, though. A purse and shoes left behind in an alley? That was bad news.

When people disappeared under those circumstances, their stories rarely had a happy ending.

But wasn't that Luxen found in the same alley? The one who was horrifically beaten? That was what Archer had said. He'd found Chas by the dumpster. And how coincidental was that? Colleen's belongings were found in the same alley where Chas had been nearly beaten to death?

That was what woke me up Sunday morning and stopped me from going back to sleep. Had Colleen seen something at the club Friday night, something like what I'd seen? Luc had said . . . God, hadn't he basically told me that people got hurt when they saw things they shouldn't? Maybe not in those words exactly, but that was how they'd come across. And he was definitely hiding Luxen at Foretoken—*unregistered* Luxen.

Did that happen to Colleen? She saw them or something, and now she was simply *gone*? Did it have something to do with what had happened to Chas? Maybe he knew something, and when he woke up, if he woke up, he'd be able to tell someone.

Then again, Chas was unregistered. Who could he tell who wouldn't jeopardize his safety?

A shudder rocked me as I flipped onto my side. I wasn't close to Colleen at all. With the exception of briefly speaking to her Friday night, we'd maybe exchanged a handful of sentences. Despite that and because of the reality of the situation, I really hoped she showed up.

As I sat up and threw my legs off the bed, I couldn't stop a horrible thought from forming. If something did happen to her, it could've . . . it could've happened to Heidi or me. I'd been in that dank, dark alley on Friday night.

I'd fallen into it, actually.

It could've happened to me when I went back to the club to get my phone. It felt like I'd tempted fate twice.

And who knew where Heidi had been until she made it to the car to wait for me? Another shudder rolled over me. That was scary to think about.

"That club is such bad news," I muttered as I made my way to the bathroom.

Colleen would probably show up to school Monday morning. The days of people simply vanishing without a trace were long over. People just didn't go missing like that. Not anymore.

I kept telling myself that the whole time I was in the bathroom and while I changed into a pair of leggings and a long shirt. Hopefully the power of positive thinking was a real thing.

I snatched my poor cell phone off the nightstand and then made my way downstairs. Mom was already awake, in the kitchen, wearing a cream-colored robe and fuzzy kitten slippers that I swore were the size of her head.

Despite her poor clothing choices, Mom was gorgeous. Her

short, sleek blond hair never looked frizzy like mine. She was tall and slender, carrying an innate gracefulness even when she wore giant kitten heads as slippers that I figured hadn't been passed down to me yet.

I had a bad habit of comparing myself to Mom.

She was like fine vintage wine, and I was the watered-down stuff that came in boxes and was sold at pharmacies.

"There you are." She held a monster-sized coffee cup between her palms as she leaned against the kitchen island. "I was wondering if you were ever going to get up."

Grinning, I shuffled into the kitchen. "It's not that late."

"I was lonely."

"Uh-huh." Walking over to her, I stopped and stretched up, kissing her cheek. "How long have you been awake?"

"I've been up since seven." She turned, watching me walk to the fridge. "Figured I'd spend Sunday in my pajamas. You know, not wash my hair or brush my teeth."

Laughing, I pulled out a bottle of apple juice. "That's hot, Mom. Definitely the not-brushing-your-teeth part."

"That's what I thought," she replied. "We didn't get a chance to chat last night. You were already asleep when I got home. You girls get into anything fun Friday night?"

Making a face, I kept my back to her as I grabbed a glass. "Nothing really. We just watched movies and ate cupcakes. Lots of cupcakes."

"Sounds like my kind of Friday night."

As I poured the apple juice, I smoothed out my expression before turning to her. "I ate so many cupcakes." Which was completely true. I probably gained five pounds on Friday night. I headed into the living room and plopped down on the couch, setting my glass on a coaster on the coffee table. Then I checked my phone. Zoe and James both had texted already. They wanted to grab lunch, but after Friday night and Saturday morning, I kind of wanted to hibernate safely in my house.

For about a month.

"You're heading to Frederick today? Right?" I asked as I walked into the living room. Even thought it was Sunday, Mom worked a lot. There were some days I didn't even see her, but before she got married and decided to become a mom, she traveled to places all over the world, investigating outbreaks of diseases. Now she did more research type work, overseeing a group of medical researchers in the infectious diseases part of the medical compound.

Her job was kind of gross.

The things I'd sometimes heard her talking about gave me nightmares. Boils and pustules. Vessels hemorrhaging all over the place, eyes bleeding and bursting. Intense fevers that killed people in hours.

Yuck.

"I brought some paperwork home to get caught up on, but I don't have any plans to head out today."

"Damn," I said, picking up the remote and clicking on the TV. "I was planning to throw a party. A massive one. With drugs. Lots of drugs."

Mom snorted as she sat perched on the edge of the chair, placing her mug on another coaster. Mom was big on coasters. They were everywhere in the house.

She asked me about school as I flipped through the channels. There wasn't much to tell her as I mindlessly continued to scroll, stopping when I saw the president was on one of the news channels.

"What's he doing on TV? It's Sunday." That was kind of a dumb question. The president, fair-haired and somewhat young—at least compared to other presidents—seemed to always be on television, giving press conference after press conference or addressing the people.

"I think that's a speech from Friday."

"Oh." I started to turn the channel, but I noticed the banner along the bottom of the screen: PRESIDENT MCHUGH DISCUSSES BILL TO CHANGE ARP POLICIES.

ARP stood for Alien Registration Program, a system that required all Luxen who stayed behind after the war to be identified and monitored. There were even websites dedicated to informing people if a Luxen was registered as living in a neighborhood or working at a certain business.

I had never actually checked out one of those websites.

"What is this about?"

Mom lifted a shoulder. "There's talk about changing some of the laws surrounding the registration."

"I figured that," I replied dryly.

When President McHugh spoke, he did so staring directly into the camera, and no matter what he said, there was always a slight tilt to his lips, like he was a few muscle twitches away from actually smiling but never fully committing. I always found that a bit unnerving, but everyone seemed to love him. I imagined his age helped, as did his appearance. I guessed he was handsome, in a rugged sort of way. Coming from a military background, he was elected in a landside the past year, campaigning on the promise to make our country safe for all Americans.

I had a feeling he didn't include the Luxen in the whole "all Americans" pitch.

Flipping the remote in my hand, I asked, "Any details on the changes?"

She sighed. "There's a push for more separation, moving the Luxen to communities where they will be safer, which, of course, is safer for us." She paused. "Also cracking down on unregistered Luxen. They have to pass the changes to existing laws to implement some of the programs he's wanting to do."

I thought about the raid at the club and the Luxen hidden in the room—the Luxen who'd seemed terrified of me. I promptly changed the channel, settling on a show about people who hoard all kinds of things in their home.

"I cannot watch this." Mom shook her head. "It makes me want to start organizing things."

Rolling my eyes, I looked around our living room—at our painfully organized living room. Everything had a place, which usually involved a basket—a white or gray basket. The entire house was that way, so how could Mom organize more? Baskets by size? Color?

But Mom was totally going to watch this. Just like me. We couldn't help ourselves. These kinds of shows were like crack.

Picking up my drink, I stilled when I heard a weird sound, something I couldn't quite place. I put my juice aside, looking over my shoulder and into the foyer. The whole bottom floor was open, one room flowing into another with the exception of Mom's office, which was a closed door accessed from the entryway. Sunlight filtered in through the narrow windowpanes on either side of the front door.

Not seeing anything, I started to face the TV again when I thought I saw a shadow move in front of a window. I frowned. "Hey, Mom?"

"What, hon?"

The shadow by the window appeared again. "I think . . . someone is at the door."

"Huh." She rose. "We shouldn't be getting a delivery. . . ." She trailed off as the handle turned left and then right, as if someone were trying to open the door.

What the . . . ?

My gaze shot to the security keypad on the foyer wall, confirming what I already knew. The alarm wasn't set. It rarely was during the day, but the door was locked—

The bottom lock turned, unlocking as if someone had used a key.

"Mom?" I whispered, unsure if I was seeing what I was seeing.

"Evie, I need you to get up." Her voice was surprisingly flat and calm. "Now."

I'd never moved faster in my life. Backing up, I bumped into the gray ottoman as Mom quickly stepped around me. I expected her to go to the door, but she moved to where I'd been sitting. She yanked one of the pillows off the back of the couch and then pulled a cushion up.

Mom took out a gun—a freaking *shotgun*—from underneath the couch cushion. My mouth dropped open. I knew we had guns in the house. Mom was in the military. Duh. But hidden under a couch cushion where I sat and napped and ate cheesy puffs?

"Stand behind me," she ordered.

"Oh my God, *Mom!*" I stared at her. "I've been sitting on a shotgun this entire time? Do you know how dangerous that is? I can't—"

The deadbolt unlocked, the click echoing like thunder. I took another step back. How . . . how was that possible? No one could unlock the deadbolt from the outside. *That* could only be unlocked from inside.

Mom lifted the shotgun, aiming straight at the door. "Evelyn," she barked out. "Get behind me *now.*"

I darted around the couch, moving to stand behind her. On second thought, I whipped around and grabbed a candleholder—the new wooden gray-and-white one I'd wanted to take pictures of later. Not sure exactly what I was going to do with said candleholder, but gripping it like a baseball bat sure made me feel better. "If someone is breaking in, shouldn't we call the police? I mean, that seems like the nonviolent way of dealing with this, and the police can help—"

The front door then swung open and someone tall and broad stepped inside, their features and form blurred out by the sun for a moment. Then the door swung close, slamming shut without anyone touching it, and the glow from the sun was gone.

I almost dropped the candleholder.

It was *him.*

Luc stood in my foyer, smiling like my mother wasn't aiming a shotgun at his face—his pretty face. He didn't glance at me. Not once as he inclined his head. "Hey, Sylvia. Long time no see."

My heart pounded erratically as my gaze bounced between the two. He knew my mom? Where I lived?

Mom lifted her chin. "Hello, Luc."

9

For a moment I didn't think I moved or breathed as I stared at Mom, dressed in a robe and fuzzy kitten slippers, holding a damn shotgun, and Luc, wearing a shirt that read DILL WITH IT, and there was a pickle underneath the words, wearing . . . *sunglasses*?

Yep. Sunglasses.

I was still gripping my candleholder. "You *know* him, Mom?"

That half grin appeared on Luc's face. "Sylvia and I go way back, don't we?"

What?

The shotgun in Mom's hands didn't shake once. "What are you doing here?"

"I was in the neighborhood. Thought I'd stop by for lunch." He took a step forward. "Was hoping I'd get a home-cooked meal."

What the what?

"Move any closer, and we will all find out what kind of lasting damage a twelve-gauge slug does to your head," Mom warned.

My eyes widened. Oh my word, Mom *was* a badass—a scary badass.

However, it appeared Luc didn't realize that yet. "That's not really neighborly. Actually, it's quite rude. Is that how you normally greet guests?"

"You know better than to come here, Luc." Mom had said his name again, confirming that I hadn't been hearing things earlier. She knew him. "And you know damn well you're not a guest."

Especially considering guests don't normally let themselves in.

Peeking over Mom's shoulder, my gaze met Luc's. The breath

I took halted as his smile deepened. There was a . . . wicked quality about that smile, a secretive twist.

I couldn't believe I'd kissed him.

Well, I hadn't kissed him. I was devoid of responsibility when it came to that. He'd kissed me and he'd also tried to *kidnap* me. I gripped the candleholder tighter.

"You know how I feel when it comes to following rules," Luc replied. "And you should also know how I feel about having a gun pointed at my head."

"I don't care how you feel about that," Mom spat back.

"Really?" Luc lifted his hand, opening his fingers. Mom gasped as her shoulders jerked. The shotgun ripped away from her grip and flew across the room. Luc snatched it out of the air.

"Holy crap," I whispered.

Still smiling, as if he were beyond pleased with himself, he wrapped his other hand around the barrel of the shotgun. "Do you know how many people are killed by guns?" He paused as he raised his brows. The scent of burnt ozone filled the air. "That's not a rhetorical question. I'm honestly curious."

Mom lowered her arms and her hands formed fists. "One short of how many are killed, I'm thinking."

He smirked. "I personally don't have a problem with guns. Not that I have any use for them. I really just don't like them pointed at me."

The sharp tang of burning metal caused my eyes to water. Luc opened his hands and the disfigured shotgun fell, clattering on the floor.

The barrel was melted in the center.

"Holy crap," I repeated, taking yet another step back.

Luc leaned to the side, eyeing where I stood behind my mom. "A . . . *candleholder*?" He laughed, and it sounded like a genuine laugh. "Really?"

Mom stepped to the side, blocking him from my view. "Don't come near her. Don't even look at her."

"Well, it's a little too late for that," Luc replied dryly, and my stomach sunk. He wouldn't. "I've looked at her." Another pause. "I've definitely been near her. Like, really close. You could say, we were so close, there wasn't any space between us."

Oh my God.

I didn't stop to think what about what I was doing. Cocking my arm back, I threw that candleholder like I was winging a blade. It spun across the room, heading straight for his head.

Luc caught the candleholder as a look of shock splashed across his face.

Mom gasped as she spun, facing me. "Evie, *don't*."

I froze, hands at my sides. Considering my mom had pulled a *shotgun* on him, I figured she'd be proud of me tapping into my inner commando and throwing a candleholder at him.

Apparently not.

"Did you seriously just do that?" Luc demanded, staring at the candleholder for a moment and then throwing it onto the couch, where it harmlessly bounced and then thudded to the floor. He pinned me with a dark stare. "You could get yourself killed doing things like that."

The robe whirled around Mom's legs as she spun on a kitten slipper. She threw her arm out as if she could ward Luc off with just her hand.

Luc's features sharpened as his purple stare shifted to Mom. Something about him looked primal, then, almost animalistic. Pure power flowed from him, filling every nook and cranny in the room. Static charged the air, raising the hair on my arms.

Was he going to go full Luxen? I'd never seen that in person, only on the television. A morbid sense of fascination filled me.

"Really?" Luc said, his voice soft with deadly warning.

My heart lurched in my chest, and then Mom lowered her hand. She seemed to draw in a deep, heavy breath. A tense moment passed. "What do you want, Luc?"

I didn't expect him to answer. I honestly expected him to go nuclear like a Luxen could, but he seemed to pull the rippling power back in, sealing it up and stashing it away. "I'm here to do you a solid, Sylvia, because I'm helpful like that."

Mom waited, every part of her body screaming that she was on high alert.

He reached into his pocket and pulled out something thin and rectangular. I had no idea what it was, and there was a good chance I was close to passing out, because my heart was pumping so fast, I felt dizzy. He tossed it into the air.

With impressive reflexes, Mom caught whatever it was. Her chin dipped. A second later she whirled on *me*. "What is this, Evelyn?"

"Oh no," Luc murmured. "The full name just came out. Someone is in trouble."

"What?" I asked, glancing at Luc while wishing I had another weapon to throw at him. Maybe a missile. That would be great.

"This," she snapped, holding up my . . . fake ID.

I gaped in disbelief. She was holding the ID that Luc had taken from me on Friday night. I'd forgotten that he still had it.

Luc winked when I turned to him.

I was struck speechless. Literally. No words. He came here, almost got his head blown off and then knocked off by a candle-holder just to rat me out? All when he could've just given it to me yesterday.

Then his words came back to me. *When I said I would see you again, I hadn't meant today.*

He'd known yesterday that he'd had that ID and he hadn't given it back to me.

I couldn't even believe it.

This wasn't happening to me. All I wanted to do with my Sunday was drink my apple juice and watch *Hoarders*. That was all.

That look hit Mom's face, the one that said I was seconds from being buried in the backyard and her ending up on some show about when mothers kill their young. "I . . ."

She tilted her head to the side, waiting.

It was Luc who spoke up, because of course he would. "Your *daughter* left that at Foretoken on Friday night."

My jaw was on the floor.

His smirk grew to a point that it took everything in me not to jump on him like a rabid platypus, and that would be bad, because a platypus was poisonous. I knew this, because, well, the internet. "I thought you would like to know she was there. More than once, I might add."

My eyes were going to pop out of my face. I couldn't believe he was doing this, especially after he'd made it scarily clear that I better not say one word about what I'd seen at the club.

Luc wasn't done yet. "She left her phone there Friday night and came back for it yesterday morning. I was kind enough to keep it safe and give it back to her."

"Kind enough?" I shrieked. "You tried to—" I caught myself at the last moment. If I said he tried to kidnap me, then I'd have to explain why, which involved a horde of illegal Luxen. As much as I wanted to see Mom go all badass on him again, I wouldn't put those Luxen in danger. Or her. He arched a brow, and I finished with a sad, "You are not nice."

He pressed his lips together as if he were fighting a laugh or a smile.

Mom didn't respond. She didn't need to. I was dead, so dead, and I was going to come back as a ghost just to haunt Luc for the rest of his godforsaken life.

Then she finally spoke. "Is that all, Luc?"

"Are you making lunch?" he asked. "I'd do bad, bad things for a homemade grilled cheese sandwich."

I gaped at him.

"And tomato soup. That would be an amazing combination," he added after a moment.

"No," Mom bit out. "I am not making you lunch, Luc."

He sighed heavily. "Well, that's disappointing."

"Is that all?" she repeated.

"I guess so." He sighed, sounding bored. He started to turn but stopped. He faced Mom again. "Oh yeah, one more thing. All bets are off now. You feel me?"

Mom stiffened. "Luc—"

"No, no." He tsked softly. "Don't think you really want to get into the details right now. So I just want to hear one thing from you, or we'll all be having a very interesting conversation that will include grilled cheese and tomato soup."

What in the hell were they talking about?

Mom's lips thinned. "I feel you."

"Perfect." Luc's gaze met mine and held it for a moment too long. A shiver slipped down my arms, rattling my bones. He turned and strolled back to the door. "Peace out."

Luc walked out of the house like none of that had just happened, quietly closing the door behind him.

And I was still standing there, half afraid to even look at Mom. My thoughts were whirling all over the place as I inched over to my right and picked up my apple juice. I downed half the glass and then put it back on the coaster.

Mom still hadn't spoken.

"Um, I didn't know Luxen could just unlock doors." I took a step back from her. "That's actually a really scary piece of knowledge that . . ."

Mom glared at me.

"That . . . um, should be more widely known," I finished lamely as I walked around to the chair and sat down on the edge. My heart was still thundering.

She inhaled noisily through her nose as a strand of her sleek blond hair fell forward, against her cheek. "What were you doing at Foretoken?" She paused. "The *first* time."

"Okay." I swallowed hard. "I know you're mad, but I have questions too. Like why would there be a shotgun hidden under the couch cushions?"

Mom's brows rose.

All right, that might not have been the best thing to ask, but it was a valid question, and I had another very serious question. "And how do you know him?"

Her eyes widened in a way that suggested she thought I might've lost my mind. "I'm the one who is in the position to be asking questions, Evelyn *Lee*. Not you."

Oh no, now the middle name just came out.

"So, let me ask one more time, and it better be the last: What were you doing at Foretoken?"

"We just wanted to go out," I said, pushing my hair off my face as I stared at the door Luc had unlocked with his *freaking mind*. How did I not know they could do that? Well, most Luxen wore the Disabler, so I'd never seen them do anything like that. "I know I shouldn't have, but I . . . I don't have a good enough reason."

"Damn straight, you don't have a good enough reason." Mom bent down, swiftly picking up the ruined shotgun. "Where did you get this ID?"

I shrugged.

"Evelyn," she snapped.

"I don't know. From someone at school." No way was I throwing James under the bus. "It's not a big deal—"

"It's a huge deal." Mom tossed the shotgun onto the other chair. "Not only is that club for twenty-one and up, as I am sure you know, it's not a safe place."

I cringed. Folding my arms in my lap, I leaned forward. "I know I messed up."

"You lied to me." She picked up the couch cushion and then slammed it into place. "That is not okay."

Feeling like I was about two feet tall, I watched her straighten up the couch. "I'm sorry."

She plucked up the candleholder and faced me. "Did you see him Friday night? Luc?"

Knowing that lying to her again wouldn't be smart but telling the complete truth would be even worse, I chose my words very carefully. "I did."

She closed her eyes as her jaw jutted out. I knew she was searching for a calm, happy place.

"It's not like I hung out with him, Mom. I just . . . talked to him."

A moment passed and then she opened her eyes again. Sitting on the couch, close to me, she held the candleholder. "What did he say to you?"

I shook my head, a little confused. "Nothing really. He just de-

manded to know why I was there and then said I shouldn't be."
I saw her shoulders relax a little. "Mom, how do you know him?
How does he know where we live?"

She didn't answer as she lowered her gaze. A long moment
passed while I waited. Mom always looked younger than her age.
She was in her late forties, but I always thought she could've passed
for someone in her thirties.

Until right then.

Faint lines were etched into the skin around the corners of her
eyes, and she looked tired. Maybe those lines had always been there
and now, with a weariness clinging to her skin and bones, I could
see them.

"Luc knew your father," she said finally.

That was the last thing I expected her to say. "How? How is
that possible? Luc's about my age, right? Did Dad know him when
Luc first arrived here?"

Mom pressed her lips together. "Honey, I don't know . . .
I don't know how to tell you any of this. I'd hoped I would never
have to, but I guess that was foolish of me. I should've known this
day was coming."

A chill skated down my spine. "What are you talking about?"

She was quiet so long, I started to get really freaked out, and
that was saying something, considering there were shotguns under
cushions and random Luxen roaming into the house, unlocking
doors. "There are things you don't know—things that the general
public has no idea about."

"Like the Luxen being able to unlock doors with their mind?"

Her lips twitched. "Bigger than that, hon."

I thought that was pretty big.

After placing the candleholder on the ottoman, she angled her
body toward mine. "There are times when decisions are made for
the better good, and sometimes that involves omitting details—"

"You mean lying?" I suggested.

Her lips pursed. "I know where you're going to take this, but
lying about going to the club is not the same thing as lying to protect someone, and in this case, the entire world."

My brows lifted. A lie was a lie, but arguing that point wasn't important. "That sounds . . . serious."

"It is. Serious enough that people have died to keep certain details unknown." Stretching over, she placed her hand on my knee. "There are things I'm not allowed to discuss because of my job—because of what Jason used to do and be part of, but . . ." She exhaled heavily. "But if I don't tell you, then I know he will, and I'd rather it come from me."

"He?" I straightened. "You mean Luc? I have no intentions of ever seeing him again. Ever. Like, never, ever going to happen."

Mom pulled her hand back and she looked like she was about to say something but had changed her mind. A moment passed and then she said, "The Luxen have been here for a very long time. For decades."

I blinked once and then twice. "What?"

She nodded. "As you know, their world was destroyed. That part was true, but they didn't come here decades ago to invade us. They came to basically recolonize—to live out their lives peacefully among us. The governments all around the world knew of their existence, and they worked hard to assimilate them—pass them off as humans—and it worked. It worked rather well until the invasion."

"Wait. I am so confused." I pushed up from the chair. "You're telling me that the Luxen have been here forever and no one knew?"

"That's what I'm saying," she answered.

"How in the world did they keep it a secret?"

She arched a delicate brow. "Honey, you'd be amazed at what has been kept secret and has nothing to do with aliens from outer space."

"Like what?" I immediately asked. "What about the assassination of JFK? Oh—what about Roswell? Was that really—"

"Let's just focus on this, okay?"

I sighed, but I refocused. "I just don't get how they could keep something like that hidden for so long. It doesn't seem possible."

"It didn't always work. People found out. There were issues, I'm sure," she said, dropping her hands to her knees. "The knowledge of other intelligent life-forms was—still is—powerful and dangerous. When it was first known that they were here, the decision was made to keep it quiet until it was deemed that society could handle such knowledge. Unfortunately, time wasn't on anyone's side. The invading Luxen came before anyone was confident that society could handle the news that we most definitely are not alone in the universe."

This was utterly unbelievable.

"Many of the Luxen who are here, the ones who registered and are following our laws, are the ones who weren't part of the invasion. Very few of the invading Luxen survived. Those who did left our planet, and it's speculated that only very few remained after the failed invasion."

Confusion swept over me as I started pacing in front of the ottoman. "If some of the Luxen had been here and living normal, nice lives, why did the others invade then? They could've been—What did you call it?"

"Assimilated."

"Yeah, that. They could've been assimilated right along with the rest of them. Why did they do what they did?"

Mom tucked a strand of her hair back. "Because the others wanted to take over. They wanted this world for their own. Those Luxen hadn't come into contact with humans until they came here, and they viewed humans as something lesser."

Then did that mean Luc had been one of the invading Luxen? Because he definitely wasn't registered. But that wasn't the important thing. Anger rose, crowding out the confusion. "This makes no sense." I threw up my hands. "If people knew about the Luxen, then they could've been prepared for an invasion. All of the technology we have now—the Disablers, the weapons? We could've already had all of that. Fewer people would've died."

"Hindsight is usually twenty-twenty."

I gaped at her. "That's your response?"

The corners of her lips turned down. "Honey, I'm not the one who made those decisions."

I was still wearing a path in the throw rug in front of the ottoman as I crossed my arms. "But you knew about it?"

"Yes."

And she hadn't alerted the world to the fact that crazy-powerful aliens were already living among us? I stopped, facing her. "How did you know, though? You work with gross viruses and—"

"I used to work for the Daedalus. It was a specialized group within the military, sanctioned by the government, that worked on . . . assimilating the Luxen. The department is—Well, it no longer exists."

My mouth formed the word. "The dao-what?"

A faint smile appeared. "Daedalus. It's from Greek mythology. He was an inventor and the father of Icarus."

"Icarus?" I vaguely remembered that name. "Didn't he fly too close to the sun and his wings melted or something?"

Mom nodded. "Daedalus had built those wings for his son."

"That's a weird name for a department in the government."

"It was more of a code name. That's how I met Jason. He also worked there."

I walked back to the chair, then sat down and listened, really listened, because Mom so rarely spoke about Dad.

Mom's gaze flickered away, settling on the television. "That's how your father knew Luc. That's how I met him, when Luc was younger."

"So . . . he wasn't one of the invading Luxen? He'd been here?" For some reason, I hoped that was the case. I didn't want to think of Luc as a homicidal alien hell-bent on killing us, even though he kind of came off as one.

Her expression tightened and then smoothed out. "He was not part of the invasion."

That made me feel a little better, knowing I hadn't been kissed by a killer alien from outer space. It was the small things that made one's crappy life choices easier to deal with.

I shook my head. "So did you guys help Luc assimilate? Or his parents?"

Mom didn't respond for a long moment. "Something like that."

That wasn't much of answer. In fact, it was so evasive, I knew there was more to it.

She tipped her head back as her shoulders stiffened. "Jason . . ." She dampened her lips. "Jason wasn't a good man."

My breath caught. "I don't understand. Dad was—He was a *hero*." There was actually a statue of him in the capital! Well, not really a statue of him. It was a weird monolith-looking thing, but still. "He was awarded the Medal of Honor."

Her eyes yet drifted shut. "Honey, awards aren't a true reflection of a person. There have been many, many people highly awarded and acclaimed throughout history who were, in the end, very bad people. Oftentimes people who were so convinced that they were doing the right thing, they were able to overlook all the terrible things they were doing in pursuit of the greater good."

"But . . ." I trailed off as my heart banged around in my chest. I didn't know what to do with that piece of knowledge. I had never been close to Dad. Not really. He had never been home, but . . . "But you've told me he was a good man. You told me all the important—"

"I lied," she cut in, opening her eyes again and meeting my wide-eyed stare. "I lied because I didn't want you to know the truth about him. And yes, it was a necessary lie, one I hoped you would never have to learn was a lie, but with Luc here, I'd rather you hear it from me than him."

"What . . . what does Dad have to do with him?"

Mom rubbed her hands down her face. "Jason wasn't very kind to the Luxen he worked with. He could . . . often be very cruel to them." She paused, and I thought perhaps she was telling a lot by saying very little. "He and Luc had a past. It's not a good one."

What Luc had said to me in the club rose to the surface. He'd said I didn't belong there. I thought maybe he was just being a jerk, but what if it was bigger than that? What if he meant I shouldn't be around him, because of whatever my dad had done to him or his family?

But if that was the case, then why had he kissed me?

I scooted to the edge of the chair. "Mom, what did Dad do?"

"He made sure that Luc lost someone very dear to him," Mom answered, and I jerked at the unexpected response. "And that is something Luc will never forget nor forgive. Because of that, Luc can be very dangerous."

My heart started thundering again. "Because he's obviously not a registered Luxen?"

"Because I used to fear that Luc would seek retribution for what Jason had done to him."

My eyes widened. "Retribution? Holy crap. Dad is—He's dead. What did he do to Luc—"

"Jason was responsible for a lot of things and he made a lot of enemies and he . . . made a lot of bad choices," she said quietly, almost as if she were afraid she'd be overheard. If Dad had enemies, then I guessed that was why we had shotguns under couch cushions? "None of that matters. I just didn't want you to learn from someone else that the man who so many people look up to wasn't a very good person."

My head felt like it was going to implode. "Should we be worried about . . . Luc coming after us?"

Her gaze held mine. "I said I *used* to fear that. The truth is, if he'd wanted to hurt you or me, he would've already done that."

"Wow. That's reassuring."

"It's not meant to be," she replied. "It's just the truth. If he wanted to use me to carry out some sort of vendetta, it would've already happened." She rose, fiddling with the sash on her robe. "Luc would never hurt you."

I opened my mouth, but my tongue got all tied up. That didn't make sense. Luc didn't know me, and if my dad had done terrible things that involved Luc losing someone, I doubted he wanted to be my best friend forever. It didn't require a leap in logic to assume that "losing someone" meant someone dying. "Are you sure we're safe?"

Mom smoothed a hand over her forehead. "Oh, honey, we are," she was quick to reassure me. "It's just always good to be prepared."

I wasn't sure if I believed her. "Are there other methods of being prepared stashed around the house?"

Another smile formed as she placed her hand on my knee. "I

wouldn't mess with the pillows too much in the window seat upstairs."

"Mom." I drew in a deep breath. "Are there any more people Dad might've pissed off who we've got to worry about?"

"We are safe, but just like anyone, we have to be careful. There are bad people out there, Luxen and human, you don't want to draw attention from. The same kind of rules that applied before the invasion, you know?"

I nodded slowly. "Stranger danger kind of stuff?"

"Yes." She moved over, sitting on the edge of the ottoman so she was directly in front of me. She picked up my hands. "What are you thinking?"

A lot of stuff. "I never should've gone to that club."

"Glad we're in agreement on that." She squeezed my hands. "Right now I'm more concerned about what I told you about Jason. I know that's a lot to process."

It was.

She brought my hands up. "I'm going to be really honest with you. Okay?"

"Okay," I whispered.

"I'm not sorry I lied about who Jason really was. You deserve to believe what everyone else does," she said, her eyes searching mine. "Sometimes the truth is worse than the lie."

10

I thought Mom was going to straight up murder me," I said, dragging my fork through what I thought might be spaghetti but had the weird consistency of soup. "Like, for real."

Lunch had just started on Monday, and Heidi sat across from me, beside James, who was brown-bagging lunch because he was obviously smarter than the rest of us.

We were waiting for Zoe to join, but she was still in the lunch line, looking like she'd rather throw herself out the nearest window.

Heidi handed my camera back to me. She'd been looking through my pictures. "I'm so sorry."

"It's not your fault," I told her, placing the camera next to my tray. "You didn't make Luc show up at my house."

I'd told them about what had gone down, leaving out the part where my mom had pulled out a shotgun and I'd thrown a candleholder. I also didn't tell them all the secret stuff Mom had told me. Didn't take a rocket scientist to know that I needed to keep that to myself. James had also kept quiet about Saturday morning, which I appreciated.

Mom had shut down any further conversation by sending me to my room, where I stayed, the rest of Sunday.

Which sucked, because I still had so many questions. Like, for example, how did Mom, once upon a time, work for an organization responsible for assimilating Luxen, which was how she and Dad—aka former national hero, now apparently a really bad dude—met Luc, but Luc remained an unregistered alien? And if Mom knew he was unregistered, then why hadn't she reported him? We all were required to do so, especially her, considering

Mom still worked for the military. What would happen if someone found out she knew him and that he was unregistered?

Was it guilt? Guilt for what my dad did to Luc?

I couldn't shake the feeling that there was so much more than what Mom had told me.

James picked up his peanut butter sandwich, and envy filled me. That looked so much tastier than what was on my plate. "I can't believe he just showed up like that. Man, my dad would've called the police in a heartbeat."

That sounded like the reasonable thing to do.

"How did he find out where you lived?" Heidi asked, fiddling with the lacy collar of her shirt. "Because I so did not tell Emery anything like that."

Unsure of how to answer her question, I shifted in the uncomfortable plastic chair. "I really don't know."

Her brows lifted. "That's kind of creepy."

"How long are you grounded?" James peeled the crust off his sandwich, dropping a long section of brown bread on his bag.

I sighed as I fantasized about knocking James out of his seat and stealing his sandwich, but that would be kind of mean. "Here's the bizarre thing: I'm not."

"You're not what?" Zoe dropped into the open chair beside me as a teacher shouted at someone in the back of the cafeteria. Zoe had a slice of pizza on her tray. I shuddered. I hated pizza. James said that meant I had no soul, but whatever. It was just gross.

"Evie is somehow not grounded," James answered, now pulling his sandwich into tiny pieces. He literally had the eating habits of a three-year-old.

Zoe's dark, naturally curly hair was pulled back in a tight ponytail today, highlighting her cheekbones. Those suckers were high and sculpted. "Not grounded?" She sounded confused. "Is that a problem?"

James finally popped a piece of sandwich into his mouth. "I'm wondering the same thing."

"It's not. It's just weird." Truthfully, I thought Mom felt so bad about the whole Dad Is a Monster speech that she decided not to ground me after sending me to my room. Or she'd forgotten, and I sure as hell wasn't going to remind her. I glanced over at Heidi. She was tapping away on her phone, and I was nosy. "Are you texting someone?"

"Yeah." She peeked up, grinning a little. "Emery wants to get together tonight."

"Like a date kind of thing?" I asked, excited and hopeful. "Like you and her having dinner together?"

Heidi nodded, and I swear, her cheeks started to turn pink. "Yep. She wants to grab dinner at that new Thai restaurant downtown." She paused. "And no, we're not going to Foretoken."

I dropped my fork and clapped my hands like an overexcited seal as I saw April heading our way, her long blond hair swinging around her shoulders. "I expect minute-by-minute updates."

Heidi laughed as April sat down across from Zoe. "I don't know if it will be minute by minute, but I will keep you updated."

"Awesome. I really wish I had a chance to meet her Friday night." As I picked up my fork, I vaguely heard April snapping at Zoe.

"Me too," she replied. "But you'll get a chance now. Especially since your mom really didn't kill you and you're not grounded."

"Wait." James had moved on to a small bag of potato chips. "Who is Emery? Does she go here?"

Heidi shook her head. "No, she graduated high school last year, but she's from Pennsylvania."

He popped a chip into his mouth. "Is she hot?"

I shot him a bland look. "Really?"

"It's a valid question." He offered the bag to me, and I grabbed a chip or five out of it.

"She's hot," Heidi answered, glancing down at her phone. "And she's smart. And funny. And she likes cupcakes and Thai food."

And she hangs out with a giant jerk-face, but I kept that to myself. I was not going to crap all over Heidi's happy parade. And besides, maybe I should cut Luc a bit of a break considering what I'd learned from Mom.

Which wasn't exactly a lot.

"So . . ." April drew the word out, waiting until everyone had focused on her. "Just a friendly update that one of our classmates is still missing."

Oh hell, I'd completely forgotten about that with all my own personal drama. That meant it was official. I was a terrible person. I also hadn't even thought about that poor Luxen who had had the crap beaten out of him.

"But is she really missing?" Zoe asked, glancing around the table. "I mean, maybe she ran away."

"To where?" April challenged. "To join the circus?"

Zoe rolled her eyes. "Wasn't Colleen dating some guy who was a senior last year? And he went to a college in a different state?"

"She was dating Tony Hickles," James answered. "He ended up going to the University of Michigan."

"So maybe she ran away to see him or something," Zoe suggested.

April frowned. I guessed to her that wasn't as exciting as some-one going missing for nefarious reasons. "Well, that's stupid."

James attempted to change the subject by asking Heidi for a picture of Emery, but it didn't work.

"You're so ridiculous," I heard April say, and I started praying to the cafeteria food gods that April wasn't about to drag me into argument number 140,000 with Zoe. For some reason, she always did. I had no idea what they were talking about.

I picked up my camera, pretending to be engrossed in it even though I wasn't looking at anything. Maybe I'd get lucky and be randomly sucked into some kind of vortex before—

"What do you think, Evie?" April demanded.

Crap.

The cafeteria food gods had let me down yet again.

James ducked his chin, hiding his grin, and then he twisted, an-gling his body so he was fully focused on Heidi as she pulled up a pic of Emery on her phone that she'd taken at the club on Friday night.

"Yes, Evie, what do you think?" parroted Zoe.

I'd rather shave off all my hair than answer any question posed in that manner. Knowing how April hated it when I took photos of her without her having checked her makeup and hair first, I lifted my camera and pointed it at her.

"You take a picture of me, I will throw your camera out the window," she warned.

I sighed, lowering that camera. "That's excessive."

"And I asked for your opinion."

I picked up my fork and stabbed my noodles, pretending I basically had no idea who these people I was sitting with were. "Huh?"

It didn't work.

April stared back at me with light blue eyes as she threw her hands up, nearly elbowing a guy squeezing into the seat behind her. She wasn't even aware of him, but that was typical April. God love her, but she wasn't aware of much of anything she didn't believe affected her.

"Have you not heard a single thing I've said?" she demanded.

"She probably tuned you out." Zoe plopped her cheek on her arm and sighed. "It's a talent I wish I had."

While James was distracted, I reached into his bag, stealing another chip.

"You know what I wish, *Ms.* Zoe Callahan?" April cocked her head to the side. "I wish you didn't dress like a toddler who got to pick out her clothes for the first time."

A noodle slopped off my fork. "Wow."

Heidi got quiet.

James suddenly decided that the people sitting behind us were more interesting, and turned completely in his seat. Hell, he was practically sitting with them now, which meant I couldn't reach into his bag of chips anymore.

Zoe leaned back, her dark eyes narrowing. "What's wrong with how I'm dressed?"

"You're wearing a onesie," April stated coolly.

Zoe was totally wearing a onesie.

"You look super-cute," I told her, and that was the truth. I, on the other hand, wouldn't be caught dead in a romper. I'd look like someone who needed Child Protective Services if I stepped out in public wearing that, but with Zoe's deep brown skin, she was rocking the pink frock.

"Thank you." Zoe flashed a bright smile in my direction and then turned a glare more powerful than the Death Star on April. "But I know I look cute."

April's brows lifted. "You may want to rethink that assessment."

I honestly had no idea how Zoe and April were friends. I swore they bickered more than they ever complimented each other. The only time I saw either do something nice for the other was last year. Some guy had bumped into April in the hallway, knocking her into a locker. Zoe put the fear of God in that boy in, like, under five seconds.

Zoe responded to April with something that was about as friendly as a kick in the throat. I started to intervene, because both could get loud, and I really didn't want our table to be the center of attention yet again, but a tray clattered off a nearby table, causing my stomach to pitch.

Classmates milled from table to table. Behind me, I could hear them talking about a party on Saturday night. Burnt food mingled with the scent of lemony disinfectant. Teachers lounged by the doors and at the back of the cafeteria, by the letters CHS painted on the wall. Outside the floor-to-ceiling windows, people sat on gray stone walls, laughing and talking, and the sky . . . I could see the September sky. It was blue and endless.

My gaze landed on the table near the door. That was where *they* all sat. The Luxen who attended our school. Ten of them. All of them beautiful. It was kind of hard not to get a little lost looking at them, especially when they sat together like that. I was sure I wasn't the only one gawking at them. I knew it wasn't polite, but I wondered why they didn't sit with anyone else.

Luxen siblings always came in threes. Two boys and a girl. Or at least that was what was said, but I'd never seen a full set of Luxen triplets in my life. We knew how many humans had died, but no one knew the number of Luxen. I imagined that was why I'd never seen a set of triplets.

I always thought they had been part of the invasion, just like everyone else believed, but now I knew differently. That entire table had probably been here since they were born, never once harming a human, but we . . . we were all afraid of them because the truth had been kept hidden.

That wasn't fair or right.

For some unknown reason, as I stared at them, an image of Luc formed in the back of my head. I could easily see him sitting with them. Well, I could easily picture him sitting at the end of the table like he was ruling over them.

Did any of his siblings survive the invasion? Were there three Lucs?

Oh dear.

"Stop staring at them," hissed April.

Feeling my cheeks heat, I swung my gaze back to her. "What?"

"At *them*—the Luxen."

"I'm not staring at them."

"Yes, you totally are." She lifted her brows as she glanced over her shoulder. "Ugh. Whatever. I don't have that big of a problem with them being here, but do they *really* have to be? Can't they have their own schools or something? Is that too much to ask?"

My grip tightened on my fork. "April . . ."

Zoe closed her eyes while she rubbed at her brow like her head was about to implode. "Here we go."

"What?" April said, glancing at the table by the doors. "They don't make me feel comfortable."

"They've been going to our school for almost three years. Have they ever done anything to you?" Zoe demanded.

"They could've before they started going here. You know that when they're in their real skin or whatever you want to call it, they all look alike."

"Oh my God," I groaned, placing my fork on my plate so I didn't turn it into a projectile. Now I knew the answer to my only question about why the Luxen sat together and didn't really mingle with the rest of us.

Because of people like April.

"I'm out." Heidi picked her bag off the floor as she rose, sending me a sympathetic look. She knew I wouldn't leave Zoe to fend for herself. There was a good chance one of these days, Zoe would snap and knock April into next week. "I got to run to the library real quick."

"Bye." I wiggled my fingers, watching her skirt the table and then go dump her trash.

April was completely undaunted. "That's the truth. You seriously cannot tell them apart. They all look like glowy human-shaped blobs. So maybe one of them did something when they first got here. How would I know?"

"Girl . . ." Zoe shook her head. "They don't give two craps about you. They are just trying to get an education and live their lives. And anyway, what can they do to you? Nothing."

"What can they do? Jesus, Zoe. They are like walking weapons. They can shoot bolts of electricity from their fingertips and they're super-strong—like, X-Men-level strong." The centers of April's cheeks turned rosy. "Or have you forgotten how they killed *millions* of people?"

"I didn't forget," snapped Zoe.

"They can't do that anymore," I reminded April even though all I could think of was Luc and the other Luxen I'd seen at the club. They were not wearing Disablers.

April's foot started tapping under the table, and that was the first sign she was seconds away from really blowing up. "Well, I hope the changes to ARP go through. I really do."

"April thinks that it's completely okay to round up people and relocate them against their will. That's what the ARP changes are." Zoe leaned back, folding her arms across her chest. "Registering them is no longer enough. They want to move them to God knows where, supposedly to these new communities designed for them. How can you be okay with that?"

I glanced over to where James was, but his seat was empty. I looked up and didn't see him anywhere. Smart boy. He'd bounced out of here like a rubber ball.

"First off, they're not people; they're aliens," April corrected her with another impressive roll of her eyes. "Secondly, last time

I checked, Earth belonged to humans and not glowing aliens who killed millions of people. It's not their right to live here. They're guests. Unwanted ones, at that."

"Hell yeah!" yelled some guy from the table behind her. Probably the one she'd almost elbowed in the stomach. "You tell them!"

Heat now crawled down my throat as I slumped down in my seat a little. April was so loud. So very loud.

"And my third and final point is that these communities aren't just to keep us safe." April folded her arms on the table and leaned forward. "They're to keep them safe too. You heard about them being attacked. Sometimes separate is better. And it's already kind of like that. Look at Breaker Subdivision. They like being around their own kind."

Breaker Subdivision was a neighborhood just like any community of homes that literally looked identical to one another. The one big thing that set it apart was the fact that only Luxen lived there.

"You sound like a politician," I told her. "Like one of those creepy ones who don't blink when they're talking into the cameras."

"I blinked. Like, five times during the very impressive speech I just gave."

I arched a brow.

Zoe pressed her lips together. "The Luxen don't want to hurt us."

"How do we know that?" April shot back.

"Maybe because there hasn't been an attack in over three years?" Zoe suggested, her tone pitching like she was explaining something to a misbehaving toddler. "That could be good evidence of such a belief."

"Just like there weren't attacks leading up to the night they made our planet their bitch?" April widened her eyes. "We didn't know they existed until they literally came zooming out of the sky and started killing everyone, but that didn't change anything."

A dull throb started in my temples as I pushed strands of hair out of my face and my gaze crept back to the table full of aliens. Could they hear April? I looked away, wanting to crawl under the table. "I'm pretty sure they just want to be left alone."

Frustration heightened the color in April's cheeks. "I know you can't be a fan of them, Evie."

My hands dropped into my lap as I stared at her, and I knew what she was going to do. She was so going to go there.

"Your father *died* because of them." April's voice was low and urgent, as if I had no idea that had occurred. "You can't be okay with them living next to you or going to school with us."

"I can't believe you just brought up her dad." Zoe grabbed the edges of her tray, and for a second I thought she might smack April on the head with it. "You know, you're like a test run at having a child who disappoints you on the regular."

April's expression was the definition of unrepentant.

"None of this has anything to do with what happened to my dad." I drew in a shallow breath. "And yeah, some of them are scary, but—"

"But what?" Zoe asked quietly, her gaze latched on to mine.

I shoved my hand through my hair and then lifted a shoulder. My tongue tied up. I struggled to get out the words I wanted to say. I didn't know how to feel about the Luxen, especially after everything Mom had told me. No matter what my dad did or didn't do, he died fighting them. And no matter if some of them had been on Team Human for years, they still scared me. What human in their right mind wouldn't be scared of them?

I just didn't know.

And I also didn't know if that was, in fact, worse than having an opinion.

April shrugged as she scooped up a forkful of spaghetti. "Maybe this discussion is pointless. Maybe none of it will matter."

I looked at her. "What is that supposed to mean?"

A small twist of a smile curled her lips. "I don't know. Maybe they'll smarten up and decide there's another planet out there more . . . accommodating to them."

11

Zoe waited for me by my locker at the end of the day as I switched out my books, grabbing my bio textbook so I could prepare for an exam tomorrow.

"Are you heading home?" she asked, resting her head against the locker next to mine.

"I should." I grinned when Zoe lifted her brows. "But it's so nice outside and I was thinking about heading out to the park."

"Taking pictures?"

I nodded. The weather was perfect for taking photos, cooling down so the leaves were changing colors. Impromptu photo sessions were why I always kept my Nikon with me from the moment Mom had surprised me with it last Christmas. "Mom didn't say I was grounded."

"Sure," Zoe drew the word out. "Good luck with that."

I closed the locker door and then hitched my bag up on my shoulder. "What are you up to?"

She lifted a shoulder. "Need to study, but I'm probably going to just sit on the couch and marathon old episodes of *Family Guy*."

I laughed as we headed down the hall toward the parking lot. Zoe's parents, both of them, had died before the invasion in some kind of freak plane accident, so she had been shipped off to live with her uncle, who was never home. I only saw him once from a distance. They used to live closer to DC, but had ended up here after everything.

"So, I only heard bits and pieces about your trip with Heidi to that club." Zoe caught the door, holding it open as we stepped out into the bright afternoon sun. "She was telling me it got raided while you guys were there?"

I pulled my sunglasses out of my bag and slid them on as we followed the mass of people going toward the parking lot. "Yeah, it was wild. I've never seen anything like that. At all."

"There's a reason why Heidi didn't ask me to go with you guys. I would've told her no."

"I couldn't tell her no. She's been going there by herself for a while now, and I just wanted to, you know, for her not to be alone." I stepped around a couple who looked seconds away from either making out or screaming at each other. "I didn't even get a chance to meet Emery."

Zoe was quiet for a moment and then she nudged me with her elbow. "So I heard there was this guy there. . . ."

Groaning, I rolled my eyes as we climbed the small hill. What did Heidi *not* tell her? "There was a Luxen guy there who was a complete ass. Is that who you're talking about?"

"That's the guy who showed up at your house?" When I nodded, she let out a low whistle. "I bet your mom freaked."

"You have no idea," I muttered dryly. Out of all my friends, Zoe was the most . . . logical one, the calmest one. There was very little we kept from each other, so keeping everything from her felt wrong.

Honestly, she should've been at the club Friday night. She would've made sure I didn't end up in that hidey-hole with Luc. "So, I didn't tell anyone else this, but when he showed up at my house, Mom pulled a gun on him."

"What?" She let out a shocked laugh.

"Yep." I kept my voice down as we neared Zoe's car. Since I hadn't gotten to school super-early that morning, I had to trek all the way to the back of the parking lot, near the football field.

"Wow," she said, laughing again. From the field, a whistle blew. "What did he do?"

"He melted the barrel." I shivered at the reminder. To have that kind of unchecked power was unbelievable.

"That . . . was all he did?" Zoe reached the door of her car.

"I think that was enough." Of course that wasn't all that Luc had done. "He actually . . ."

"What?"

My cheeks started to burn. I wanted to tell her—tell someone—but at the same time, telling someone felt like that meant I was thinking about it. That I cared about it.

I wasn't thinking about the non-kiss. Well, except for last night, when I couldn't sleep, and the night before that.

Zoe nudged my arm.

"He wasn't wearing a Disabler," I said instead, shoving thoughts of kissing aside. "I don't think he's registered."

Leaning against the back door of her car, Zoe crossed her arms. "I think there probably are a lot of them who aren't registered."

"Yeah."

She was quiet for a moment. "Anyway, what April brought up at lunch was so wrong."

"Which part?"

She rolled her eyes. "All of it, but especially bringing up your dad like that. It was messed up."

"It was." I dug a thick bobby pin out of the pocket of my jeans, then bent over and gathered up my hair. "But that's April."

"I don't know." Zoe squinted as she stared out over the football field. "Sometimes she worries me."

Twisting my hair into a bun, I managed to keep my sunglasses on and shove the bobby pin into the thick mass. "She always worries me." I straightened. "There are days when I don't even know why I'm friends with her."

"There are days I wonder how I haven't pushed her in front of a bus," Zoe admitted.

My smile faded as I thought about the conversation with Mom. If April had known my dad had done bad things, it probably wouldn't have changed anything she'd said, because my father's death fit her narrative—her agenda when she talked about the Luxen.

"You okay?" She moved several curls out of her face.

"Yeah." I smiled. "Why?"

Her brows lifted. "You had a pretty interesting weekend."

And she didn't even know all of it. "Yeah, I did, but I'm okay. Totally."

She studied me a moment and then pushed away from the car. "All right, I've got to run. Text me later?"

"Yep." I waved good-bye to her, then headed behind her car and started rooting around for my keys. I made a promise that I would get to school earlier from now on, because this hike sucked. I found my keys just as my car came into view. I unlocked it, opened the back door, and tossed my bag onto the seat.

I didn't even know how it happened.

I must've left my bag half unzipped, because the next thing I knew, a rainbow of notebooks slid out, slipping onto the gravel. My camera inched out next. Gasping, I dropped my keys and lurched forward, catching the camera before it hit the hard ground.

Closing my eyes, I let out a ragged breath. "Oh, thank you, baby Jesus."

"Here you go."

Startled by the deep voice, I lost my precarious balance and fell backward, plopping onto my butt. My head jerked up as I clutched my camera to my chest. A guy stood next to my car. Brown hair brushed dark sunglasses. A warm smile curved his lips as he picked up my notebooks. My gaze flew back to his face.

"These are yours, right?" he asked.

I eyed the notebooks. "Yeah. They are."

His head tilted to the side. "Do you . . . want them back?"

For a moment I didn't move and then I snapped forward, onto my knees. I grabbed the notebooks. "Thank you."

"No problem." He stepped back as I got up. A dimple appeared in his right cheek. "See you later."

Holding my notebooks, I watched him pivot. Some type of leather messenger bag thumped off his thigh as he cut around the back of my car, walking through another row of cars.

"Huh," I murmured. I didn't recognize the guy. Granted, the sunglasses had shielded half his face, but he had to be a student. From what I could see of his face, he looked pretty cute. I really needed to start paying more attention to who I had class with.

Shaking my head, I shoved my notebooks back into my bag, zipped it up, and then shoved the door closed. I bent over, snatching up my keys. Still holding on to my camera, I opened the driver's-side door and then came to a complete stop. A weird feeling hit me. The tiny hairs along the back of my neck rose.

It felt like . . . like someone was watching me.

Maybe I was just being paranoid, but I scanned the parking lot. There were people, lots of them, and no one was paying any attention to me, but the feeling didn't go away. Even when I got into my car and turned it on, the sensation lingered like summer's heat.

As I was walking the path along the still waters of Centennial Lake, I lifted my camera and stepped back. Composition of a photo pretty much came down to the rule of thirds. Of course, it didn't work for all photos and I didn't follow the rule for outdoors ones. I always liked photos where the object was slightly off-centered.

I snapped a picture of one of the largest trees, loving the contrast of its leaves against the deep blue of the sky. Then I zoomed in on the burnt gold and red leaves.

I didn't like to look at my pictures until I got home and was able to load them onto my computer. If I got caught up in checking them out, I'd end up just focusing on one image and miss everything else around me.

Keeping to the edge of the pathway, I was careful not to bother the joggers and people walking their dogs. There were a lot of people out, and as the day progressed, the park would be packed. I could already hear childlike shouts and giggles coming from the playground.

I came to Centennial Lake often, at least once a week for the last year or so. I loved being outside, taking pictures even though I knew I probably wasn't that good at it. Mom said my film was great and that I had talent. So did Zoe and Heidi. James wasn't interested unless the photos were of hot chicks in bikinis. Usually April laughed at my pictures. That was if she was paying attention when I shared them.

I doubted Mom or Zoe would tell me I was terrible. Sucking didn't matter, though. It wasn't why I took pictures. I did it because of how it made me feel.

Or how it *didn't* make me feel.

My brain just sort of emptied out while I had a camera in my hand. I didn't think about anything—about how scary the invasion had been. I didn't think about the surreal quality of the last four years or what had happened the night at the club. I sure as hell didn't think about the kiss that didn't even count as a real kiss. Or everything my mom had told me.

The camera put a wall up between the world and me, and it was an escape, one I looked forward to. I cut off the pathway and trekked up a small mound that overlooked the playground, then sat down. Laughter and squeals drew my attention and I lifted the camera, catching a small girl darting from the slides to the swings, her pigtails bouncing. Another kid, a little boy, nearly belly-flopped off the swing, letting the seat spin back. I caught the empty seat swinging, snapping a picture of it floating, the seat cockeyed in flight.

I sucked in a shallow breath, feeling a sudden burn in the back of my throat.

I slowly lowered the camera and watched kids race back and forth from one playground set to another. Everything about them was carefree and happy. Innocent. They were lucky. None of them remembered that utterly all-consuming fear. None of them remembered what it was like to go to bed wondering what kind of world they were going to wake up in come morning, if there would even be a world. They had the freedom the rest of us had had the minute and second before our lives had imploded.

The invasion had been so traumatic that I had a hard time remembering anything before it. I mean, I could remember things, but those memories were fuzzy and faint compared to that night the Luxen came and the days afterward. I'd looked it up once, to see if that was common, and it was. These kids, though, they'd never have—

Stop.

Closing my eyes, I forced a long, deep breath out. When I held the camera, I didn't think. When I took a picture, I didn't feel.

Today was not going to change that and ruin it.

Pressing my lips together, I shook it out—shook my shoulders and arms, wiggled all the way down to my butt planted in the grass. It probably looked weird, but I pictured all the fears and worries being rattled right off me, and it worked. I opened my eyes again, and the unwanted knot of emotion was gone.

Once I got myself in check, I lifted the camera again, moving away from the playground and over the walkway. I started to get a long shot of the lake, but my attention was snagged. My finger slipped over the zoom button before I even knew what I was doing.

Blue Mohawk?

What the hell?

It was the guy from the club. It was so him standing on the edge of the pathway, hands shoved into his pockets. In the daylight, his blue hair was even more striking against his pale skin. I bet he was a redhead. He wore a black shirt with some kind of symbol on it. Two snakes, mouth to end.

What was his name? Kent. Yeah, that was his name.

He turned toward the hill I sat on. Sucking in a sharp breath, I jerked the camera away from my face. There was no way he could see me. He was human, but God, it was almost like he'd looked right at me.

I thought about the feeling I'd had in the school parking lot.

Well, now I was being paranoid, because those two things had nothing to do with each other.

I shook my head and then scanned the pathway down below. No Kent. Frowning, I craned my neck to see if he'd gone around the bend. It shouldn't be hard to see him. He kind of stuck out. And what was he doing here? Yeah, this was a public park, but what was the likelihood of seeing him at the lake, especially when I'd never seen him here before, and right after—

"Fancy seeing you here."

Instantly I recognized the deep voice coming from behind me. My stomach dropped at the same time my heart rate kicked up.

Twisting, I looked up . . . and up some more. I nearly dropped my poor camera.

Luc.

He crouched so we were face-to-face. Somehow I'd forgotten how striking his eyes were up close. A purple so intense, it reminded me of the most vibrant of wolfsbane. "Surprised to see me?"

"Yeah," I said, checking out his wrist. Still no Disabler. Just that leather cuff and weird stone. "A little."

One dark brow lifted. "You probably thought you were never going to see me again. You probably even hoped for that."

I laid my camera down in the grass, figuring it was better to have my hands free at this point. "Honestly? After my mom pointed a shotgun at you, I figured I *would* never see you again."

He laughed, but it made every muscle in my body tense. "Yeah, usually that would deter people, but then again, I'm not like most people."

"That's the understatement of the year."

Letting his hands hang between his knees, he nodded slowly. "True."

Mouth dry, I glanced around, but I didn't see Kent anywhere. Actually, it seemed like no one was near us. Luc gave off this vibe, like an invisible barrier that kept people back from him. "I didn't tell anyone about what I saw Saturday."

"I know." His gaze flickered over my face. "I make you so incredibly nervous, don't I?"

Warmth crept into my cheeks. It was true. He made me nervous on nearly every level, even ones I didn't quite understand, and the fact that he noticed this ticked me off to no end.

I rose to my knees, meeting his stare head-on. "Yeah, you make me nervous."

"Because you think I'm a Luxen?"

"It has nothing to do with what you are." I pressed my palms into my thighs. "You make me nervous because the last time I saw you, you unlocked the door and entered my house without permission, and before that, you tried to kidnap me."

"We're still disagreeing on what kidnapping involves, I see."

"You tried to kidnap me, Luc."

"Hmm," he murmured. "That means I like you."

I arched a brow. "Okay. That's messed up on about a thousand different levels."

"Probably. I don't people well."

"Gee, really," I replied dryly.

He seemed to consider that for a moment and then said, "I have good reasons for why I thought it would be better for you to stay there."

Both of my brows lifted now. "And I'm sure most serial killers have 'good reasons' for cutting up their victims and eating them too."

Luc's lips twitched. "That's a bit extreme."

"You're *a bit* extreme."

His gaze lowered, his thick lashes shielding his eyes. "You're a bright girl. I know that. You saw more than one Luxen without a Disabler. You also saw frightened Luxen hidden. You were there when we were raided. I know you can put two and two together." Those lashes lifted. "Obviously that knowledge you possess is dangerous, and it requires me to be *a bit* extreme to protect what I'm doing."

As much as I hated to admit it even to myself, I understood. Reluctantly. "What are you doing?" I asked. "Besides . . . hiding them?"

He gave a little shake of his head. "You're not ready for that." A sigh shuddered through him. "I'm not ready for that."

That didn't make much sense. "Why?"

"Because I can't trust you. Not like that."

I was kind of offended by that. "We're talking about trust? When you entered my locked home and proceeded to melt a shotgun barrel with your bare hands?"

A small grin appeared on his lips. "I did do that."

I gaped at him. "And I'm also pretty sure the last time I saw you *illegally* in my house, I tried to knock your head off with a candleholder, so I would think you'd realize *I* didn't want to see *you*."

Luc laughed.

Anger rushed over the confusion and fear, squelching out the nervousness. "Do you think I'm funny?" I demanded.

"Well." His gaze moved to the sky like he was really thinking hard about this. The sun glanced off his angular cheekbones, creating shadowy hollows under them, and my fingers itched to capture the moment with my camera. "Yeah, I kind of do think you're funny."

"Well, I don't think you're funny," I snapped. "At all."

He arched a brow again, and when he spoke, there was a playful quality in his tone. "If I thought everyone who wanted to knock my head off didn't want to be my friend, then I'd be friendless."

My jaw clenched down. "Wow. That's something to be proud of."

"I like to think so." The curve of his smile said he knew how much he was getting to me. "You take pictures?"

I almost answered his question. The "yes" was burning on the tip of my tongue, but I shut that right down. "Why are you here?"

"I just happened to be around and I saw you."

"Oh, just like you happened to be outside my house on Sunday and you just happened to have my ID with you? Which, by the way, you could've given back to me on Saturday."

"Yeah." He bit down on his lower lip, and it was ridiculous how much that drew my attention, so I forced my gaze up. "How much trouble did you get in for that?"

"A lot," I gritted out.

"Not exactly surprised." He focused on the lake. "Sylvia is . . . she's a hard-core woman."

It was still super-weird that he knew my parents. Part of me knew I should get up and get the hell away from him, but nope. I was still perched on my knees. For some reason, as I stared at him, I thought about that guy who'd been hurt. "How is he? Chas?"

A muscle flexed along his jaw. "Better. He woke up this morning."

"That's good news, right?" When he nodded, I bit down on my lip. "Did he tell you what happened?"

"He was jumped. Didn't see the person."

My brows creased. "It's got to be hard to jump a Luxen."

"It is. Really hard," Luc agreed. "Which is very concerning."

I looked away, thinking about Colleen. "Do you know that one of my classmates has gone missing? I saw her Friday night at the club, and her purse and shoes were found in that alley."

"I'd heard that."

My gaze crawled back to his. "Do you think what happened to Chas is related to Colleen?"

"I wouldn't see why."

I wasn't so sure about that. "Have you contacted the police or anything, about what happened to Chas?"

"No." He laughed as if I'd suggested the most ridiculous thing possible. "No way."

I looked back at him, eyes narrowing. "I get that you—"

"You don't get anything, Evie."

I sat back on my legs and lifted my hands in surrender. "Whatever, dude."

"The police aren't going to care about an unregistered Luxen nearly being beaten to death." Those eyes churned a restless purple. "If anything, they'd immediately blame Chas for the girl's disappearance."

"And you're sure he had nothing to do with it?" I asked.

A smirk formed as he laughed under his breath. "Oh, because he's a Luxen, he's automatically responsible for some human girl—"

"That's not what I'm saying," I argued. "Maybe he saw something and that was why he was hurt."

"He didn't see anything."

I drew in a shallow breath. "Well, I'm glad he's okay."

Luc was quiet as he watched me. "Me too."

I looked away then, drawing in a shallow breath, and then I refocused on him. "You know, Mom told me."

Shock splashed over his face as his gaze flew back to mine. "She did?"

I nodded. "She told me about . . ." I glanced around, but there was still no one near us. "She told me about how you guys were here long before the invasion."

His expression smoothed out. "Oh, really?"

"She also told me about my dad."

Everything about Luc changed in that moment. His features hardened and his shoulders tensed. His gaze was glacial as it locked on to mine. "She did?"

"She said he was responsible for you losing someone . . . close to you?"

His pupils seemed to stretch, and wow, that was . . . different. "He was."

Feeling a little out of my element, I rose from my haunches and my mouth just started running. "I didn't know my dad was like that. I didn't know my dad at all, it seems. Obviously. But I mean, he wasn't around a lot, and now I think maybe Mom and Dad weren't getting along—" What in the world was I telling him? I shook my head, refocusing. "None of that is important, but what I'm trying to say is . . . I'm sorry."

His eyes widened slightly as he stared at me. "Are you apologizing for him?"

"I . . . think so? I don't even know why, which would usually mean that's a crappy apology, but mainly because I don't know exactly *what* he did, but I just know that my mom wouldn't lie about something like that—"

Luc's laugh was harsh.

My lips started to turn down. "Are you laughing while I'm trying to apologize for my father?"

"Yeah, I am." Straightening, he rose. "You don't need to ever apologize for a damn thing that man did."

"Oh." I was still for a moment and then scrambled to my feet so he wasn't some giant towering over me. "That still doesn't—"

"I'm not here to talk about Jason Dasher," he cut in.

I took a tiny step back. "Then why are you here?"

His head tilted to the side, and a slow grin tipped up one side of his lips. "I don't know," he said, pausing. "Maybe I was looking for you."

My hands tightened on the camera as my stomach dipped and twisted. Good. Bad. Both. "I think that's pretty obvious."

He chuckled as he leaned forward about an inch. "And here I thought I was in stealth mode."

"Not exactly." I glanced down at the camera. "So why were you looking for me?"

"Why aren't you running away?"

My gaze shot to his. That was a good question, but whatever. "Is this how every conversation is going to go? You answer a question with a question?"

"You do realize you just did exactly that."

Irritation prickled over my skin, as did reluctant amusement. "I think it's weird to ask someone why they aren't running away from them."

"Maybe, but I—" His head swung to the left and his eyes narrowed. I followed his gaze, unsure of what I was going to see, but I expected *something*. I didn't see anything. He sighed heavily. "Unfortunately, I need to go."

"Uh, okay."

Luc's gaze slid back to mine. "Do you know how easy it was to find you? The answer is really easy. In a city that has—how many humans? A little over a hundred thousand? It took nothing for me to find you."

My heart banged around in my chest. "Why should I be worried about how easy it is to find me?"

"You never considered that before?"

"That's not something I've really ever thought about," I answered truthfully, because seriously, who thought about that unless they were trying to hide? Or had something to hide?

His eyes held mine. "You should probably start doing that."

12

The house was too quiet when I got home, so like any other normal person out there, I turned on every light—and I mean, every light, even the hallway bathroom. *And* turned on the TV in my bedroom.

It still felt too dark in the house.

I'd uploaded the pictures I'd taken at the park and was flipping through them, but I didn't really see any of them. My mind was someplace else as I sat on my bed.

Namely, it was still in the park.

What the hell was up with Luc? After he said that creepy thing that kind of felt like a warning, he'd just strolled on off like he hadn't freaked me the heck out. And I like to think anyone in my shoes would've been creeped out. Why did it matter how easy it was to find me?

Shivering, I rubbed my hands down my arms. I just didn't get why Luc felt the need to search me out in the first place. It was literally the weirdest conversation I'd ever had.

Ever.

And I'd had some weird conversations with Zoe and Heidi, the kind you didn't want to repeat and you hoped no one was listening to.

My phone dinged from where it rested beside my laptop. I leaned over and picked it up to see it was a text from Heidi. Excitement sparked to life when I saw it was a picture of her and Emery, their cheeks pressed together. Emery was smiling, and wow, she was truly a stunning girl. Her skin tone was rich and earthy next to Heidi's paler skin. Of course Heidi's lips were puckered, like she was blowing a kiss at the camera. It looked like they were at a restaurant.

I quickly texted back: *You guys look adorable.*

Then I added about a dozen exclamation points, which earned me a heart emoji, the kind that exploded into little baby hearts. I sent another text, telling Heidi to call me when she got home so she could tell me all about her date.

I tossed my phone back onto the comforter. I was still too antsy to go through the pictures I'd taken. I scooted off the bed, and my sock-covered feet whispered against the hardwood floors as I decided to grab something to eat, because shoving chips into my mouth was the only way to kill time when I was feeling antsy.

Stopping near the window seat, I frowned. I walked over to it and lifted the gray cushion to see if there was a handgun or a sword stashed inside.

There wasn't.

Thank God.

I'd half expected a gun or knife to slip out of the pile of towels in the linen closet that morning when I grabbed a clean one. I honestly didn't know what to think about Mom having weapons hidden. Part of me kind of understood even without all she told me on Saturday. Things had been tense in the weeks and months after the invasion; it had been scary. Any noise sounded like an explosion, and for a long time it felt like we were waiting for the end to come. So I guessed having weapons within reach wasn't too bad of an idea.

As I dumped about three handfuls of chips into a bowl, I glanced at the clock on the stove. It was close to eight, and Mom still wasn't home. It seemed like she was working later and later each week.

I missed her.

I *wished* I missed Dad.

My entire body clenched with guilt.

Since I didn't have access to therapy to sort out all those messed-up feelings, I added another handful of chips to my bowl and made my way back upstairs. Munching on the crispy, salty goodness, I started flipping through the pictures I'd taken once more.

I almost missed it, since my head wasn't all there, but something caught my attention as I flipped through the pictures of the swing set. Right after I'd taken a picture of the swing, I'd zoomed out and snapped another picture without realizing it. Two people stood behind the swing set. Wait. My eyes narrowed as I clicked on the zoom. A chip fell out of my open mouth.

That was . . . I leaned in, squinting. I'd taken a picture of April. Hell, I hadn't even realized she was there. It made sense that she'd be at the playground, though. I knew she had a younger sister, so one of those little girls was probably her.

But there was something weird about the photo.

There was this odd double exposure effect where April stood. That was why I almost didn't recognize her, but it wasn't a normal double exposure. There was this shadow type affect surrounding the upper part of her body, as if someone were standing directly behind her.

That was super-odd, but that had to be it, because the rest of the picture was fine. There had to be someone behind her. Did April know?

Shaking my head, I zoomed out and started clicking through the pictures mindlessly, but I gave up and promptly fell down a rabbit hole of watching short videos of people making fancy cupcakes. I lost about an hour doing that, because I moved on from cupcakes to cakes, and then all I wanted from life was a giant chocolate candy bar.

After logging on to my Facebook page, I hit the "most recent" button and started scrolling through new updates. I needed to be doing homework, but I didn't budge from my laptop. My finger moved over the track pad as I mindlessly scrolled, stopping when I saw an update from my ex, Brandon. He'd posted a picture of a girl, and it took me a moment to recognize the blonde.

I leaned in, squinting at the smiling selfie. I knew her. She was in my chem class. I'd seen her today. Her name was Amanda— Amanda Kelly. I quickly read the caption under her picture and my heart dropped.

"No," I whispered, sitting back.

Amanda was reported missing this afternoon by her grand-parents. The post read that she hadn't come home from school.

School had ended only a handful of hours ago, so she might not be missing, but there had to be a reason why her grandparents were freaking out. I read the post again, and it didn't look like it had been reported to the police. The contact number belonged to her grandparents.

God.

I stared at the picture in disbelief. Colleen was missing. And what if Amanda was too? Both went to our high school and had vanished mysteriously the same weekend? That was . . . that was way too coincidental.

Or maybe her grandparents were just overreacting? That was possible, because it wasn't like with Colleen, who had been miss-ing since Friday night. Maybe Amanda—

A crash come from downstairs, causing my heart to lurch in my chest. My head shot up.

What the . . . ?

I snatched the remote off the bed and muted the TV, and for a long moment, I didn't move as I strained to hear any other noise. There was nothing, but that didn't stop the wave of goose bumps from spreading over my skin. I was frozen for a moment, and then I grabbed my cell phone. I knew it wasn't Mom, because I didn't hear the garage door open under my bedroom. I swung my legs off the bed and then crept out into the hallway to peer down into the foyer. I held my breath and, when I didn't hear anything, realized I had two options.

Go back into my bedroom, sit down with the laptop, and look for a local exorcist, because obviously random, unaccounted-for sounds meant there was a demon in my house. Or go downstairs and investigate the strange noise to determine that it wasn't a demon. But what if someone was breaking in?

With all the lights on in the house?

That seemed unlikely.

I inched toward the stairwell and headed down them, stopping halfway when I remembered something very important I'd learned recently.

Luxen could unlock doors.

Oh crap.

What if it was a Luxen helping themselves to the bag of chips I knew I'd left on the counter? A shiver crawled along my arms, and I looked down. I was still holding the remote. What the hell was I going to do with the remote? I started to turn back around, but stopped. What was I going to do? Call the police because I heard a noise?

I was being stupid.

Taking a deep breath, I went down the rest of the steps, stopping at the bottom. Front door was shut, but . . . but the French doors to my mom's office were ajar, cracked open.

I froze.

Those doors were always closed. Always. Had Mom forgotten to lock them? That wasn't impossible, but it was strange.

Leaning forward, I peered into the rest of the downstairs. Everything looked normal. I shuffled into the living room, making my way through the dining area we never used. The kitchen looked untouched, and I could see the bag of chips, still where I left them. I stopped by the gray upholstered dining room chair, inching closer to the kitchen. There was nothing—

I sucked in a sharp breath.

The back door was wide open and the night air was spilling in, creeping across the tile floor.

I so did not leave the back door open.

Nope.

Goose bumps returned with a vengeance as I took a step back, my hands clenching the phone and remote control. I doubted a demon had opened the door. Oh God, I should've just called the police. I should've called—

The wisps of hair at the nape of my neck stirred. Something touched my cheek. Soft. Quick. Warm. Air lodged in my throat as icy fear seized every muscle in my body. Instinct exploded as my ears buzzed. Heart lurching into my throat, I slowly turned around as panic dug in.

Nothing was there.

I lifted my hand to my cheek. Good Lord, if someone were standing behind me, I would've had a heart attack, right then and there. Dead before I was eighteen, and that would suck so bad.

Luxen could open doors that were locked, and they were also fast—fast enough that one could run past me, *touch me,* without being seen. It was possible, but why? Why would one be in this house? I seriously doubted it was Luc. I didn't know him well, but I had a strong suspicion he would've made himself known.

Obnoxiously so.

Hands shaking, I kept backing up, past the dining table, and then I turned around.

Mom's office doors were closed.

The breath I took got stuck. Silence fell as I stared at the closed French doors. I lifted my phone and then jerked as a knock sounded from the front door. For a moment, I didn't move. I couldn't. My pulse was thundering, blood roaring. The knock came again. I glanced over my shoulder. Whoever was in here wouldn't be knocking on the door, right?

It was like moving in slow motion. One step in front of the other until I pressed into the door and peered through the peephole.

Zoe.

Relief nearly cut my legs out from underneath me. Throwing the deadbolt, I yanked opened the door. "Zoe!"

She must've seen something in my expression, because concern filled hers. "Are you okay?"

"Yes. No." I stepped back, looking over my shoulder at my mom's office. "I think someone was in here."

"What?" Zoe stepped into the house. "Why do you think that? Have you called the police?"

"No. It just happened." I swallowed hard, lifting my phone. "I was upstairs and I heard something fall over down here. I don't know. It was a loud noise and I came downstairs. I didn't see anything at first, but then I saw that the back door was open and—"

I turned and my eyes narrowed. The back door was closed. "Wait. It was *just* open."

Zoe stepped around me, her gaze following mine. "Did you close it?"

Clutching my phone harder, I shook my head. "No. I didn't even go near it."

She started for the door, and I quickly followed, practically snapping at her heels. She reached for the door. I started to tell her to stop, but when she turned the handle, the door didn't budge. "It's locked."

"What?" Not believing her, I shot around her and tried the door myself. She was right. The door was locked. "That's impossible."

Zoe stared at me.

"Well, it's not impossible. Luxen can unlock doors. That means they could probably lock them, right?"

"Right." Her gaze searched mine. "But why would they do that?"

"I don't know." I twisted. "Those doors were open. I swear."

Zoe didn't say anything for a long moment and then she charged forward, back toward the front of the house. "Let's check it out."

I didn't get a chance to protest that possibly unwise life choice, because Zoe was already climbing the steps. Not wanting to be left behind, I quickly caught up with her. Every room was checked, and in less than five minutes we were back downstairs, in the living room.

"You don't believe me," I said.

She placed a hand on my arm. "You're shaking. So I know something happened, but, Evie . . ."

"But it looks like nothing happened." I slowly shook my head, feeling like I'd lost my mind a little. "I heard something. I felt someone. They walked past me. Touched my cheek—"

"Touched you?" Zoe's brows lifted.

Nodding, I brought my fingers to my cheek. "That's what it felt like." I walked to the couch and sat down on the edge. "I don't understand."

Zoe followed me. "What were you doing upstairs?"

"Just looking at cupcake videos," I said, and Zoe pressed her lips together. "Then I got on Facebook and I saw that Amanda's grandparents reported her missing. . . ." A shudder racked me. "Maybe reading that, I let my imagination get away from me."

Zoe sat down next to me and glanced at the front window. "Maybe. I mean, the mind can do crazy things, right? Especially after everything we've all been through with the invasion. It can play tricks on you. You okay?"

"I'm fine. Just freaked out." I ran my palm over my knee as something occurred to me. I twisted toward Zoe. "What are you doing here?"

She laughed at my question. "I was craving Walkers and I grabbed a burger. I texted you."

"You did?" I glanced at my phone. "There's no text from you."

"I guess it didn't go through. Weird." She frowned. "Anyway, I thought I'd stop by and see if you heard from Heidi yet."

Zoe rarely just stopped by my house. Come to think of it, I couldn't recall a time when she was here with my mom home. Moving a loose strand of hair back from my face, I glanced at the closed and *locked* back door. "She texted me a picture of her and Emery earlier. I think they were at a restaurant." I exhaled roughly. "Did you hear about Amanda?"

"I saw something when I was at Walkers. She was at school and it's only been a couple of hours, but . . ."

I dragged my gaze back to her. "But what?"

She lifted one shoulder. "But I guess something else must've happened for her grandparents to think she's missing after such a short period of time."

"I was thinking the same thing." I leaned forward and placed my phone on the ottoman. My head was in a thousand places as I sat back. The run-in and weird conversation with Luc competed with Amanda's possible disappearance. And whatever the hell happened here tonight was still taking center stage.

And I really, really wanted a giant candy bar now.

"You sure you're okay?" Zoe asked again.

I nodded even though I had a hard time believing that my mind had tricked me into hearing what I did, seeing two doors open, and feeling . . . feeling what I had. I leave bags of chips open all the time. Not doors. I wasn't stupid.

If someone had been in here, they'd been in my mom's office.

That left two questions.

Who and why?

Smothering a yawn, I grabbed my English textbook out of my locker and shoved it into my bag.

"You look like you just woke up five seconds ago," James commented.

I glanced up at him. He had his baseball hat on, turned backward. I gave him about five minutes before someone yelled at him to take it off. "I overslept."

Which was the God's honest truth. I hadn't been able to fall asleep easily last night, since I was expecting a door to randomly open and close all night long. When I did finally pass out, my alarm seemed to go off minutes later.

I hadn't told Mom what had happened last night.

By the time she got home and Zoe had already left, I was beginning to doubt everything and it felt silly trying to explain what I thought had happened.

"I can tell." He stared over my head as he slipped his cell phone into his pocket. "Here comes April."

I groaned under my breath as I pushed a strand of hair out of my face.

"And she looks surprisingly . . . chipper this morning."

"Chipper?" I coughed out a dry laugh as I rooted around for the granola bar I knew I had in my locker. "Is that the word of the day for you or something?"

"No." James paused. "Gadzookery is."

Wrinkling my forehead, I stopped lifting books and looked at him. "That cannot be a real word."

"Yeah, it is. Look it up. You might learn something."

I knelt down, rolling my eyes.

"Hey." April stopped behind me and there was a pause. "Didn't you wear that cardigan yesterday, Evie?"

Closing my eyes, I counted to ten before I answered. "Yeah, I did, and most people wouldn't point something like that out."

"I'm not most people," she replied, and James was right. She sounded awful *chipper* this morning.

"I've got to run." James was such a punk. "I'll see you guys later."

April slid into his spot. "I don't think he likes me."

"I don't know why you'd think that." I lifted up a binder at the bottom of my locker, and there it was. One lonely, little chocolate chip granola bar. I snatched it up. It was mine, all mine.

"Who knows? It's whatever." She waited as I got up. "Are you going to Coop's party this weekend?"

I closed the door and faced her. There was nary a wrinkle on her white blouse. With her dark skinny jeans and her hair sleeked back in a ponytail, she looked like a very expensive personal assistant. "Not sure. You?"

"Of course." Her blue eyes glimmered like she'd downed a million cups of coffee. "You should definitely go."

"Yeah, we'll see." I lifted my bag to my shoulder as I pushed away from my locker. I spotted Heidi's fire-engine-red hair, and the moment she saw April with me, she winced and wheeled around, heading in the opposite direction.

Traitors.

All my friends were traitors.

"You know who I heard was going to Coop's party this weekend?" April chattered on as we walked. "Brandon."

I slid a long look at her. Why would I care if my ex was going to a party? "So?"

"And I hear he's not going alone." She reached up, twisting the end of her ponytail as we neared the bathrooms on the main floor. "I think he's actually seeing someone."

"At the risk of sounding repetitive . . . so?"

One side of her lips curled. "You haven't heard? He's been getting super-close to Lori—"

A scream cut her off—a bone-deep shout of terror that raised the tiny hairs all over my body. There was a small cluster of people by the bathrooms, like normal.

The scream came again, louder and closer, and then the girls' bathroom door flew open. A girl burst out of it, her face the color of fallen snow.

April dropped her ponytail. "What in the hell?"

"Her eyes!" The girl shrieked as she skidded into the group lingering by the bathroom. "She's dead and she didn't have any *eyes!*"

13

As I sat on one of the stone tables outside of the cafeteria, I squinted as the bright morning sun glared down on us. "I can't believe that just happened."

Heidi was sitting on the bench next to my feet, her dark sunglasses shielding most of her face. "I heard the screams. I thought it was a joke at first . . . until I heard what she was screaming."

I dipped my chin as I dragged my hand around my neck, scooping up my hair and bringing it to one side. As long as I lived, I would never forget the sound of that girl's screams.

We'd all been evacuated the minute a teacher checked the bathroom. Some of us had been sent out to the back parking lot and the rest of us were here, milling around or in small clusters. The police showed up within minutes of us being sent outside, and I'd only seen a handful of teachers since then. Everyone was pretty quiet, speaking in hushed voices or comforting one another. Every so often someone's phone would ring. The school district had sent out an alert that there was an issue at the school. Knowing that Mom probably wouldn't get the call or my text for a while, because she didn't take her phone into the labs, I still let her know that I was okay.

Someone's parents wouldn't be getting that text today.

Heidi twisted as Zoe came around the corner. She dropped down beside Heidi. She'd left a few minutes ago to see if she could find out anything.

"I think they're going to cancel school for the rest of the day." Zoe placed her book bag on the table. "I peeked through the front entrance, and the entire hallway is blocked with police tape."

"It's basically a crime scene now." I shivered despite the warmth of the sun. "They probably won't be able to let us inside for a while."

Heidi's phone dinged and she pulled it out from her bag as she asked, "Did you hear who it could've been?"

Zoe shook her head as she swung a leg over the bench. "I'm never going to be able to use that bathroom again."

"Ditto," I murmured, opening my backpack. I pulled out my camera and popped off the lens. I was aware that Heidi and Zoe were watching me, but they didn't say anything as I started snapping photos of everyone standing around, focusing on how their shadows looked on the cement. I liked the contrast.

It was probably weird that I was doing this, but Heidi and Zoe didn't say a word. This wasn't the first time they'd seen me whip out a camera at the most inappropriate time.

Taking pictures was about more than clearing my mind. Sometimes the camera was . . . It was kind of like a shield between me and what was happening. It helped distance myself, so I didn't feel too much.

Maybe I *should* look into photojournalism when I graduated instead of nursing.

As I lowered the camera, I spotted James jogging around the corner, crossing the common area. He stopped by a group, clapping his hand on another guy's back before he made his way over to us.

"Have you heard anything?" I asked, putting my camera away.

"Yeah." James dropped his bag onto the cement ground. "It was Colleen."

"What?" I gasped.

He climbed onto the table and sat next to me. "I was talking to a few guys. One of the teachers was standing nearby, talking to Jenny—the girl who'd found her in the bathroom. From what I could hear, it sounded like Colleen had been . . . you know, gone for a while. I don't know how Jenny could tell that, but that's what I heard."

"Holy crap." Heidi lowered her phone to her lap. "Oh my God, that—"

"Doesn't make a lot sense?" Zoe finished for her, the corners of her lips turning down. "I thought the last time she was seen was at Foretoken on Friday night."

"That's right." I glanced at Heidi. She was staring straight, her face pale. "Her purse and shoes were found in the alley. There's no way she'd been in that bathroom since Friday."

"I used that bathroom yesterday," Zoe pointed out. "Someone would've noticed. At least, I hope so."

"She was in the last stall and it was unlocked," James explained, rubbing at the back of his neck. "Supposedly Jenny went in there and saw that the door was cracked open a little. She didn't think anyone was in it, so she pushed it open, and there . . . was Colleen. Said she was slumped next to the toilet."

"God." Heidi shuddered. "That's just horrible."

My stomach twisted as I folded my arms. Part of me had been hoping that she'd run away to see her boyfriend, like Zoe had suggested. Deep down I think I knew that hadn't been the case, not when her shoes and purse had been left behind in an alley, but I didn't think *this* was what had happened.

Zoe slumped against the table. Tight curls fell forward as she bowed her head. "She's in my communications class. She was just there, you know, on Friday."

"And you guys saw the posts about Amanda, right?" Heidi folded an arm across her stomach. "I saw this morning that she still hadn't returned home."

Zoe nodded slowly. "I saw that."

Silence fell between us, because seriously, what did any of us have to say? We'd all suffered some sort of loss, whether it was before the invasion or afterward. Both of Zoe's parents were gone. Heidi's uncle had been in the army and had died fighting. James had lost an aunt and a cousin. We all knew what grief felt like. Been there, done that, and we had the emotional baggage to prove it. And we all knew what the surprise of death felt like. It was that alarm-like jolt every time you realized someone was no longer there when they had *just* been there. And we all also knew what fear felt and tasted like. Still, with all our experience, none of us knew what to say.

"I heard something else," James said quietly.

I was almost too afraid to ask. "What?"

"You heard Jenny screaming about her eyes, right?" He reached up, turning his baseball hat around to the front. "They were . . . I heard they were burned out completely."

Zoe sat up straight. "Burned out?"

James nodded as he leaned around me. "Nothing but the sockets left."

"Oh God," Heidi moaned as my stomach churned some more.

"That wasn't all," he added, looking around at all of us. "She had burn marks—like, the skin was charred. At least that was how Jenny described it. Like she'd been electrocuted."

Zoe's lips parted as icy fingers of dread trailed down my spine. Oh no. My gaze connected with hers, and I knew she was thinking the same thing I was. There were two ways a person could end up looking like they were electrocuted. One way was touching a live wire and not living to regret that really bad life choice. The second was far scarier than accidentally dropping a plugged-in hair dryer into a tub. There was something out there that could kill, and when it did, it often looked like electrocution . . . if there was anything of that person left behind.

A Luxen.

Buses pulled up out front, and school was officially canceled for the day. We walked to our cars, the usual excitement of an unexpected day off nowhere to be found.

"Are you guys going home?" Heidi asked, digging out her keys.

"I am." Zoe stopped in front of the older truck she drove. "I think I'm just going to go back to sleep and pretend today hasn't happened."

Heidi smiled faintly. "I was telling Emery about what happened, and she wants to meet up and grab something to eat, you know, if you guys are interested."

"I'm going to pass." Zoe opened the driver's door. "Maybe next time?"

Heidi nodded as she glanced over at me. "What about you?"

Truthfully, the last thing I wanted was to be alone. "Are you sure it's okay?" I waved good-bye to Zoe as we skirted around her truck.

"Of course!" Heidi nudged me with her arm. "You're the most amazing third wheel, remember?"

I laughed as I pulled my keys out. "So does that mean you and Emery are officially a thing?"

"I think so. We had a really great time last night." As we stopped by my car, she hitched her bag up on her shoulder. "And we made plans for later in the week, too."

"Awesome. You still need to fill me in on everything."

"I will," she promised, brushing her hair back. "We're going to that restaurant near the park—"

"The one with the stacked waffles?" My stomach grumbled despite everything. "I'm totally in."

We split up, and I ended up following her through downtown. At one of the stoplights, I checked my phone and there were still no messages from Mom. I tossed my phone back into my bag and thought about last night. The panic and fear of thinking someone had been in my house felt like nothing compared to what had happened to Colleen.

My empty stomach continued to twist anxiously. If what James had said was correct, then it was likely a Luxen had done that to her. But why? Why would a Luxen possibly grab Colleen from the alley, hurt her, and then leave her body in a bathroom at school?

Why would anyone do that?

An insidious thought crept in. Anyone, human or not, would only leave a body in such a public place if they wanted the body to be found in a very public way.

But why?

I didn't have any answers.

Heidi was already out of her car and waiting when I pulled into the parking garage. I grabbed a spot where I could simply pull out when it was time to leave, because I sucked at backing up in crowded parking lots, then snatched up my purse off the backseat and shoved my phone into a little pocket in my bag.

I joined Heidi in the dimly lit section of the garage. "Make today feel normal and tell me about your date."

"It was a lot of fun. After dinner, we did the most normal and corniest thing possible. We went to a movie." Heidi paused as we reached the escalators to take us to the street. She always had to look down and wait several seconds before stepping onto an escalator. "I had an amazing time. I really like her." Her cheeks turned pink in the sun. "I know I keep saying that. I probably sound like a dork."

"You don't. You sound adorable."

She smiled, but it was brief. "I'm sorry. It feels so weird talking about the date after what happened."

"I know." I sighed as I touched the railing. "Going to breakfast feels weird too, but honestly, I'm glad we are. I really don't want to be sitting at home, mentally playing police detective."

Heidi snorted. "Ditto. Especially when my mind immediately goes to dark places. Like, I'm already convinced there's a serial killer in our midst, picking out his next victim." She stopped, looking at me. "Both Colleen and Amanda have blond hair."

My eyes widened as I absently touched *my* blond hair. "Uh, thanks for making that connection."

"Sorry." She smiled weakly. "I've been watching way too much true crime TV."

"You may not be far from the truth, though." I shuddered. "I mean, both having blond hair probably doesn't mean anything, but if Amanda really is missing—"

"It has to be tied to Colleen," she finished the thought. "It's way too much of a coincidence."

I started to tell her about what had happened last night, but stopped myself. After this morning, voicing what I *thought* had happened to me just seemed so stupid compared to what *did* happen.

We reached street level and walked the half block to the restaurant. Opening the door, I looked back at Heidi. "Is Emery here or should we grab a table?"

"She's meeting us, so we should grab a table." She followed me in, pushing her sunglasses up onto her head.

Since it was Tuesday, we didn't have to wait, and were immediately seated at one of the booths. I took the seat across from Heidi, sliding all the way to the window. I picked up a napkin, and started fiddling with it. "Did you know Colleen very well?"

Heidi had grown up in Columbia, unlike Zoe and me, who were transplants after the invasion. I was pretty sure Colleen was from this area too.

"When we were younger, like in elementary school, we used to play together during recess and sometimes afterward, but we kind of grew apart when we got to middle school. I don't even remember why. It was something that just happened. Now . . ." She trailed off, resting her head against the booth. "I wish I knew why we stopped being friends."

I folded the napkin. "We never really talked. Nothing more than the bare minimum, you know? I saw her Friday at the club. We talked for a couple of seconds, and then I think someone called her name and she went back on the dance floor."

"I didn't see her." She leaned forward. "Do you . . . Do you think a Luxen really did that?"

"I don't know." Unease blossomed as I lowered my voice. "But why else would she look like she'd been electrocuted—in a school bathroom, almost four full days after she disappeared?"

Her shoulders tensed as she turned to the window. "Oh, here comes Emery."

I turned to look, but she was already out of my line of sight. Nervousness grew as I waited for her join us. I wanted Emery to like me because Heidi liked her so much. Nothing sucked more than one of your best friends' significant other not being able to stand you.

A wide smile broke out over Heidi's face as she scooted all the way over to the window. "Hey."

I looked up, plastering what I hoped was a normal, welcoming smile on my face as I waved my hand. "Hi."

Emery grinned down at me as she murmured back the same greeting before sliding into the booth next to Heidi. Emery looked over at her, and there was a moment where neither quite knew how to acknowledge the other person. Should they kiss? Hug? Just smile? They were at that adorably awkward stage where every moment and every act counted, the stage I'd never . . . Wow, I'd never experienced that with Brandon.

Holy crap, how was I just now realizing that?

Whenever Brandon and I saw each other, even after the very first date, it was always a kiss and then he'd start talking about the football game he had coming up or I would ask about his classes.

None of those moments had counted, not for me and not for him.

They counted for Heidi and Emery, though.

They hugged, and when they pulled back, Heidi's normally pale face was flushed and there was a pinker tint under Emery's deeper-hued skin.

Ugh. They were so cute.

I wish I hadn't left my camera in the car. Taking a picture of them together would've been perfect.

"I'm really sorry about what happened," Emery said, tucking her dark hair behind her ear. Up close, her green eyes were the muted color of moss. "It's unbelievable."

"It really is," Heidi agreed. "I was just telling Evie that I used to hang out with Colleen in grade school. We weren't close over the last . . . well, in forever, but it's still so sad."

"Did you know her?" Emery asked me.

I shook my head. "We never really talked beyond the basics."

Emery's gaze flickered to the window and she drew in a shallow breath. "So, not to change the subject or anything." She focused on me. "Please don't be mad at me."

My brows rose as I glanced at Heidi. "Why would I be mad?"

"I didn't come alone," she said, and muscles I didn't even know I had clenched in my stomach. "Well, I tried to. It didn't work out that well."

"What do you . . . ?" Heidi's eyes widened as her gaze focused on something or someone behind me. "Oh my word."

I didn't have to look behind me to know. On a cellular level,

I just knew, and my heart started throwing itself around in my chest. My pulse picked up as a shadow fell over our table. I knew it wasn't our waitress, and I had no idea how I felt.

But I did look.

Slowly, I lifted my head and looked to my right, and there stood Luc, his bronze hair a mess of waves and curls. He was wearing silver aviator sunglasses, the kind with lenses so reflective, I could see my own wide-eyed stare in them. My gaze was drawn to the clean, hard lines of his jaw and then lower, over the broad width of his shoulders, and then to his chest.

His shirt read MUGGLE IN THE STREETS, WIZARD IN THE SHEETS.

My mouth gaped open.

"Like my shirt?" he asked, dropping into the space beside me.

"It's . . . nice."

"I think so." He threw his arm over the back of our booth. "Kent got it for me." The ever-present half grin faded. "Sucks about what happened at your school, to that girl."

"Yeah, it does." I shot a look across the table, and saw that Heidi sort of resembled a fish out of water. "You know the girl who was at Foretoken when she disappeared?" I blurted out before I had a chance to stop myself. Luc and I had briefly talked about her when he found me near the lake. "I talked to her that night."

One single brow rose above the sunglasses. "I didn't know you talked to her." He looked over at Emery, and for some reason, I got the distinct feeling that not a single part of that had been news to him. "What has happened to her is unfortunate to hear."

Way unfortunate.

His head cocked to the side as he leaned forward, extending his arm toward Heidi. The gesture caused his shoulder to press into mine, and I scooted toward the window, earning some space. His grin returned, tipping up on one side. "I don't think we've actually met. I'm Luc."

"I know." She shook his hand. "I'm—"

"Heidi," he answered for her. "It's nice to meet you. Emery has nothing but wonderful things to say about you."

Flushing once more, she glanced over at Emery. "Is that so?"

"Just telling the truth," Emery replied with a shrug. "Luc heard I was coming to meet you guys."

"And I invited myself along." He returned to his normal sprawl. "I had to do it."

"Really?" Heidi replied.

Luc nodded as he finally pushed the sunglasses up. "I knew Evie would be disappointed if I didn't show."

A strangled-sounding laugh burst out of Heidi as my head whipped around toward Luc so fast, I thought I was going to give myself whiplash. "What?" I demanded. Luc looked at me, and whatever I was about to say died on the tip of my tongue. "Your eyes!" I gasped in a whisper.

He dipped his chin, and somehow the little distance that I'd gained was lost. "Contacts," he whispered, winking. "Special ones. And yes, they really mess up the RAC drones."

My mouth dropped open for a second time. "That's a thing?"

"There are a lot of things that are a thing," he replied, and I blinked hard. He looked away. "Well, hello there."

For a moment I didn't know who he was talking to, but then I saw the waitress.

"What can I get you all to drink?"

The girls got waters, and Luc ordered a Coke. I started to order one of the sweet teas, because I knew they made it the way I liked, with tons of sugar, but I ordered a Coke.

"A Coke?" Heidi asked, sounding as surprised as I felt. "Don't you normally order Pepsi?"

I did, but I wanted . . . I wanted a Coke for some reason. Not exactly a big deal. I shrugged. "I guess I want a Coke."

"The last time I accidentally brought you a Coke, you threatened to stop being my friend."

I laughed. I had threatened that.

The waitress shuffled off, and I was back to staring at Heidi, desperately wondering how I had ended up eating breakfast with Luc.

It was *weird*.

It felt like eons ago that I'd seen him at the park, and I hadn't even begun to process the bizarre conversation with him or what had happened over the weekend, and now he was sitting *right* here.

The drinks arrived quickly and we placed our orders. Of course, I ordered the tower of waffles and a side of extra-crispy bacon. I grabbed my Coke, gulping down the sugary goodness.

"Thirsty?" Luc eyed me closely.

Feeling my cheeks heat, I put my glass down and shot back, "You're good at pointing out the obvious, aren't you?"

Luc's lips curved into a grin. "That's my superpower."

"Nice," I replied dryly.

Heidi cleared her throat as her gaze flickered to Luc. "So, how did you and Emery meet? I never heard about that."

"Well, that's kind of a sad story." Luc's finger tapped along the back of the booth.

Emery toyed with the edge of her fork. "My family didn't . . . survive the invasion."

"Oh my God, I'm sorry to hear that." I glanced over at Heidi, and that part didn't seem like it was news to her.

"Thank you," Emery murmured, and then lifted her gaze, looking at Luc. "Things were kind of a mess afterward. You know how everything was. I ended up on the streets and Luc took me in."

Surprise flickered through me. "He took you in?"

Luc nodded, those fingers still tapping behind my shoulder. "I'm charitable like that."

"He did the same for Kent," Emery added, her fingers stilling over her fork. "He'd lost his family too and had no place to go until he found Luc."

That piece of information was unexpected, because my impression of Luc was not charitable, but more important, Luc and Emery looked roughly the same age. How in the world would Luc be in the position to take anyone in when he was fifteen?

Unless he was lying about his age.

"Emery is my age," Luc replied, and my entire body jolted. "And I was more than capable of helping her out."

My eyes narrowed on his profile. Seriously. It was like he was inside my head, because I knew damn well I didn't ask that question out loud. Wait. Could he be?

No. I'd never heard that any Luxen could do that.

A half smile appeared as his gaze slid to mine. Our stares connected, and the effect was instantaneous. Everything around us faded, and there was just us, and this . . . this sensation of falling. I couldn't look away as this feeling surfaced, rushing to the top.

I've been here before.

My breath caught as a wave of tight shivers rippled over my skin. That thought didn't make sense. I hadn't been here with him before.

Luc inhaled sharply, and he moved without me noticing. He was closer. His warm breath danced across my cheeks and then my mouth. Air hitched in my lungs for a second time. Those well-formed lips of his parted, and now I *really* wished I had my camera. And I . . . I couldn't stop myself from wondering what those lips felt like—tasted like—because that brief kiss-that-wasn't-a-kiss hadn't told me what I needed to know.

"What's going on in that head of yours?" he asked in a soft voice.

The hold that seemed to have forged itself out of the tense air around us was broken. I snapped out of it, jerking back and nearly smacking into the window. What was going on in my mind? Nothing but stupid—a whole lot of stupid.

My gaze swung across the table.

Heidi and Emery were staring at us like they were watching one of those really terrible but addictive reality shows.

Warmth exploded across my cheeks as I decided staring at the table was an awesome thing to do. My heart was pounding in a silly way. What in the world was I thinking? Luc was attractive. In all honesty, he was truly beautiful, and he apparently had a nice streak in him. Somehow he'd taken care of Emery and Kent when they needed help the most, and I'd seen him with Chas at the club, but I wasn't even sure I liked Luc.

I wasn't even sure he liked me.

Thankfully, the food showed up at that moment, and I focused on shoving as much waffle into my mouth as humanly possible while Heidi and Emery chatted. I stayed quiet, as did Luc, but every part of my being was painfully aware of his every movement. When he picked up his glass or cut into the omelet he ordered. He'd shift, and I'd catch that woodsy pine scent of his, and when he did speak, the deep timber of his voice echoed through my veins. By the time breakfast wrapped up, every muscle in my body was stiff and sore. I felt like I'd run a marathon as we filed out of the restaurant.

I lingered behind, giving Heidi and Emery some space as they walked ahead. Luc apparently was of the same mind, because he slowed his long-legged pace, walking beside me.

Walking beside Luc was . . . interesting.

People had one of two reactions when they neared Luc. They either gave him wide berth, nearly stepping into the street to avoid brushing up against him, or they did a double take, male and female. Their gazes would glance over him and then bounce back and they wouldn't be able to look away. With his sunglasses on and contacts in, no one should be able to tell what he was by appearance, but it was the vibe he emitted, even with his lazy swagger.

We didn't speak, not until we neared the entrance to the garage. Luc easily glided in front of me, stopping so we were standing next to the building, away from the foot traffic.

My heart was tripping all over itself as I lifted my chin. "Do you need something?"

"I need lots of things," he replied, and warmth cascaded through me, because my mind belly-flopped right into the gutter. The grin that appeared made me wonder just how apparent my thoughts were. "They seem to really like each other."

"Oh." I glanced around him. Heidi and Emery had already entered the garage. "I think they do."

"You know what that means?"

"They'll start dating?"

Luc chuckled as he stepped in. "We'll be seeing lots of each other."

"I don't know about that." I folded my arms.

"I do."

I tilted my head to the side and lifted a brow. "I think you're wrong."

"Hmm," he murmured, looking out toward the street as a car zoomed by, blaring its horn. A moment passed and then his head turned back to me. Even with the sunglasses, I could feel the intensity of his gaze. "You don't like me, do you, Evie?"

The bluntness of his question was jarring. "You weren't exactly nice to me when we first met. Like, at all."

"I wasn't," he agreed.

I waited to see if he would add on to that statement, and when he didn't, I sighed with irritation. "Look, I could go into extensive detail about all the signals you've been throwing off, but I really don't feel like putting that much effort into it. You don't seem to like me either, Luc."

"I like you, Evie." His hand lifted with startling quickness and he picked up a piece of my hair. "Lots."

I snatched my hair free. "You don't know me well enough to like me, and if you do like me, you have a terrible way of showing it. Terrible."

Somehow he got closer, and I didn't even know how, but when he spoke, his voice sent a shiver curling down my spine in an oddly pleasant way. "You'd be awed and amazed by what I do know."

I resisted the urge to retreat.

"And I already told you. I don't people well."

"Not peopling well is a crap excuse," I retorted, and started to step around him, but a sudden thought occurred to me. I stopped, refocusing on him. "Were you in my house last night?"

That half grin kicked up a notch. "If I was in your house last night, you would've definitely known."

My stomach dipped like I was standing too close to the edge of a steep cliff. "I don't know what that means."

Luc opened his mouth.

I lifted a hand. "I don't *want* to know what that means."

He dipped his chin. "I think you know exactly what it means."

I thought I did, but that was beside the point.

"Why would you ask if I was in your house last night?" he asked.

When I started to tell him it didn't matter, I stopped myself. I found that I wanted to tell him—tell someone, to see if they, too, thought it was my imagination, like Zoe had. "When I was home last night, I heard a crashing sound downstairs, and when I went down there to check—"

"You hear a random noise in your house, you go downstairs and check it out?"

"What was I supposed to do? Call the police and say, 'Hello, officer, I heard a noise downstairs. Can you come check it out?'"

"Yes," he said. "Unless you're equipped with a shotgun, and you just might be because of Sylvia, you don't go downstairs."

I shook my head. "Whatever. I went downstairs, and the back door was open even though I know damn well I'd closed and locked that door. And while I was standing there, I *felt* someone standing behind me, but when I turned around, no one was there. Then the back door slammed shut."

Everything about Luc changed in that instant. The teasing quality to his voice and the curve of his lips were gone. "What else happened?"

"My . . . mom's office door was open and it's always locked. Always." I shifted my weight from one foot to the other as the scent of exhaust fumes rose. "One of my friends, Zoe, actually came over, and I think she thinks I was overreacting, but I know what I saw. What I heard and . . ."

"And?" he asked quietly.

I leaned against the side of the building and looked away. "I felt . . . I swore I felt someone touch me." I waited for him to say something obnoxious, but when he didn't, I drew in a shallow breath. "Mom went into her office last night when she got home, like she always does, but she didn't mention anything. If something was taken or messed up, I think she would've said something to me. Like, asked if I'd been in the office."

Luc was staring at me.

"I know Zoe thinks I left the door open, but I know I didn't. It had to be a Luxen. How else could someone move so fast without me ever seeing them? I know it sounds bizarre, but—"

"No." Luc's jaw was as hard as his tone. "If you think someone was in your house, Evie, then someone was in your house."

My heart turned over heavily. It was equally nice and disturbing to have someone believe me.

"You didn't see anyone, though?"

I shook my head. "Like I said, they were fast. But why would a Luxen come into my home and not take anything and just leave?"

Luc didn't answer for a long moment. "Well, that is the question of the day, isn't it?"

I nodded.

"But you know what the more important question is?" he asked. "What if a Luxen was in your house and they did take something? You said Sylvia's office door was open, but it's normally locked."

"It's *always* locked." My gaze flew to his. "Why wouldn't she mention that then?"

Luc didn't answer for a long moment, and when he spoke, he didn't answer the question. He posed another one. "How well do you think you know Sylvia Dasher?"

14

Wednesday morning's local news was consumed by what had happened to Colleen, and Amanda's disappearance.

Murder.

Kidnapping.

The reporters openly speculated that it had been a Luxen attack—an unregistered Luxen attack—and that one was also behind Amanda's disappearance. They didn't say why they thought that, but the why didn't seem to matter to them. They'd already made up their minds.

When I arrived at school later that morning, news crews from every major network were parked out front, grabbing and interviewing students as they stepped off the buses.

The whole day felt off. At lunch, even James was subdued. I imagined it would be that way for a while. No one had heard from Amanda, and without anyone saying anything, I knew we all feared the worse.

She would turn up just like Colleen.

Mom had texted saying she wouldn't be home until late, so I was left to my own devices. After everything that had happened in the last week, that meant my brain was working overtime and what Luc had asked me yesterday had haunted me on and off over the last twenty-four hours, and it was back with a vengeance, pecking away as I walked into the quiet house. Why would he ask me something like that about my mom?

Why hadn't I asked myself that yet?

Because I'd learned firsthand this weekend that there was a lot I didn't know about my mom or my father. I had no idea they'd been involved in the Daedalus—hell, I hadn't known about the Luxen making this planet their home sweet home for decades.

Mom was a bucket of secrets.

Dropping my keys and bag on the dining room table, I shivered as I stood in the same place I had last night when I'd felt the *presence* behind me. Someone had been in here and they had been in Mom's office.

Why?

Maybe focusing on this was pointless, but it was better than thinking about what had happened to Colleen and what could be happening to Amanda. That was what I didn't want to dwell on while I was home alone.

I walked through the living room and into the foyer. Bright light streamed from all the windows and everything was where it should be, but the house seemed strange to me now.

Cloudy, somehow.

The glass French doors were closed, and a thick white curtain shielded the little square windows. I'd never been in Mom's office. Never had a reason to. Someone could be living in there for all I knew.

Biting down on my lip, I reached out and wrapped my hand around the cool, tarnished gold handle. My wrist twisted. The door was locked, as always.

Would be really nice to have that nifty Luxen ability right about now.

"Wait," I whispered. Luc had that awesome breaking-and-entering talent. He could easily get into her office.

But seriously? Would I ask him to do that? I didn't even know how to get in touch with him. . . .

Actually, I did know how to get ahold of him. There were two ways.

I pivoted and went to where my bag was on the dining room table. I snatched my phone out of the top pocket, ignoring the little voice in the back of my head that was demanding to know what the hell I was planning to do. I hit the second contact on my phone.

Heidi answered on the third ring. "Hey, girl, what's up?"

"Um, nothing. I was wondering if Emery was with you?"

There was a beat of silence. "Yeah, she's right here."

"I know this is going to sound really weird, but can I talk to her for a moment?" I folded an arm over my waist and started pacing.

"Is this about Luc?"

I tripped over my feet. "What? Why would you ask that?"

"Why else would you be calling me to talk to Emery?"

She was right, but I still lied. "There could be tons of reasons why I'd want to talk to her. Like your birthday is coming up. Maybe I want to plan something with her."

"My birthday is in April, Evie. It's only September."

"Yeah," I drew the word out. "I'm just planning ahead."

"Uh-huh," Heidi replied. "So, this is about Luc?"

I sighed and rolled my eyes. "Yes, but it's not what you think."

"Sure." She laughed. "Hold on a second."

Before I had a chance to reply, Emery was on the phone. "What can I do for you?"

What in the world was I doing? I had no idea, but I was pacing again and my mouth was running. "I know this is going to sound weird, but I was wondering if you could . . ." I trailed off as I stopped in front of the couch.

The cushions were where they were supposed to be, but all I could see was Mom whipping the one cushion off, pulling out a shotgun—and pointing that shotgun at Luc.

"If I could what?" Emery asked.

Squeezing my eyes tight, I shook my head. "I was wondering if you could give me"—I cringed—"Luc's phone number."

"Yeah," she answered immediately. "I can have Heidi text it to you."

I started to tell her that would be fine but stopped. Again, what was I doing? Besides the absolutely insane fact that I was about to reach out to Luc and invite him to my house to help me break into my mom's office, how would I know if anything was missing? I didn't even know what the inside of her office looked like. What could I find when I didn't even know what I was looking for?

But I still wanted in there.

"Are you still there, Evie?" Emery asked.

I nodded and then rolled my eyes, because duh, she couldn't see me. "Yeah, I'm still here. It's just I . . . I don't know why I'm asking for his number. I needed help with something and could use his unique . . . talents, but I . . . I don't really know him and this was probably a really bad idea. I'm sorry to bother you two."

"You're not a bother." It sounded like she moved and then I heard her say in a low voice, "Is everything okay?"

A weak smile crossed my lips. That was sweet of her to ask. "Yeah, everything is fine. I'm just being dumb."

"All right, so now it's my turn to sound weird, but hear me out. I don't know what you need help with, but whatever it is, Luc will do it," she said. "You can trust him. Out of everyone you've ever met, you can trust Luc."

Heidi texted me Luc's phone number and I ended up staring at the text for five full minutes, unable to bring myself to call him. I really felt like something was wrong with me, because there was a huge part of me that trusted what Emery had said in spite of everything that indicated otherwise.

There was no good reason to believe what she said.

I'd met Luc just six days ago and it had been a rough six days, but in a way, it felt like I'd known him a lot longer than that, and that probably wasn't a good thing.

My phone rang suddenly, and I almost dropped it. An unknown number had popped up with a local area code. It took me a second to vaguely recognize the number.

"Oh crap," I whispered, my eyes going wide. It was Luc's number. Of course, Emery had probably contacted him and told him I'd asked for his number.

Scrunching up my face, I squeezed my eyes shut as I squeaked out, "Hello?"

"So, I got this interesting text from Emery," came the deep voice that twisted my stomach all up in knots. "She said you asked for my number."

Why did I do that? Why did I answer the phone? "I did."

"And she said you needed help with something," he continued. "However, that was about five minutes ago, and you haven't texted or called, so I'm dying of curiosity."

I walked over to the couch and plopped down and closed my eyes. "I had a temporary moment of insanity."

Luc chuckled. "I think I should be offended by that statement."

"Probably," I muttered, pressing my fingers to my forehead. "You didn't have to call me. I would actually prefer that you forget I asked for your number."

"Well, that's never going to happen."

"Great." I sighed. "Couldn't you just lie to me?"

"I would never lie to you," he replied without a second of hesitation.

I frowned. "Why do you say things like that?"

"Like what?"

"Like . . ." It was hard to put into words. "Never mind."

He sighed. "What do you need help with, Evie? Tell me. The world is your oyster and I'm your pearl."

My frown increased. "That doesn't make any sense."

"Makes perfect sense."

"I just want you to know that I rolled my eyes so hard, they rolled down the back of my throat."

His answering laugh tugged at the corners of my lips. "Tell me why you need my help."

Falling back against the couch, I sighed again, heavily. "I wanted to get into my mom's office and see if there was something in there that would explain why someone was in the house on Monday, but I don't even know what to look for."

"And you thought I'd know?" A door shut on his end.

"No. I thought you would be able to unlock the door for me since you have unique talents suited for criminal behaviors."

"I can unlock the door."

"I know, but it's pointless, because I have no idea what to look for. I'm not a detective. I've never even been in the room." I kicked my feet up onto the ottoman. If Mom saw that, she would knock my feet right off it. "It was a stupid plan and it's your fault."

"How is your lack of creativity when it comes to sleuthing my fault?"

"Because you said—" I deepened my voice. " 'How well do you think you know Sylvia Dasher?' and now I'm paranoid. That's your fault."

"I think that was a very valid question."

It was, which irritated me. Luc was right. I thought I knew my mom, but I also thought I knew my dad, and obviously, I hadn't known him at all.

"I have an even better question for you," he said.

"Oh, goodie gumdrops. Can't wait."

His soft laugh annoyed me greatly. "Why do you think you will find something in the office?"

Tension crept into my muscles. "If there was someone here, a Luxen, he or she was in that office." I thought about what my mom had said my father was involved in before his death. "There had to be something."

"Are you sure that's the only reason?" When I didn't answer, he said, "Or do you think it's because there just might be something else she's keeping from you?"

Closing my eyes, I took a breath, but it didn't do any good. How would he know that? That ever since she told me about my father, I was wondering if there was more she hadn't told me?

"That's it," Luc said quietly. "Hit the nail on the head."

I didn't say anything. I couldn't.

"And maybe deep down, you know there are things I could help you with." His voice was soft, coaxing. "Things that Sylvia hasn't told you about. Things I know she won't."

My eyes opened. "Like what things, Luc?"

"I won't come over and open a door that's going to lead you nowhere," he said. "But if you come to the club tomorrow, after school, there'll be a lot of doors to open that'll lead you somewhere."

15

So." Heidi plopped down in the seat next to me, cradling a stack of Eastern Europe maps. We all were in the library during English, collecting research books for our next paper. I had no idea why she had maps. I was confident that her paper was on Alexander Hamilton. "Did Luc help you with whatever you needed last night?"

Zoe looked up from a thick tome, raising an eyebrow. "Come again?"

I shot Heidi a look, but she ignored me. I sighed. "Remember me telling you about the guy named Luc?"

"Yeah, the guy who busted up in your house and melted a shotgun." Zoe slowly closed the book, keeping her pointer finger between the pages. "You were with him last night?"

"No," I whispered, leaning forward. "I asked for his number, because I needed help with something that required his . . . talents."

Zoe's brows lifted. "My brain just took that in several different directions."

"Mine too." Heidi giggled, smoothing her hands over her maps.

"God. No." I glanced over as April shuffled past our table. She stopped a few feet away. I lowered my voice even more. "I wanted to get into my mom's office and the door was locked. He can help with that."

Zoe stared at me a moment and then moved a curl out of her face. "Okay. I have several questions. Did you invite him over to your house?"

"No. I didn't text him." I turned to Heidi. "But someone told him I asked for his number."

Heidi shrugged. "Wasn't me."

"I know," I deadpanned. "And why do you have maps of Eastern Europe?"

Glancing down at her pile, she sighed. "I've always wanted to travel to Europe."

"But you're supposed to be working on a paper about Alexander Hamilton," I pointed out.

Zoe snapped her fingers, drawing my attention back to her. "Focus. Why do you want to get into her office?"

"It's a kind of convoluted story."

"Does it have to do with what happened Monday night?"

Heidi's forehead wrinkled. "What happened Monday night?"

I quickly told her about how I thought someone had been in the house and had gone into my mother's office. "So, I thought maybe Luc could help me get into the office."

"You thought someone was in your house?" Heidi whispered, her eyes going wide.

"We didn't see anyone and the doors were locked," Zoe added, and then lifted her hands when I frowned at her. "Not that I don't believe you. There was just no sign of anyone being there."

Heidi sat back. "That's really creepy, especially with everything that's going on with Colleen and Amanda."

"Yeah, it is." I breathed in the scent of musty books and stale air. "When Mom came home, she never mentioned anything being weird about the office, but . . ." I hated what I was going to say. "But I don't know if she would if she noticed something, you know? I don't think I . . . I really know her. Like, I do, because she's my mom. Duh. But obviously, at the same time, I don't. I know that doesn't sound like it makes sense."

Zoe was quiet, her gaze serious. "What do you think she's lying to you about?"

"I don't know. I mean, someone was definitely in the house, and the whole thing with her and Dad knowing Luc. I just think . . . I think there's more." It was hard to explain without spilling all the secrets, and I wanted to tell them, but instinct told me that there were some things I seriously needed to keep to myself. "Anyway, Luc didn't come over last night, but—"

Someone shushed us.

Zoe lifted her head, pinning a dark look onto some unfortunate soul somewhere behind me. "But what?"

I curled my fingers around the edge of my book. "I think Luc knows something about Mom and my dad." *And about me,* whispered a weird voice in the back of my head. Shivering, I ignored it. "He pretty much insinuated that he did and that he would tell me."

Well, I guessed that was what he meant in his very obnoxiously mysterious way of his.

I thought Zoe looked surprised, but her expression smoothed out so quickly, it had to have been my imagination.

"What could he possibly know?" Zoe asked.

"I don't know." I looked between the girls. "But I'm going to find out."

I ran into James as I walked to my car after school. "What are you up to?" he asked. "I'm starving, so I thought I'd do you a sweet favor and let you accompany me on my excursion to find the juiciest and thickest hamburger this fine town has to offer."

I laughed as I pulled out my sunglasses and slid them on. "I'd love to, but I have something I have to do. Maybe tomorrow? Or Saturday? I heard Coop canceled his party."

"I heard the same. He's doing it next weekend instead. Guess he wasn't . . . in the mood after what happened."

Dead and missing classmates kind of dampened the whole party vibe.

"I also heard you have plans today after school," he said as we stopped by my car. "You're going to that club."

Dammit. "Which one of them blabbed?"

He folded his arms. "I'll never tell."

I'd told both of them I'd been planning to go to the club, and now I was regretting it. "If you knew what I was doing, then why did you ask me to do something?"

"Thought I could possibly woo you with hamburgers instead."

He stepped aside as I moved toward the driver's-side door. "Do you think it's smart to go back there?"

No. I didn't think it was smart at all.

"I mean, you know I don't have anything against the Luxen, but there were a ton there unregistered. Then there's what happened to Colleen, and Amanda is still missing. . . ." He cleared his throat. "And that Grayson dude freaked me out."

If he thought Grayson was freaky, which he really was, it's a good thing he hadn't met Luc.

"And when that blue-haired dude took me home, I thought you were being kidnapped or something."

My lips pursed. Luc *had* tried to kidnap me, which made the fact that I was going back to the club willingly seem even more idiotic. "Aw, are you worried about little old me?" I teased, punching him lightly on the arm. "I'll be fine."

"Uh-huh. Fine. I'll go eat juicy grilled hamburgers all by myself." James started to turn and then stopped. "Can I ask you something?"

"Sure." I opened up the car door.

He seemed to consider what he was about to say. "Are you, like . . . getting involved with someone there?"

"What?" I tossed my bag onto the front seat and then turned back around to face him. "Like, am I interested in someone? Luc?"

James nodded.

I laughed, but it sounded weird to my own ears. "You haven't had a chance to meet him, but if you did, you would know how ridiculous that question is."

That was partly true. How could I be into Luc? I wasn't, but . . . I was. And while I should be worried about going to that club, I wasn't, and I couldn't even explain why. It made no sense, especially when I'd promised my mom I wouldn't go back there, made Heidi swore she wouldn't, and I hadn't even wanted to go there in the first place. I couldn't put my finger on it, but there was this weird sense of—of what? Safety? Familiarity?

There was a good chance I was losing my mind.

He raised a brow. "He's a . . . He's a Luxen, right?" When I nodded, he looked away and then refocused on me. "Just be careful, Evie. Colleen was at that club when she went missing, and now Amanda is gone. It feels like, I don't know, they are the beginning of something."

Walking up to the red doors of Foretoken, I felt like I was seconds away from stealing something pricey at a ritzy department store. Like I was about to shove a car payment's worth of perfume under my shirt.

Not that I knew what it felt like to do that, but I imagined a shoplifter felt the same mix of anxiety and excitement I was currently drowning in.

A huge part of me couldn't believe I was actually doing this. I hadn't told Luc I would last night. For all I knew, he might not even be here.

Knowing that, I was still here.

Drawing in a shallow breath, I lifted my hand, but before I could touch the red doors, one of them inched open. Gasping, I took a step back. I'd expected to see Clyde. That wasn't who I got an eyeful of.

Luc stood just inside the entryway to Foretoken.

He wasn't completely dressed.

As in, he was shirtless.

And there was a whole lot of naked chest in front of me—naked chest and stomach.

My brain sort of shorted out on me. I didn't even know where to look. I shouldn't look at all, but I couldn't help myself. I *wanted* to look and I wanted my camera in my hand, to take a photo of those . . . angles.

His jeans were zipped but unbuttoned, and they hung indecently low—like, so low, they had to be held up by alien superpowers. He had those muscles on either side of his hips, the kind that formed indents. I didn't even know what they were called, but boy, oh boy, did he ever have them. There was a faint dusting of hair that disappeared below the jeans.

A flush of warmth hit my cheeks as I dragged my gaze up, over his abs—he had abs for *days,* each one cut and defined. His chest was sculpted, and as he lifted an arm, clapping his hand over the doorframe above him, I watched, sort of dazed, as the muscles along his ribs moved and flexed in interesting ways.

Luc was . . . holy crap, he was *ripped*.

I'd figured he was in shape based on the few, brief times I'd *accidentally* touched his stomach or chest, but thinking about what he had was nothing compared to what he actually had.

This wasn't real.

That was what I kept telling myself as my gaze flickered south again, to that interesting trail of hair. His body wasn't real. It was just a mask the Luxen wore. Luc really looked like a human-shaped jellyfish. This . . . very beautiful body wasn't real.

Thinking that didn't help.

At all.

Because his body looked totally touchable and real.

"Do you want me to take one of those creepy, self-indulgent selfies of my stomach and send it to you?" Luc asked. "Then you can check me out whenever you want, even when I'm not around."

Oh my God.

Heat filled my cheeks as my gaze snapped to his face. He'd obviously just gotten out of the shower. Damp hair teased his forehead and temples. No contacts today. Eyes back to that weirdly beautiful purple. "I wasn't checking you out."

"Really? Because you were staring so hard, it felt like an actual touch. Not a bad touch. You know, not the kind with the dolls and years of therapy."

Oh my *God* . . .

"A good touch. The welcomed kind that puts you in therapy for a whole different reason," he added as he moved aside, holding the door open. I noticed then he was barefoot. "But we can pretend like you weren't checking me out."

"I wasn't," I seethed, refusing to look at him at all.

Luc stepped around me. "Whatever makes it easier for you to

sleep at night, because checking out someone you think is an alien? Oh, the horror."

I blew out a long, steady breath. "You *are* an alien."

Luc widened his eyes at me. "You know nothing, Evelyn Dasher."

"Did you just quote *Game of the Thrones*?"

"Maybe," he murmured.

"And why aren't you wearing a shirt? Did you forget how to put one on?"

"Putting on clothes is *haaard*."

"Apparently buttoning your pants is too," I muttered, flushing again.

He laughed as he opened the second door. "Why are you wearing a shirt?"

Slipping past Luc, I shot a glare at him as we walked into the dimly lit, quiet club floor. "Are you seriously asking that question?"

He raised a shoulder as he brushed past me. "I thought it was as valid as your question." He looked over his shoulder as he walked ahead of me. "You know. As valid as asking any other stupid question."

My eyes narrowed on his back—his *really* nice back. He had these muscles all up and down his spine. I stopped by the dance floor, briefly closing my eyes. What was I doing? "This was a mistake."

He turned to me, and I sort of wished he didn't, because the struggle was real when it came to focusing north of his shoulders. Not that that was any easier. "Why would you think that?"

"Why?" I barked out a short, harsh laugh. "You're being an ass."

"Because I acknowledged that you were so obviously checking me out and you reacted like I accused you of drinking the blood of babies on the Sabbath?"

My nose wrinkled and my gaze dipped. I had no idea what his skin felt like, but I imagined it was like silk stretched over steel. *Dammit*. I needed to stop—

He stepped in, and my back straightened. "Let's start over. Completely. You'll pretend that the mere idea of being attracted to me doesn't freak you out, and I'll pretend that you're not thinking about how I'd feel under your fingers. Hmm? Sound like a plan?"

My jaw hit the floor as the heat splashed down my throat. I stepped forward, pointing a finger at him. "I am not thinking that."

His grin spread. "Stubborn and a terrible liar. I guess some things never change."

"You haven't known me long enough to know that I'm a crap liar."

Turning away, he ran a hand over one of the tables. "I know you just as well as you know yourself."

"Whatever." Irritation flared. "You know what I know? I know that you like to say crap that makes no sense just to hear yourself talk."

Luc chuckled in a deep, would've-been-nice kind of way if it had been coming from anyone else. "Hell, you do know me."

"I have to agree," came a voice from behind me. I turned, spying Kent. I had no idea where he'd come from, but he was carrying a bottle of water. "That sounds exactly like the Luc I know."

"You're not supposed to agree with her." Luc reached the bar area. "Bro code, dude. Bro code."

Kent winked as he walked past me. "She came alone."

I'd just picked my jaw off the floor to have it fall again. "You were checking me out to see if I came alone?"

"Of course we did," Luc said. "We're not stupid."

I gaped at him. "You told me to come here. Why would you think I brought someone with me?"

"Because you did last time," he explained. "And I have a feeling you don't quite know why you did come."

I snapped my mouth shut.

Luc started walking again. "So we were just making sure there weren't any surprises."

Kent moved closer to me. "I don't think we've formally met. You're Evie. I'm Kent. I like long walks in dark cemeteries and I want to have a pet llama before I die."

I blinked. "A llama?"

"He's a bit obsessed with llamas," Luc chimed in.

"Hell yeah. Who wouldn't be? I mean, they're like God got confused, you know? He already made horses and sheep, and decided, let's mix that together, and voilà—you get a llama," Kent explained. "Freaking ah-mazing. Have you ever met a llama?"

"No," I murmured.

"That's a shame. Anyway, we'll be taking this." Before I could react, he'd slipped my backpack off my arm. He smiled when I spun toward him. "Only until you're ready to leave."

"Are you serious?" I demanded. "What do you think I'm hiding in there? A bomb?"

"We can never be too careful," Luc called from the hall. "And you did threaten to call the police once."

I whipped back around, finding him waiting for us. "I told you I wouldn't have actually done that! And I thought we were starting over and pretending to actually like each other."

"We're selectively pretending certain things didn't happen."

"God," I groaned as disappointment trickled into my veins. It was obvious he didn't trust me completely, and I didn't know why that bothered me, but it did. Which was stupid, because it wasn't like I trusted him either. "I thought we . . ." *I thought we were past all that.* Man, that was such a stupid thought, I couldn't even begin to explain.

His gaze sharpened. "We what?"

I drew in a deep breath. "I do not like you."

Luc bowed in my direction, sending a shock of hair over his forehead.

"Don't be mad at him. You can never be too safe nowadays. I mean, have you seen the news? Just the other day, a known Luxen community center in Denver was bombed."

I hadn't heard that.

"Someone walked right in, put a backpack down, walked out, and blew up a bunch of innocent people, including humans. So, we're careful." Kent hitched my bag over his shoulder. "But I won't let your bag out of my sight." He brought it around to his chest and hugged it close. "It'll be my new best friend."

My gaze flickered over him and his Mohawk. The hair had to be standing up a good seven inches. "Okay."

"I thought we could chat upstairs, where it's more comfortable," Luc intervened. "You coming?"

This was how I figured most horror films started out, but in for a penny, in for a pound . . .

So I sighed my annoyance and trekked after Luc. He held the door to the stairwell open for me. I walked through and started up the stairs.

Luc easily caught up with me, and Kent was right behind him. Trying to shake the nervousness, I trailed my hand along the railing.

Miraculously, they were quiet as we rounded the second floor. Luc kept walking, continuing up several flights of stairs, and I vaguely wondered if it would kill them to have an elevator.

Not even out of breath while I was seconds from dying, Luc opened the door to the sixth floor. This hallway looked like the one on the second floor except it was wider and had fewer doors.

"I'm gonna make myself scarce with your bag." Kent walked past us, whistling what sounded like a Christmas song under his breath, and opened one of the doors down the hall. "You two kids behave yourselves! Don't do anything I wouldn't do."

My eyes widened. As Kent disappeared into the room, Luc said, "Kent is . . . Well, he's different, but he kind of grows on you."

"Yeah." Legs burning, I forced one foot in front of the other until Luc stopped outside a wooden door. My heart flip-flopped in my chest. "How's Chas?"

"Better. He'll be back to hundred percent by tomorrow."

"He's lucky," I said, and Luc looked over at me. "I mean, if he were human—"

"He wouldn't have survived the attack," he finished for me. "And if he wore a Disabler, he wouldn't have been able to heal himself."

I worried my bottom lip, looking down. "Is this . . . your room?"

"More like my apartment."

His apartment. Right. Not like he just had a bedroom in his parents' house. For all I knew, he had been hatched from an egg somewhere.

Luc lifted an arm, brushing his hair from his face. My gaze followed the movement of all his skin and muscles. He dropped his arm as he faced me.

Our gazes connected, and I found I couldn't look away. There was something entrancing about his stare, and for a long moment neither of us spoke. A weird edginess surfaced, the same I felt when I'd been here on Saturday, and it seeped into the hall and settled over my skin like smoke. It was like being near an electric storm. I half expected the overhead lights to dim or explode.

He lowered his gaze, breaking the connection. His voice was low. "I'm glad you came."

I blinked. "You are?"

A moment passed. Dark, impossibly thick lashes lifted. Amethyst eyes latched on to my eyes once more. "Yeah. I didn't think you would."

I crossed my arms and shifted my weight from one foot to the next. "Would you blame me if I hadn't?"

"No." A wry grin formed.

Warmth hit my cheeks. "You were right earlier. I'm not even sure why I'm here."

The grin spread as he turned, pressing his finger against a pad. Fingerprint read and processed, the lock unclicked. High tech right there. "I know why."

My stomach tumbled a little. "Why?"

Luc opened the door. "Because I'm going to tell you a story."

16

A story?

That was not what I'd come here for. I wanted to know what he knew about my mom—about what secrets she could possibly be keeping. But the moment I stepped inside the slightly chilly room and Luc flipped on an overhead light, I wasn't thinking about what he could know.

This was not the kind of dingy apartment I was expecting.

My wide gaze traveled across the long length of the room. With the exception of two doors, which I guessed led to a bathroom and maybe a closet, the large space was entirely open. There was a huge living room with one of those deep moon-pit-style couches seated in front of shuttered, floor-length windows. A massive TV sat across from it, perched on a metal-and-glass stand. Floors were hardwood throughout, and flowed into a bedroom. The bed—*oh my*—the bed was on a raised platform. Two long wooden dressers butted up one side of the room, next to a clean desk. Only a laptop sat on the surface.

Looking around, I saw nothing personal. No pictures. No posters. The walls were all bare. Luc brushed past me as I stepped in farther and spied a guitar in the corner by the TV.

Luc played the guitar?

I peeked at him. He was walking into the kitchen area, one long-fingered hand trailing over what appeared to be a slab of slate countertop. Did he play the guitar shirtless?

I rolled my eyes. I did not need to know the answer to that question. "This is your place?"

"Yep." He walked to a stainless-steel fridge.

I shook my head. "How is that possible? How do you own this—own the club? You're only eighteen and I didn't think Luxen could own property?"

"They can't, but that doesn't mean they haven't found a way around those laws. My name isn't on any documentation, but all of this is mine."

"You mean it belonged to your parents?"

He laughed under his breath. "I don't have parents."

I frowned. Luxen totally had parents, but then I figured out what that must've meant. Luc's parents were dead, either before the invasion or during. Maybe they had—

"They didn't leave me money, either," he cut in, and my eyes narrowed. "I knew a guy once who had been really good with money. His name was Paris. Learned a lot from him."

Paris? What an odd name. Sounded familiar. Wait. That was a real person in history, right? "Where is Paris now?"

"Dead."

"Oh. I'm . . . I'm sorry."

His back was stiff as he lifted a hand, thrusting his fingers through his hair. "Do you know? Wait. Of course you don't." He laughed, dropping his hand as he twisted. "Paris was like a father to me. He was a good man, and I . . . I got him killed. That's not an exaggeration. I involved him in something—something reckless, before the invasion, and he died for it."

I didn't know what to say to that.

"I'll get back to that part. You want to know why I keep saying I'm not a Luxen? It's because I'm not."

I cocked my head to the side and folded my arms. "Why do you keep saying that?"

"Because it's the truth." He faced me, and I sort of wished he'd kept his back to me. "I'm an Origin."

I blinked once and then twice. "You're a what?"

One side of his lips kicked up. "An Origin. The offspring of a Luxen and a mutated human."

Several moments passed as I stared at him. "A mutated human?" A hoarse laugh escaped me. "You know what, I think I just need to find Kent and—*Holy crap.*"

Luc was suddenly *right* there, towering over me. He wasn't touching me, but he was close enough that I could feel the heat radiating from his bare skin. "I have no reason to lie to you. None. You need to understand that I have absolutely nothing to gain." His gaze met mine. "And everything to lose by telling you what the vast majority of the world doesn't know."

I swallowed as I held his stare. "What do you have to lose?"

A long moment passed before he answered. "Everything."

My heart lurched in my chest. "Then why would you risk everything by telling me anything?"

"Good question." His head tilted slightly. "But you want to the truth and I'm feeling chatty. The question is: Are you willing to listen?"

Part of me wanted to find my bag and get the hell out of here, but I did want the truth and I could decide when this was all over if he was lying or not. I nodded. "I'm willing to listen."

"Perfect." He turned, and in a blink of an eye, he was in front of the fridge, door open. He grabbed two Cokes. "There's a lot the public doesn't know."

Our fingers brushed as I took the Coke he offered me. I thought about what my mom had said about the public not knowing everything. My grip on the can tightened. "Does it have to do with the group my father worked in? The Daedalus?"

A wry twist of his lips appeared as he nodded. "Why don't you take a seat?"

Exhaling roughly, I looked around and decided the couch was the safest place. I walked over and sat on the edge. It was a wide and deep couch, and if I scooted all the way back, I'd have to roll out of it.

"Your mother told you that the Luxen had been here for a while, right? And that the Daedalus worked on assimilating them into society, hiding them. That's not all they did." Luc strode past me, placing his unopened can on the end table. "You see, the Luxen are hard to kill, something the world learned during the invasion."

Shivering, I twisted and watched him.

"It's not just because they're powerful, able to tap into what they call the Source and utilize it as a weapon." Luc stopped by a dresser, yanking a drawer open. "It's also because they can use it to heal themselves, which is what Chas did when he returned to his true form. But the really interesting thing is what they can do to humans with that power."

"Kill them?" I asked, popping open the can.

He chuckled as he pulled out a long-sleeve black shirt. Thank God. "They can heal humans."

My hand jerked, and carbonated goodness seeped over my fingers. "What?"

As he pulled a shirt over his head, I looked away before I got caught up in watching all those muscles doing weird and interesting things. "Luxen can heal anything from minor scrapes to near-fatal gunshot wounds. Of course, they have to want to do that, and most never did before the invasion, because their way of life—their safety—harbored on the fact that humans didn't know they existed. Running around and healing people with their hands is going to draw attention. People who did know the truth ended up disappearing. Even now. People who know the truth go missing. The truth is dangerous."

A shudder worked its way through me. And now I was going to know the truth.

Tugging the hem of his shirt down, he faced me. The shirt only helped a little. "And healing humans can have strange side effects. If they healed a human multiple times or if it was a massive job, like legit saving someone's life, it could change the human."

I took a sip of soda as Luc made his way back to the couch. "Mutate them?"

"Yep." He sat down next to me. "In some cases, not all, the human would take on some of the Luxen's characteristics, able to use the Source. They would be stronger and they wouldn't get sick."

I mouthed that word. *Hybrid.* It sounded like something straight out of a science-fiction novel. "But those hybrids are still . . . human, right?"

"Yes? No?" He shrugged. "I guess that's up for debate, but what isn't is that everything changed once the Daedalus realized the Luxen didn't get sick and that they could heal humans. Groups like the Daedalus started out with the best of intentions. They studied the Luxen, seeing if they could use their genetics to cure human diseases, everything from"—exhaling roughly, he looked away—"the common cold to certain cancers. The Daedalus knew the key to eradicating diseases was in Luxen DNA. They developed treatments and serums derived from Luxen DNA. Some of them worked." Another terse pause. "Some of them didn't."

Stunned, I stayed quiet and listened.

"It blew the door off what was possible when they learned that the Luxen could mutate humans, turning that human into a hybrid of sorts.

"Sometimes the human wouldn't mutate. They'd become normal again. Other times they . . . sort of self-destructed. There's some . . . mysticism involved in the mutation of a human, so the Daedalus studied that, coming up with treatments to insure that the mutations took hold. The Daedalus was dedicated to improving human life. They were doing some good. For a while."

I had a feeling things were going to take a sharp turn.

"Studies turned into experiments, the kind that violated probably every level of ethics that ever existed. It didn't take long for them to realize that a Luxen could breed with a human he'd mutated, producing children that were in many ways more powerful than a Luxen." He paused. "And the Daedalus experimented on them—many generations of those children. Keeping some around. Destroying others who didn't meet their expectations."

Revulsion rolled through me as I leaned forward, placing my can on the floor. "Oh my God."

"Many of those children never met their parents." Luc's features sharpened like a blade. "Then . . . the Daedalus was partnered with the Defense Department. It became more about creating soldiers than about curing diseases. Entire generations of those children grew up in labs and hidden facilities. Some never stepping outside. Many died in the same twelve-by-twelve room they were raised in. Others were planted into the military, government positions— billion-dollar companies."

My jaw was practically in my lap. This was . . . This was wow.

He put his hand on the couch beside my thigh and leaned in. "Whatever passion some of those doctors had in the beginning became twisted." Slowly, he lifted his gaze to mine, and I sucked in an unsteady breath. "Especially when they started forcing the breeding."

Sick to my stomach, I wanted to look away from Luc, but it felt like that was like looking away from the truth, from what I knew he was going to say.

Luc lifted his arm and slowly began rolling the sleeve of his shirt up, exposing a powerful forearm. He looked over his shoulder, raising his other hand. Something flew off the kitchen countertop and landed in his hand. I realized it was a knife, a very sharp one.

I tensed.

"When you cut a Luxen, they will heal in a couple of minutes, sometimes longer, depending on how deep." The sharp point hovered over his taut skin. "When you cut a hybrid, they, too, will heal. Not as fast, but definitely quicker than a human."

I clasped my hands together. "Luc—"

Too late.

Pressing down, he dragged the knife over his skin, slicing deep. Bluish-red blood beaded on his flesh. Before I could launch myself off the couch to grab towels, the skin closed over the wound, sealing it up.

"Holy crap." No blood. No cut. It was like he hadn't just sliced his skin open. My gaze shot to his.

"But a child of a Luxen and a hybrid—an Origin—heals immediately."

Understanding flared to life as I glanced down at his arm and then back to his striking face. "You . . . You're one of those kids?"

He nodded and then leaned to the side, placing the knife on the end table. "Watch."

I was so watching.

A faint white glow appeared over his pointer finger. Leaning away, my eyes widened to the size of saucers. "Don't—"

"It's okay." The light washed over his hand, licking down his arm. "Origins aren't transparent. . . ." He grinned. "Like jellyfish."

I could see that. His arm was fully formed underneath the intense light.

"Origins' eyes are like mine. Same color. Same kind of pupils."

I forced my gaze to his. Who had eyes like his? The guy I'd seen with Chas. "Archer. He's an Origin?"

As Luc nodded, the glow warmed his features like he was leaning over a candle. That explained the weirdness of his pupils, something I'd never seen on a Luxen. "There used to be more Origins. There aren't . . . many left."

I bit down on my lip. "What happened to them?"

Luc didn't answer for a long moment. "That's another story for another day."

My gaze flicked up his face and then back to the whitish glow humming over his hand. Some bizarre, innate urge to touch him— the light—woke up inside me.

"You can," he said, voice low and deep. "You can touch it. You won't be hurt."

My heart skipped a beat as I lifted my hand. "Can . . . can Origins read minds?"

A secretive smile played over his lips. "Some of us can."

Oh hell no. I froze. "Can you?"

"I can."

I started to draw back. I'd been right all along. Good Lord, the kind of stuff I thought around him? The bad? The really bad? The really embarrassing?

"I try not to do it. Like, I don't go peeping in people's thoughts. Sometimes I can't help it, especially when a person is broadcasting loudly." His gaze met mine. "You are . . . quiet most of the time. I've only picked up a few things unintentionally. Just parts of thoughts."

"Why would I believe you're not reading my mind on purpose?" If I had that ability, I'd totally be doing it every five seconds.

The light around his hand pulsed. "Because if I did read your mind, I probably wouldn't like what I found."

Startled by his blunt honesty, I was at a loss for words. Part of me wanted to apologize.

"Touch the light," he coaxed. "I know you want to. And it's not from reading your mind. It's written all over your face."

Luc was right.

I wanted to.

Probably a sign of insanity.

Swallowing hard, I reached out. Time seemed to slow as my fingers neared the glow. The air was warm around his hand. Not hot. Tensing, I tipped forward. My fingers parted the light, and a jolt of electricity danced over my skin. The light spread from Luc to me. It felt like a soft hum.

My breath caught.

Touching the light didn't hurt. Not at all. It felt like I was running my fingers through sunbaked air. Little tendrils of light flicked out, curling around my hand.

This wasn't just *light,* though. It was power—pure power that could be harnessed into a weapon—a weapon that had killed my father.

I pulled my hand free, pressing my palm into my leg.

The light dimmed until Luc's hand and arm looked normal. His pupils looked weird once more, as if they were stretching.

I cleared my throat. "What else can you do?"

Luc didn't answer for a long moment. He just looked at me in a way that made me feel like I was some kind of jigsaw puzzle he couldn't piece together. Our gazes collided and held. My breath caught. Something . . . something hot and unwanted flared to life between us.

His throat worked on a swallow as he looked away. "We're susceptible to the same weapons as the Luxen—Tasers and electric pulse guns are not our friends. Anyway, everything that a Luxen can do, we can do better."

"Wow." I laughed, pushing the odd feeling aside. "That's extremely modest of you."

A small grin appeared. "I knew someone once who said modesty was for saints and losers."

My brows lifted. "That sounds like someone who was very grounded. And likable."

Luc chuckled. "If you only knew . . ."

Silence fell around us, and I had so many questions. Like an entire night's worth of them. "So you . . . you never met your parents?"

Luc shook his head. "Nope. Pretty sure they're both dead."

"I'm sorry."

He raised a shoulder as he rolled his sleeve back down.

I was staring at him, at the planes and angles of his face. I knew I shouldn't ask this, but kind of couldn't help myself. "Did you grow up in one of the labs?"

"I did." His lashes lifted.

"What . . . was that like?"

He looked away, and I didn't think he'd answer. "It was like nothing. There was no sense of . . . self." His jaw worked as his gaze trekked over the bare walls of his apartment. "There were no friends. No family. No worth beyond what we were created for. An Origin was just a single entity, but at the same time, all Origins were the entity. We were kind of like computers in a way. All of us. Programmed from birth to obey until . . ."

"Until what?" I asked quietly, innately knowing this wasn't something he talked about a lot. Maybe ever.

He was still staring at the empty walls. "Until I became self-aware. Sort of like Skynet. You know, *Terminator*? I just woke up one day and was like, I'm smarter, faster, and deadlier than those who created me. Why was I letting them tell me when I could eat and sleep, when I could leave my room and when I could go to the bathroom? So I stopped obeying."

I imagined that didn't involve him just walking out a door. "What were you created for?"

"The basics," he replied. "World domination."

I choked on a laugh. "That's basics?"

"Isn't that what every idiot who goes down the wrong path in life wants? Maybe it doesn't start out that way. The Daedalus believed they were on the good side. They're the heroes in the story, but before they know it, they're the villains. Same with the Luxen who invaded Earth. They wanted to dominate, because they thought they were the better species. And the Daedalus? They wanted a perfect army, a perfect government—a perfect species. That was us. That was me."

"God, Luc. I'm so—"

"Don't. Don't apologize." He looked at me. "You had nothing to do with any of that."

"I know, but . . ." Pressure clamped down on my chest. "Did my parents have anything to do with those experiments?"

"Are you really ready for that answer?"

My breath caught. "I am."

"Jason was one of the people who oversaw the Daedalus. He knew exactly what they were doing and how they were doing it."

I already suspected as much, based on what Mom had told me, but still, that was a punch to the stomach. "And Mom?"

He picked up his soda, popping open the can. "I never saw Sylvia at any of the facilities, but there is no way she didn't know what they were doing—what her husband was doing. She may not have been part of any of the experiments, but she sure as hell was complicit."

I didn't want to believe that. Mom was a good person.

"Good people do terrible things when they believe in what they're doing," Luc commented.

"You're reading my mind."

He turned his head toward me. "You're broadcasting very loudly."

My eyes narrowed.

One side of his lips tipped up. "I'm not saying Sylvia is a bad person. There were a lot of decent people in the Daedalus who believed they were making the future a brighter, safer place."

"But . . . that doesn't make what they did okay. What you've described to me is horrific."

"It was." His eyes met mine. "And I didn't even tell you half of what they were responsible for."

My stomach twisted as I squeezed my eyes shut. I didn't know what to think. I couldn't picture Mom knowing about forced breeding and children being raised in cells, and being okay with that. If so, it was . . . It was sickening, and I wasn't that surprised that Mom had left all of this out when she told me about the Daedalus.

"You know what I've realized?"

"What?" I opened my eyes again.

Luc watched me. "Most people are capable of doing horrible things or looking away from them while they're doing amazing things. People aren't one-dimensional."

"I know, but . . ." I trailed off, staring at my hands. My mom was kind of my hero. She was badass and strong. She kept it together after the invasion and Dad's death. I didn't want her *tainted* like this, but it was too late. The truth had a way of erasing the past you knew.

Smoothing my hands over my legs, I exhaled roughly.

"I mentioned a man's name earlier. Paris? I said that I got him killed. That's true," Luc said quietly as he rose from the couch, and I turned my attention back to him. He was staring at me, his eyes a little wide. "And the really messed-up part of it? He knew what he was getting into. He knew why I was risking him, risking everyone, and he went along with it. And I know if there was a rewind button on life, he would've done the same thing—if not for me, for *her*."

I had no idea what he was really talking about, but there was no mistaking the hint of pain and sorrow that pinched his striking features. "Who is . . . her?"

"That's the story I'm going to tell you." He paused. "If you still think you have the brain space for it."

I nodded slowly. "I think I do."

He backed up and leaned against the wall. In that moment, he looked almost normal. Like he could be any teenage boy out there, but it was his eyes that set him apart. Not the color, but what was in them. An aged weariness churned in the purplish hues.

"I knew a girl once," he said. A wry grin appeared on his lips. "You know that saying, right? All great stories start with a girl? It's true, and this girl . . . she was special. Not because she was the most beautiful. Not that she wasn't, because I thought she was the most beautiful thing I'd ever seen, but that wasn't what made her special. She was the kindest and strongest human I'd ever met. She was brilliant and she was a fighter, surviving unimaginable things."

A twinge of sorrow blossomed in my chest. I already knew this story wouldn't have a happy ending.

His eyes drifted shut as he tipped his head back against the wall. "She was probably my only real friend—no, she *was* my only true friend. She wasn't like me—an Origin. She wasn't Luxen or a hybrid. She was just a human girl, a tiny thing, who had run away from her home just outside of Hagerstown—a house without a mother, and a father who cared more about getting drunk and high than he did caring for his child."

Hagerstown? That was where I was from—where I lived before the invasion. What a hell of a coincidence. The world truly was small sometimes.

Luc continued, his eyes still closed. "Somehow she made it from Hagerstown to Martinsburg, a town in West Virginia. I didn't find her. Paris did, and yes, he was a Luxen. He came across her one night. I don't even remember what he was doing, but I guess he felt bad for her, so he brought her back with him. She was this filthy, mouthy little thing, about two years younger than me." The grin appeared again, this time a little sad. "I didn't like her very much at first."

"Of course," I murmured, trying to picture a much younger Luc.

"She never listened to anything Paris or I told her, and no matter how annoyed I'd get with her, she was my . . ." He let out a heavy breath. "She was my shadow. Paris used to call her my pet. Which is kind of offensive when you think about it now, but yeah . . ." A shoulder lifted. "We tried to keep what we were a secret from her, because this was before the invasion, but that lasted all of about fifteen seconds. She wasn't scared when she learned the truth. If anything, it just made her extraordinarily curious . . . and more annoying."

A small grin tugged at my lips as I picked up my soda. Now I pictured a young Luc with an impish little girl tagging along behind him.

"Eventually, she grew on me." The sad smile returned. "She was like a little sister I never wanted, and then as she grew older, as *we* grew older, she became something entirely different to me." His eyes closed as a shudder worked its way through him. "I respected her before I even really knew what respect meant. She'd been through so much in such a short life. Things that even I couldn't comprehend, and I was never quite worthy of her—of her friendship, her acceptance and loyalty."

A knot formed in my throat. "What was her name?"

His striking eyes held mine as his head tilted to the side. "Nadia. Her name was Nadia."

"That's a pretty name." I toyed with the tab on my soda can. "What . . . what happened to her?"

"Jason Dasher."

A piercing pain hit my chest as I looked away. I'd known it before I'd even asked it, hadn't I? My father—the man who I'd just learned was responsible for horrible experiments on innocent Luxen and humans.

My mother's words came back to me. *He made sure that Luc lost someone very dear to him.* Oh God. My father had done something to this girl—this girl who Luc spoke of so reverently that it was obvious he had been madly in love with her even at a young age. And probably still was, even though it was painfully clear she was nothing more than a ghost now.

"You apologized at the lake for what he did, but you don't know what he did. Sylvia does, but she hasn't told you."

Curiosity filled me, but so did a hefty dose of dread. I wanted to know, so I would just have to deal with whatever terrible things my father had done. "What did he do?"

He stopped in front of me and knelt with the fluid grace of a dancer. "There is so much you do not know or understand."

"Then tell me," I insisted, my fingers denting the can.

A shadow flickered over his features. "I don't know if—" Luc stopped and turned his head toward the door. A second later there was a knock. "One moment." Sighing, he rose and went to the door. Grayson stood on the other side. "I thought I made it pretty clear I didn't want any interruptions?"

Widening my eyes, I lifted my soda and took a sip.

Grayson cast a dismissive glance in my direction. "Unfortunately, this couldn't wait. It has to do with the . . . packages that were left here last night."

Packages? Wait. Hadn't that one guy with the gorgeous green eyes mentioned packages? Daemon was his name.

"What's going on?" Luc demanded.

Grayson sighed as he glanced to where I sat. "Let's just say they ran into some unexpected problems."

"Dammit." Luc was already on his feet, walking toward the door. "Sorry," he said to me. "I need to handle this."

"It's okay." Bad timing, but I totally understood.

He hesitated for a moment. "This may take a while."

In other words, I needed to leave. I stood. "All right. I guess. . . ." My gaze met his, and I didn't know how to say good-bye after everything I'd learned.

Luc turned to Grayson. "I'll be right there."

Grayson looked like he'd rather not leave, but he pivoted stiffly and then disappeared from my sight. Luc faced me, his gaze searching mine as I inched forward. "Are you okay with everything?"

I placed the soda on the counter and nodded. "Yeah. I mean, it's a lot to learn, but I . . . I believe you." And I did. All that information was a lot to make up, and I couldn't fathom why he'd lie about any of it. "I have a feeling, though, that there's more."

He looked down at me. "There is." His body moved, and before I knew what he was doing, the very tips of his fingers touched my cheek. The contact carried a muted static charge. He lowered his head, and I felt his nose brush my other cheek. When he spoke, his tone was oddly rough. "Peaches."

I inhaled sharply. "It's . . . it's my lotion."

"You've said that before." Luc lingered there, his warm breath puffing against my skin. "I'll call you, okay?"

"Okay," I whispered, feeling like every breath I took wasn't enough.

He pulled back, letting his fingers slip from my cheek. "Kent will see you out."

I looked behind him, and yep, there was Kent standing in the hallway, holding my bag. I could feel my face heat as I walked out of the room.

Kent grinned at me.

Feeling about seven different kinds of awkward, I turned to say good-bye to Luc, but he wasn't there. "Whoa." I twisted back to Kent. "Where'd he go?"

"He's fast." Kent handed me my bag.

I glanced up and down the hall. It was empty. "Is he invisible?"

Kent laughed. "Sometimes it feels that way. Come on, honeybuns. I'll lead you out."

Honeybuns? I had no idea how to respond to that, so we got to walking, all the way down the six flights of stairs. The club floor was empty as he led me to the entrance. I didn't see Clyde or anyone else.

"I'm sure I'll be seeing you again," Kent said, opening the front door.

"Yeah." I gripped the strap of my bag. "Um, thanks for keeping my bag . . . safe."

He grinned. "It was an honor, Evie."

I laughed, shaking my head. "Bye."

"Peace out."

My head felt like it was in a million places as I walked out to where I'd parked. I unlocked the door and sat inside, placing my bag on the passenger seat. I hit the ignition button and then looked over at the closed red doors.

An Origin—Luc was an Origin. Something I didn't even know existed until an hour ago. And there were hybrids. Good Lord. I slowly shook my head as I wrapped my hands around the steering wheel. Closing my eyes, I squeezed the wheel. What had my father done to that girl? To Nadia? My mom had to know. I couldn't ask her. If I did, then she'd know I'd talked to Luc, and I seriously doubted she'd be okay with that.

And there was more he hadn't told me? What else—?

Someone knocked on my window, causing me to gasp. My eyes flew open. "Holy crap," I whispered.

Chas stood outside my car.

It was definitely Chas, minus the bloody and beaten face. As he stood there peering through the window, his hands on the roof of my car, he didn't even look like he'd been within an inch of his life a handful of days ago.

I hit the window button, sliding the window down. "Hey."

His gaze, an intense shade of blue, flickered over my face. "You were there—Saturday. When I was found?"

Glancing behind him and not seeing Luc or Kent, I nodded. "Yeah. I'm sorry about what happened to you, but I'm glad to see you're . . . doing better."

"Thanks." He stared down at me. "Your name is Evie, right?"

I nodded again. I had no idea why he was out here, talking to me.

He looked to his left and his shoulders tensed. Those eerie, intense eyes focused on mine. "You need to stay away from here."

Caught off guard by the statement, I jolted. "Excuse me?"

Chas knelt down so we were at eye level. "I know you don't know me, but you saw what happened to me. You need to stay away from here. You need to stay away from Luc."

17

I didn't get much sleep Thursday night. I couldn't clear my head long enough to relax. What I'd learned about Luc and the Daedalus kept replaying over and over, as did Chas's extraordinarily weird warning.

Stay away from the club—from Luc.

Why would he say that? Because I was human? I wanted to believe that was the only reason, but instinct told me it was more than that. *You saw what happened to me.* Yeah, I'd seen that. It would be a long time before I forgot what I saw.

What sucked most was that I knew I couldn't talk to anyone. Besides the fact that I doubted anyone would believe me if I started talking about secret government groups, Origins, and hybrids, Luc didn't need to tell me how important it was that I keep my mouth shut. I didn't want to say something and put someone in danger.

People who know the truth go missing.

That wasn't a pleasant thought.

I spent the night twisting and turning, falling asleep only for a few hours before I needed to get up. I was in a weird mood all day Friday, made worse by the fact that I hadn't heard from Luc. Not that I expected him to be in touch—well, I guess I sort of did. And I could've just texted him, but that felt . . . It felt weird. Like, I don't know, too personal? And that didn't make sense. Friends contacted friends all the time. Except, were we friends? How could I be when I'd barely scratched the surface of who Luc was? When even admitting that there were moments—rare moments—when liking him on a basic friendship level made me feel . . . weird?

So I didn't text him.

And he didn't text me.

That wasn't a big deal. Not at all. Nope.

"Are you okay?" Heidi asked as we walked out to the parking lot after class.

"Yeah." I glanced up at the thick clouds blocking the sun. "Why?"

She nudged me with her arm. "You've just been really quiet all day."

Had I? "I didn't get much sleep last night."

Zoe caught up with us as we began to clear the hill. "You look like you could use a nap."

I laughed under my breath. "Yeah, I really could."

"Did Luc keep you up last night?" Heidi grinned.

"What? No." I'd already told them about my trip to the club yesterday. Of course, I'd left out, well, everything. When they asked if I learned anything about my mom, I'd . . . I'd lied, and I hated doing that. "I just couldn't sleep. Did Emery keep you up last night?"

"I wish," Heidi said, and sighed.

I was about to ask if she'd spent time with Emery last night, but Zoe stopped in front of me as we reached the entrance of the parking lot. "What in the hell?" she said.

Curious, I stepped around her. There was a car parked in the middle of the parking lot, right where cars drove through to get out. It was a newer model. A Ford. A few people stood back from it.

"Isn't that . . . Amanda's car?" April suddenly walked past us, her blond ponytail swaying.

"I don't know," Zoe answered.

April slid past a small group. "Yeah. That *is* her car and it's running."

I trailed behind April, glancing at Zoe. She shrugged. Amanda hadn't been in chem today, but if that was her car and it was running, then was she . . . ?

It happened so fast.

"Oh my God." A girl stumbled back from the car, dropping her bag just as the driver's side came into view.

I saw it—saw everything before I had a chance to look away, to not see what would forever be imprinted in my mind.

Amanda was sitting in the driver's seat, her posture rigid. At first glance I thought she was driving—I thought everything was okay—but then I saw that her head was tipped back against the seat, her long blond hair falling over her shoulders. Then I saw her face.

Someone screamed.

Someone grabbed my arm.

Someone was tugging on me.

But I saw her face through the windshield.

I saw where her eyes should've been, but they were just burnt-out black sockets.

"How are you handling everything?" Mom asked as she picked up a lid and placed it on a pot later that night.

I watched my Mom from where I sat on the kitchen island, my chin in my hands as she dumped popcorn kernels into a pan. Popcorn nights were kind of a tradition in our house whenever we both were home. Normally we chatted about school and watched really goofy movies, but tonight was different.

Amanda Kelly was dead.

She had been murdered in the same way Colleen had.

It looked like she'd been electrocuted, but we all knew that was what it looked like when a human was killed by a Luxen using the Source. Colleen. Amanda. Both killed in the same way. Both left at the school in a very public manner, to be found.

I shuddered.

Police had arrived before any of us could leave the parking lot. I think we were all questioned. I had no idea if Amanda had been kept like Colleen, alive for days after she'd disappeared. I wasn't even sure I wanted to know.

"Evie?" Mom said softly.

I peeked up at her. "Yeah, I'm okay. Just . . ." I lifted a shoulder. "I was thinking about everything."

Mom came around the island. "I wish you never had to see anything like that."

"Me too."

She cupped my cheek in her cool hand. "I'm sorry, hon."

My gaze lifted to hers, and I wanted to ask what other terrible things had she seen. She worked for the Daedalus. I knew they were responsible for things just as horrific as what had happened to Amanda and Colleen. I looked away and her hand fell to the side. "Do you . . . do you think a Luxen is responsible?"

"I don't know." She turned, walking back around the island. She clicked the stovetop on and blue flames roared to life. "It seems to be that way."

"Why? I mean, why would they do something like that, knowing how people already feel about them?"

"Why does a human kill innocent people? A lot of times we don't have all the clues or answers. I think sometimes some people are just . . . evil, and I imagine it's the same for the Luxen." One of the kernels popped, smacking off the lid as she looked over her shoulder at me. "I just want you to be extra careful, Evie. Pay attention to your surroundings. Listen to your gut. Just like it was after the invasion."

Pressing my lips together, I nodded. "So you think there is, like, a serial killer Luxen?"

Mom turned back to the stove, shaking the pan. "I don't know what to think, but being careful and vigilant never hurts."

I twisted my hair in my hands and tapped my foot off the base of the island. "I wonder if the cops will figure out what it has to do with the school."

"I wonder the same." As the popping slowed, Mom turned off the stove and moved the pot to one of those trivets I never used. "Are you sure you're okay?"

Was I? I'd seen a . . . a dead body today. From a distance, but I'd seen enough, and my head was wrapped up in everything Luc had told me. So I guess I was okay, all things considered.

It was killing me not to talk to my mom about everything I'd learned, and my mind raced to come up with a plausible way to bring up what Luc was and what he'd said about the Daedalus without her suspecting I'd been in contact with him.

What did Mom know?

"So, I was . . . thinking about what you told me about Dad." I kept twisting my hair, searching for a way to broach the topic with her. "You said he was responsible for taking something from Luc. A girl, right?"

Mom glanced up, and a long moment passed. "I never said it was a girl, Evie."

Oh crap. She hadn't? I couldn't remember. My heart thundered in my chest. "Yeah, you did. You said it was a friend. A girl."

"Did I?" She stared at me for a long moment and then sighed. "I don't know the details surrounding what Jason did. I just know he did something he shouldn't have."

She was lying. Anger sparked deep inside me. She was totally lying. "It had to be pretty major for you to be worried about Luc."

"I don't want you to stress over what I told you about your father. Not when this terrible stuff is happening to your classmates. Okay? What your father did is in the past."

But it wasn't.

Exhaling roughly, I let go of my hair and hopped off the stool. It was time to change the subject before I blurted out things that showed I knew too much. I walked over to the counter and grabbed a large bowl. "Do you have to work this weekend?"

"I may head in for a few hours tomorrow." She pulled the lid off the pot, revealing fluffy white heaven. "What do you have planned?"

I sat the bowl on the island and then grabbed the saltshaker, dumping a salt mine's worth on the popcorn. "Nothing, really. Might take some pictures. I have a paper to work on."

"How about you work on the paper first and then go take pictures?"

"That sounds too reasonable."

"Or stay in, especially after what happened this last week." She switched the popcorn to the bowl as I walked to the fridge. "What movie do you want to watch tonight?"

"I think I saw that movie about the haunted doll was available."

"You want to watch a horror film?" Surprise filled her tone. "Since when?"

I raised a shoulder as I opened the door. "I don't know. In the mood for something different." Scanning the fridge, all I saw was a sea of blue. I frowned, craving a Coke. "There's nothing to drink."

"What?" Mom laughed. "There is a whole fridge full of soda."

"Yeah, but I want a Coke."

"A Coke? You never drink Coke."

I shrugged again as I reached in, grabbing two bottles of water. "Do you want the spray butter?" I looked over my shoulder, finding Mom staring at me with her lips parted. "Uh, why are you looking at me like that?"

She blinked once and then twice. "Nothing. Leave the butter where it belongs."

"All righty then." I closed the door and headed toward the living room. Mom was still at the island, though, staring down at the bowl of popcorn like it held the answers to life. I set the bottles on the end table. "Is everything okay?"

"Of course." Lifting her chin, she picked up the bowl and smiled, but as she drew closer to me, there was a forced quality to the smile. She placed the bowl next to the water and then picked up the remote. "Haunted dolls, here we come."

I was editing photos on my laptop, trying not to think about haunted dolls or what I'd seen at school today, when a soft glow of light seeped into my bedroom.

Frowning, I looked over at the window. The curtains were drawn, but they didn't block the light from the motion detector. I waited for the light to flip off, which it did pretty quickly whenever there was an animal like a deer in the front yard.

The light stayed on.

I set the laptop aside and tossed the covers off. I got out of bed and made my way over to the window, drawing the curtain back as I peered outside. There was a small roof outside my window, more like a two- or three-foot ledge, and that was where the motion detector was. It cast a bright spotlight down onto the driveway and part of the front yard. I saw nothing out there beyond the tree. Wind was moving the limbs, but that wouldn't set the light off.

There had to be an animal out there.

Or a creepy-as-hell haunted doll.

Or a psychotic, killer Luxen.

Probably a deer.

My phone suddenly dinged from somewhere. I let go of the curtain and went back to the bed. Didn't see the phone anywhere. Groaning, I lifted the blanket and spied it halfway under a pillow.

Snatching it up, I saw there was a number on the screen. My stomach dipped as I immediately forgot about the motion detector. It was Luc. I knew it was, because I hadn't saved his number. I opened the text and my stomach tumbled even more.

Come see me tomorrow.

Sometimes I wondered if I ever made good life choices. As Clyde let me into Foretoken on Saturday, that was the question I was asking myself.

At least it wasn't a half-naked Luc answering the door.

Though a very bad part of me was kind of disappointed.

Kent was waiting for me in the center of the gloomy, quiet dance floor.

"You came back!" He clapped his hands as he strode forward.

My steps slowed. "Did you think I wouldn't?"

"I try not to be too hopeful." He threaded his arm around mine and started walking toward the back hallway. "Luc will be happy."

I didn't know what to say to that.

"And I mean, he'll be really happy."

I shot him a look.

He chuckled. "Hey, it's a good day for us when boss man is happy."

"Luc is your boss?"

"In a way," he said, and that was all he said.

Kent basically escorted me to Luc's apartment, knocked on the door, and then skedaddled, disappearing back into the stairwell before Luc even answered the door.

My heart rate was all over the place while I waited for Luc, and it had nothing to do with the walk up the stairs.

Before I had the chance to have deep thoughts about my actions, the door opened and there he was.

Wearing a shirt.

That deep violet gaze flicked over me as he stepped back, holding the door open. "Come on in," he said, running a hand over his damp hair. "Want something to drink? Eat?"

Nervous, I shook my head and walked toward the couch. A three-wick candle burned on the end table, and it reminded me of mahogany and spice. I could feel his gaze on me as I sat on the edge of the couch and as I looked around the room.

I couldn't help it. I thought about what Chas had said to me, and look where I was?

"What did Chas say to you?"

My head swung in his direction. It took me a moment to process the question. "You're reading my thoughts!"

He stepped toward me. "You were practically screaming them at me."

I shot up from the couch. "You shouldn't do that, Luc. Seriously."

"Okay. I'm sorry. My bad, but he . . ." His head tilted to the side. "He told you to stay away from me?"

I threw up my hands, feeling terrible that Luc now knew what Chas had said to me. I wasn't even sure why I felt bad about it. "Obviously you know that answer."

"What the hell?" he muttered, thrusting his hand through his hair.

Crossing my arms, I stared at him. "Do you happen to know why he would say that to me?"

He dropped his hand. "Not exactly, but I'm going to find out."

"I don't think he was trying to start something—"

"You don't know him well enough to make that assumption."

"And I don't know you well enough to know if I should've listened to him," I snapped back.

Luc was quiet for a moment. "But I think you do. You're here. Are you regretting that?"

"I . . ." How could I answer that? I sat back down. "I don't know. Some really crazy stuff has been happening and I make bad life choices."

His lips twitched and the line of his jaw softened. A moment passed. "The next time someone says something like that, tell me."

"You think it's going to happen again?"

"I hope not."

"Well, you seemed busy, and I—"

"Didn't want to get Chas in trouble? And no, I'm not reading your thoughts to pick up on that." He sighed as he pulled his phone out of his back pocket and placed it on the kitchen counter. "Chas won't be in trouble. You don't need to worry about that. He and I will just have a chat."

"You really have no idea why he'd say that to me?"

Luc was quiet for a long moment. "Do you know what I'm doing here?"

I had a good idea of what went on here. "Uh, well, I guess you're hiding Luxen—unregistered Luxen."

"I'm not just hiding them. I arrange for them to leave, to go someplace safe. The guys who were here on Saturday? Daemon and Archer? They help transfer the Luxen."

"So 'the package' is the unregistered Luxen?" I rubbed my palms over my bent knee. "Why . . . why are you moving them someplace safe? Does it have to do with the changes the president wants to make to the registration program?"

"I think you know that history has proven that anytime a certain group of people has been placed in their own *communities,* bad things come from that."

History had proven that. Knots twisted up my stomach. "Do you think it will go through? Those changes?"

"I think anything is possible when the public is being fed nothing but fear," he said, and I thought about Colleen and Amanda. What had happened to them surely wasn't helping how humans viewed Luxen. "We want to be prepared for if and when those changes are implemented."

I stopped moving my hands and clenched my knees. "How can I help?"

Luc's brows lifted in surprise. "You want to help Luxen?"

Did I? "The Luxen have been here forever, right? Most of them just want to live their lives like we do." I thought about what my mom had said. "And there're bad Luxen just like there're bad humans. That doesn't mean all of them are bad."

"Right," he murmured, tilting his head.

"And I . . . I don't want to be on the wrong side of history, you know?" I felt my cheeks warm.

Those odd eyes fixed on mine. "You can help by doing what you're doing. Keeping what I am a secret. Keeping what I do here a secret."

I thought there was way more I could be doing. "I'd never tell anyone about this." I lowered my gaze and thought of something. "Does the task force know what you are? Do they know about Origins?"

"Very few do. Higher-ups? Yes. The ones who do the raids? Most likely not."

I was weirdly reassured about that and I didn't want to look too closely at the whys. "So, something went wrong with the moving of the Luxen?"

He nodded. "Someone tipped off the task force. They were ambushed. The family you saw? They were captured."

"God." My stomach twisted. I didn't like the fact that the dude had choked me, but it sucked hearing that they had been captured. "What about Daemon and Archer?"

"They got away. They're actually on their way back here, since they need to lie low before they attempt to go home."

"And it'll be safe for them to come here?" I asked. "You guys were raided."

"I'd rather shoulder that risk than their homes be jeopardized."

I opened my mouth, but I didn't know what to say to that. That was brave and crazy.

"We'll be okay here," he said, walking over and sitting beside me. "We'll always be okay."

I glanced at him. "Always?"

"Always," he repeated. He'd leaned toward me at some point. Or maybe I'd leaned toward him. I wasn't sure. But there were only a few inches separating us. "I heard that the missing girl was found."

"She was." Looking away, I cleared my throat. "I saw her. Not close up, but I saw her eyes. They were burned out, Luc, and she'd been placed in her car, in the middle of the parking lot. She'd been left there like—"

"Like someone wanted her to be found that way. Just like with the other girl."

I nodded. "The public thinks it's a Luxen."

"It sounds like one." Luc touched my arm, and I drew in a shallow breath as I looked over at him. "I'm sorry you had to see that, and I think I need—" His gaze shot toward the door, and a second later there was a knock. He sighed as he rose and went to the door.

A wicked sense of déjà vu rolled over me, and I tensed. It was Grayson. He didn't even look at me. "I know you probably want to murder me right now." Grayson's voice dropped, but I could still hear him. "But we have guests. The kind that meant I had to send Kent away."

"Great." Impatience dripped from that one word. Luc glanced over his shoulder at me. "I'm sorry, but—"

"It's okay." Because what else could I say? "We have the worst timing."

A strange look flickered over his face. "Always."

My brows knitted. "Can I come with?"

"No," he was quick to reply. "I'll be right back. Turn on the TV, watch a movie, and make yourself at home. I won't be gone that long."

My eyes narrowed. Luc was out of the room before I could respond, closing the door behind him. Sighing, I looked around the room once more. Any other time I would be beyond interested in snooping around his apartment, but I was interested in a whole different kind of snooping. I wanted to know what was going on that required Kent, a human, not to be present.

I wandered halfway across the room, toward the guitar, and then stopped. Luc didn't tell me I had to stay in the room. He just told me that I couldn't go *with* him. So if I found my way out of the room and downstairs, then it wasn't like I wasn't listening to him.

Not that I had to listen to him anyway.

Pivoting, I made up my mind and didn't give myself a chance to really think about what I was doing. I slipped out the door, relieved to see that no one was standing guard. I made my way to the end of the hall and entered the stairwell. Going down six flights of steps didn't suck as badly as walking up them, but I really needed to start exercising or something, because the muscles in my legs were already starting to burn.

Sweating more than I should've been considering I was walking *down* steps, I reached the main level and slowly opened the door. I crept into the dim hallway, keeping close to the wall as I neared the opening to the club. I stopped at the end and peered around the corner.

I saw Grayson first. He was standing by one of the high, round tables, his arms crossed. My gaze shifted to the right and I could see only Luc's profile, but it was enough to recognize the bored indifference etched into his striking face.

My fingers curled around the edge of the doorway as I saw a muscle clenched in Luc's jaw.

I saw a guy first. He was tall and dark haired, and standing next to him was someone who was obviously a sibling—a sister. She was the feminine version of him. Same black hair and identical height, and where his features were masculine, hers were delicate. The other guy was darker skinned than them, as if he spent a lot of time in the sun.

None of them wore a Disabler.

And all of them looked like rejects from Bikers 'R' US. They were decked out in leather—leather pants, leather jackets.

"We know you help our kind." The one I deemed the Brother stepped forward. "And you're saying you can't?"

Help? Duh. They were unregistered Luxen—Luxen looking to leave here—but why wouldn't Luc help them?

"I do help others." Luc sounded just about as enthused as he looked. "But I don't help those like you."

"Like us?" the sister parroted his tone, her gorgeous face pinching. "What is that supposed to mean?"

Luc tilted his head to the side. "You know exactly what that means."

"I don't know what you've heard about us." Suntan Man's tone was more gentle as he smiled. "But we're not here to cause trouble. We just need to lie low for a couple of days, and then when you deliver your next package, we go with them. That's all."

"And why exactly do you guys need to lie low, Wayland?"

Suntan Man winced only slightly. "There have been a few mis-understandings."

"Yeah." Luc snorted. "I'm sure they were *misunderstandings*. Like I said, It's not that I can't help you. It's that I *won't*."

"That's bullshit," seethed the brother.

"I would watch your tone, Sean." Grayson lifted his chin. "Or there's going to be another misunderstanding."

Sean sneered. "You better watch how you talk to me, traitor."

Grayson's arms unfolded as a faint white glow shimmered over his shoulders. "What did you call me?"

"You heard him," the sister chimed in, smiling cruelly. "You sided with them. Fought against your own kind. What else does that make you?"

Holy crap, these Luxen were so not on Team Human. A chill powered down my spine. They were the invading Luxen.

"Intelligent?" Luc suggested. "Unlike you, Charity, and your brother. And your friend Wayland."

Sean stretched his neck from one side to the other. "Why are you making this so difficult? We are Luxen and you help us. We need to get out of here and we know we can't do that without you."

"That's correct." Luc moved so that his back was to the hall. "I help Luxen worthy of living out their lives without having to look over their shoulders. I do not help Luxen who signed up for the whole Make Earth Their Bitch club."

Yep.

They were definitely not friendlies.

A startling thought occurred to me. Were they responsible for what had happened to Colleen and Amanda? Maybe they thought murdering a human was a misunderstanding? But if it had been them, why would they have left the bodies in such obvious places?

"And why is that, Luc?" Charity glided in front of her brother, and Luc momentarily blocked her from my sight. "Why would you even care about the humans? They should mean *nothing* to you. I don't even understand how you can surround yourself with them. If I breathe too deeply, I can smell their leftover sweat and . . . perfume. Peaches."

Peaches?

I sniffed the air around me.

Uh-oh.

"This conversation bores me," Luc replied, his fingers moving idly at his sides. "I'm going to give you a minute to leave here and this city, because I'm feeling generous today. That minute starts now."

"Do you think we're afraid of you?" Sean's stance widened. "We know what you are. You can't take all three of us."

"Oh really?" Luc chuckled. "Then you don't know what I am if you think I can't take the three of you."

Grayson grinned as he reached into his pocket, pulling out a sucker. "Cosign."

Wayland raised his hands. "Now, everyone, let's just calm down—"

"You're down to thirty seconds," Luc reminded them.

"Screw that." Charity stepped to the side. "Screw *this*."

"Twenty seconds," Luc counted.

Her beautiful face twisted as she lifted a hand. "You know what. We don't need your help."

"Charity," warned Wayland.

"Ten seconds."

Her chest swelled. "Fine. We're leaving." She took a step back. "But first? You've upset me. I'm thoroughly disappointed with the great and powerful Luc."

"Oh Lord," murmured Grayson. He'd unwrapped his Blow Pop and shoved it into his mouth.

"I guess I should just show you how disappointed I am." Bright white light erupted from her arm, spiraling down to the tips of her fingers. She tapped into the Source. "Hey, Peaches," she called out, and I froze from my not-so-hidden place. "You didn't have to die today, but you can thank Luc for that. Oh wait. You can't, because you're going to be *dead*."

18

Someone cursed as light exploded from Charity's fingertips and arced across the room, coming straight at me. There wasn't even time to scream.

I was going to die.

Without warning, something—no, *Luc*—crashed into me. The impact knocked the air out of me. He brought me down, twisting in midair and hitting the floor, taking the brunt of the fall. For a brief second I was splayed out on top of him, hip to hip, absolutely stunned. "That was . . . *fast*."

Luc rolled quickly, shoving me underneath him as the plaster exploded above us, sending puffs of drywall dust into the air. "God, you *still* don't listen to anything I say."

"Wait. What?" I whispered.

"Stay put," he said to me, and then sprung up, spinning around. "That was a huge mistake."

I rolled onto my belly, lifting my chin.

Stalking forward, Luc lifted a hand as I sat up, scrambling to my feet. A rush of air whipped through the corridor, lifting my hair and sending the strands flying across my face. The next second, Wayland was scooting backward, across the dance floor. Sean slammed into the wall and slid up it, pinned several feet off the floor.

"Wow," I murmured.

Charity charged Luc—straight up charged him like a linebacker.

Gasping, I shot forward, skidding to a halt when Luc stepped into the attack. He dipped as she swung at him. White light crackled from her open palm. Luc caught her outstretched arm as he rose, twisting her backward. She flipped through the air, but Luc caught her before she hit the floor.

Grayson pulled a stool off the table and sat down, shoving the Blow Pop back into his mouth.

Luc held Charity there with one hand around her throat. He lifted her up. "Normally I don't like to do this, but you just tried to kill Peaches, and I find myself partial to peaches. Even the edible ones. *Don't*"—Luc gripped her other hand before it connected with his arm—"*even try it*."

Luc threw her back. She hit the floor, rolling several times. He prowled forward as she shot to her feet. Charity slipped into her true form. Her veins lit up. My breath caught. A white sheen filled the club as the light in her veins seeped into her skin, replacing bone and tissue. Heat flared like the air was kicked on, and I shrunk back, pressing against the bar.

The glow was so intense, like staring into the sun. Within moments, Charity was incased in light. She went after him again.

"Wow," Grayson said, cocking his head to the side. "She does not learn."

"Nope." Luc stepped to the side, nothing but a blur. He caught her by the throat again, bringing her to her knees. He was seemingly oblivious to the crackling light stretching out toward him.

Sean fell from the wall, landing in a crouch. He popped up and darted across the dance floor. Without taking his gaze off Charity, Luc threw out his other hand. Sean shot into the air, flipping sideways, right over Grayson's head. He landed in one of the shadowy alcoves.

"You know, you could help, Gray," Luc gritted out.

"Nah." He swirled the stick around in his mouth. "Looks like you got it all handled."

Luc rolled his eyes as he focused on Charity. "I didn't want it to come to this." A different kind of light rippled over his arm as he knelt down. "But you do not threaten what is—"

Charity's scream drowned out the rest of what Luc was saying. Her arms flailed out as her back bowed. Her light flickered rapidly, like a bulb that was going to burn out.

Sean's roar sent a bolt of fear through me as he pushed to his feet.

"No!" Wayland shouted a second before he went all Luxen.

It was too late.

Her glow receded just as the brighter light, the light radiating from Luc's hand, burst from her eyes and open mouth, streaming to the ceiling of the club where it seemed to roll harmlessly across the studs and beams.

Luc let go.

Charity hit the floor, her arms outstretched, her knees bent. I pressed my hand to my mouth. She looked like . . . like what my mom had said, like Chas when he was slipping back and forth between the two forms when he'd been injured. Her skin reminded me of a translucent shell with empty, dull veins and features that were *almost* human but not quite.

Wayland shot across the floor, making a beeline for Luc, who was stepping over the body. Sean was running out of the alcove, bypassing Grayson, who looked like all he was missing was a bowl of popcorn.

The two male Luxen launched themselves at Luc. I didn't think. Spinning around, I grabbed the closest thing possible—a heavy bottle of amber liquid. Cocking my arm back, I winged it as hard as possible. The bottle smashed into Sean, shattering upon impact.

"A bottle?" Grayson laughed. "Did you just throw a bottle?"

"At least she's helping," Luc shot back, lifting his hand.

"Hey." Grayson pulled the sucker out of his mouth. "I'm here for moral support."

I cringed as Sean shook the broken glass and liquid off and slipped back into his human form. His eyes narrowed on me.

Luc opened his fist, and it was like an invisible lasso caught Wayland around the waist. Whipped right off the floor, he was thrown into the air and then he just—he *levitated* there.

Sean shot toward me, and I reached blindly behind me, grabbing for another bottle. Then he wasn't coming at me. It was like a giant invisible arm swept him across the floor. Sean crashed into the table Grayson sat at. They went down in a tangle of legs, arms, and chairs.

Luc chuckled. "Moral support, my ass."

With wide eyes, I picked up another bottle as one of the top-pled stools flew across the floor, shattering against the wall. Grayson was on his feet, his usually perfectly coifed blond hair falling into his face.

"You made me drop my sucker." Reaching down, he gripped Sean by the collar of his shirt and lifted him up. "And it was my favorite. Sour apple."

Striding toward Wayland, Luc cocked his head to the side. "I would say I'm sorry about this, but that would be a lie. I'm not." Luc closed his hand.

Bones cracked like thunder. Wayland's body twisted and churned, his arms and legs breaking at impossible angles. His body folded like an accordion, collapsing into itself and squashing Wayland's light like he was nothing more than a bug.

"Oh my God," I whispered as horror rose inside me. When Luc said he could do everything a Luxen could do but better, he hadn't been joking.

Luc's head whipped around. His pupils glowed like diamonds as he lowered his hand. Wayland fell to the floor, and I knew he was dead before he even landed. Luc's gaze dropped to where I clutched the bottle. That muscle flexed along his jaw and then he turned away.

Grayson suddenly skidded across the floor, thrown by Sean. "We came to you for help!" shouted Sean. "And this is how you respond?"

Spinning toward Sean, Luc stiffened.

"You're going to regret this, so help me." Sean moved so fast, he was nothing more than a bolt of streaking light.

But he didn't make it far.

I saw him at the door, yanking on the handle. It wouldn't budge. Luc stalked toward him. In his true form, Sean burst away from the door as Luc stopped in the center of the dance floor. A faint whitish glow appeared over Luc's form. The air crackled and thinned, as if the oxygen were being sucked out of the entire room. I tried to take a breath, but it burned. I stumbled back, bumping into the shelf. Liquor bottles rattled.

"I am done with this," Luc said, closing his hand into a fist.

The light around Sean's body pulsed to an intense, nearly blinding white light. He jerked, falling to his knees. His back bowed as he threw his arms out. The light around him began to flicker rapidly and then it went out. Stopped. Oxygen rushed back into the room as Sean toppled forward, unmoving. A dark pool of blood appeared under him, seeping across the floor.

My wide gaze lifted from the fallen Luxen to where Luc stood. The hazy glow receded back into him. So that was the difference between a Luxen and an Origin. The latter was able to kill by closing its hand.

Dear God.

"Well." Luc sighed, looking at the floor—at the bodies. "That escalated quickly."

Grayson shoved a hand over his head, pushing his hair back from his face. "That it did." He looked over at me. "I think the girl is traumatized."

Still holding the bottle of liquor, I glanced at the bodies. They looked so . . . weird. Like props from a science-fiction movie.

Luc slowly turned to me. His chest rose with a heavy sigh. "I'm pretty sure I told you to stay in the room."

"No." I forced my gaze away from the dead Luxen. "You said I couldn't come down with you."

He walked over to me, ignoring the bodies as if they weren't even there. "You do realize that meant the same thing." He stopped in front of me and reached out, prying my fingers off the bottle. He placed it back on the bar behind me as his eyes met mine. "Are you okay?"

My hands fell to my sides. "Yeah."

His gaze flickered over my face and he seemed to draw in another deep breath. His voice was low when he spoke. "I had to, you know? I had to do that. Those Luxen were not good Luxen."

I swallowed. "I sort of figured that out."

"I've had a few run-ins with Wayland. He knew better than to bring them here."

"They were invading Luxen, right?" When he nodded, I exhaled roughly. "That's why you wouldn't help them?"

His gaze searched mine. "I didn't help them because they have no respect for human life. That's why."

My heart pounded in my chest.

"Wayland knew that any Luxen who would be a threat to a human would not receive my aid."

"If they knew that, then why did they come to you?"

"Because they were desperate." Luc looked away then, and I saw that Grayson was no longer on the club floor. "The task force is ferreting out unregistered Luxen every day, and I have a feeling they'd done things that had brought unnecessary attention to themselves. They were bad."

Having heard the way they'd spoken told me that, but would things have escalated like they had if I hadn't been here? Guilt formed an uneasy knot in my stomach. "I should've stayed in your room."

"Yeah." His gaze slid back to mine. "You should've."

"I'm sorry," I whispered, fully understanding that if I'd stayed in the room, things might not have—

"Things would've ended the same way," Luc cut into my thoughts. "Whether you stayed in the room or not, but you could've been hurt."

"Don't read my mind."

He stared at me, somewhat unapologetically.

I sighed heavily. "They were scary, Luc."

"They are. Most Luxen care for humans. Some don't. Those Luxen were dangerous." He leaned in, placing one hand on the bar, beside my hip. His lashes lowered. "I'm sorry you had to see that. I'm sorry you could've been hurt."

I really could've been.

"She called you Peaches?" A faint smile tugged at his lips as he lifted his gaze. "I kind of like that."

My nose wrinkled. "I don't."

"It works for you."

"It's just . . . lotion."

"No." He let his head fall back. "It's more than that."

I had no idea what to say to that. My gaze started to trek back over to the bodies. "Are all Origins capable of what you did?"

"No." Two fingertips curled under my chin, guiding my stare away from the fallen Luxen. Luc lifted my head. He didn't speak as our gazes connected. Silence stretched out between us. I should have been frightened of him, especially after seeing *that*. I should have been running out that door and screaming at the top of my lungs.

But I wasn't.

I wanted to be, because that seemed smarter, feeling that way.

But I wasn't.

"Most weren't as . . . skilled as I am," he said, and I couldn't suppress the shiver skating over me. "But there were a few who were a hell of lot scarier than me. Ones who . . ."

"Who what?" I whispered.

"Origins that lacked all humanity." His thick lashes lowered, shielding his eyes. "Ones I thought I could change—teach them to be empathetic, to be more human. I learned that even though we want to believe that there is never a lost cause, there are examples of such. There are times when there is nothing we can do to change an outcome."

"I don't want to believe that there are people out there who are lost causes," I admitted. "It feels too defeatist."

His fingers dipped, barely grazing the center of my throat. A different kind of shiver skated over me. "It's being realistic, Peaches."

"Don't call me that," I said, pulse thundering as the pupils of his eyes faded into a fuzzy black.

"What in the world did I miss?"

We both turned, finding Kent standing by the stage. Luc stepped back, and I felt like I could breathe again.

"I have to cut our time together short," Luc said, dragging a hand over his messy bronze hair. "I'll make sure you get home safe."

"Wait. Why wouldn't I get home safe?"

"Luxen come in threes, and from what I know of Sean and Charity, they have a brother. He may be dead already or he may come walking through the doors any minute, looking for his siblings."

Holy crap, that was right. Luxen were triplets. I'd just never seen a complete set of them.

"Grayson is making sure no one is lingering outside right now, but I'd rather be safe than sorry and have you out of here just in case."

Kent looked over at us. "Seriously? Why are there dead Luxen on the floor? And better yet, who is cleaning that up? Cuz it ain't me."

Luc ignored him. "You're okay. Just didn't want to take chances."

I suddenly remembered what Sean had said about misunderstandings. "Wait. Do you think they had something to do with what happened to Colleen and Amanda?"

A weird look flickered across Luc's face, one I couldn't read because it was gone before I had a chance to really figure it out. "They could be," he said, but for some reason, I didn't think he believed that. He took my hand, pulling me out from behind the bar. "If there is another one, Grayson will find him."

"Really? Because Grayson literally just sat there that whole time," I pointed out. "The only thing he seems capable of finding is a lollipop."

Kent snorted. "Sounds like Grayson."

"It'll be okay," Luc said, his gaze flickering over me as he led me to Kent. "I'd just rather you be home at the moment and not here."

Kent's brows lifted. "Oh wow, tonight sounds like it's going to be fun. Can't wait. Still not cleaning up that mess."

"But—" I paused as Kent patted my shoulder. I shook my head, turning from him. "Wait. We haven't—"

"We'll get time," Luc cut in. "I'll make sure of it, Peaches."

My lips thinned. "Don't call me that."

"I'll be in touch," he insisted. "I promise, but I need you to go." His hand tightened around mine. A heartbeat passed and then he tugged me to him, chest to chest. He dipped his head and his breath moved against my temple. The contact startled me. "Do this for me. Go home." His lips brushed my skin. "Please."

Unsettled and thrown off, because I had a suspicion he didn't say please a lot, I did what he asked when he let go.

I left.

19

I woke early Sunday morning, jerking straight up in bed, gasping for air. My hand flew to my throat. It hurt. The skin, the fragile bones. Like someone had their hands around my neck, squeezing. . . .

I'd been dreaming.

That much I knew, because moments ago, I'd been back inside that club with those Luxen, but Luc hadn't been there. Instead it had been a man who looked like Sean and he'd been choking me.

"God," I whispered, willing my heart to slow down. "It was just a nightmare."

But there were tiny bumps all over the bare skin of my arms, and my throat *hurt*. I lowered my hand, and my gaze trekked around the dark room. The comforter was at the foot of my bed, kicked off in my sleep. Everything was quiet, and I could make out the still shadows of my dresser and desk. The clock on the nightstand read only twenty minutes after three.

Way too early to be awake.

I pushed it out of my face. I shouldn't be surprised by the fact that I was having nightmares after . . . well, everything. Who'd blame me? Especially considering I didn't really think for one second that the Luxen who Luc had fought had been responsible for what had happened to Colleen and Amanda. It wouldn't make any sense, since they were trying to get out of this city without drawing attention.

I pressed my lips together as my stomach knotted. What if there was also a very ticked-off Luxen sibling out there now, seeking revenge? On top of everything else? And wouldn't that be my fault? If I'd stayed in Luc's room—

"Stop," I said. "Just stop."

This was the last thing I needed to be stressing over if I wanted to fall back to sleep. I reached for the blanket piled at the end of the bed but stopped when a sharp pain skated along my stomach.

"Ouch." Frowning, I straightened and placed a hand on my stomach. I jerked. The area was tender.

Carefully, I leaned over and turned on the bedside lamp. Buttery light filled the room as I sat back. I wrapped my fingers around the hem of my sleep shirt and pulled it up.

"Holy crap," I said, and gasped.

Three long, jagged welts cut into my skin, right above my navel, like a cat . . . or a demon had gotten ahold of me. They weren't open scratches and they didn't look like they'd bled at all, but there were definitely three marks.

What in the world?

I looked around my room again, like it held the answers or something. Then I poked at the welts. Wincing at the spike of pain, I pulled my hand away. I let go of my shirt and walked into the bathroom. From there, I did a full-body scan. There were no other scratches, but there was a bruise on my right hip, probably from when Luc had tackled me.

The scratches had to have happened during that. But how? I didn't know, but that was the only thing that made sense unless I'd done it to myself while sleeping. The nightmare was pretty vivid, so Lord only knows what I could've done.

I grabbed the bottle of peroxide out from underneath the sink and with a couple of dabs with a cotton ball, I determined that I'd done my due diligence when it came to not developing a flesh-eating bacteria.

I turned off the light, hurried back to bed, and all but dived under the covers. I closed my eyes, squeezed them tight, and tried not to think about Luc, the club, or anything, but it was a long time before I fell back to sleep.

My mood plummeted as I walked into the cafeteria on Monday and saw that the only options for lunch were pizza and salad. Both looked like they'd been sitting out over the weekend.

"What kind of fresh hell is this?" I muttered.

James laughed as he brushed past me. "Want half of my sandwich?"

"Yes." I followed after him like a lost puppy, practically snapping at his heels. "Please and thank you."

Finding Heidi already at our table, I sat down next to her and dropped my bag onto the floor while James grabbed the seat across from me.

He opened his bag and pulled out the ziplocked piece of peanut butter heaven. "I should make you work for this," he said.

"That would be incredibly mean and opportunistic," I told him, extending my hands. I wiggled my fingers. "Yummy. Yummy in my tummy."

"Do you know what that song actually meant?" Heidi said, peeling the lid back on her Lunchable. I hadn't seen anyone else eat them since middle school, but Heidi loved them. "The whole yummy-in-the-tummy part?"

James pulled apart the sandwich. "Probably something dirty."

"It is." Heidi picked up a cracker, placed her ham on it, and then topped it off with a slice of cheddar. "Just think about something that involves being with a dude that could end up being yummy in the tummy."

"What? Ew." I wrinkled my nose. "That's gross."

"It's true. Look it up." She offered me a cheese-and-ham-cracker stack.

"Thank you." I placed it next to my sandwich. "Look at me, piecing together an amazing lunch from parts of my friends' lunches."

"You really need to start bringing your own." Zoe dropped into the seat beside me. She had a salad, because of course she did. "Or try eating something green."

My lip curled.

"So, you guys hear that Coop's party is back on for Friday night?" James took a swig of his water. "You guys are going, right?"

Heidi continued to build her cracker delights while I tried not to think about how weird it was to have such a normal conversation. "I don't think so."

"Oh, so you go and get an older girlfriend, and now you're too cool for us and our childish high school parties," teased James.

"Pretty much," she replied.

I laughed. "At least you're honest about it."

"Speaking of being honest—" Zoe's eyes narrowed. "What in the hell?"

I followed her gaze as James twisted in his seat, spying April and a handful of students. April was marching—legit marching—across the cafeteria, her blond ponytail swinging in a way that made me want to cut my hair. She was holding some kind of poster in her hands and had a handful of minions with her.

"I have a really bad feeling about this," Zoe said, sighing.

My gaze flew to the table of Luxen, and I tensed. Connor, the dark-haired Luxen who'd been at the club when I went back to get my phone, was the first to notice April. His mouth moved and the rest of the Luxen looked up.

Heidi craned her neck to see over the table behind us as April grabbed a free chair and pulled it across the floor, creating a horrible screeching sound. She planted the chair in the middle of the cafeteria and then stepped up on it with the aid of one of the guy minions.

She held her hands up in the air and flipped her poster over. My mouth dropped open.

In the center of the poster was the typical alien face, the one with the pointy chin and big black eyes. The face was even colored green. Over it was the circle-backslash symbol.

"Holy crap," muttered James.

A second later her minions lifted their signs. They were all the same.

"Are you kidding me?" I said, lowering my sandwich.

"I wish." Zoe pressed her lips together

"Listen up, everyone!" April shouted, and it was like a switch was thrown. The cafeteria quieted, because, hello, there was a girl standing on a chair holding a "Just say no to aliens" sign. "We have the right to be safe in our schools and in our homes, and we don't have that safety. Colleen wasn't safe here—not from them! Neither was Amanda!"

My gaze shot to the Luxen table, and I saw that Connor was still but his face was devoid of emotion.

"They shouldn't be allowed to go to school with us. They're not human. They're aliens!" April continued.

"They shouldn't be here!" shouted one of the guys standing with her. He rattled his sign as if that helped get the point across. "They don't belong!"

Pink splashed across the face of one of the younger Luxen. She dipped her chin, letting her brown hair fall forward.

April's eyes gleamed as she shook her arms. "No more Luxen! No more fear! Come on. Say it with me! No more Luxen! No more fear!"

Those with her picked up the chant. Someone behind us stood, yelling the same. I turned in my seat as Heidi cursed. "Where are the teachers? Jesus!"

"No more Luxen! No more fear!" The chants rose from several other tables. Students lumbered to their feet, climbing onto their seats. Their fists pumped the air, reminding me of those dancing at Foretoken.

Not everyone was chanting.

Others stayed quiet, exchanging awkward looks. I shifted toward Zoe. "This is so wrong."

Zoe lips pursed. "I cannot believe I was ever nice to her."

"You and me both." Anxious energy rose from the pit of my stomach. I should do something. We *needed* do something. I looked away from Heidi's pale face and shifted toward Zoe. "We need—"

"That's enough! Everyone, get off the chairs and shut up!" Coach Saunders, the phys ed teacher, stalked down the middle of the cafeteria. "Right now."

April's chin jutted out stubbornly. "You can't stop me. It's my right to protest. That's what being a human means."

James slowly turned around. "I don't think April knows what the whole right to protest thing means."

"He can't stop us," April told those around her. "Come on! No more Luxen! No more fear! No—"

"Your right to protest doesn't extend to the middle of cafeteria, Ms. Collins." Coach Saunders snatched a poster out of a boy's hand and tossed it aside. "Get down now and, all of you—every single one of you, get to Principle Newman's office."

A few of April's minions stopped right then and there, but April kept shouting her lame chant until a female teacher showed up and practically yanked her right off the chair. That didn't quiet April down. She was still yelling as she was escorted out of the cafeteria.

"Wow." James slowly faced us. "Doesn't she make you feel all warm and fuzzy?"

Heidi snorted.

"She makes me feel things, all right." Zoe stabbed her lettuce with a fork. "But more like cold and prickly."

The table where the Luxen usually sat was now empty.

As I glanced over my shoulder, I saw that some of the shouting students were still standing, their gazes fastened on the doorway, where you could hear April's distant chants.

They looked . . . *woke*.

Like they'd just experienced something enlightening and found a righteous path laid out before them. A reason. A cause. A purpose. They were nodding as they looked among one another, faces I'd recognized and saw nearly every day for the last four years. Nice girls. Smart guys. Clever people.

I saw my ex, Brandon.

He was standing by the windows, his floppy brown hair golden in the sunlight. His warm, friendly smile was gone, replaced by a thin, hard line. He was slowly nodding too, as if he were answering April's call.

He yanked his chair back, climbed up onto it, and then jumped onto the table. "No more Luxen! No more fear!" He thrust his fist into the air. "No more Luxen!"

I yawned loudly as I switched out my textbooks at the end of the day. I needed to grab my chem book, since I had a feeling there was going to be a quiz tomorrow.

"You doing anything later?" James asked. He was lounging against the locker next to mine, staring down the hall. Part of me wondered if he knew he was staring at the girls' bathroom.

"I think I'm just going to go home and sleep. Today has been exhausting." I started to close my locker. "So I'm thinking about napping the evening away."

"Want company?"

My entire body jerked. That question had so not come from James, but from a now-familiar voice. My breath caught, and I slowly turned to my left.

Luc stood there.

Wearing one of those slouchy knit beanies. Dove gray. He looked good in it. Really good, even though it had to be seventy outside and he was wearing a short-sleeve shirt.

I blinked hard, thinking he had to be a mirage, because he couldn't be here. But he was still there, standing in the hallway of my school.

One side of his lips kicked up. "Hey, Peaches."

Knocked out of my stupor, I shut the locker door. "What are you doing here?"

"Recon." He was wearing those damn contacts.

"Recon?"

"Yeah." The other side of his lips tipped up. "Thinking about enrolling in good ole Centennial High."

I gaped at him. He couldn't be serious.

"Who's this, Evie?" James asked.

"Luc." He answered, leaning around me and extending a hand before I could say a thing. "And you're James."

James's gaze flicked to Luc and then back up. His shoulders tensed, and he didn't take Luc's hand.

Luc arched a brow.

Oh dear.

"You're the friend who let her roam around the club when she went to get her phone." Luc tilted his head to the side. "You're a good friend."

"All right," I said as I gripped Luc's arm. A charge of electricity, much more benign than before, passed through my palm. "Glad you two have formally met. Can you excuse us?" I asked James. "I've got to talk to him."

His jaw worked. "You going to be okay with this guy?"

Luc laughed, and it was a sound of warning. "That's an interesting question coming from—"

"I'm fine." My grip tightened on Luc's arm.

"Ow," he murmured, even though I know it didn't hurt him.

"He might not be," I finished. "Seriously. I'll text you later. Okay?"

James didn't look like he was going to back off, but after a moment he nodded. "Text me."

"I will." I smiled and then pulled on Luc's arm, tugging him away from James and my locker. I waited until we were halfway down the stairs before I let go of his arm. "Seriously. What are you doing here, Luc?"

"I kinda like the arm-grabbing thing," he replied, shoving his hands into the pockets of his jeans. "Very dominant of you. Maybe I'm the submissive type in, you know, the—"

"Shut up," I hissed. "Why are you here?"

"How can I shut up and answer your question at the same time?"

I shot him a death glare. "Luc."

"I was in the neighborhood." He opened the door and then held it as I walked outside. Pretty sure he let it swing closed in someone's face. "Thought I'd stop by and say hi."

I had no idea what to say to that, so I dug out my sunglasses and slipped them on. "You're not seriously thinking about enrolling, are you?" I didn't even know if that was possible or not.

Luc snorted as he fell in step with me. "No. I would be so bored out of my mind, I'd probably set the entire school on fire."

"Wow."

"Just being honest." He squinted as he glanced over at me. "There really is nothing new I could learn in school."

"Really? You know everything?" Gravel crunched under my feet as we neared the area where Amanda's car had been idling. I focused on Luc, not wanting to think about her sitting in that car.

"Pretty much."

The desire to prove that wasn't correct got the better of me. "Okay. Who was the twelfth president of the United States?"

"Zachary Taylor," he answered immediately. "And he wasn't president very long. He died of a very upset stomach. Side note, there's still much debate over what exactly caused his death."

"Okay. The fact you know the latter part is odd, but whatever. Tell me the square root of five hundred and thirty-eight?"

He laughed, which was unnecessary because he was already getting an absurd amount of double takes from nearly everyone passing by us. "Twenty-three point one nine—and you know what? You don't know the answer to that question."

That was true. "How do you know? I'm a math genius."

"If that were true, you wouldn't have asked that question."

My eyes narrowed.

"Taft was one of the last presidents to preside over the addition of a new state. Currently there are eighty-eight known constellations. Beard hair grows twice its normal rate while on a plane."

"What?"

"It's true. Another thing that's true? Honey never spoils. Look it up. It's also hard to access memories without moving your eyes. Try doing that one day," he said. "Water can boil and freeze at the same time. Cats always land on their feet because of physics. And there's enough DNA in one human to stretch from the sun to Pluto seventeen times."

"School *would* bore you." I stopped by my car.

"Not if you were in class."

I ignored the weird flutter in my chest. "Uh-huh."

His grin teased at me. "Can I come home with you?"

"Come again?"

"Well, that came out kind of wrong, didn't it?" He chuckled as he stepped forward, and I had to tilt my head back to meet his gaze. "I want to come home with you."

My heart did a cartwheel and then face-planted itself against my ribs. "I still don't think that came out right, Luc."

"It came out just the way I wanted it to."

That flutter grew, and I did everything in my power to ignore it. "Are you going to finish our conversation from this weekend?"

"If that's what you want."

"Why else would I talk to you?" I shot back.

He laughed again under his breath. "I like to think there are other reasons you'd talk to me, Peaches."

"Don't call me that." I opened my car door. "My mom would flip if she came home and saw you there."

"I'd be gone before she got home."

I hesitated. "How would you know that?"

"I'm fast. The moment you heard her pull up, I'd be out of the house." He paused. "In a jiffy."

He was fast. I knew that, but still. "I don't know."

Luc was quiet for a moment. "You came to my place. How is this any different?"

It didn't seem like it should be, but it was. Allowing him to come to my house was different.

"Are you afraid of me?" he asked after a moment.

His question startled me. I should be afraid of him, especially after seeing exactly what he was capable of, but truth was, I wasn't afraid of him.

"No. I'm not." I took a deep breath. "You can come home with me, but you have to promise you'll be good before my mom gets home."

"Pinkie swear."

I rolled my eyes. "Get in the car."

Grinning, he walked around to the passenger side and climbed in just as I was turning the car on. I glanced over at him. "So, um, what did you end up doing with your weekend?"

"Patrolling."

I waited until two girls passed my car, and then I pulled out. "What does that mean?"

"It means I was out making sure we didn't have a psycho Luxen hanging around, hell-bent on revenge." He stretched out his long legs, letting his elbow rest on the open window. "Good news is that we didn't see any signs of Sean and Charity having another sibling."

"That's good." My stomach tumbled. "Right?"

"Right."

He didn't sound like it was a good thing. I glanced over at him. Luc was staring out the window. "What are you not telling me?"

He didn't answer.

Anxiety spiked. "Luc."

"Everything." Luc looked at me as we reached a stoplight. "I still have everything to tell you."

Luc didn't tell me anything when we got to my place. Once we got to my house, he'd turned on the TV and started searching for alien movies.

Yep.

Alien movies.

For three hours, he raged about how alien invasions in Hollywood almost always got it wrong. He was kind of right. Real aliens didn't look like giant insects, but when I pointed out *Invasion of the Body Snatchers,* I'd stumped him.

It was a weird afternoon, but it had been . . . amusing. And it had also felt . . . normal. Like I'd done this before, and honest to God, I'd never sat and argued about which aliens were freakier: the ones from *Independence Day* or from the old *Alien* franchise.

He was skilled at avoiding questions, and talented in the art of distraction. As promised, he'd left right before Mom came home, but he didn't tell me anything remotely useful.

Luc didn't show up at my locker on Tuesday.

That was a good thing, because if he did, there was a good chance James might've punched him, and that would've ended badly . . . for James.

After school on Tuesday, I'd grabbed something to eat with Zoe and Heidi, and we met up with Emery. I was with them when I got a text from Mom saying that she wouldn't be home till late, and the girls ended up hanging out at my place until it grew dark outside. Mom came home about twenty minutes after they left.

Tuesday felt normal, like it used to be before Colleen and Amanda . . . and Luc, and I didn't realize how badly I needed time with my friends until then. Where we just ate a ton of junk food and talked about nothing . . . nothing scary.

Normalcy didn't last long.

On Wednesday, April and her minions took to protesting the Luxen at the entrance of the school. Their group had doubled in size since Monday.

I couldn't stay quiet any longer. April and I weren't the closest, and on most days I didn't consider her a friend, but I had to try to talk some sense into her, because she was getting everyone riled up.

I waited for her after our third-period class, catching her in the hallway. "Hey." I slung my backpack over my shoulder. "Can we talk real quick?"

"Sure." She was shoving a thick monstrosity of a binder into her bag. "What's up?"

My hand tightened around my backpack strap. "What are you doing, April? With the whole protesting thing?"

She stopped and looked up. "Excuse me?"

"Why are you doing this? The Luxen here haven't done anything wrong, and you're—"

"I'm what, Evie?" Her face pinched. "Vocalizing my right to be safe in my high school?"

"You are safe."

She laughed as she stepped to the side, continuing to jam her binder into her bag. "You're an idiot if you think any of us are safe anywhere. You saw Amanda. You know what happened to Colleen."

I stiffened. "I clearly remember what I saw, but that doesn't mean all Luxen are dangerous. Or that any of the Luxen who go here are responsible."

"How do you know that? Did you ask them?" she replied.

"I don't need to ask them. I don't walk around assuming every Luxen is a murderer."

"Well, you should." She yanked up the zipper on her bag. "I really thought that you, out of everyone, would be standing with me. Your father—"

"Stop bringing up my father, April. You didn't know him." We were starting to get stares, but I didn't care. "What you're doing is wrong and super-disappointing."

"Disappointing?" She laughed as she flipped her ponytail over her shoulder.

"Yeah, that's what I said."

"You know what? You've disappointed me." April pivoted on her heel and stalked off, her sleek ponytail swaying with each step.

I disappointed her? I almost laughed, but nothing about this was funny.

Talking with April had gone about as well as expected, but at least I'd tried. Maybe Zoe could try talking to her. She knew April better.

My conversation failure with April pecked away at me for the rest of the day, only sliding into the back of my mind when I walked out to my car and saw Luc waiting for me, leaning against the car, ankles crossed and hands resting on the hood.

There was a small group clustered together across from him, openly checking him out. He was grinning like a maniac when I walked up to him, and somehow, thirty minutes later, he was at my house again.

"Do you want something to drink?" I asked, walking into the kitchen. "I don't have any Coke."

"Whatever you have is fine." He lingered by the dining room

table as I grabbed two fruit punch Capri Suns. Turning, I tossed one to him. He easily caught it. "Can I ask you something?"

"Sure." I pulled the plastic off my straw.

"Is there trouble at your school?"

I stabbed my straw through the little hole in the Capri Sun and looked up. "There've been protests. You've heard about that?"

"I've heard some things."

"How?"

His smile turned secretive.

"Why do you always do that?"

"Do what, Peaches?"

"Seriously. *That.*"

He bit down on his lower lip and then let it pop free. "You're going to have to be more detailed."

I slurped up a good amount of the Capri Sun in one gulp. "You're always evasive. Like, when you talk, it's only ever half the story. You still haven't told me anything you promised you would."

"I've told you a lot." He finished off his drink. From where he stood he tossed the empty container, and the damn thing actually landed in the garbage. I hated him. "And I've actually told you something pretty major that has nothing to do with what I am."

"Bull."

Luc shrugged. "You just haven't been paying attention."

"That's not true." Irritated, I fought the desire to wing my packet at his head. "I'm super-observant."

He laughed. "That is not true."

"You know, you can leave." I sucked my drink dry and then tossed it at the trash. It smacked off the trash can and plopped onto the floor. I sighed. "I have homework to do and you're annoying."

"If you actually wanted me to leave, I wouldn't be here."

I picked up the damn packet and placed it in the trash. When I straightened, the movement tugged on the tender skin of my stomach, causing me to suck in a sharp breath.

"Are you okay?"

Straightening more carefully, I nodded. "Yeah."

His head tilted to the side. "You're lying." There was a pause. "What happened to your stomach?"

My mouth dropped open. "Get out of my head, Luc."

He moved too fast. A second later his fingers had a fistful of my shirt, and the next thing I knew, he was pulling the fabric up.

"Luc!" I shrieked, grabbing his wrists, but it was too late.

Waves tumbled over his forehead as his chin dipped. "What the hell, Peaches? What happened to your stomach?"

I tried to pull his hands away, but it was no use. "I don't know. It's—"

"You think this happened at the club, when I took you to the floor?" His gaze shot to mine. "I did this?"

"Luc! Seriously. Stay out of my head. It's rude."

His jaw hardened. "I didn't know I hurt you."

"I . . . I didn't know either. I didn't notice until later. It's not a big deal." I tugged on his wrists again. "They're just scratches."

"Scratches?" His gaze dropped to my stomach, and I sucked in a shallow breath. "Peaches, I think they're burn marks."

"What?" I temporarily forgot about the fact that he was staring at my belly.

"Burn marks. Like you touched a flame for too long. I must've done it when I grabbed you." He let go of my shirt, but whatever relief it brought was short-lived, because he placed his palm just below the fading scratches.

I gasped.

The contact, flesh against flesh, took the air right out of my lungs. The touch was intimate and unnerving. My gaze shot to his, and I thought I saw his eyes widen just a fraction, as if the feeling of his skin against mine had the same intense effect on him. His palm was warm, almost too warm against my skin.

Luc's throat worked on a swallow as his lashes lowered halfway. "I'm sorry."

"For what?"

"Hurting you," he said, his voice deeper, rougher, as he lowered his head. "I should've been more careful."

"It's okay." I shivered as his forehead touched mine. It wasn't a shiver of fear. It was something else. Anticipation? Yes. And it was *more*. Tension built in the space between us. I closed my eyes. "You were trying to stop me from getting blown up."

"Yeah. There was that." His head tilted just the slightest, and I felt his breath against . . . against my lips. Was he going to kiss me again?

Would I let him?

His hands slipped away, and Luc backed off a good foot, but the tension was still there, crackling in the air between us. Slowly opening my eyes, I pressed my lips together, unsure if I should feel grateful or disappointed that he hadn't kissed me.

The corners of his lips tilted up.

Oh no. "You're not reading my thoughts right now, are you?"

"I would never do such a thing."

Yeah. Right. "I don't even know why I let you come home with me."

That smile of his was really starting to concern me. "Oh, you know."

Luc stepped toward me again, and I tensed. His gaze never left my face, and I had the distinct urge to run away from him and . . . and run toward him. The latter made no sense. He stopped, his brows pinching as he reached into the pocket of his jeans and pulled out his phone. He looked down at it. The frown turned into a scowl as he glanced up. "Do you mind if I turn on your TV?"

"Uh, sure."

As he walked into the living room, Luc extended his arm and the remote flew off the coffee table and landed in his hand.

My brows lifted. "That's handy and also incredibly lazy."

Luc winked and, of course, looked good doing it. The TV came on and he quickly turned it to one of the local channels. The moment I saw the reporter standing out in front of a brownstone, a somber expression on her face, I knew this was going to be bad news.

The reporter was speaking and it took a few moments for my brain to catch up with what she was saying. "All four victims, the youngest three years old and the oldest thirty-two years old, lived in this home. Neighbors are saying that they were a quiet family and very hardworking. I've learned that the children were close in age, and it is believed that all four of them were murdered sometime last night."

Dread filled me as the screen switched to a male reporter behind the news desk.

"This comes on the heels of the murders of Colleen Shultz and Amanda Kelly, two seniors from Centennial High School. Ms. Shultz was found in the school restroom last Tuesday, and Ms. Kelly was found in her car in the school parking lot on Friday," he added. "Early reports indicate that all four victims have been murdered in the same manner as Ms. Shultz and Ms. Kelly. It is also believed that an unregistered Luxen committed these horrific crimes. I'm learning that these types of incidents are not isolated to Columbia, or even Maryland. Over the last two months, there have been suspicious deaths in Virginia, West Virginia, Pennsylvania, and Tennessee. Attacks by unregistered Luxen are on the rise, and many people are asking what, if anything, will be done? How can we be safe—"

Luc turned off the TV and cursed under his breath. A muscle popped along his jaw. "There's no way."

I sat down on the edge of the couch, horrified by the news and terrified by the implication. "What do you mean?

When there was no answer, I twisted away. The living room was empty. I shot to my feet and spun around.

Luc was gone.

And my stomach didn't hurt with the sharp, careless movement. I looked down and pulled my shirt up, exposing smooth, unblemished skin.

"That's not possible." I lifted my gaze.

But it wasn't impossible, was it? Luc had said that as an Origin, he could do this. He'd also said Luxen could heal humans. Scratches. Bumps. Bruises. Wounds. I let go of my shirt.

Luc had healed me.

20

I just don't like him," James was saying as we walked into school Thursday morning. "And it has nothing to do with what he is."

That was good to hear, since James had no idea what Luc really was. "He doesn't make good first impressions."

"No kidding?" He snorted as we neared my locker. "I know you say you're not involved with him—"

"And I'm not," I told him for the umpteenth time. That was the truth. Luc and I were barely friends. I decided that was probably a good thing—a great thing. *Really*. Something about him left me . . . unnerved and confused, and I didn't like it. At all.

Luc was an unknown variable, and that made *me* feel like a mess. And I didn't need any messy stuff right now. Not when the world felt like it was on the verge of imploding again.

James nudged my arm. "You know, I'm just concerned."

"Why?" Right now I thought there were a lot more important things to be concerned with. Like who'd wiped out an entire family yesterday, and was it related to what had happened to Colleen and Amanda?

And Luc's reaction to it? It was like he knew something. What, I had no idea, and I hadn't heard from him since he'd literally disappeared from my house.

"I don't know," he said as I opened my locker door and grabbed my books. "Ever since you went to that club with Heidi, you've been different. And don't ask me how. It's just a feeling."

It was too early in the morning for these kinds of deep thoughts. "I'm the same Evie as before . . . and before that . . . and before that, too."

James was quiet for a moment. "Well, that looks like it's going to be a problem."

At first I didn't know what he was talking about, but I followed his gaze and saw that he was checking out one of the younger Luxen boys. He was at a locker several feet away, by himself. I thought maybe his name was David . . . or Danny. Something like that. The metal band around his wrist gleamed in the light as he gripped the edge of the locker door. He was alone, but he wasn't going unnoticed.

Two older guys were standing across from him, by one of the glass cases full of really crappy senior art projects that had been completed last year. I recognized the guys as part of April's protesting pack, which was out in front of the school again.

Except for these two.

They were eyeing the younger boy like a pack of hyenas sizing up a baby gazelle for dinner. Not good.

"You know," I said. "I tried talking to April about what she's doing."

"I bet that went well."

I bit down on my lip as I closed my locker door. The young Luxen was obviously aware of the guys. His knuckles seemed to be bleached white, and it appeared as if he were stalling, probably hoping they'd leave first.

The two guys didn't look like they were going anywhere.

Nervous energy buzzed through my veins. I could just walk away. I didn't know the boy. A horrible voice whispered, *Why get involved?* It had nothing to do with me . . . but didn't it?

Straightening the strap on my bag, I made up my mind. "Do you know those two guys?" I asked, jerking my chin in their direction. "Are they jerks?"

James nodded. "Yeah, they're dicks."

"So, they're probably not eyeballing the boy because they like his shirt and want to know where he got it so they can buy one?"

"Nope."

I drew in a deep breath. "I'm going to see if he needs someone to walk with him to class. I mean, I'm not going to say it like that, because that would sound weird and awkward, but you know, I'm just going to . . . be there."

James pushed away from the locker beside me. "I'll join you."

Thankful I wasn't going at this alone, I walked toward the young Luxen. His head jerked up and swung in my direction before I got within a foot of him. His shoulders were stiff as wariness crept into deep ocean-blue eyes.

"Hi," I blurted out. "I don't think we've ever met. My name is Evie, and this is James."

The Luxen glanced at James, and then those startling blue eyes centered on me. "Daniel—I'm Daniel."

Aha! I almost had his name correct. "You're a sophomore?"

He nodded as James angled his body, blocking Daniel from the other guys. "Yeah. You guys are . . . seniors?"

"Yep," I chirped a bit too happily. "Do you have class on the second floor? James and I do."

"I do." He closed his locker door. A moment passed. "Why are you guys talking to me?"

I blinked at the blunt question.

"You've never talked to me before, and I've seen you guys every day at your locker since the start of school."

"Well, is there any better time than now to start talking?" James dropped a hand on the smaller boy's shoulder. "Since we're heading upstairs, we'll keep you company."

"Uh-huh." Daniel's gaze dropped to James's hand, and then he arched a brow. I honestly thought he was going to tell us to take a hike, which would be a really bad thing, because the two hyena boys were looking like they were working up the nerve to say or do something. "I know why you guys are doing this."

Prepared to deny the truth until I ran out of oxygen, I opened my mouth, but James said, "Then you know it's probably a smart idea to let us walk you upstairs. Because that's Andy and Leo standing over there. Let me give you a quick character breakdown for you. They're both linebackers on the football team. They have a tendency to *accidentally* knock students down, and they have one-half of a fully working brain between the two of them."

Daniel's lips twitched. "And let me guess, they're not fans of the Luxen?"

"I'm going to say that would be a reasonable assumption." James patted his shoulder and then dropped his hand. "So, what class do you have?"

"English."

"Then let's go." I stepped around so I was on his other side. "I can't be late. I have this phobia of walking into class after the bell rings. Freaks me out when everyone stares at me as I take my seat and the teacher gives me that disappointed, annoyed stare."

Daniel didn't respond as he swung his backpack over his shoulder, but he started walking, and we followed him, caging him in from either side. As the three of us made our way to the second floor, gazes followed and silence fell, broken only by hushed whispers. Tension cloaked the stairwell, as suffocating as a heavy blanket. James appeared to be immune to it, because he talked about some investment TV show he'd been watching at night. Or maybe he was trying to distract Daniel or himself.

Maybe he was trying to distract *me,* because the tips of my ears were burning, and every time I looked around us, I saw gazes turn from wary to outright hostile.

"He shouldn't be here," someone said in a whisper that carried, and then another said, "You know one of them killed Colleen and Amanda." Someone else responded, but I couldn't make out what was said.

"They killed that family," another said, louder.

Daniel's cheeks began to turn pink.

My stomach sank as those words settled into me. If it all was hard for me to hear and to see, I couldn't even imagine what it felt like for Daniel. There could be a hundred people like James willing to serve as a barrier for Daniel, for the other Luxen, but no one could be there every day, in every class.

Deep down I knew that whispered words were going to turn

into actions, and things would escalate. Fear would turn to hatred, and that was a deadly combination. The school was a powder keg, and it wasn't a matter of if it would blow.

It was only a matter of when.

Walking to my car after class, I kept expecting Luc to pop up out of nowhere, but as I glanced over my shoulder and scanned the parking lot, I didn't see him.

I thought about messaging Zoe and seeing what she was up to, because I didn't want to go home. Mom probably wouldn't be there for hours. She'd been working super-late every day this week, something to do with foreign officials visiting.

Pushing my hair back as the wind picked it up, I cut between two absurdly large trucks, making a mental note yet again to get to school in a timelier manner. Walking this far *sucked,* which meant I probably needed to walk more. I slipped out between the trucks just as someone stepped in front of me.

"Whoa." Jerking to a halt, I stopped myself a second before I face-planted into a chest. A hand gripped my arm, steadying me as I looked up. It was a guy—*that* guy. It took me a moment to recognize him and those dark sunglasses. He was the guy who'd helped me pick up my spilled notebooks. "Hey."

He smiled as he let go of my arm. "This is becoming a habit—meeting in the parking lot."

"It is." I lifted the strap of my bag, settling it in on my shoulder. "I should really pay more attention to where I'm walking. Sorry about that."

"You should, but then I wouldn't benefit from your lack of paying attention." His tone was light, teasing even.

The corners of my lips curved up as I wondered who this guy was. "I don't think . . . we've met before. I mean, outside of me dropping my stuff all over the ground."

His head tilted slightly. "Oh, but we've definitely met before."

"Oh." Embarrassed, I felt my cheeks heat. "Do we have a class together? I'm sorry. As you can tell, I'm not really observant."

If Luc were here to hear me admit that, he'd be doubled over in laughter.

The smile on the guy's face grew as he shook his head. "We don't have class together."

My grin faltered.

"I don't go to this school," he added, placing his hand on the fender of the truck he stood next to. "And I'm not from . . . around here."

Confusion filled me as I stared up at the guy. "Then I don't remember how we've met."

"I'm beginning to see that. Understand that." He paused. "Which is very interesting to me. I can't figure it out."

I had no idea what this guy was talking about, but I honestly didn't want to find out. A chill powered down my spine as primal instinct sparked alive. Something about this conversation, this guy, wasn't right.

"Well, it's nice seeing you again." I stepped to the side, deciding I needed to listen to whatever inside me was saying it was time to end this conversation. "But I have to get going—"

"Don't run off just yet." With his other hand, he reached up and lowered his sunglasses. "Not before I tell you what we have in common."

Surprise rocked me as I saw his eyes. They were the same startling shade of violet as Luc's, and just like Luc's, the black line of his irises were fuzzy. "You're . . ."

One side of his lips kicked up. That dimple in his right cheek appeared. "An Origin?" His voice dropped low. "Yes. That is what I am."

Luc had made it sound like there weren't many Origins in existence, but there was definitely one standing in front of me.

"Luc would be correct. There aren't many of us left."

I gasped, realizing he was reading my mind.

"And you know what? Luc could tell you exactly why there aren't many Origins left." Metal dented under the hand resting on the truck. The paint immediately smoked and peeled back. My eyes widened. "Don't," he murmured, straightening his sunglasses with his other. "Don't draw unnecessary attention, *Evie*."

My heart thundered. Why, oh why, didn't we have retinal checks at the entrances of the parking lot? Then again, Luc had those contacts, and I had a feeling this Origin would've found a way around them.

"Because if you draw attention to us, then I'm going to have to make a scene," he continued. "And I've already made quite a few scenes. I think you've witnessed at least one of them."

The next breath caught in my throat as I realized what he was talking about. "You . . . you're responsible for what happened to Amanda? Colleen?"

"Well, I wouldn't say I was a hundred percent responsible." The easy grin remained fixed.

I tried to draw in a shallow breath, but it did nothing to ease the pressure clamping down on my chest as I glanced around. People were near their cars, but no one was looking at us. Why would they? From a distance, he just looked like some normal guy, especially with the sunglasses on.

"Evie," he said my name so softly. "Are you paying attention to me?"

"Yes." My gaze shot back to his.

"Good. Now ask me who else is responsible."

My heart was tripping all over itself as I forced the words out. "Who else is responsible?"

"Good girl." He took a slow, measured step forward. The paint on the truck rolled back, hanging limply in the wake of his touch. "Luc is. He's about eighty percent responsible."

"How—"

"So are you," he cut me off. "After all, I thought I was grabbing you that night at the club. I mean, I'd only seen you from a distance, talking to Luc, and that girl was wearing the same color dress. She was a blonde. Honest mistake. Kind of worked in my favor, though, especially when I grabbed another blonde. *That* was on purpose. You know, just to do it."

Horror froze every muscle in my middle as what he said sunk in. I thought about what Heidi had said about both of them being blondes. It had been a pattern, a terrifying pattern.

"Because I got to see you up close and personal in this very parking lot. I knew you weren't that second girl." The easy tone of his remained level. "But she knew you."

A horn blew in the distance, causing me to jump.

"It was so easy to find you."

Luc's warning came back to me with a vengeance. *Do you know how easy it was to find you?* Christ. He hadn't been joking around.

"I don't understand—"

"Neither do I. Well, some parts of this little story," he said. "I don't understand you. Yet. But I'm figuring it out. Going to your house helped."

Oh my God. He was the one in my house that night—

"Yes," he intruded into my panicked thoughts. "More than once, actually. You should really set that alarm system. I mean, what good is having one when you don't use it? Then again . . ." He laughed, a sound so at odds with what he was saying. "It wouldn't have stopped me. I was so close, I left my mark behind."

Horror gave way to nausea as understanding filled me. I stumbled back a step. "You scratched me?"

"Well, yeah, and I was choking you." His smile spread to both sides of his mouth. "Just a little."

"Just a little?" Bile climbed up my throat. Terror turned my blood cold as my heart ended up somewhere in my throat. My hand closed into a fist. I'd been so close—

"To dying? Yeah, but not as close as you have been before. *Don't*—" His voice rose and his tone sharpened. "Come any closer."

I thought he was talking to me at first, but I wasn't trying to get near him. Then my gaze shot behind him. Standing between the bed of the truck was Emery. Behind her was . . . *Connor.* What was Emery doing here? I didn't see Heidi. And why was she with Connor?

"You two come any closer, I will have to do something that would be considered inappropriate," the Origin said, never looking behind him. Not once. "Something that would make Luc very upset, and you guys don't want that. Right? You know what happens when Luc is . . . disappointed."

"I don't know who you are and I don't even care at the moment, but it seems like you know Luc and what happens when he's angry. You do not want to get on his bad side," Emery warned as the wind picked up, tossing the longer hair across her face. "Trust me on this."

The Origin smirked. "Oh, trust me, I know exactly what happens when Luc is angry."

Air lodged in my throat. I stared at Emery, really looked at her. Her eyes weren't . . . they weren't a muted green anymore. They were the color of the brightest moss, and her pupils—her pupils were all white. My mouth dropped open.

Emery wasn't human.

She'd been wearing contacts the day at breakfast. Heidi's girl-friend was a Luxen!

"You have no idea who is really around you, do you? I guess you'll figure it out in due time." The Origin drew my attention back to him. "But in the meantime, I have a question I want you to ask Luc. Would you do that for me? Please?"

He gripped my arm before I even saw him move. I gasped as he yanked me forward and my bag slipped off my shoulder and hit the ground. His grip tightened, causing me to cry out. "Ask him if he'll play with me?"

"What?" I whispered.

It happened so fast.

There was a crack from *inside*. Red-hot pain, the kind I'd never experienced before, shot up my arm, stealing the next breath I took. I couldn't even scream as my legs gave out.

The Origin let go, and my knees slammed into the asphalt. Doubling over, I pressed my arm to my stomach. Someone cursed, but I could barely hear them over the pounding of my blood.

He broke my arm.

Holy shit, *he broke my arm*.

The stranger stepped around me as I tried to breathe through the throbbing pain, casually walking off like he hadn't just snapped my bone with a twist of his hand.

Emery was there in a second, kneeling in front of me as she gripped my shoulders. "Are you okay?"

"No," I said with a gasp, rocking backward as another wave of sharp, burning pain shot through me. "He broke my arm. Like, for real."

"Dammit." Emery looked over her shoulder at Connor as she wrapped her arm around my waist. "I've never done the healing thing before, and you're wearing a Disabler. Call Luc."

"Luc?" I said, and gasped again, my head not working right. "I need a hospital. Doctors. Pain meds—*strong* pain meds."

"We have something far better than that." Emery hauled me to my feet with striking ease. "Come on."

My gaze darted around the parking lot. I saw Connor was on the phone, his mouth moving fast.

Heidi was suddenly there, her face pale. "What happened?"

"I thought I told you to stay back." Emery walked me out between the trucks. "But of course you didn't listen."

"You should've known better than that." Heidi grew closer. "Holy crap, what happened to your arm?"

"Some guy broke it," I gritted out. "And I need a hospital."

"Some guy?" Heidi repeated.

"I don't know who it was, but that's not important right now," Emery said. "Grab her bag. We've got to go."

"To the hospital?" I suggested, wheezing through the pain. In the back of my mind, I remembered the whole Luxen and Origin healing thing. Hell, Luc had healed those marks on my stomach, but my arm was *broken*. I wanted a doctor. I wanted pain meds. Lots of them.

Connor turned, sliding his phone into his pocket. "He said he'll meet you."

"Thank you." Emery ushered me past a group of people. They were starting to pay attention. "Heidi."

She came running to our side, carrying my bag. The world spun a little. A car door opened in front of me. It wasn't my car, but I was suddenly in the backseat and Heidi was crawling in beside me. Another door slammed shut.

"Let me see your arm." Heidi scooted close as the engine turned on. Emery—Emery *the Luxen* was driving.

I stared at her face, taking short, quick breaths. "How bad is it? I can't look."

"Um." She glanced at the front seat. "I don't see a bone, but it's swollen and really red."

"Okay," I whispered. "Not seeing . . . a bone is a good thing, but I don't know if I can feel my fingers."

"It'll be okay." Tears gleamed in her eyes. "I promise."

Needing to believe her, I nodded as Emery peeled out of the parking lot and gunned the engine. I swallowed hard and tried to focus on anything other than the breath-stealing pain. "It was him—he killed them. Colleen. Amanda."

Heidi blinked and then pushed her hair back from her face. "Oh God."

"He didn't say who he was?" Emery demanded from the front seat.

"No. But he knew Luc. He knew me. He . . . he was at the club when it was raided. I . . ." The pain was getting worse. I felt like vomiting, and there was a good chance I might. Squeezing my eyes shut, I pressed down against the seat, onto my side, legs curling and uncurling, but it did nothing to help with the deep, inescapable pain.

"Evie?" Heidi placed her hand on my leg.

Sweat dampened my brow. "I think I'm going to be sick. Oh God, th-this really hurts."

"I know. I'm sorry." Heidi's trembling fingers pushed my hair back from my face, tucking the hair behind my ear. "We're going to get it fixed. I swear."

"There he is." Relief was evident in Emery's voice. "Finally."

I kept my eyes shut as I felt the car pull over. A car door flew open, and the sounds of traffic poured in, along with the scent of exhaust and . . . and *pine*. Evergreen. I pried open my eyes and turned my head.

Luc replaced Heidi. He cursed.

I panted through the pain. His hair was a mess of waves and curls, like he'd been in a windmill.

"H-how did you get here?"

"Ran." Concern filled his face, darkening his eyes. The front passenger door opened and then Heidi's face appeared between the two front seats. "Get us to the club," he ordered. "Now."

"I need a *hospital*."

Luc leaned over me, and those churning violet eyes became the only thing I saw. "You need me."

"Wha—"

"I'm going to touch your arm." And then he did just that, curling one hand around my elbow. "And this is going to hurt, but only for a second."

Panic dug in. My wild gaze swung around the car, glancing off Heidi's stricken face to Luc's. His jaw was hard, and extreme concentration was etched into his features. "Wait. Please. I know you can heal, but I want—"

The pupils of his eyes flared white. "I'm sorry."

Luc folded his hand over the center of where the worst of the pain was coming from, my forearm, and my arm caught *fire*. My back bowed as my head kicked back. A scream ripped through me as the ceiling of the car warped, fading out and then rapidly coming back into stark clarity. My legs straightened, and I didn't know how I didn't kick Luc through the door, but he was still there, holding onto my arm.

"Stop!" Heidi cried out. "You said he could help her. He's hurting—"

"He's making her better," Emery said. "I promise, Heidi. Just give him a second."

This wasn't helping. At all. It was nothing like the brief warming I'd felt before.

The pain pulsed and flared through my entire body, obliterating all thought until there was no pain and nothing . . . nothing but swamping heat.

21

Warmth flowed, seeping into bone and tissue. I was floating, like I was in the warm ocean waters of the south. I thought of the beach, but I . . . I couldn't remember when I'd actually gone to the beach.

Memories still came together, of the bright sun and pale, gritty sand, of sitting with my toes just touching the frothy waters. There was laughter, and I knew I wasn't alone. I was safe, *always* safe—those images broke apart before I could hold on to them.

I knew I'd never been to the beach. Neither of my parents had been the vacationing kind. There hadn't been time after the invasion, and before . . .

Why couldn't I remember before?

You know why, whispered a voice. *Before never existed.*

I was floating again, and thinking became overrated. There was this voice, this deep melodic voice whispering in my ear, telling me to give in, and that voice was warm and *safe.* So, I gave in to the warmth settling over me. I let it lull me deeper, guiding me back into the abyss, where I stayed and stayed. Maybe it was minutes, maybe it was hours, but I finally, *finally* opened my eyes.

I wasn't in the backseat of some car, writhing in unbelievable pain. I was on a bed, a very comfortable bed. Swallowing against the dryness in my throat, I looked around the room. The moment I recognized the bare walls and exposed brick, my heart stopped.

Luc's apartment.

What happened came rushing back to me. I'd been leaving school and run into this Origin—he'd broken my arm and Luc had done something. Something big, because my arm barely hurt.

He'd healed me, for real this time, and that was huge. He didn't have to do that. They could've taken me to a hospital. Wait. Oh God, was I going to turn into a mutated human—

I shifted and my leg bumped into something hard. I stopped moving. I was so not alone. I breathed in deeply, my heart stuttering when I recognized the woodsy scent surrounding me.

Oh dear.

I looked to my left, and devastatingly beautiful features registered. Yep, that was Luc lying next to me, and I couldn't even begin to fathom how this had come about.

My eyes widened as I took in the sight of him. He was half sitting up, his back against the wooden headboard, and his chin was dipped down. Thick lashes fanned the skin under his eyes. His arms were folded over his stomach and his chest rose and fell deeply, as if he were asleep.

What in the world?

If I had had my camera, I would have taken a picture of him in that moment. Probably sounded creepy as hell, because he was asleep and all, but Luc at rest was a stark contrast of hard lines and unyielding softness.

Okay.

I needed to prioritize, and taking pictures of a sleeping Luc was nowhere on the list of things I needed to do. Unable to help myself, I glanced over at Luc. Eyes like polished amethyst jewels stared back at me. Every muscle in my body froze, causing my arm to throb.

"Hey there, Peaches," he murmured.

"Hi," I whispered. I was really out of it, because I knew there were a lot of important things we needed to talk about, but those problems, terrifying ones, seemed muted and far away. "Why am I in your bed . . . with you?"

One side of his lips kicked up. "I was dozing." His gaze dipped and then he sucked his lower lip in between his teeth as his lashes lifted. "Damn, Peaches . . ."

The next breath I took got stuck as what had happened rushed to the forefront of all my jumbled thoughts. "God," I whispered, shuddering. "Luc, that guy—he's responsible for what happened to Colleen and Amanda. Maybe even that family."

The sleepiness vanished from his features. "I wanted to wait to make sure you were okay before we talked about this—"

"This can't wait." My heart thundered in my chest as residual fear kicked in. "He admitted to killing them. He said—" My voice cracked. I couldn't bring myself to say what I needed to.

Luc picked up on it. His lips thinned. "He thought he was grabbing you when he took Colleen? After he saw you talking to me?"

For once, I wasn't mad about him for peering into my head. "Yes. God." I felt like I was going to be sick. "Colleen is dead because he thought she was—"

"Stop." His fingers touched my chin, drawing my gaze to his. "She is not dead because of you. What happened to her isn't your fault. Okay?"

I drew in a shallow breath. "Okay."

"I have a feeling you don't really believe that."

It was hard to believe that when you knew someone had been killed because they were mistaken for you. My guilt, misplaced or not, wasn't important right now. "I met him before—I mean, in the parking lot of school. My stuff fell out of my bag and he helped me pick the stuff up. He hadn't given off any 'Hey, I'm a serial killer' vibes then. He was nice, and I thought he was a student, but it was him. And he was in my house that night and he said he left his mark on me the second time."

Understanding flared in his eyes. "Those marks on your stomach."

"You didn't do it. It was *him*." Nausea twisted up my insides. "He's been in my house. Twice." I looked away from Luc, squeezing my eyes shut. "He knew you, Luc, and he wasn't a Luxen. He was an Origin. I saw his eyes. They were just like yours."

Luc was so quiet, but I could feel the red-hot fury pouring off him. It charged the air in the room. "He didn't happen to give you a name or anything useful?"

"No. I thought there weren't many Origins left?"

"There aren't," he growled. "What did he look like?"

"About my age." I opened my eyes, willing my heart to slow down. I wasn't in that parking lot. I was safe. For now. "He had brown hair and the same color eyes as you."

"Anything else you remember?"

"He was wearing sunglasses nearly the entire time, but he . . . he had a dimple in his right cheek and . . ." I trailed off as I remembered what he'd said to me right before he broke my arm. "He asked me to ask you something, but I don't think I heard him right."

The pupils of Luc's eyes were starting to turn white. "What did he say?"

I shook my head. "He wanted me to ask you if you'd . . . play with him."

Everything about Luc changed in an instant. He was off the bed in a nanosecond.

His hands were curled into fists at his sides.

"What?" I asked as a kernel of panic took root. "What, Luc?"

"How old did you say he looked?"

"Around my age, give or take a year."

"He was definitely a teenager? This is important, Peaches. You're positive that he was a teenager?"

"Yes." I stared up at him. "I'm positive. Why? Do you know who it is?"

Lifting a hand, he thrust his fingers through his messy hair. "There's only one person I can think of, but he's . . . God, he would only be about ten years old now."

I choked on a hoarse laugh. "He definitely wasn't ten years old."

There was a flicker of relief skittering across Luc's features, but it was brief. "It cannot be."

"What are you not telling me?" I started to sit up, but the room spun a little. "Whoa."

"What's wrong?"

"Just a little dizzy." I felt out of it. Like I was waking up after being sick from the flu.

He was next to me again in an instant, on the bed and reaching for me. I jerked, but he was fast. His fingers grazed my cheek and then sifted through my hair, curling along the back of my skull as he shifted. He rose up on his other arm so that he hovered over me. I gasped as warmth radiated from him—from his *fingers*. It was the same feeling I'd felt before, when he'd touched me in the car.

The warmth soaked my body. "Wh-what are you doing?"

"Fixing you."

"Should you be doing that?" The tingling sensation rippled down my spine, spreading out through every nerve ending. I bit down on the inside of my lip, twisting restlessly, drawing one leg up. "I . . . I don't want to change into a mutant."

Luc's chuckle held a rough edge. "You mean hybrid? You're not going to turn into one."

"How do you know?"

"I know things." There was a pause. "Did that bastard do anything else to you?"

"No. Just my arm."

"Just your arm?" His voice hardened. "He nearly snapped it in two, Peaches. The dizziness could be left over from that."

I closed my eyes, remembering the stomach-twisting pain.

"Are you still dizzy?" he asked as his hand slipped down to the nape of my neck.

"No."

"That's good." His voice sounded deeper.

I could feel my pulse speeding up. "I know you told me that you can heal, but I don't understand how this is working. It seems impossible."

"It's the energy. It can be channeled into a human to repair bone, tissue, and muscle, even nerve damage. Wounds." He paused. "Like I said before, we can heal almost anything that was caused externally, but we cannot heal damage from an internal source."

"Like a virus or cancer?" I asked, recalling bits of that previous conversation.

"Some cancers they were successful at healing." His voice thickened. "But nowhere near all of them."

All of it sounded insane, but he had healed me, and his touch was doing something right then. My eyes were still closed, but I felt the bed shift under me—under us—and I knew he was closer. I wanted to smack myself. I should be telling him to stop doing whatever it was he was doing because I was okay and this seemed dangerous in a way, but the languid heat was making its way down my arms and over my chest, clouding my thoughts and common sense.

Luc was quiet for a long moment. "You scared me today."

My heart skipped a beat as I opened my eyes again. I was right. Luc was close. Our mouths were separated by what felt like just inches. "I did?"

"When I got that phone call and Connor said you were hurt, I . . ." He closed his eyes, his features tensing. "It terrified me."

I didn't know what to say to that, because it didn't seem like anything scared Luc.

His hand was gone from the back of my head, but was now trailing down the side of my neck, eliciting a wave of acute shivers. The healing warmth from his hand was gone, but the heat was still there, curling deep in the pit of my stomach. His breath coasted over my cheek and he opened his eyes again. "Are you sure you're feeling better?"

My lips parted as I pressed down into the pillow. "I am. Thank you."

"You shouldn't thank me."

"I just did."

"This shouldn't have happened to you." The tips of his fingers coasted over my not-so injured arm, to where my hand rested on my stomach. "I'm sorry."

Electricity danced across my skin, following his touch. My breath hitched as his finger reached the tip of mine and then halted.

"It's not your fault."

An eyebrow lifted. "It's not? This . . . thing that came after you did so because you were seen talking to me. Right?"

"You just told me what happened to Colleen wasn't my fault. How can you blame yourself for this?"

"Because I can." His palm moved maybe half an inch and then

flattened against my stomach, right below my belly button. Little tingles shimmied across my midriff.

"You didn't break my arm or tell the guy to do that. You fixed it. You made it better."

Luc's gaze lifted to mine, and his eyes reminded me of liquid fire and . . . hunger. I'd seen it before, in the way Emery looked at Heidi, and I was suddenly thinking about what it would be like for us to be in a bed under different circumstances, with his hand where it was and his eyes full of so, so much.

That half grin slipped from his mouth as a certain intensity settled around his lips. My whole body tensed as he lowered his forehead to mine.

"What . . . what are you doing now?" I asked.

"I really don't know." He inhaled deeply and it came out in an unsteady rush. "Actually, I'm lying. I know what I'm doing."

I had a good idea of what he was doing too. My toes curled against the soft blanket, and my hand had a mind of its own. It left my stomach and landed against his chest. He jerked at the contact and then shuddered. My eyes widened at his response. His pupils started to glow and it had nothing to do with anger. Then his eyes closed as his head tilted to the side, lining our mouths up. I shouldn't let this happen. I knew that. There was an entire football field length of reasons why: he was infuriating half the time, and I had a feeling he was keeping so much from me. Funny that the biggest reason, the fact that he was definitely not human, didn't even register.

But I wanted this kiss—a real one that wasn't stolen.

I've wanted this for forever.

That thought caught me off guard. Forever? There had been no forever. I hadn't known him for forever, and most of the time I had, I'd wanted to punch him. In the throat.

The wanting, though? It was consuming and pounding, undeniable and *new*. My fingers stretched out over his chest. I could feel the heat from his body through the thin shirt. I'd never experienced anything like this before.

And it was a little terrifying.

I pushed against the chest. "Luc, I . . ." I didn't want to say. I didn't know what I was feeling.

He shifted onto his side. "It's okay. It's—Wait a second." Luc sat up swiftly, his gaze flickering over me like he was looking for something. Then his eyes widened.

"What?" I sat up, relieved that the movement didn't make me dizzy. I looked down at my arm again, making sure it hadn't healed all wonky, in case that was why he was looking at me strangely.

Touching it lightly, I winced at the dull spike of pain. My arm had been broken and . . . and now it wasn't. That was the proof in the pudding right there. Mind. Blown. Overwhelmed, I lowered my arm to my lap. "I feel like I need to thank you again."

"Don't." A muscle flexed in his jaw. "I'm the last person you should be thanking."

"Why?"

He turned his head to me, his expression unfathomable. "Something is wrong here."

My mind raced back to what we'd almost done. We had been heartbeats away from kissing. Was that what he was talking about? There was a knock on the door.

Luc turned. "Come in."

The door opened to reveal Emery and then Heidi, peeking around Emery's shoulder. "We just wanted to check on her," Heidi said.

Emery had the same look on her face as Luc did. Like she was looking for something around me that wasn't there.

I was starting to get a little worried.

"You don't see it either, do you?" Luc asked her.

Emery shook her head as Heidi stepped farther into the room. "See what?" Heidi asked.

"I don't know." I looked at Luc. "What are you guys looking for? And why are you staring at me like I have a second head?"

"I know why," Emery interjected.

Heidi looked at her. "Care to fill me in, babe?" she asked.

Emery glanced at Luc.

"Why are you looking at him instead of telling me?"

Luc rose from the bed. "I have to go."

"What?" My voice cracked. "Can't whatever you need to do wait?"

"No." Luc laughed, and it was nothing like the laugh I'd heard before. It was cold and sent chills over my skin. "*This* cannot wait."

22

W here do you think Luc went?" I asked. "Did he go looking for the guy?"

Heidi and I were sitting on Luc's couch. Ten minutes had passed since Luc had bolted out of the room like the building was on fire. Emery had followed him, but she said she was coming back.

"I don't think so," Heidi answered. "When you were out of it in the car, it sounded like Connor was trying to track that guy down."

Connor.

I'd forgotten that he'd been there. That was another person I needed to thank. I glanced down at my arm, still unable to get over the fact there were only bruises. Healing broken bones in moments? Unbelievable, but it'd happened. Awe-inspiring and overwhelming. It was amazing.

Part of me could understand why that would capture the attention of doctors and researchers. What would normally take a surgery and a cast to fix, Luc had done in minutes.

"As soon as Emery gets back, we'll get you to your car." Heidi pulled her legs up and wrapped her arms around them.

I lowered my arm to my lap.

"Is it hurting?"

I shook my head. "Just a little, but nothing like before. It feels like I just banged it into a wall instead of it being broken."

Emery returned then, walking into the room. She sat beside Heidi. "Sorry about that. I just wanted to let Grayson know what was going on."

"It's all right." Heidi smiled at her.

She was seriously a Luxen. How had a pair of contacts tricked me? I gave my head another shake. "So, I have questions."

Emery smiled weakly. "I figured as much."

My mind was going blank as I tried to process everything that had happened. "Why were you and Luc looking at me strangely?"

"This is where things get complicated."

I looked over my shoulder and saw Kent. He was wearing a shirt I imagined Luc would wear. On it was a picture of a T. rex trying to hug another T. rex, but with their short arms, that wasn't happening.

"Really?" I murmured, wondering if Luc would be thrilled that everyone was in his apartment. "Things are just now getting complicated?"

Kent strolled into the room, carrying a can of Coke. "So, you know about the Daedalus and everything, right?"

I nodded and then glanced at Heidi. Apparently that wasn't news to her, either.

"Your government knows damn well the Luxen can heal humans, and they also know not every Luxen is equally skilled at doing it. Some are better at it than others, and those really interest them. Those were the ones your government stole." He sat on the arm of the couch, closest to me. He handed me the Coke. I took it. "I didn't misspeak about the whole 'your' government thing. I claim no ownership of that hot mess express, but that's not the biggest risk when it comes to healing humans."

I frowned, deciding not to follow him down that rabbit hole for the moment. "So what's the bigger risk? Mutating them?"

"Someone has been filling you in on things." Kent grinned. "But obviously not everything."

Catching my eye, Heidi unfolded her legs. "I don't know all the details, but what they're about to tell you? I believe it."

At this point, I believed in the chupacabra.

"So, you know that the Luxen have been here for decades and decades, if not longer. They didn't come to take over or hurt people," Emery explained as I clutched the can of soda. "They came because their planet was destroyed in a war with . . . with another race of aliens, and they were looking for a new place to live. My ancestors basically came here to recolonize."

Alien planets, plural? Wars between alien species? Recolonization? This had just veered straight into science-fiction territory, but I was here for this. I popped open my can and then took a long, healthy gulp, welcoming the carbonated burn.

I needed to focus on one thing at a time here. "Planets?"

"We come from a planet that's, like, a trillion light-years from here." Emery leaned forward. "We weren't the only planet with intelligent life-forms on it."

That had been the big question after the invasion. Were the Luxen the only aliens out there? We'd been assured that was the case. "You're not the only aliens?"

She shook her head. "We come from Lux. That was our planet, but it was destroyed by a species known as the Arum."

I opened my mouth, but what the hell was I going to say? So I snapped it shut again.

"My people had been locked in a battle with them for many, many decades. Centuries, really." Her knees bent, straining the ripped jeans. "We were taught that we were the innocent ones, but there's rarely a war where there's a truly innocent side, and long story short, we basically destroyed each other's planets."

"The Luxen came here first." Kent tapped his bare foot off mine. "The Arum followed."

"Wait." I lifted my free hand. "Back up a second. Who or what are the Arum?"

"They are like us in some ways. They don't come in threes, but in fours. They can assimilate human DNA, so they blend in just like we do, but where we kind of glow when we're in our true form, they can be solid . . . or turn to shadows."

"Shadows?" I repeated dumbly.

"Shadows," Kent reinforced.

I stared at his profile. "You've got to be kidding."

"I have a better sense of humor than that," he returned. "They look like shadows to us, because that's the only way our brains can process what we're seeing: relating their form to something famil-iar. They aren't really shadows."

"Oh," I murmured.

"They can feed off Luxen, steal their abilities."

"How do the Arum feed? Are they like vampires?"

Kent laughed. "Not really. They also don't bite. They . . . well, they can do it through touch or inhaling."

"Inhaling?"

"Exactly that. So, okay. You know that humans have electricity inside them—electrical signals running throughout the body? The Arum can feed on that even though it does nothing for them. When they do, it disrupts the signals the human's body is sending. Massive heart failure, basically."

"Wow," I whispered. "That's . . . that's scary."

"Can be," he answered. "Arum are very powerful, but they do have some weaknesses. For example, beta quartz hides Luxen from them by dispersing the energy they naturally put off, and it dis-rupts Arum's visual fields. Obsidian is deadly to Arum."

"Aren't those gemstones or something?"

Kent nodded. "Obsidian is volcanic glass. It's deadly to an Arum, fracturing their entire cellular makeup."

Well, none of that sounded even remotely real, but I vaguely remembered hearing something about beta quartz before, right after the invasion, when people were learning about the Luxen. "All righty then." I took another sip. "And the Arum are . . . still here?"

Heidi nodded. "We've probably even seen them, Evie, and just not realized they were different from us or the Luxen."

I wasn't sure if I believed any of this, but I was experienc-ing next-level curiosity. "And they're dangerous? Do they wear Disablers?"

"The Arum roll low-key and the Disablers wouldn't work on them. Right now there's a weird peace between the Luxen and the Arum, but the Arum are . . . Well, the need to feed off Luxen is really hard to ignore." Kent ran his hand over his Mohawk. "With-out feeding, they aren't as powerful as the Luxen. Hell, they're basically the same as us. Or a Luxen with a Disabler. Plus not every Arum is on the peace-loving train. There's a lot of baggage between the Luxen and the Arum. Not everyone can let it go."

"Okay." I scooted forward, holding on to the empty can of soda. "So, the Luxen and Arum are here and they've been here . . . doing stuff. Got it." I paused, twisting toward Heidi. "What does that have to do with the risk of healing a human?"

"Well . . ." she said, drawing the word out. She twisted her red hair into a thick rope. "I think I'll leave that to them to explain."

Emery took a deep breath. "The Arum can sense Luxen. The only thing that stops them from doing so is being surrounded by beta quartz. I'm talking large deposits, usually natural ones found in mountains all over the world. We used to live in communities that were near natural deposits of quartz, but that changed after . . . well, after the invasion. Most of our old communities were destroyed."

I wish I had more Coke. "Okay."

The look on Emery's face said she knew I was a couple of steps away from sensory overload. "When we heal a human, we leave a trace behind on them. To an Arum, it's almost like the human is lit up. They're surrounded in a glow. The Arum find humans with a trace as tasty as Luxen."

"What?" My back straightened. "So, I'm glowing and an Arum shadow creature is going to eat me?"

Kent coughed out a laugh. "Boy, I just took that the wrong way."

Emery rolled her eyes. "Normally, they would find you—or they could. They'd see your trace, and if they were hungry for some Luxen goodness, they'd either use you to get to the Luxen or use you as a snack. It wouldn't just put the Luxen in danger, but also his or her friends and family. See, an odd side effect of the Disablers is that it blinds the Arum to the Luxen, so . . . they've been really hungry. They can't search out most Luxen now."

"Normally?" I'd caught that word.

"Normally," she said, her gaze roaming over me. "If a Luxen heals a human, then we usually stay very close to them, just to be sure they aren't in a danger, but you . . . you don't have a trace, Evie."

Relief made me dizzy. "Oh God, I thought you were going to say I was as bright as the sun or something. This is good news, right? I'm safe. My mom is safe. Well, safe from the Arum thing. I'm not going to be some weird shadow alien's snack. All I have to worry about is bone-breaking Origins."

"Well . . ." Kent took my empty can. "I'm just a lowly human, but apparently if she doesn't see your trace, then that might not be a good thing."

I focused on Emery. "Why?"

Emery lifted her hands. "Because *every* human who's ever been healed always has a trace on them."

"Well, I'm human, so—Wait, but Luc—"

"Luc is an Origin," Kent confirmed. "But it works the same way. Origins leave a trace behind."

My gaze swung to him. "Then what does that mean?"

Kent lifted a shoulder as he stood. "I have no idea. Anyway, I have to go." He patted my head, easily moving out of reach when I swatted at his hand. "People to see. Stuff."

I glared at him, super-annoyed. "Well, that was a lot of help when it comes to clearing things up for me."

He winked at me. "Obviously, you understand how important it is to keep this quiet. If not . . ."

"Yeah, you'll go after everyone I know and love?" I shot back.

Kent winked. "That's my girl." He walked out of the room, throwing up a peace sign.

I turned to Emery. "God, why does everyone have to be so annoying?"

Emery gave me a sympathetic smile. "I know all of this sounds made-up."

It did.

"But it's the truth," she continued. "Look, I'm going to go check on a few things. I'm sorry about what happened to you today. We'll make sure it doesn't happen again." She started to get up.

Emery didn't get very far, though.

Catching her hand, Heidi pulled her back down for a kiss. Not exactly a quick one either. The tips of my ears were burning by the time they broke up, and Emery sashayed out of the room.

"You really, really like her, don't you?" I asked.

Heidi laughed softly. "I do. You know, I knew what she was the first night I met her. It never mattered to me. At all."

There was a lot I wanted to talk about, but the really important one won out. "Why didn't you tell me what Emery was?"

Heidi dragged her palms over her knees as her gaze fell to the carpet. "I didn't think you'd . . . approve."

"Really?"

She glanced at me. "Really. You haven't . . ."

I haven't what? I'd never been anti-Luxen. Then again, I'd never been really vocal either way in the past. I'd mostly been . . . quiet. Staying quiet was just as bad as being against them, and I had to get real with myself and take ownership for why she would've thought that. Because deep down, I had said things in passing that would've made her think that.

But when I looked at Luc or Emery, it was hard to see them other than how they presented themselves. It was hard to remember why I was scared of them, even when I'd seen Luc go all badass on the Luxen.

But here I was, obviously not afraid of Luc or Emery.

"I don't care that she's a Luxen." And that was the truth. I held her gaze, grinding my teeth as the pain in my arm heightened. "It's risky, though."

"I know," Heidi replied, voice low. "But it's worth the risk. *She's* worth it."

"You're worth it. I'm sorry," I said, meaning it. "I really like Emery, and I don't think it's wrong. I really don't." Saying those words made me realize it was the truth. "I just worry if someone were to find out—"

"Like I said, it's a risk we're both willing to take. We're careful. Usually when we're out, she's wearing contacts. Very few people know what Emery is."

"Okay." I was still worried though.

Heidi smiled a little. "What about you and Luc?"

I frowned. "What about him?"

She lifted a brow. "You were out for a few moments, but he was upset about how hurt you were, and from what I gather from Emery, Luc is never not chill. He pretty much operates on *calm* and *calmer*."

I didn't know how to respond to that. Mainly because I had no idea what I thought when it came to Luc. I was all over the place.

Heidi leaned into me, throwing an arm over my shoulder. "Things are really kind of bizarre now, aren't they?"

I laughed dryly. "My mind is blown." I made a poofing sound. "And then I'm not glowing?"

"It's probably a good thing."

"Yeah." I dragged my hands over my knees. Staring at her profile, I began to wonder why exactly she sounded more nervous about that than she did about me having a trace. I was human. So, why wasn't I glowing?

About an hour later Emery and a very reluctant Grayson drove me back to my car. They followed me home. Emery stayed, and a few minutes later Heidi showed up. By then there was just an occasional twinge of pain in my arm.

Mom wasn't home, and I figured that for once her ever-increasing late nights were a blessing. The girls stayed until the sun set. They didn't say it, but I knew they were there because of what had happened.

Once they left, I went to my bedroom and sat staring at my laptop screen. I'd actually googled Arum. What I learned was that *arum* was actually an arrow-shaped plant that sometimes had berries.

Definitely nothing about aliens.

And that wasn't at all helpful.

I went several pages deep on the search, and stuff really just got weird at that point. I didn't know what I was expecting to find. An in-depth explanation of the different types of aliens? If there really were aliens called Arum and the government didn't want us to know about them, then there wouldn't be anything for me to find, so I had no idea what I was doing.

I closed my laptop, pushed it to the edge of the bed, and then I just sat there, staring at the corkboard of photos above my desk. They were pictures of my friends and me. Halloween. Christmas. Random shots. Some from this past summer, but summer felt like a lifetime ago.

Luc had been right.

Everything had changed.

And now there was a guy out there—a superpowerful Origin who had a major problem with Luc and had used me to get to him.

I almost couldn't believe any of it happened, that it was happening. Some creepy guy had come after me, had killed because—

I sucked in a sharp breath as I closed my eyes, lowering my head to my hands. Was this guy going to come back? A chill curled down my spine as a terrible sense of foreboding washed over me. He'd been in my house, in this room while I slept—while my mother slept down the hall.

He'd . . . touched me and I'd had no idea. He'd *choked* me, and I'd thought it was a dream. What was stopping him from getting in here again? I knew that if he wanted to kill me, he could. I'd seen what Luc was capable of, and if this Origin was half as powerful, I didn't stand a chance.

Icy terror pooled in my stomach. And what about Luc? Would he be safe? He was strong and fast, but . . .

Dropping my hands, I opened my eyes again and exhaled raggedly. I could sit here all night and worry about the Origin, but it wasn't the only concern. My throat constricted. I knew so much now, things I had to keep secret. Staying quiet wasn't going to be easy, but who would believe me? No one.

My gaze drifted to my bedroom door.

Did my mom know about the Arum and healing?

The moment that question entered my thoughts, I squirmed with unease, because of course she did. I knew she did. She worked for the Daedalus, but she conveniently left out the whole part about healing humans and a whole other alien race when she'd told me about it.

What else was she keeping secret?

I snatched a thick bobby pin off my nightstand and gathered up my hair, twisting it into a bun and then shoving the bobby pin in. I went to grab my laptop again when a text came through.

Are you awake?

It was that unknown number again, and my lips parted on a soft inhale. It was Luc. One of these days I just might add him as a contact. I sent a quick yes back to him.

Incoming.

I jolted. Incoming? What the hell did that mean? I lifted my head, clutching my phone—

A rapping came from my bedroom window.

"No way," I whispered, eyes wide.

The sound came again.

I scurried off the bed, then briefly glanced at my closed door before I rushed around the bed. No way was Luc outside. It was impossible to get up to my window. No trees and only a small roof over the bay window. The only thing that could've gotten up there was a pterodactyl . . . or someone who wasn't exactly human.

Which would be Luc.

Or the psycho Origin.

I drew back the curtain and gasped.

Crouched on the small roof was most definitely not a pterodactyl.

Luc grinned like he wasn't perched outside my bedroom window, and when he spoke, his voice was muffled by the thick glass. "Knock, knock."

23

I gaped at him through my window in a state of suspended disbelief. This had to be a weird dream, one induced by psychotic Luxen and weird internet searches.

Luc lifted a hand. "I brought you a Coke. A nice, fresh Coke." And he had. He was holding a red-and-white can in his hand. "Not a Pepsi."

My heart sped up. What in the world?

Luc waited, his face lit only by the moonlight. Mom was going to flip out if she came home and caught him here. Wait. Was I seriously considering letting him in?

I was.

Which meant I'd officially taken a left turn into Baddecisionville, population: Evie. Cursing under my breath, I unlatched the window and shoved it open since I hadn't set the house alarm yet. "Are you out of your mind?"

"I like to think I was never in my mind," he replied. "Can I come in?"

I stepped back and extended an arm. "You're already up here."

A wide smile broke out across his face and then he came through the window, landing gracefully and silently. I, on the other hand, would've fallen right through, likely face-first. He straightened, offering the Coke. "I'm a very special delivery boy."

I took the can of soda, careful that our hands didn't touch. "Yeah . . ."

Standing as close as we were, it was hard not to acknowledge how tall he was, how he seemed to take over. My room wasn't small, but with Luc in it, the space didn't feel big enough. His presence overwhelmed the room as he turned in a slow circle.

Thank the Lord I was wearing a pair of leggings and a super-baggy shirt, because I was amazingly braless at the moment.

He plucked up my left hand and lifted my arm. "How is it feeling?"

"Almost perfect." I slipped my hand free and stepped back. "I know you said not to thank you, but thank you for . . . fixing my arm."

Luc didn't say anything for a long moment. "It could've been worse."

Knowing that was true, I folded my arms across my stomach.

"He hurt you because of your . . . association with me," he continued, his eyes churning restlessly. "He will pay dearly for that."

I was chilled by his words; I knew that was a promise.

Luc turned and walked away.

"What are you doing?" I whispered as he headed to his left, running his fingers over the spines of books haphazardly stacked on the built-in shelves next to my dresser and TV. "If my mom catches you here, she will shoot you. Like legit whip a gun out of a pillowcase and shoot you."

He grinned. "She would."

My mouth dropped open as I threw up my hands. "And that doesn't concern you?"

"Not really." He pulled an old, tattered book off the shelf. His brows rose as he read the title. "*Claimed by the Viking*?"

"Shut up." I stalked over to him and snatched the book out of his hand. I put it back on the shelf. "My mom is—"

"If you were so worried about your mom, you probably shouldn't have let me inside." Luc picked up another book, this time a thin hardcover on photography. He quickly grew bored with that, and placed it back. "But alas, your mom isn't home."

"How do you know that?" I followed him as he moseyed on past my dresser and to my cluttered desk.

"I'm omniscient." Luc touched—touched *everything*. The pens and highlighters, the heavy five-subject notebooks stacked on top of one another. He picked up the hot-pink miniature stapler, clicked it once, and then put it back. His long fingers drifted over loose papers.

"Oh, come on."

"She's been working really late, hasn't she?"

"Yeah, it's not at all creepy that you know that."

He chuckled as he looked over his shoulder at me. "Maybe your momma isn't working late. Maybe she's hooking up with someone."

"Ew. No way is she—" I stopped myself, not wanting to even think about my mom hooking up with someone.

"She has needs too, you know." He refocused on my desk, picking up my world history textbook.

I shot him a death glare. "Please stop talking about her like that. It really weirds me out."

"Yes, ma'am." He leaned in, squinting at the photos.

My heart sped up for no good reason. I stayed where I was, plastered against the wall, near the window. "How did you even get up here?"

"I ran and then jumped." He touched a Halloween photo from last year. It was Heidi and Zoe at James's house. They were dressed as Jokers—green hair and purple suit. I'd gone as Harley—old-school Harley Quinn. Finding the perfect jester suit had not been easy. It also hadn't been that flattering, which was why all pictures of me from that night had been burned. "I'm skilled like that."

I rolled my eyes.

He chuckled, and the sound was . . . annoyingly nice. "All these photos and none of you as a kid. None of your mommy and daddy?"

"That's not strange. We didn't get a chance to grab the photo albums after the invasion. All that stuff was left behind."

"Every single picture?" He turned to me. A moment passed. "Where were you when the invasion happened and what were you doing?"

I thought that was kind of a weird question, but I answered it anyway. "I was at home. It was early in the morning and I was asleep. Mom woke me up and told me we had to leave."

"And?"

"It's all . . . kind of a blur. We left when it was still dark outside." The details from that day had faded over time, and I thought a lot of it had to do with the fear and panic that had crowded the events. "We moved to a location in Pennsylvania and stayed there until it was safe."

After a long moment, Luc looked away.

"What about you?" I asked.

"I was in Idaho."

"Idaho? That's . . . unexpected."

"Do you know there's actually a theory where people believe that Idaho doesn't exist?"

"For real?"

"For reals. It's a conspiracy theory. Something like government mind control. Not that the government doesn't have the power and methods to pull something like that off, but I can one hundred percent confirm that Idaho is a state."

"All righty then." Curiosity was getting the best of me even though I should have been demanding that he leave. "Were you alone when it happened?"

He shook his head. "I was with people I knew."

"Friends?"

A strange, wistful smile appeared. "Depends on the day."

Oookay.

"You actually met two of them briefly."

I thought about that for a moment. "Daemon and Archer?"

He nodded. "They got back tonight. I'm sure you'll be seeing them again." He glanced over at me. "Is there a reason why you've attached yourself to the wall?" he asked, those striking eyes shooting to mine. "I don't bite."

A warm flush splashed across my cheeks. "Why are you here, Luc?"

"Because I wanted to see you." He backed up and then sat on my bed, his gaze never leaving me.

"Make yourself comfortable," I said dryly.

"Already did."

My eyes narrowed. "You . . . you shouldn't be here."

His lashes lowered. "You're right. More so than you even know." Before I could question what the heck that meant, he said, "I wanted to talk to you about what happened today."

I peeled myself off the wall and inched my way to the bed. "Talk."

A wry grin appeared as he rubbed a hand along his chest, above his heart. "Connor didn't find the Origin who attacked you, but he did give the same description that you gave me, and even though it's impossible, what that Origin said to you reminded me of one I once knew."

I sat on the bed, keeping a healthy distance between us. "Once knew?"

He nodded as he dropped his hand. "There's something I feel like I need to tell you." He bit down on his lower lip. "I probably shouldn't, but I think you need to know this. It's not something Grayson or Kent knows. Or Emery, who you've figured out by now is a Luxen."

"Yeah, I've figured that out." I picked up the Coke he brought and popped the tab. "What do you have to tell me?"

His shoulders stiffened. "When I said there weren't many Origins left, I know this because . . . I'm the reason."

"What? How?"

Luc's gaze slowly lifted to mine. "Because I . . . I killed most of them."

My lips parted on a sharp inhale. "I . . ."

"You don't know what to say? Most wouldn't." He rose from the bed. "When I told you that I was created in a lab, that all Origins were, it wasn't an exaggeration. We were engineered from embryo to adulthood. It took the Daedalus countless *batches* to perfect what they were designing, and even then, they weren't satisfied. They continued doing experiments, changing the serums and injections. Most of us don't even know what was given to us."

The horror from when he first told me about the Origin resurfaced. I watched him walk to the window he'd climbed through.

"Only a very small percentage of Origins were considered stable."

He pulled the curtain back, and moonlight peeked in, slicing across his cheekbones. "Some didn't make it to their first year. Others lasted longer before whatever was given to them went bad. And there were some who were extremely violent, dangerous to everyone and everything around them, and they were . . . they were put down in the labs, usually through lethal injection."

"Dear God." I set my soda aside and pulled my legs up onto the bed. "Luc, I'm—"

"That's not the worst part." There was a quick twist of his lips as he let the curtain go. "There was a new batch of Origins, ones who the Daedalus were particularly excited about. I learned of them right before the invasion. There were being kept in a facility in New Mexico, and after the Daedalus collapsed, I freed them. I freed them, because I knew if I didn't, they would either be terminated or shipped off to someplace else."

Luc turned to me. "You see, I thought I was doing the right thing. I brought them all to a place where I believed they would be safe. They were young, Peaches. No more than five years old."

My heart squeezed. I had a feeling this was going somewhere very bad.

"I left them with people I trusted, people I knew would take care of them because I couldn't stay. I had other things I had to do, and those people did take care of them. They tried." Luc walked back toward the bed. "Except those kids . . . I should've left them in the lab."

"What happened, Luc?"

A muscle flexed along his jaw. "It started with small things—things that would be normal dealing with any child. They'd want something and when they couldn't have it, they'd throw tantrums. Except their tantrums resulted in houses catching on fire and people getting thrown into walls."

My eyes widened.

"I don't know why I thought of them as normal kids. Origins are highly intelligent, and I am not saying that to pat myself on the back. Even at five years old, they could outsmart any adult. They could plot and work together to get what they wanted, whether it was a bowl of ice cream or to stay up late. The people I left them with realized quickly that socializing them was going to be issue, especially when their intelligence became manipulation and their manipulation became violence."

Luc sat down, closer than before. Close enough that I caught the outdoorsy scent, the mix of pine and burning leaves. "Two of them attacked someone—someone who cared for them all—because she wouldn't let them have an extra cookie. A cookie, Peaches. They threw her through a third-story window over a cookie."

Stunned, I stayed quiet and listened.

"She was okay in the end, but only because she's a hybrid—you know, a human who has been mutated. If she hadn't been, they would've killed her. That was when I went back." He paused. "I thought I could, I don't know, change them, because there was one of them who was . . . stable. I thought he was a good sign, and that since they were like me, I could instill patience in them, and empathy and, you know, basic humanity. I didn't want to accept that it was hopeless. I couldn't." A harsh laugh parted his lips. "If anything, my presence made it worse. It was like putting two betta fishes in front of each other. Nothing I did worked. Separating them. Punishing them. Rewarding them. I couldn't lock them up. They were way too smart and powerful for that."

I remembered what he'd said about being a realist before. That some people were lost causes, and I was thinking I was about to find out why he believed that.

Luc's features sharpened like a blade. "Then they attacked again, and this time, they killed someone. A Luxen, and they couldn't be with the people I left them with. Then they came at me, all of them except one. They sure as hell couldn't be out in society, running amok. As much as I hated it, I realized that freeing them had been a big mistake."

He put his hand on the bed beside my bare feet and leaned in. "I had to take care of them, Peaches." Slowly, he lifted his gaze to mine, and I sucked in an unsteady breath. "Do you understand what that means?"

Stomach churning, I wanted to look away, but I didn't. "I think I do. You had to . . . terminate them?"

Pain filled those beautiful eyes. "I did, and it was possibly the worst thing I'd ever had to do. I had no choice, Peaches. They were hurting people. They were killing, and they were only children. I couldn't fathom what they would become as they grew older."

I slowly shook my head. "That's . . . Luc, I don't know what to say. I really don't."

He held my gaze for a long moment and then looked away. "Daemon and Archer were two of the people I left them with." His jaw worked as his gaze trekked over the corkboard of pictures. "It was Daemon's wife who had been thrown through the window. It was one of their friends who was killed. They knew what I'd done. It's . . . it's one of the reasons why I haven't gone back to see them since then. I don't like being reminded of all that."

I remembered Daemon asking about why Luc hadn't visited, and of course, Luc had given some vague-as-hell answer. Now I understood why. How could he have explained that to me before?

How was he able to do it now?

"The one who I thought was okay? He . . . he got away. His name was Micah." A wry twist pulled at his lip. "That kid was like a brother to me. No idea where he is now. It's probably a good thing, but what that Origin said to you today reminded me of Micah. He was always trying to get people to play with him. He was just in desperate need for attention or something."

My brows knitted. "The Origin I saw today was a teen."

"I know. It can't be Micah. He'd only be about ten now, but it's obviously an Origin who knows what I did. Perhaps one who has come across Micah or something, but I . . . I'm not surprised. When Chas was attacked, I knew it had to be an Origin to get the upper hand on him. I think that's why he tried to warn you away."

Holy crap . . .

"And I began to suspect that one was around. We can sense one another, but that isn't always perfect, especially when other Origins are around."

"Like Archer?"

He was still for a moment and nodded. "I didn't think what happened to the girls had anything to do with what happened to Chas. Not at first, but when I saw you in the park, I sensed an Origin."

I stilled. Probably even stopped breathing.

"From there, I tried to keep an eye on you. If not me, then Grayson." He didn't look at me. "Or Emery. I know you probably hate hearing that, but I was worried whoever was around was going to come after you. I was right, and obviously I didn't do a good enough job at keeping an eye on you. He still got to you. More than once."

I didn't even know what to think as I stared at the hard cut of his profile. He'd been watching me? Had people watching me? Part of me wanted to be pissed off. A huge part, because that was just freaking creepy. "Did you guys set off the motion detector before?"

He raised a brow as he glanced over at me. "I didn't, but I'm pretty sure Grayson did."

"So, that's why you've been hanging out with me? The same reason Emery and Heidi—"

"No, that is not the reason why I've been hanging out with you." His gaze met mine. "I could keep watch and you'd never know I was there."

"Well, that's creepy."

"You're mad."

"I'm—I don't know. I mean, yeah. I think anyone would be freaked out by the idea that people have been watching over them."

"But?"

"But I kind of get it. Okay. I do get it. It's still creepy." I looked away. "But I also may be a target of a psychotic Origin, so there's that."

"There is that."

A long moment passed before I spoke again. "Do you think he's out for revenge?"

"I think its something like that. I think now he's just messing with me."

"Why? If he hates you because of what you had to do with the other Origins, then why doesn't he come for you?" I asked. "Why go after other people?"

"Like I said, to mess with me." His throat worked on a swallow. "I think with high levels of intelligences also comes the high level of sociopathic tendencies. Sometimes I think with each batch of Origin, they were getting closer and closer to creating the perfect serial killer and not human."

I gaped at him. "Wow."

He slid a look at me. "Anyway, I brought you something. A gift."

My brows rose as he shifted and reached into his pocket, pulling out an object that was small and black, and kind of reminded me of the pedi thing I used in the shower.

"Wait. Is that a Taser?"

"It's a stun gun."

I frowned as I resisted making grabby fingers at it. "Aren't they the same thing?"

"Actually, no. A Taser can be used from a distance and close contact. A stun gun only works at close contact. Kind of surprised not every human is outfitted with one of these." He lifted a shoulder. "Cartridges are inside, and its ready to be used. All you have to do is press this against the skin and hit the button," he explained. "It will take a human down for a bit, but it will incapacitate a Luxen, hybrid, or Origin for a couple of minutes, if not longer if they're weakened or wounded." He offered it to me. "Use it wisely."

"As in not against you?" I took it, surprised by how lightweight it felt.

Luc smirked. "See that button? When you slide it up, the light will turn red. That means it's ready to go. Then you just push the button."

Because I had to, I did just that. The little light flipped red and then I pushed down. Electricity crackled between the prongs. "Cool."

Luc was leaning back, nodding slowly.

Grinning, I placed it on the nightstand. "Thank you."

One shoulder lifted. "I don't plan for you ever to have to use it. Until we find the Origin who came after you today, you're going to be stuck with one of us."

"But—"

"That's not up for discussion, Peaches."

"Don't call me that," I snapped. "How can you always be watching me? That's not even feasible."

A faint smile curved up his lips, but it didn't reach his eyes. "I'm not going to let him hurt you again."

"Why?"

He blinked. "You're asking me why?"

"Yeah, why do you care? I mean, you barely know me, Luc. Why do you—"

"Not want to see you hurt or dead? Gee, I don't know. Maybe because I'm a decent Origin?"

"So, you protect all helpless humans you come across?"

"Not all of them," he said slowly. "Only the special ones."

"Luc."

He sighed as his gaze returned to the pictures. "Only you would ask a question like that."

"Only you would answer the question all evasively," I shot back.

"Because I know how much you love it," he replied. "I know the sight of me probably disgusts you at this point, but you're going to have to deal with me being around for a little longer, like it or not."

"Wait. What? Why would you say that?" I asked, genuinely confused. "That you would disgust me?"

"I don't?" His gaze inched back to mine. "I just told you that I killed a bunch—"

"I know what you told me," I cut in, not wanting him to have to say those words again. "And I don't know what to say to that. The only thing I can think of is that it's not fair that those kids were raised to become something like that. It's not fair that people who tried to take care of them turned into victims. And it's sure as hell not fair that you had to be put in a situation where you had to do something like that."

Surprise widened his eyes. "You really think that? That I had to do that?"

"What else could you have done, Luc? I wasn't there. I didn't know these kids, and I . . . don't know you all that well, but I think I know you would've done that only if it was your last option."

"It was." His voice was low. Hoarse.

"I'm sorry." When he opened his mouth to speak again, I rushed on. "I'm sorry for all of you. For those kids and for you—I'm just sorry, and . . ." Anger flowed over me in a powerful wave. "And I hate that my mother—and my father—had a role in this. You have no idea how hard it is for me to not say something to my mom. I have so many things I want to say to her."

Luc was quiet, oddly so.

Wanting to offer some level of comfort, I reached out. I hesitated with my hand a few inches from him, but then I placed my hand on his upper arm. Luc jerked as if my touch had scalded him, but he didn't pull away. "I don't know what you must be feeling or felt when you had to do that."

He folded his hand over mine. "Someone who obviously has a problem with me broke your arm today, and you're wanting to make me feel better?"

I lifted a shoulder as I slipped my hand out from under his. "I guess so."

Luc opened his mouth as if he wanted to say something, but then he looked away.

I followed his gaze. Something occurred to me. "You never had any of that, did you?"

"Had what?"

I leaned a little closer to him. "Friends you went to parties with. Dressing up for Halloween. Sleeping in for no reason. Changing your Facebook profile pic three times in an hour just because you could? Pictures? Memories?"

"Memories? I have memories. Some of them are . . . actually beautiful," he confessed. "Those memories came after my time with the Daedalus."

At once, I knew who he was talking about. "Your friend? What was her name? Nadia?"

His shoulders tensed.

"You miss her, don't you?"

Luc laughed, but it was without humor. "With every single breath I take."

Wow. My heart squeezed in my chest as curiosity filled me. "Were you two together?" The question sounded ridiculous, because if my father was involved in her death, that had to be more than four years ago. Luc would've only been fourteen and she would've been thirteen. Then again, I'd seen some super-intimate young 'uns before.

"Like, *together*?" He laughed again, and once more, there was little softness to the sound. "I never would've been that lucky."

Aww. My shoulders slumped. That was sweet and kind of sad, all things considered. "Did you . . ." Wondering if I was pushing too hard, I dampened my lips. "Did you love her, Luc?"

His eyes closed, and that beautiful face was stricken. Utterly broken wide open as he reopened his eyes and said, "With every breath I take."

The knot in my throat expanded, and I suddenly wanted to cry. He said *take* and not *took*. Even though she was gone, he was still in love with her. That was beautiful in the way only heartbreak could be.

Luc turned away from my pictures. Shadows clung to his gaze. "None of that matters now. You can't go back. The past is the past. Nadia is . . . She's gone. And so is the Daedalus, and soon there will be one less Origin to deal with."

Pressure clamped down on my chest. "And it has to be you?"

"It has to be." He let his head fall back. "Sometimes I wonder if everything we went through changed anything in the long run."

"What do you mean?"

Luc didn't answer, but he didn't move back, either. Our faces were only several inches apart. Neither of us said anything.

A long moment passed, and I pulled back, running my hands

down my face. Leaning against the headboard, I yawned. "My brain feels like it's going to implode."

"We wouldn't want that to happen. It would be messy."

I peeked over the tips of my fingers. "So, what are we going to do?"

He smoothed his hand over the comforter. "'We'?"

"About psycho Origin guy?"

Drawing his bottom lip in between his teeth, he grinned a little. "We aren't going to do anything. I will find him. I will take care of it."

"And I'm just supposed to sit around and twiddle my thumbs?"

"Yeah." He paused, his hand stilling. "Or you could sit around and read a book about Vikings claiming some fair maiden."

"Shut up," I grumbled. "I have to do something, Luc."

He lay down on his back, resting his hands on his stomach. "What can you do, Peaches? Not trying to be a jerk, but you can't fight an Origin. You're . . . you're damn lucky you're sitting here."

My stomach took a tumble. "I know that, but there has to be something."

He turned his head toward me. "That's why you have the stun gun. Just in case. But other than that, you're going to stay as safe as possible."

My eyes narrowed even as my heart started to kick around in my chest as the fear began to take hold again. I didn't want to think about that Origin, even though I had to.

One side of his lips tipped up. "Deal with it."

"You're annoying."

"It's a special talent of mine."

I cleared my throat as I peeked over at him. He was watching me from his super-comfy position on *my* bed. "So, the whole not glowing thing? Is that something I should be worried about?"

A shadow flickered over Luc's face. "Honestly?"

My stomach dipped. "Honestly."

"I don't know. You're human. You should have a trace." He shifted onto his side, propping his chin up with his fist. "Maybe you're an angel."

I blinked. "Come again?"

His grin crept across his face. "Because it's like you fell from heaven."

The tips of my ears burned. "Did you . . . seriously just say that out loud?"

"I did." He chuckled. "And I have more."

"Really?"

"Yep. Get ready for them. No woman or man can resist these," he said, biting down on that lip. A moment passed. "Life without you is like a broken pencil. Pointless."

I had no words.

"Struck speechless. Can't blame you. How about this one? Good thing I have my library card, because I'm so checking you out."

"Oh my God." I laughed. "That's terrible."

"As bad as this? You know what's on the menu?"

A smile tugged at my lips. "What?"

"*Me 'n' u,*" he replied.

I rolled my eyes.

"Did you just come out of the oven?" he asked.

"Oh God."

"Because you're hot."

"Please stop."

"Well, here I am. What are your other two wishes?" he replied.

I shook my head.

"I'm lost."

"Yeah, you are," I muttered.

He flicked my calf. "Can you give me directions to your heart?"

I shot him a withering look.

"You remind me of peaches. Sweet—"

"Don't even finish that sentence." I held up my hand. "I think it's time that you leave."

"I can't."

"What do you mean you can't?"

"Because you've swept me off my feet."

Letting out a reluctant laugh, I nudged his leg with my foot. I knew what he was doing. Distracting me from thinking things that were likely going to haunt my sleep tonight. "You seriously need to leave before I staple your mouth shut."

"Okay. I'll stop, but I'm staying until your mom gets home. Deal with it."

I started to protest, but then I thought about Heidi and Emery. Anxiety buzzed under my skin. "You think that guy is going to come here?"

"I don't want to take the chance." His eyes met mine. "I shouldn't have taken the chance in the first place. I'm not doing it again."

"If my mom catches you here—"

"I'll be gone the moment she walks into this house," he assured me. "She won't even know I'm here."

"I have the stun gun," I reminded him, nodding at the night-stand.

"I know, but I'm really hoping to prevent you from having to use it."

Letting Luc stay here wasn't particularly wise, but neither was ignoring a credible threat, and truth was, I . . . I really didn't want him to leave. Especially since that guy had gotten in here twice.

The fear I'd been trying to suppress all evening tore through me once more. My next breath went nowhere. *Keep it together.* I was safe. For now. And I could deal with this. After all, I'd dealt with the invasion. I'd survived that.

Luc's hand curved over mine, causing me to jerk. My eyes flew to his. "You know," he said, his gaze searching mine, "it's okay to be afraid."

A knot formed in the back of my throat. "Is it, really?"

"What do you mean?"

"I don't know." I lifted a shoulder. "Being afraid clouds your thinking. It gets in the way. It makes you weak."

"Sometimes. And sometimes it clears your thoughts and makes you stronger and quicker." His fingers slipped under mine and then he was holding my hand.

Flutters picked up in my chest, like a nest of butterflies stirring. I tried to stamp down the feeling, but it was there. I averted my gaze.

"Okay," I said finally.

Luc let go of me, then sat up and extended his hand. The TV remote flew from the desk to his palm. I really wished I had that talent.

I stayed quiet as Luc got himself situated, which somehow ended up with us shoulder to shoulder at the head of the bed. He turned on the TV. "I wonder if there are any Arnold Schwarzenegger movies on."

Slowly, I turned my head to him.

"What?" he asked.

"That's random."

"He's just so quotable," he reasoned, flipping through the channels.

I really couldn't respond to that and I really couldn't believe I was sitting here, next to Luc in bed while he searched for old Arnold Schwarzenegger movies.

Life was strange.

And I had a feeling it was about to get stranger.

24

When I woke several hours later, I was staring at the TV. Confusion swept through me. There was some kind of infomercial playing, but I couldn't figure out what it was since the volume was low.

The soft light from the TV cast flickering shadows throughout the bedroom. It was still nighttime, and I. . . .

Oh my God.

For the second time in only a handful of hours, I wasn't alone in a bed. I was lying on my back, and there was a warm, heavy arm tossed over my waist, and a leg—an actual boy leg—tangled between mine. My eyes went wide as they shifted from the TV to the ceiling, and my heart skyrocketed into uncharted territories.

Luc was right next to me, so close that I could feel his breath against my temple.

I remained very still, close to holding my breath.

How did this happen? I remembered Luc listing all the memorable Arnold Schwarzenegger lines, and there had been a lot, before he ended up settling on some crime show about murders. Totally a weird combination to fall asleep to, but I had, and here we were, together. At least we were on top the comforter, but I didn't think that made much of a difference.

At least Mom hadn't checked in on us, because I would've known if that happened. Her screams of rage would've woken me and—

Luc's entire body shifted.

It wasn't much, maybe just half an inch, but it was *everything*. His thigh shifted against mine, *between* mine, and his arm moved. Somehow, I didn't even know how, his hand was flat against my stomach. My bare stomach. His fingers moved in a small, unconscious way, dragging over the skin near my navel. I bit down on my lip as I squeezed my eyes shut.

I had no idea what to do. I should get up or wake him up. Do something, but I did nothing. I lay there as a sweet fire built under my skin, making it difficult to remember exactly why this was wrong, because it didn't feel that way. It felt *right*.

Every part of my body was aware of his. The strength in his hand, the hardness of his thigh, and the steady dancing of his breath, and we were lying together like we'd done this a thousand times.

Oh boy, I was wide-awake now.

He was a super-attractive guy, and I'd been through a lot. Had had my arm broken, and stuff—other stuff had happened. I was vulnerable to doing and thinking stupid things. Plus my hormones were kicking into high gear, shooting lightning through my veins. Yep. That was exactly why I was letting myself sink farther into his warmth.

I should really wake him up.

I should probably also run from the house with my arms flailing.

I didn't.

Luc moved, his hand sliding back across my stomach to curve around my waist. He squeezed, and then—*oh my*—he was pressing into me, pulling my shoulder to his chest, his leg to—

Oh gosh.

This sound came from him: a sleepy growl that sent shivers pounding down my spine. I kept my eyes closed, swallowing a sound that would have embarrassed me as his long, tapered fingers brushed the band of my leggings. His breath and then his lips coasted over my temple.

I knew the exact moment Luc woke up.

He stiffened against me. I didn't even think he breathed for a good half a minute. I didn't move, keeping my breath as deep and even as possible. I didn't want him to know I was awake—awake this whole time.

Which was probably pointless, since he could read my thoughts and could be doing that right at this very moment.

God, I hoped he wasn't.

Luc lifted his hand first, seemingly one finger at a time, and then he moved his leg. He stayed close though, for just a couple of moments. I waited, the tips of my fingers tingling. His breath drifted over my cheek. He seemed to hesitate, and then I felt his lips press against my forehead.

I stopped breathing, and my heart, well, my heart sort of imploded.

The mattress bounced slightly as Luc left the bed. I stayed completely still, my ears prickling until I heard the window slide open. Cold air seeped into the room, cut off as the window came back down. I heard the lock latch into place, and I didn't move for a good minute or two after that.

Luc had kissed my forehead.

That was . . . so sweet, and it made my heart feel all gooey, and that was dumb, because he was still in love with some dead girl, and I didn't even really like him. I mean, I did like him. He was kind of growing on me. Like mold—if mold was ripped and hard and hot and—

"Ugh," I groaned.

Okay. I needed to be real with myself. I *did* like him.

I rolled over and planted my face into the pillow and inhaled. Oh God. The pillow smelled like him. I flopped onto my back once more, letting out an aggravated curse.

I needed help.

Seriously.

I was running late for school—so late.

Having finally fallen back to sleep sometime close to dawn, I'd dozed right through my alarm. I ended up barely having time to shower, leaving only time enough to twist my hair up in a wet bun and to grab the cleanest pair of jeans I could find.

I saw that it was rainy and overcast, so I pulled a thin black thermal on over my head and then grabbed my backpack. On the way down the steps, I shoved up my sleeve to check my left arm.

The bruise was almost completely gone, having faded overnight into a pale blue mark. Still, my stomach dipped. The Origin had—

Wait. Dammit. I'd forgotten the stun gun.

Cursing under my breath, I ran back to the bedroom, snatched my new best friend off the nightstand, and shoved it into my bag. Once again, I was stomping down the steps. I was going to grab a granola bar and then break several speeding laws.

Mom was in the kitchen, sitting at the island. She held a mug in her hand, but she didn't look up as I zoomed past her, heading for the pantry. "Hey," I called out. "I'm running super-late. I just need to—"

"Slow down," she said. "There's no need to rush."

"Oh yes, there is." I threw open the pantry door. "I'm going to be so late, and that means I'll have to park all the way in the back of the school parking lot. I'm way too lazy to make that walk twice."

"Honey, we need to talk."

With the conversation with Luc so fresh, talking to her was the last thing I wanted to do at the moment. Hold up. Did she know about Luc being here last night? I slowly turned around, feeling like the fact that Luc had been in my bed—had kissed my forehead— was tattooed all over my face. "About what?"

She lowered her mug. "Why don't you put your bag down and have a seat?"

Unease blossomed in my stomach as the bag slipped from my shoulder to my elbow. "Why?"

"Evie, come have a seat."

I opened my mouth, but I finally noticed her—really looked at her. Mom hadn't showered yet. Her shoulder-length hair was secured with a barrette, and several strands had fallen free. Based on the wrinkled blouse and dark trousers, I wondered if she'd slept in her clothes from yesterday—or slept at all.

My mouth suddenly dried. "What's going on, Mom?"

Her brown eyes met mine and she seemed to pale before my eyes. "Come sit down."

For some reason I wasn't sure I wanted to hear what she had to say. Maybe it was instinct. "I have to get to school."

"Evelyn, we need to talk now."

I hitched up my bag, walking away from the pantry without grabbing a granola bar. I made my way to the island.

"Luc paid me a visit yesterday, while I was at work."

The bag slipped off my arm and hit the kitchen floor this time.

"How he got as close as he did unnoticed is beyond me." She took a sip of coffee. Her hand trembled, but her hands never shook. "I know what happened yesterday."

I stared at her from the other side of the kitchen island.

"He told me that you were attacked by an Origin and that he healed you," she added.

I felt dizzy. Well, now that confirmed my mom knew about the Origins, but I already knew that, didn't I? But why hadn't Luc mentioned this little meeting to me last night? He'd had ample time. Tons of time. I placed my hands on the island, but I felt like I was still moving.

The mug shook as she placed it back on the gray tile coaster. The coasters belonged to a set I'd gotten her for Mother's Day last year. "I really think you need to sit down."

My heart was pounding so fast, I thought I'd be sick. "I don't want to sit down."

Her face pinched as she briefly closed her eyes. "I'd hoped I would never have to have this conversation with you. I see now that was foolish. I should've known the moment Luc walked through that door that I was . . . that I was on borrowed time. I should've told you the truth then."

Pressure clamped down on my chest. "About what the Daedalus was really doing?"

The breath she took rattled her body. "I can see that you've been talking to Luc. It was bound to happen. After all, I expected as much. He told me the deal was off the day he brought your ID to me. I'm just shocked that he hasn't told you himself . . . but I knew. I could tell by the tiny changes in you. The Coke. The horror movies.

That wasn't something we expected. Then again, we'd never done what—"

"What does this have to do with a soda or a movie?" Tension seeped into every muscle. "What do you need to tell me? And are you going to be a hundred percent honest now?"

She flinched then, as if I'd cursed at her. "I need to tell you who you really are."

25

There was a buzzing in my ears, and the only thing grounding me was the cool granite under my palms. "What does that even mean?"

Mom tucked a thin strand of her hair back. "I want you to know that no matter what, I love you. I need you to remember that."

"What?" I stepped back from the island as my earlier anger seeped away, replaced by concern. "Why are you saying that? Are you sick?"

"I'm not sick," she said, drawing in a shaky breath. "Evie, there's no easy way to say this, so I'm just going to say it. I've only been your mother for the last four years. From what I know, the mother who bore you died when you were just a small child. A drug overdose."

My brows lifted. What in the hell? Something was really wrong with Mom.

"And before you came to me, you had a different name, a whole different life," she continued, her gaze slowly tracking over my face. "Your real name is not Evelyn Dasher."

"Okay." I bent down, picking up my bag as concern exploded in my gut. I reached into the front pocket for my phone. "We need to call someone. I don't know who, but there has to be—"

"We do not need to call anyone," she interrupted. "There is nothing wrong with me. I'm telling you the truth, honey."

"Mom—"

"Your real name is Nadine Holliday."

Every muscle in my body froze as the phone slipped from my fingers, falling back into the pocket. I lifted my gaze to hers.

"That was your name—*is* your name." Her upper lip thinned. "But you were called Nadia for short."

"No," I whispered. My brain sort of emptied of all thought. For several precious moments there was nothing in my head. Nothing but the buzzing, which was now louder and more incessant.

"That's what Luc called you. Nadia."

A jolt traveled through my system. *"No."*

"You were a very sick girl when I first met you. A blood cancer. And while some of the treatments we'd developed had been successful with less-invasive cancers, yours was very aggressive. You were dying, and Luc had tried many different things," she continued, even as I began to shake my head. "He knew that we—the Daedalus—had different serums, but nothing he'd been able to get his hands on had worked."

I backed up, bumping into the sink. This couldn't be real. I was dreaming. I had to be. That made more sense, because nothing she was saying was possible.

"Luc came after Jason. He was going to kill him for the things he'd done to . . . all those innocent people, but Jason . . . he knew about you. Jason knew you were dying, and he was ever the opportunist. He bartered his life for yours. There was a new serum that the Daedalus had just designed, right before the invasion. We / . . . we called it the Andromeda serum, and the Daedalus had amazing success with it. Jason offered the treatment in return for his life, and Luc . . ."

Her shoulders tensed as she exhaled roughly. "Luc was desperate. He had to be to let Jason live, because Jason had—" She cut herself off with a quick shake of her head. "Luc brought you here, just after the war with the invading Luxen ended. I met him in this room for the first time, in this kitchen. I met *you* for the first time that day. Jason had already told me what to bring."

Nothing she was saying made sense. We'd lived in Hagerstown before the invasion—

Hagerstown.

Luc had said Nadia had been from Hagerstown.

A shudder worked its way through me.

"You were so sick. Just this small thing struggling for every breath and heartbeat, and Luc was near rabid when it came to you. He would've sacrificed everyone around him if that meant you'd live, and he did. In a way, he sacrificed you. He knew there was a good chance what it meant if the Andromeda serum was successful—"

"Stop." I held up my hand as if I could ward off what she was saying. "Just stop. This is insane and impossible." I started around the island, having no idea where I needed to go, but knowing I just needed to get out of there.

I couldn't listen to this.

Mom rose from the stool, moving faster than I'd ever seen her do before. So fast, I jerked back with a gasp. She cradled my cheeks in her cool palms. "Listen to me, honey. You were given your Andromeda serum. That serum acted like a virus once inside your body. It attacked the cancer cells as it reshaped your genetic material, the very core of who you were. Like any virus, it causes a fever, an extremely high one. Most of our subjects we tested didn't even survive the fever, but I cared for you myself. I stayed by your side, day and night—"

"Stop it!" I shouted, trying to break free. "Why are you saying this stuff? Why are you doing this?"

Mom dropped her hands to my shoulders and gripped them, holding me in place with surprising strength. "You lost your memories, just like we told Luc would happen. It was the fever, but you survived it and you . . . became Evelyn."

Wrenching free of her grasp, I darted to the side. "Do you know how insane all of this sounds?"

"The Andromeda serum had alien DNA and now so do you," she continued. "Not enough to trigger a retinal scan or simple blood work unless extensive typing is done. That was why there was no trace when Luc healed you. That was why he came to me last night. He wanted to know what we—what I had done to you when I healed you."

"I have alien DNA in me?" I laughed.

Mom wasn't laughing. "You do."

"Oh my God." Another laugh burst out of me, sounding brittle. "This is absolutely nutty, and I don't even know what to say to you right now."

"It's the truth."

"No. It's some kind of joke I'm missing the punch line to." I started around the island again.

You're still so incredibly stubborn.

My throat threatened to seal up. I pushed Luc's words from my mind. "And I just need you to stop—"

"I need you to listen to me." Mom turned. "The moment you walked into that club, everything changed. Luc saw you and he's back in your life now. It's only a matter of time before he tells you the truth, and things are about to—" She took a deep breath. "You needed to hear this from me. Not him."

I spun around, facing her as my heart kicked against my ribs. "This is not real. You're telling me that I'm not Evie. That I'm this dead girl."

"Nadia never died."

"Yes, she did. Luc told me she did."

"Did he say those words exactly?" she asked. "Did Luc ever say that Nadia died?"

"He—" I snapped my mouth shut and then dragged my hands over my hips. Luc had never said that Nadia was dead. He only said that she was . . . that she was gone. Throat dry and stomach cramping, I kept backing up. "It doesn't matter what he said. It's not possible. I remember me. I—I know who I am. How do you explain that?"

"You don't remember, Evelyn. You just remember what I wanted you to," she replied quietly. "We can't implant memories, not yet, but the mind is an amazing thing. It's so susceptible to *impressions,* and that's what we did—what I did. When you woke up and after—after Jason was gone, it was just you and me, and I gave you the impression of Evelyn's life."

"Jesus." I smoothed a hand down my face. There was a good chance I was going to be sick. "I don't have *impressions*. I remember Dad and—"

"Tell me what Jason's voice sounded like," she demanded, coming around the island.

I opened my mouth, but I . . . I couldn't. I hadn't been able to in . . . I hadn't been able to. "He sounds like a guy," I said, blinking rapidly.

"Tell me what our old house looked like in Hagerstown?"

I knew what it looked like. The memories were there, but I was too overwhelmed to see the house in my mind. I had those memories; I knew I did. I just needed to concentrate.

Tears filled her eyes. "Tell me what I said to you the morning of the invasion and where did we go?"

"You—You told me that everything—" I squeezed my eyes shut. What had she said? Everything was a blur. "I was too panicked. I don't remember, but that means nothing."

"Honey, it means what it means. You weren't with me when the Luxen invaded. You were wherever Luc had you." She pressed her lips together. "There is not a single thing you can tell me about elementary school or your tenth birthday. What you have to pull from, the well you've drunk from these last four years, are stories I told you while you had the fever, while we cured you."

Panic started to dig in with razor-sharp claws. "How is that possible? How can you stand there and tell me that I have no memories, or that the ones I do have are fake? That's impossible. You're my mom and I'm Evie. That's who I've always been!"

Mom shook her head.

As I stared at her, a horrible, terrifying thought occurred to me. What if . . . what if she was telling the truth? There had been that weird sense of déjà vu when I first saw Luc in the club. There were all those times when Luc spoke as if he knew me. And the deal— he'd kept mentioning this deal.

Mom stopped in front of the island, placing her fist against her chest. "I'm still your mother. I am—"

"Stop," I demanded. "I just need you to stop. Please. Because this can't be real."

"It is." Her chest rose, and then she lifted her other hand to her eyes, making a pinching motion. When she lowered her hand, she dropped something on the island—two brown contacts.

My gaze flew to hers, and I gasped.

Mom's eyes weren't brown anymore. They were the color of the summer sky, before a storm. A vibrant, unnatural shade of blue.

"No," I whispered, shaking my head.

She smiled as tears tracked down her cheeks, and those tears disappeared as the veins under her skin filled with beautiful, luminous light. The glow spread, seeping into her skin and replacing the tissue. Within moments, she was fully encased in light.

Suddenly I remembered when Luc had come into the house and Mom had lifted her hand as if she was about to do something. Luc had dared her to do it. I hadn't understood then what was happening, but I did now.

Luc had known. . . .

He had known that Mom was a Luxen.

But she wasn't my mom—not my biological one. I knew that now. No matter how much I wanted to deny what she was telling me. I knew enough about the Luxen to know they couldn't have children that weren't Luxen.

"God." The room tilted. I felt faint, dizzy, and I couldn't deal with this. I couldn't process the truth that was *glowing* back at me. My feet were moving into the living room before I realized what I was doing or where I was going. Then I ran back into the kitchen and grabbed my bag off the island. I spun and went for the garage door.

"Honey!" she called out.

I stopped and looked. She was back to normal. Well, except for her eyes. They were still the eyes of the Luxen.

"Please," she said again, her eyes glistening. "Please just sit down and we will talk. We will—"

"No."

She took a step toward.

"Don't." My voice cracked. "Don't come near me."

She stopped.

My entire body trembled. "Just stay away from me."

I pulled the door open, stepped out, and smacked the button on the side of the wall. The garage door groaned open as I yanked the car door and tossed my bag onto the passenger seat. Muted daylight poured into the garage as I rounded the front of the car—of the Lexus that had belonged to Dad.

But he wasn't my dad.

Because if Mom wasn't my mom, then he wasn't my dad. . . .

But she was the only mom I knew, and I loved her. I *knew* her.

My hands were shaking as I climbed into the car. I started it as the garage door swung open. Mom stood there, calling my name, but I gunned the car in reverse. Tires squealed as I backed out of the driveway. I made it to the end of the driveway when movement out of the corner of my eyes caught my attention.

I slammed on the brakes and then looked to my left. "What the hell?"

A man strode across my front yard, a tall dark-haired one I recognized immediately. *Daemon*. What was he doing here? My gaze flew to the open garage and I saw Mom.

Daemon appeared at my driver's door, tapping on the window. I hadn't even seen him move. He was in the yard and then right there.

In a state of stunned disbelief, I rolled down the window.

He bent over, placing his hands on the open window. "Where you heading to? I doubt it's school."

I blinked once and then twice. Then it hit me. Daemon was here because of Luc, because of that Origin. Holy crap, how long had he been out here? I clenched the steering wheel as I stared into eyes that were impossibly green.

Mom was saying something as she walked forward, but I couldn't look away from the Luxen. I remembered the look on his face when he first saw me at the club. I remembered Luc quickly shutting him up, but Daemon had looked at me with surprise. I'd chalked it up to me being a human. . . .

"Do you know who I am?" My voice was hoarse, unfamiliar to my own ears.

An easy smile formed on his lips. "Why don't you turn the car off and step out? Go inside. Okay?"

"What is my name?" I asked, my knuckles aching from how tightly I was clenching the steering wheel.

Something flickered over his face. "Let's head inside. You shouldn't—"

"What is my name?" I shouted, my voice giving out on the last word.

"Hell," he muttered, glancing toward the garage. "Call Luc."

My stomach plummeted all the way to my toes. I didn't want them to call Luc. I didn't want them to do anything.

Pulling my foot off the brakes, I slammed my foot down on the gas pedal. Daemon cursed as he jerked back. The car flew out into the street, fishtailing. With my heart racing, I shoved the gear into drive and floored it. Wind and rain poured in through the open window as I sped through the subdivision.

None of this was true. It was too unbelievable to believe, too out there to even consider.

But Mom was a Luxen.

And she said I was that girl—that girl who Luc claimed had been his only true friend. The girl he'd admitted some ten hours ago he was still in love with.

That was the deal. I stayed away if you stayed away.

No.

No way.

I wasn't her.

My name was Evie.

That was who I was.

I passed the entrance as I dragged in deep, even breaths, hitting the open stretch of road.

My name is Evelyn Dasher.

Tears blurred my vision as I eased off the gas. *My mother's name is Sylvia Dasher. My father—*

Daemon suddenly appeared in the center of the road, several yards away. Screaming, I slammed on the brakes. The wheels lost traction on the rain-slick asphalt. The car spun out, and by some act of God, I didn't lose control. The Lexus coasted to a stop.

Dragging in deep, uneven breaths, I watched Daemon start toward me. My hands slipped off the steering wheel as emotion boiled up from deep within, like a shaken soda bottle. I smacked my hands over my face and opened my mouth to scream, but there was no sound. Nothing came out. I pressed my forehead against the steering wheel, my fingers curling into my skin. This couldn't be happening. This couldn't be real. I dropped my hands, clutching my knees as my stomach roiled.

I actually might get sick.

"That was fun," Daemon said, and then the door opened on its own accord. "But I need you to get out of the car."

Slowly, I lifted my head and numbly unhooked my seat belt. I stood on legs I couldn't feel as rain pelted me in the face.

"Come on." His voice was softer, and so was the sudden grip on my arm. He walked me around to the passenger side. "My job was to make sure you got to school safely. Been a while since I played bodyguard. Not doing a great job at it."

I got in the car. Before I could blink, Daemon was in the driver's seat, closing the door and rolling up the window. He shoved his hair, wet from the rain, back from his face.

My breath caught. "I don't want to go back there."

"If you don't go back there, then you're going to Luc." He looked over at me. "Those are the two choices."

I wanted a third choice—actually, I did want to see Luc. "The club."

"Sounds like a plan." The car started moving and he looked over at me. "Seat belt. The last thing I need right now is Luc losing his mind if you end up going through a window or something."

"You stepped out in front of the car," I reminded him as I buckled up. "That could've caused an accident."

"I made sure it didn't," he replied.

Go figure. It hadn't been my driving skills that had prevented a wreck. I looked out the window, not really seeing anything.

Maybe that woman back there wasn't my mom. Maybe a Luxen had assimilated her and she was pretending to be my mom.

Stop.

That was my mom. It sounded like her—smelled like her and talked like her. As much as I wanted to believe that wasn't her, it was. So did that mean what she claimed was true? That I wasn't Evelyn? That I was this other girl? That everything I'd known and believed . . . since, well, since I could remember, was a lie?

"You doing okay over there?" Daemon asked.

I closed my eyes against the burn. "Did you . . . did you know me before you saw me in the club?"

There was a long pause, so long that I didn't think Daemon was going to answer. And when he did, I wished he hadn't. "Yeah, I knew you."

I left Daemon in the hallway downstairs and climbed the six damn flights of steps. I went to Luc's door, closed my hand, and beat my fist off it like I was the police about to serve a warrant.

The door swung open and there was Luc. Hair damp like he'd just gotten out of the shower and still . . . painfully beautiful to look at.

Surprise washed over Luc's face as he stepped back, letting me inside the apartment. He closed the door behind him.

"Aren't you supposed to be at school?" He'd changed from last night. Gone was the Henley, and in its place was a black shirt. I was guessing Mom hadn't been able to get ahold of him. "Did something happen?"

I was never quite worthy of her—of her friendship, her acceptance and loyalty. . . .

Seeing him after what I'd learned this morning was like being smacked in the face and told it was a kiss. If what I had been told was true, he had been. . . . he had been—God, I didn't even know. But it was wrong. It was beyond wrong.

I'd asked Luc about Nadia last night, if he still loved her, and he'd said—

He'd said, *"With every breath I take."*

I didn't stop to think. I only acted.

My hand shot out and my palm smacked across his cheek with stinging force. His head snapped to the side and then swung back. Luc's pupils widened as horror gripped me.

I'd hit him.

I'd never hit anyone in my life.

And I didn't even feel bad about it.

Red blossomed along his cheek. "Was that for last night? Because I didn't leave before your mom got home?" He paused, eyes flashing. "Or was it because you lay there and pretended to be asleep while you wished I'd stayed?"

My hand cocked back again, but Luc was prepared this time. He caught my wrist and hauled me forward. Air pushed out of my lungs at the chest-to-chest contact.

"Hitting is not nice," he said, his voice steely. "Pretty sure they taught that in kindergarten, Evie."

"Evie?" I laughed, and it sounded even more wrong. Worse than brittle. It sounded near hysterical.

His brows knitted and then smoothed out as understanding seeped in. His mouth opened, but he didn't speak as he dropped my wrist as if my skin burned his.

Words festered and finally boiled over as I stumbled back a step and kept going, until my back hit the door. "Why didn't you tell me you saw my m-mom yesterday?" My voice cracked on that one, powerful word. "When you were with me last night, why didn't you tell me you'd talked to her?"

He started toward me, his long-legged pace eating up the short distance.

"Don't," I said, voice barely above a whisper. "Don't come near me, Luc."

He halted, his amethyst eyes wide and endless. "What did she tell you?"

"Oh, let's see. She explained that she didn't give birth to me. Apparently my birth mom died of an overdose? Now, if I was simply adopted, that wouldn't be a big deal, because a mother isn't always by blood." I dragged my hand over my hair, smoothing the strands down. The bun had slipped and was falling free. "But according to her, she's only been my mom for about four years, and that's kind of a big deal."

Luc's hands closed at his sides.

"And you know? I didn't believe her, because that sounds bananas, but then she turned into a Luxen. Right in front of me."

He closed his eyes.

A knot expanded in my throat and moved to my chest. "But you already knew what she was. Didn't you?"

He didn't answer.

"Didn't you?" I shouted, hearing my voice snap.

Lashes lifted. "I knew."

"Of course you did. And you know what else she told me this morning? She told me why I didn't have a trace on me. Because supposedly I was given some kind of weird serum," I said, swallowing against the knot. "But you know that, too."

"Damn her." Exhaling heavily, Luc walked away from the door and sat on the edge of the couch. "I didn't know she was going to tell you. If I had, I would've been there."

Knots formed in my stomach, twisting up my insides. He said that like he meant it, and a distant part of me knew he spoke the truth.

"Been there for what, Luc? Were you going to be there and hold my hand while she told me that whatever memories I think I have, I don't? Were you going to share coffee with her while she told me that my name isn't Evelyn Dasher?"

He looked like he wanted to get up, but he stayed put. "I would've been there to make sure you were okay. Helped you understand who you—"

"Don't say I'm not Evelyn. That is who I am." My voice warbled. "My name is Evie."

"I know." He softened his voice. "You're Evie."

My muscles tensed. "So, let's say that this isn't some kind of dream and it's real. Why didn't you tell me the truth? You had chances. Especially when you told me about her—about what happened. You could've told me then."

"I could've." His gaze searched mine. "But would you have believed me? Honestly? If I told you that you were really Nadia Holliday, but your memories were wiped, would you have listened to me or walked away?"

I inhaled raggedly. Truth was, I wouldn't have believed him. I was having a hard time believing . . . Mom. Closing my eyes, I shook my head. "If it's true, why did you leave me there—leave me with them? I was supposed to be your bestest friend in the whole world. You said you lo—" Unable to finish that, I opened my eyes again. "Why would you leave me with them?"

His pupils turned white. "I never really left you."

26

Pressure squeezed my chest. Denial was the best defense against the confusion and raw pain springing forth inside me. My mouth moved for a good half a minute without words, and then finally, I said the only thing suitable: "Is this a joke? A really bad joke that—"

"It's not a joke." His voice turned hoarse. "I made a deal with them to save your life. It was the worst and the best decision. Worst because I am incredibly selfish. And best because I had to do something incredibly unselfish."

"I don't—"

"You don't remember. I know. But I remember. I remember everything every damn day of my life."

I stared at him. "Don't say that."

His eyes burned bright. "Did you come here, hoping I'd lie to you now?" He rose then. "I'm done lying. You want the truth? Here it is. I never stopped thinking about you. I never forgot. I never stopped looking out for you. You forgot me, and that's okay, because you had no choice, but—"

"Stop it!" I shouted. "I know who I am. My name is Evie. That has *always* been my name."

Luc shot forward, gripping my shoulders. "Listen to me. You are Evie now, but you've only been Evelyn Dasher for about twelve hundred and seventy-eight days and about roughly eight hours, and yeah, I could tell you the seconds if you want to get really detailed."

My lips parted.

"But you were Nadia for nearly thirteen years prior to that."

"Stop saying that." I wiggled my arms free, stepping back. "The memories I have right now aren't fake." I curled my hands into fists. "They are real—"

"You prefer Coke over Pepsi. How do you think I knew to give you one?"

The image of Mom—of her reaction when I'd asked for a Coke—formed in my thoughts, as did what she'd said earlier. I always drank Pepsi, because . . . that was what had always been in the house. . . .

"That's the funny thing about what they did to you. They wiped your memories, but there are still these innate personality traits there. There are still parts of you." He crossed the distance between us. "I know you like horror movies and hate the ones that make you cry."

"Congrats, did you look at my Facebook profile?" I snapped.

Luc grinned, undaunted. "You were always interested in photography, even before. You used to whine until Paris would take you to the Potomac River so you could take pictures."

"I don't even know who Paris is."

"You did, though. He was like a father to you." Luc kept going. "You have the same nervous twitch."

I drew back, scowling. "I don't have a nervous twitch."

"Yeah, you do. You rub your hands on your hips and knees when you're anxious." He arched a brow. "You're doing it right now."

I pulled my hands off my hips and then folded my arms across my chest.

"Do you still want me to keep going? You constantly mess with your hair. It's another thing you do when you're nervous or don't know what to do with your hands." He stepped in, tilting his head to the side. "I know you don't like pizza."

My heart flopped over as I stared at him. "Heidi told you that."

"No." Bending so his cheek brushed mine, he said, "But I'm right, aren't I?"

He was, but I couldn't answer.

Luc lingered close, too close, his cheek just touching mine.

"Here's something you don't remember and Sylvia couldn't have known." A heartbeat passed. "You were my first kiss."

I gasped.

"Granted, we were kids, so it wasn't much of a kiss." He drew back, the bridge of his nose dragging over my cheek. "It was my favorite kiss."

I squeezed my eyes shut.

Luc's voice was low. "And I stayed away like I promised Sylvia, because I knew if I didn't, I wouldn't be able to walk away. I stayed close, but I never went near you. I never went *looking* for you. You were why I left those Origins with Daemon and them. I couldn't leave you here by yourself. Not for years," he continued. "You have always been the only priority to me that mattered."

The floor felt like it was shifting under me.

I remembered moving into the house in Columbia, and I remembered my first sleepover and the first crush I had and those memories—

Those memories were all wispy and smoky, existing on the fringes of my consciousness, and as I tried to pull them forth, they slipped out of my grasp.

Had they always been like that?

Oh my God, I didn't know, because I never really thought back in detail. I didn't think beyond the invasion—

I remembered that, though. I remembered the fear and I remembered the way things were before, but . . .

Panic dug in deep, and I sidestepped Luc.

"You don't have clear memories because they aren't real memories," he said softly. "And you never questioned it, because you had no real reason to."

"Stop it," I hissed, spinning toward him. "Stay out of my head."

"Kind of hard to right now."

I dragged my hands over my hips and then stopped when he shot me a pointed look. What Luc was saying was too much to believe—having this entire life I couldn't remember, dying and being given a second identity.

I lifted my chin. "So I'm your long-lost BFF forever and I was given some kind of super-serum that not only healed me, it wiped my memory and implanted false impressions but somehow doesn't stop me from breaking out in pimples at least once a month?"

He frowned. "Well, yeah and no. The fever stole your memories. Not the serum."

"But why did you leave me?" I cried out, surprising myself with the rawness behind the question.

"Do you think I wanted to?" he shouted back, startling me. His features sharpened. "I never trusted Sylvia or Jason and they didn't trust me, but I . . . I was desperate, and you had agreed. 'One more chance.' That's what you said to me, because I'd already given you all these other serums and they didn't work. Then you made me promise to let it go if it didn't work. You made me promise to let you go so the end would be *peaceful*." His voice caught, broke a little. "And I agreed."

Hearing him say these things, talk about decisions I'd supposedly made as this . . . this Nadia girl was beyond unnerving.

"Jason knew I was coming after him. So he came to me first. He bartered for his life. He offered to heal you, but I had to stay away. I had some big issues with Jason, as he did with me, but it was more than that. The cure came with a deal. . . ." A muscle began to tick along his jaw. "I would have to give you up. Walk away from you, from the only real friend I had, from the only person I'd ever truly trusted. The only person I ever . . ." Trailing off, he shook his head. "I made the deal. I would walk away and I would stay away if you were safe. I agreed. You agreed to it, but you . . . didn't know you wouldn't remember me or anything. I knew if I told you that, you wouldn't do it."

I moved backward and then shook my head again, not wanting to hear what he was saying but knowing I couldn't stop him.

"I agreed to their terms, but I stayed close to make sure you were okay and that nothing strange was happening to you."

"And yet you still left me with people you didn't even trust?"

Luc flinched—actually flinched. "Like I said, I was desperate, but that wasn't part of the original agreement."

"What was supposed to happen to me once they wiped my memory and healed me?" I laughed harshly.

"You were supposed to be placed with a family, but as I left the house the day you woke up from the fever, the esteemed Jason Dasher tried to renege on the deal. He attempted to kill me."

My breath caught as the trembling throughout my body picked up. "Did you . . . Did you kill him?"

His jaw hardened. "That's what some think. I might've even let people believe it, but I didn't."

I couldn't look away from him. My mind leapt to the conclusion. "Are you saying . . . ?"

"Sylvia killed him. She was there when he tried to do me in. She took him out. That's why I let you stay with her."

Holy crap.

"This is too much." Lifting my hands halfway, I stopped, because I had no idea what I was doing with them.

"Sylvia promised me that she would give you a good life, that no matter what happened, she would keep you safe, and she did. I made that deal and she honored it. I know, because I never really left. I always knew you were okay."

"You . . . kept tabs on me?"

Luc didn't deny it.

"Christ." I gasped, unable to even comprehend it. "This just keeps getting worse."

A muscle flexed along his jaw. A long moment passed. "If I had to do it all over, I would. Without a fucking doubt, I would do it again, because the only other option would be that you wouldn't be standing in front of me—pissed off, but breathing. Alive and so damn beautiful that it sometimes kills me a little each time I look at you."

I stared at him, and even though every part of my being wanted to deny what he was saying, what I'd learned today, I saw the truth in his tense expression. I saw it in the way he dragged in a heavy breath, and I saw it when I talked to *her*. To *Mom*. The truth had been in her tears.

I sagged, leaning against the wall. My skin felt stretched too thin. Oh God, this was true. This was real, but . . . "I'm not her anymore." Tears clogged my throat. "I'm not Nadia. My name is Evie."

His gaze met mine. "I *know*. She's gone," he said again. "And you are here."

I . . . I couldn't deal with this.

I had to get out of there. I needed time. I needed space. My body trembling, I pushed off the wall and walked to the door.

"Where are you going?" he asked, his voice hoarse.

"I don't know, but I'm sure you'll find out, right?" I looked over my shoulder at him. "You'll have someone follow me. I just don't want it to be you. I want you . . . I want you to stay away from me." I turned and opened the door. "I wish . . . I wish I never came to this club."

27

I didn't go home.

I didn't go to the park.

I drove and drove until I couldn't concentrate any longer. Even though my life was hot mess express at the moment, I really didn't want to accidentally take out a family of four. I pulled into a shopping center and turned off the car. I let my head fall back against the seat.

Yesterday I'd been worried about some kind of psychotic Origin out to kill me, and today my entire life had imploded.

I stared at the ceiling. "How is this possible?"

None of it sounded like it could be, but why would *she* lie and why would Luc lie? What did they have to gain by telling me that my entire life was one big fat façade?

They wouldn't.

A huge part of me knew that it was the truth. There was nothing to gain by the lies. Nothing.

When I'd felt like the world was on the verge of imploding, I hadn't realized it was *my* world that had been hours away from self-destructing.

I squeezed my eyes shut. "My name is Evelyn. My name is . . ."

I couldn't remember what it was like to be a kid. In the quiet, I searched and searched my memories. There were glimpses of running and laughing, the scent of wet soil and the sound of rushing water, but nothing concrete. How had I not noticed that before? Could it be as simple as what Luc had said? That I hadn't noticed, because I simply hadn't thought to?

Sounded unreal, but it wasn't like I'd spent time each day reminiscing about the good old days or something.

My phone rang, jarring in the silence.

I reached into my bag and pulled the phone out. Heidi. I started to answer the call but stopped. Luc could've told Emery what had happened. Or it could just be that I wasn't in class and Heidi had snuck out into the hall to call me. Either way, she was too close to Luc.

Too close to *everything*.

I silenced the phone and then saw there were several missed calls and texts. One from *her*. Several from Zoe and Heidi. A text from James. I dropped my phone back into the bag. Did Heidi know what Luc had told me? It was possible. He could've told Emery and she could've confided in Heidi.

The back of my throat burned as I lowered my head to the steering wheel. I fought back tears as I closed my hands into fists, pulling my elbows into my stomach. The movement didn't even hurt my arm.

My arm that had been broken less than twenty-four hours ago.

I would do it again, because the only other option would be that you wouldn't be standing in front of me.

"Oh God," I whispered, a sob racking my body, but I didn't let the tears fall. I refused to.

My phone rang again. Cursing, I grabbed it and was a second from pitching it through a window, but saw that it was Zoe. I stared at the picture of us. We were making duck faces in our selfie.

She had nothing to do with this or Luc.

I answered, croaking out, "Hello?"

"Evie! God." Her voice was hushed. "Where are you?"

I glanced out the window. "I'm outside of a Target. Where are you?"

"I'm hiding in the bathroom at school, calling you. Is there a reason why you're there and not at school?" she asked. "Your mom called Heidi this morning, asking if you came to school."

Mom.

"We waited until lunch to see if you would show up, but when you didn't and then didn't answer any of our calls, we started to get really freaked," she said. "You know, considering how class-mates are disappearing left and right."

I should have thought about that.

"Especially since I heard someone say some guy jumped you in the parking lot after school. Heidi said that wasn't true, but I'm not so sure."

"That's not true." I didn't want her to worry. "I'm fine."

There was a beat of silence. "If you're fine, why aren't you at school?"

I pushed my hair back. "Mom and I—We got into this huge fight this morning. I just couldn't go to school."

"About what?" she asked.

I pressed my lips together as I blinked back hot tears. "Noth-ing." I cleared my throat. "It's nothing. Look, I haven't eaten. I'm going to grab something at Target."

"Wait—I can leave school and come meet you."

"That's not necessary. I'm okay."

"Evie—"

I winced at the sound of my name. "I'm fine. Seriously. Go back to class. I'll text you later."

Not giving her a chance to argue, I hung up the phone. I sat there for a couple of moments, and then a sudden, shattering thought occurred to me.

Who the hell is Evelyn Dasher then?

Better yet, did she even exist?

Thirty minutes later I walked back into my house. It was empty and quiet. Her car was gone. Wasn't exactly surprised. Knowing her, she was probably at work.

I stopped in the middle of the living room. Actually, I didn't know her. At all. I just knew what she let me see, which was a lie.

I picked up the wooden candleholder, the really nice gray-and-white one that I still hadn't taken a picture of. I walked over to the office doors and slammed the heavy base through the square window by the lock. Glass shattered, pinging off the floor.

The sound was frighteningly satisfying.

Reaching inside the gap, I unlocked the door. It swung open with a rush of cold air. I stepped into the room, seeing it for the first time.

Looked like any normal office. Built-in bookshelves lined with medical tomes. A neat, dark cherry oak desk with a desktop computer sitting next to a large desk calendar. There were bins—organizing bins everywhere, under the window seat and on the bookshelves.

I stalked toward the nearest one, a gray cloth bin under the window seat. Bending down, I picked it up and peeled the lid off, dumping the contents onto the floor. Receipts fluttered. Hundreds of them. I grabbed the next bin and it was heavier. I turned it upside down, and envelopes fell out, along with a black handgun.

The gun thumped off the floor.

"Jesus," I muttered, leaving the gun where it fell. I stepped over it and got to work. Every bin came down. Every single one, and there was nothing—not a damn thing in any of them who told me who Evelyn Dasher was or if she ever existed.

Not until I pulled open the bottom drawer of the desk, which took using a hammer I'd found in the garage and prying it open. In the process, wood splintered, and I really didn't care.

A photo album.

I found myself staring down at a freaking photo album.

There supposedly hadn't been any that had survived the invasion. That was what I'd been told. That was what I'd believed to be the truth. Surprise, surprise. That was also a damn lie.

I dropped the hammer onto the floor and then snatched up the photo album and carried it over to the window. I sat down and yelped. I stood and ripped the cushion back.

Another shotgun.

"Are you freaking kidding me?" I picked it up and propped it against the wall. Then I sat back down. "Geez."

Drawing in a deep breath, I cracked open the photo album and there, right on the first page, was a photo of my *mom* and who I knew immediately to be Jason Dasher. They were younger, probably in their twenties. He was in a full military uniform with awards and shiny things on his breast and shoulder. She wore a pretty white dress and had flowers in her hair.

She wasn't wearing contacts.

Her eyes were as blue as they'd been this morning.

Hands shaking, I flipped the glossy pages. There were more pictures of them, in places that appeared to be far from here. Tropical, I was guessing, based on the palm trees. There were a few of her in what appeared to be army greens. Candid snapshots taken of them both, and it was evident that there had been a relationship between them. I didn't know how many pictures I'd flipped past before I saw her.

Evelyn Dasher was real.

It was the three of them.

Jason and Sylvia Dasher stood behind a girl who had to be about nine or ten, give or take a year or so. Both had their hands on her shoulders. Peeling back the clear film, I pulled the picture out.

She had a cherub face—round with big cheeks. Freckles like me. Long blond hair. Brown eyes.

"Holy Christ," I whispered. She looked like me. That was like climbing the Mount Everest of messed up and sticking a freak flag on the top of it.

I couldn't believe what I was seeing.

Was this why the door to her office was always locked?

I put the picture aside and kept turning the pages. There were more pictures—a birthday party with a cake. There was a number eight candle in the middle of it. There were first-day-of-school pictures—photos with her in a frilly blue dress and black shoes. In between the pages, there were blank sheets—sheets where there had to have been photos once, because perfect square white marks stood out in stark contrast against the faded yellow of the rest of the page.

I came upon another birthday picture. She had this little cone-shaped hat on and she was smiling so brightly at the camera. There was another cake, and the man crouched next to her was him: the man whose face I couldn't remember, whose voice I couldn't hear.

But that wasn't the part of the picture that was an undeniable stab to the chest.

Behind her, hanging from the ceiling, was a sparkling banner. It had unicorns on either side of the words—words that spelled out HAPPY BIRTHDAY, EVELYN.

Evelyn.

That wasn't me.

She looked like me, like we could be cousins, but that wasn't me.

All these photos, and none of you as a kid.

Luc had said that to me. Luc had said so much. My hand trembled as the picture blurred. How was I supposed to . . . How was I supposed to process this?

How was I supposed to understand this?

That I was holding a picture of Evelyn Dasher and she wasn't . . . wasn't me.

28

H ere." James thrust a red cup in front of my face. "Looks like you could use this."

Catching the strong scent of alcohol, I frowned. "What's in this?"

"Just try it." James plopped down on a lounge chair, stretching his legs out. "Trust me. Whatever you got going on right now that you absolutely refuse to talk about, this will definitely take your mind off of it."

My mind was off of *it,* because I just wasn't going to deal with it at this moment. Nope. I was Captain Nope at the moment.

I'd left the photo album and that picture of the three of them on the window seat and walked out of the house. By then, school was over and I called the one person who I was rarely tempted to confide in.

James.

I'd forgotten all about Coop's party until James told me to meet him there.

So here I was, sitting by a pool like my entire life hadn't blown up this morning, pretending I hadn't seen Grayson in my rearview mirror as I parked. I ignored him and he ignored me. Perfect.

I had no idea what I was going to do tonight, but I didn't want to go home. I peeked at James. He'd probably let me stay at his place, sneak me in right under his parents' noses.

But that would be kind of weird.

Hearing the laughter and shouts and the steady thump of music coming from inside the house was also kind of weird after everything that had happened.

I took a drink and immediately regretted it. Fire poured down my throat and hit my nearly empty stomach.

"What's in this drink?" I asked again, flapping one hand in front of my face.

James chuckled as water splashed over the pool patio, drawing my attention. It didn't feel warm enough to swim, but that hadn't stopped anyone. Neither did the lack of bathing suits. I was seeing waaay more than I ever needed to.

I sat beside his legs, to stay out of the reach of the cold water.

"A little of this and a little of that."

I frowned. "It tastes like gasoline—gasoline on fire."

"It's not that bad."

Pressing my lips together, I shook my head and then leaned over his legs, placing my cup on the table. "It's bad."

"You're such a lightweight." He knocked his foot against my hip. "Drink up."

"Nah. I think I'll pass." I folded my arms in my lap. "I'm driving."

"You could always crash here," he suggested. "Half the people here will."

I shook my head as my gaze crawled back to the pool. I saw April standing on the other side, her arms across her chest as her mouth appeared to be moving a mile a minute. A small group surrounded her, obviously enraptured by whatever hateful crap she was spewing.

I dragged my gaze from her, to those in the pool. So many smiling faces. It was almost like Colleen and Amanda hadn't died. Okay. Maybe that wasn't fair.

Or maybe they were just having fun, letting loose to remind themselves that they were very much still alive. My gaze dropped to the cup, but whatever the hell devil mix that drink was wasn't going to prove that I was alive—that I was real and not a fraud. If I drank, it would probably make it worse.

What was I going to do?

Could I go home and go to bed, wake up tomorrow and pretend everything was okay? How could I?

"Can I ask you something?"

"Sure," James replied.

I exhaled roughly. "What would you do if you found out you weren't really James?"

"What?" He laughed.

It sounded stupid. "Never mind."

He stared at me a moment and then sat up. "Like if I found out I was adopted or something?"

Yeah, no. That was not what I was going for, because this was nothing like finding out you were adopted. I would've been cool with that. Shocked. But cool. I lifted a shoulder.

"That's not what you're asking." He dropped his feet to the patio next to mine. "You mean if I found out I wasn't *me*?"

"Yeah," I whispered.

His brows furrowed in the flickering light from a nearby tiki torch. "Why are you asking something like that?"

"I don't know." I feigned casual indifference. "Just something I read about online earlier. You know, one of those . . . kidnap stories." Man, I was proud of how fast I'd come up with that. "Where a kid was taken at a young age and was basically given a whole new identity."

"Oh." He scrunched his fingers through his hair. "I guess I would want to figure out who I was and why I was taken. I'd hope there'd be a good reason for it. Not something creepy." He paused. "Though I doubt there's ever a non-creepy reason for taking a child."

I hadn't been taken.

I'd been given away . . . to be saved.

Swallowing hard, I let my head fall back. The stars were out in full force, blanketing the sky. Somewhere up there was where the Luxen had come from. Crazy.

"Evie?"

I sucked in a sharp breath and then shook out my shoulders. "Yeah?"

"Are you okay?"

"I'm perfect. Just in a weird mood." Time to get moving before

I did something stupid, like blurting out everything, for example. I stood, needing to use the bathroom. "I'll be back."

"You better."

Waving my hand, I turned and made my way around the pool and across the deck, entering the back of the house. The kitchen was packed, and the air was sticky, smelling of perfume and spilled beer.

Coop's parties were popular, so people were everywhere. I had no idea what his parents did for a living, but they were never home on the weekends, and their house was huge. Unfortunately, there was a line for the downstairs bathroom, so I crossed what I thought was a marble floor and held on tight to the railing as I climbed a set of stairs.

I wasn't at all surprised to see that the upstairs hallway wasn't vacant. I turned sideways and slid past a couple who looked like they were literally seconds away from making a baby right then and there, and two girls who appeared to be on the verge of vomiting all over the place. Yikes.

Wait.

I stopped and looked over my shoulder. Was that guy Coop? From what I could see of his fair head and face, I was pretty sure that was him. It was his house. Why wasn't he in, I don't know, his bedroom? For a moment I was filled with such envy. I wanted to be him. Well, not him. Just anyone who honestly didn't find out that they were some dead girl.

Well, Nadia hadn't died. That was the whole point of all of this. Right? I shook my head and started walking again.

"Bathroom. Bathroom," I murmured, keeping my arms folded tightly across my chest. "If I was a bathroom, where would I be?"

Probably somewhere far, far away from here.

Passing a few doors that were cracked open, I spied a closed one at the end of the hall that I figured had to be a bathroom. I picked up my pace, thinking I might not make it. Thankfully I did because it *was* a bathroom. A few moments later, I was washing my hands.

Drying my hands with a nearby towel, I looked up at my reflection. My cheeks were a little flushed. It was my face. My hair.

My eyes. My mouth. I was Evie, because . . . because I'd been told I was her. I closed my eyes.

What was I going to do?

I couldn't stay in the bathroom all night. Though at least that would be a plan. I opened my eyes again and pushed away from the vanity. I opened the door and stepped back out into the hall-way. Coop and whoever he was practically eating the face off of were still at the end of the hall, completely oblivious to me. The green-around-the-gills girls were gone, though. I'd started walk-ing, making it halfway down the hall, when I heard a voice.

Zoe.

"I don't think you should be here right now," she was saying.

What in the hell? I stopped. Zoe never came to these parties. Ever. What was she doing here?

Placing a hand against the wall, I strained to hear what she was saying and who she was talking to.

"It's probably best you just take a step back," she continued. "Give it time. This is a big deal and we have it covered."

I held my breath, waiting to hear a response.

And it came in the form of a deep, slightly melodic tone that was familiar—too familiar. "I've done nothing but give it time."

My breath stalled in my chest, and for a brief second my brain completely emptied. It was like a switch had been thrown, suck-ing all thoughts right out of my head. I knew that voice. It made no sense, but I *knew* that voice.

It was *Luc*.

"I know," Zoe replied softly.

Oh my God, Zoe was talking to Luc.

I didn't even know where to start with this. Luc had never men-tioned Zoe, and vice versa, and I'd talked to her about him before. Why wouldn't she tell me that she knew him?

Why wouldn't Luc . . . ?

A chill moved down my spine as I pushed away from the wall. There was only one reason why she wouldn't have told me. I stepped in front of the door and slammed my fist into it, knocking it wide open.

"Hi!" I chirped, stalking into the bedroom. "Funny to see you two here."

Shock splashed over Luc's face, and seeing that would've been funny under any other circumstances. "Shit."

My entire body was shaking as I focused on Zoe. Her eyes were so big, they could've popped out of her face. "So I'm guessing this friendship isn't a recent one, is it?"

Zoe stepped forward. "Evie—"

"Are you sure that's the name you want to use?"

Her pretty face tensed.

The door swung shut behind me, and my narrowed gaze zeroed in on Luc. "I want to know what the hell is going on, because I'm literally this close to flipping the hell out. And I mean a full-on flip-out that's going to draw a lot of attention."

"We're here because you are." It was Zoe who spoke. "Things are a little dangerous right now, with the Origin—"

"I don't care about him." My hands closed into fists as I zeroed in on Luc. "I don't care about any of that right now. I told you—"

"I know what you told me," he said, features sharp. "But I'm not going to leave you unprotected until I know it's safe for you."

"Grayson followed me here. So I'm not unprotected, and there is no reason for you to be here. Or is there?"

Luc's jaw locked down. "We can explain everything, but I think we should go someplace else first."

I was breathing heavy. "We're not going anywhere. I want to know why you two are in here talking!"

"Because I'm what he is," Zoe replied, and then for the second time in one day, I watched someone pull out contacts. Zoe's eyes were the same shade as Luc's.

My mouth dropped open.

What felt like an entire minute passed before I could speak. "Are you freaking kidding me? Is there not a single person around me who hasn't lied to me? My mother. Heidi. Him." I stabbed my finger in his general direction. "And now you?"

"Heidi?" Zoe asked, her brows knitting.

"The whole Emery-being-a-Luxen thing."

"Oh," she said, blinking. "Heidi hasn't told me that. She doesn't know what I am or that I know Emery."

I threw up my hands. "Is that supposed to make this better?"

"No." She cringed. "But it's not like an everyone-knew-but-you kind of thing."

Luc took a step forward. "Evie—"

"You. Shut up."

He shut up, but he did not look happy about it.

"And you? You're an Origin?" When she nodded, I laughed and it was scary sounding. "I thought all the Origins—"

"I told you that some were still around." Luc knew where I was going with that. "I told you that some were okay."

I couldn't even deal with all that. I refocused on Zoe. "And you've known Luc for how long?"

"A little longer than you," she replied, clasping her hands in front of her. "And I don't mean as Evie. I've known both of you about the same length of time."

Floored, all I could do was stare. "What?"

"I don't think this is the place for this." Luc's voice was gentle. "You've been through a lot today."

Pressure clamped down on my lungs as I turned to Zoe. "What does that mean, Zoe?"

Her face contorted with sympathy, and that—*that* terrified me. "I knew you before you were Evie."

"What?" I screeched, my hands opening at my sides.

She nodded. "I met you three or four times, whenever I'd see Luc after he . . . Well, that's a long story. But the three of us? We used to play Mario Bros. together."

"I always won," Luc felt the need to add at that moment.

"And when you . . . you became Evie and you stayed with Sylvia, that's when I came to Columbia," she explained. "Luc couldn't be around you. That was the deal he'd made, but that deal didn't extend to me."

My mouth dropped open and my legs almost gave out on me.

"Are you saying . . . are you saying you purposely became friends with me so you could watch over me? That—"

"No," she was quick to insist. "We knew each other before. We were friends. Not extremely close, but you liked me."

Luc nodded. "You liked her. You . . . you liked everyone. Even Archer. You don't remember this, but you met him the first time he was out in the real world, and was incredibly socially awkward. You ate breadsticks with him."

I remembered Archer from the club. Not the Archer I . . . ate breadsticks with.

"I don't think that's helping, Luc," Zoe said.

There were several long moments where I didn't know if I wanted to laugh or cry. Or scream. Screaming until my voice went hoarse sounded like a good plan at this point.

"When you called me today, while you were at school, you . . . you knew what happened today?" My voice shook.

"Luc called and gave me a heads-up," she admitted. "I should've said something right then. I was going to. I swear. But I didn't want to do it over the phone."

"Yeah, because doing it in person is easier." I took a breath, but it didn't help the sudden dizzy feeling. "This is why you never came around my house when my mom was home, isn't it?"

She had the decency to look sheepish. "I couldn't risk her realizing what I was."

"Because you always knew she was a Luxen?"

Zoe nodded.

Staring at them, I didn't really see them. Not anymore. "I . . . I need space right now."

"I understand that, but—"

"You don't understand that," I cut Zoe off. "How could you possibly understand this—any of this?"

She started to speak, but I couldn't be in that room any longer. I couldn't be around either of them. This was too much. My legs stared moving, and I pivoted, relieved when I found that the door was open for me.

I bumped into the couple, drawing them apart. I murmured an apology and hurried through the hall. My heart was racing as I went down the spiral staircase, and I felt—oh my God, I felt sick. Like I might hurl.

Hurt brimmed to the surface as I pushed past the dancing bodies, making a beeline for the door. I couldn't deal with this. It was too much. Disappointment curled low in my stomach, slushing through my veins like muddy water.

Zoe was my most logical friend. She was the one who I always trusted to stop me from doing something stupid, and she was the last person I'd ever expected to be lying to me.

Skirting the edge of the packed pool, I ignored my name being called out and kept walking. I pushed open the gate and stalked down the driveway, my hands curling into fists yet again. Reaching the road, I drew up short and ended up staring at the dark houses across the street. "Where in the hell did I park?"

Way down the block.

I had no idea where I was going. I was just going. Maybe get on the interstate and head west, keep driving until I ran out of gas. I figured—

Evie . . .

Tiny hairs rose all over my body. My name. I heard my name, but it hadn't been—It didn't sound like it had been out loud. More like it had been in my head, but that made no sense.

Okay.

I had been through a lot in the last twenty-four hours. Attacked. Had my arm broken and healed. Found out I wasn't even Evie. So I shouldn't be surprised that I was hearing voices. That seemed like the most expected thing to be happening.

Evie . . .

There it was again. I stopped, frowning. What in the world?

Slowly, I turned around even as every part of my being screamed that I should hightail my behind right back to the party, but that wasn't what I did. I stepped out onto the sidewalk. "Hello?"

I scanned the street and sidewalk, seeing nothing but cars. I walked toward the corner, sticking close to the large retaining wall. I reached the corner and looked around. Nothing. Nothing at all . . . My gaze dropped.

Something was lying there. Like a bundle of clothing. I stepped closer, squinting. The streetlamps cast a dim glow, and I knelt down. The clothing looked rumpled, but there was a shape to it. I breathed in sharply and there was the scent of . . . of burnt flesh.

I jerked back and stumbled to the side. That wasn't just clothes. Oh my God, that wasn't just clothes at all. Two legs were stretched at an awkward angle. A torso twisted to the side, and a mouth gaped open, skin charred at the corners. Burnt sockets where eyes should've been. The entire face was charred.

I dragged in gulps of tainted air as I pinwheeled backward. Horror seized me. Oh God, that was a body—a body like Colleen's and Amanda's, and the bodies of that family. I spun around, blindly reaching for my phone and stun gun, but I'd left both of them in my car.

Because I was an *idiot* in the middle of an utter breakdown—

The streetlamp popped, exploding in a shower of sparks. I whirled as the one across the street blew out too. One after the other, all the way down the street, lamps burst, pitching the entire block into darkness.

My mouth dry, I backed up and then turned. Darkness blanketed the sidewalk, blocking out the cars parked along the road. It was so dark, it was like I'd lost my vision. I exhaled roughly, and my breath puffed out as a misty cloud in the air. Goose bumps spread across my flesh. The temperature felt like it had dropped twenty or more degrees.

He was back—oh God, I was such an idiot, and I was going to get myself killed.

The darkness suddenly shifted and it—it *pulsed*, expanding and deepening, reaching out toward me in thick tendrils. Icy air stirred around me, lifting the hair off my shoulders and sending it flying across my face. A startled scream burst out of me as the thing took shape right before my eyes.

Oh crap.

That wasn't a shadow or darkness. I didn't even think it was the psycho Origin. This was something straight out of nightmares. Was it an Arum? Emery and Kent had said they looked like shadows, but hearing about them and actually seeing something like them were two very different things.

Instinct flared to life once more, demanding I listen to it, and this time I gave in. I spun around and took off, running as fast as I could. I darted into the night, utterly blind in the cloaking darkness. Panic dug in, but I kept going—

My legs and hips slammed into something hard—something metal. The impact knocked the air out of my lungs and my legs out from underneath me. I screamed as I lost my balance, falling backward. I threw out my arms, but there was nothing to grab on to except cold air.

I went down fast, my back and shoulders slamming into the sidewalk a second before the back of my head collided with cement. Raw pain exploded all along the base of my neck and skull, shooting stark white-hot pain down my lips. Light burst behind my eyelids and then . . . then there was nothing.

29

For the second time in I don't even know how many hours, I woke up and had no idea how I'd gotten where I was, but I recognized the damn brick walls.

Luc's place.

Jackknifing upright, I scanned the dimly lit room. For a moment I thought I was alone until I saw Luc rise from the couch like a wraith.

"You're awake," he said, his voice flat. Distant.

I scooted to the edge of the bed. "Why am I here?"

"Well . . ." He walked around the couch but stopped at the edge of the raised platform. "I believe you might've knocked yourself out by . . . running into a parked car."

"I did?" A brief image of running panicked into the darkness surfaced. I sighed. "I did."

"You took a pretty nasty hit to the head." He leaned against the back of the couch, staying to the shadows of the room. "You weren't seriously injured, but I . . . I fixed it."

"With your special magic healing fingers?"

"Something like that."

I pushed my hair back. I couldn't believe I'd actually knocked myself out by running into a car. God officially hated me.

"I once knew of a girl who walked out in front of a speeding truck," he said. "Well, that's the story I heard."

Walking out in front of a moving truck sounded a lot better than running into a parked car and knocking myself out. "Is that supposed to make me feel better?"

"Not really." A moment paused. "We were only a moment behind you. Zoe wanted to give you space. Well, the illusion of space. I shouldn't have listened to her. If I'd just gone after you, you wouldn't have seen that."

I looked over at him, my stomach turning. "The body—"

"The police were called. I think they're still there. The party was shut down."

A shudder worked its way through me. "Did you . . . hear who it was?"

"Yeah."

When that was all he said, dread set in. I clasped my knees. "Who was it?"

"Some guy who went to your school. I think his name was Andy. At least that's what Zoe said."

"God," I whispered, looking away. Andy was one of the guys who'd been eyeballing the young Luxen at school. What I knew about Andy wasn't good, but I wouldn't want him or anyone to die like that. It was terrible.

I folded my arms across my stomach. "This is going to make stuff at school so much worse."

"Probably," he agreed. "The Origin must've followed you there."

I frowned. "I don't think it was him, though. I saw something there. I think—no, I know I saw an Arum."

"What?" He pushed away from the couch, nearing the platform.

I squeezed my knees. "It was just like Kent and Emery said it would look. I thought it was just shadows at first, but then the shadows moved and thickened. The temperature dropped and . . . there was something there." I shivered. "That's why I ran."

"An Arum can't kill a human like that. They can assimilate some of the Luxen ability if they feed, but when they kill a human, it doesn't look like what happened to the guy. It had to be a Luxen or an Origin." He paused. "Or possibly a hybrid, but let's stick to the first two as possible suspects. And we already know there's a ticked-off Origin murdering people."

"I know what I saw. It wasn't my imagination. And before I saw the body, I heard my name, but—"

"It was in your head?" he interrupted. "The Arum, when in

their true form, speak on a different wavelength. It sounds like it's in your head, but that's just how your human ears process the sound. But that doesn't explain how an Arum would know your name."

"It doesn't." I lifted a shoulder. "Then again, maybe another one of my friends is an Arum for all I know. It could be James."

He snorted. "Arums don't interact with humans on that kind of level. They stick to themselves. Usually in dark, damp places."

"I'll have to take your word for it." The moment that came out of my mouth, I tensed. I couldn't just believe what he said. Not now.

Luc exhaled roughly. "The Arum could've sensed the Origin and was tracking him, but instead of finding the Origin, the Arum found you."

"And I ran."

"Into a parked car."

I shot him a look.

"Running was the smart thing to do. That's what you need to do if you ever come face-to-face with an Arum or a Luxen who is trying to hurt you," he stated. "You cannot possibly fight them. There is no training a human can do to be able to take one out. Running is why you're still alive."

"Well, this convo is making me feel a lot better about everything."

"It's just the truth. It's not meant to make you feel better."

All righty, then. I glanced at the clock on the nightstand and saw that it wasn't even midnight yet. "Where is . . . Where is Zoe?"

"She's here. Not down in the club, since it's open, but she's here." His shoulders seemed to tense. "Do you want me to get her?"

"No," I replied quickly, standing. "I don't want to see her."

Luc folded his arms across his chest. "Don't be so tough on her."

"Excuse me?" I turned to him slowly.

"Don't be so tough on Zoe. The girl cares about you—"

"She lied to me! Are you serious right now?"

"Zoe lied to you, because what could she tell you, Peaches? There was nothing she could do without you thinking she was crazy. You were never supposed to find out the truth."

"Well, I did, didn't I?" Anger rose swiftly. "And don't call me that."

"The fact that she's an Origin and knows the truth about who you are doesn't change that she's your friend."

In the back of my mind, I knew Luc had a point. Hell, he was probably right, but I wasn't ready to face that. "It's the fact that everyone I know and care about has been lying to me. That's just not something you easily forgive."

"But you could try understanding."

Pressing my lips together, I shook my head. "Whatever."

"Whatever? Fine. Let's move this conversation to something else that's important."

"Oh great," I snapped. "Can't wait to hear this."

He ignored me as he stepped up on the platform. "What in the hell were you thinking? There is a psychotic Origin on the loose and what do you do? You spend all day driving around, practically wearing a neon 'come break my other arm' sign."

"I—"

"Then you go home, leave your freaking house in a mess, scaring the shit out of Sylvia, causing her to think something happened to you."

My eyes widened. "How do you know that?"

"Because I was there, watching over you to make sure you didn't end up dead."

"Oh my God, that's not okay! I told you that I didn't want you doing it. You could've had Grayson or Daemon—"

"Pretty sure after the stunt you pulled this morning, that was enough punishment for Daemon," he shot back, eyes afire. "And then you go to a party. A *party,* knowing there's an Origin who apparently wants to use you in some cliché revenge plot? Are you out of your mind?"

I was about five seconds from being out of my mind. "Why am I even here with you? I told you I didn't want to see you again."

His lips twisted into a smirk. "Do you want me to take you home then, to Sylvia?"

"No."

"Then congrats, you're stuck with me."

Turning to him, I closed my hands into fists. "That doesn't mean I have to stand here and listen to you."

"Damn straight you do. What you did tonight, by going to that party, was absolutely, fundamentally—"

"Want to use another adverb?"

"Yeah." His jaw locked down. "How about irresponsibly, recklessly, and carelessly *immature*?"

I sucked in a stuttered breath. "You're acting like I just found out today that my parents are getting divorced and I'm overreacting."

"I don't think you're overreacting. I cannot even fathom what you must be thinking or feeling, but that doesn't mean you made smart choices today." Luc's lips formed a thin, hard line. "I didn't spend half of my godforsaken life trying to keep you alive for you to just throw it all away!"

I sucked in air, and something, something exploded inside of me, like a buckshot, and I got right up in his face, putting my hands on his chest. He caught my wrists. "I don't belong to you, Luc! My life doesn't belong to you! No matter what you did for me."

Luc drew back as if I'd slapped him. "I never said you did."

My entire body was trembling. "I want to make something very clear. My name is Evelyn. You can call me Evie. That is who I am, no . . . no matter who I used to be."

"I know," he said solemnly, his gaze never leaving mine. "Nadia doesn't exist. Not anymore."

I wasn't exactly sure what happened next. Maybe he pulled my hands back to him, or maybe that was all me, but suddenly my palms were flat against his chest. He was wearing a shirt, but the heat of his body seemed to burn through the cloth, searing my palms.

Neither of us moved.

We both seemed frozen, and then Luc did move. He lifted a hand, placing it over mine—over the hand that rested above his heart.

My gaze darted to his and I found it difficult to breathe. The fluttering was back in my ruined chest, overshadowing the wrecked feeling that threatened to pull me under and never let me resurface. The fluttering rapidly became something else, a burning and tingling that spread much, much lower.

My fingers curled into his shirt. What was I doing?

Luc was, well, he was Luc. He wasn't even really human. As I stared up at him, I had to admit to myself that I'd stopped caring about the whole not-being-human thing after the first time I'd seen him shirtless.

I was that shallow.

I fully accepted that.

Whatever.

But what was I thinking?

I was thinking about stretching up on the tips of my toes and kissing him. That was what I was thinking about. And I didn't want to think anymore—think about who I really was or all the lies that now made up my life.

I just wanted to feel—feel what I never did when I was with Brandon. I just wanted to feel—feel *real*. Like I was a person who existed and who had a past and a future.

Luc's eyes flared a sudden deep and stunning violet. His gaze lowered to my mouth. An intense emotion rolled across his face. Luc let go of my hand and stepped back, but for once I was quicker than him. I stretched up and slid my hands up his chest, to his shoulders, and I brought my mouth to his.

I kissed Luc.

The first touch of our lips was like hitting a live wire. Little darts of pleasure shot through my veins as the flutter in my chest spread lower. My lips tingled from the contact and my skin flushed, and Luc . . . he just stood there, as still as a statue.

He wasn't kissing me back.

He wasn't doing anything.

Oh holy Lord, what was I doing? I was kissing Luc, and he wasn't even touching me. His hands were at his sides, and I was hanging on to him like a feral octopus.

I needed help.

Serious help.

I let go and rocked back a step and then two. My legs bumped into the bed. The wrong kind of heat—murky, sweltering heat—suffocated me while Luc stared at me like I'd lost my mind, and there was a good chance that I had.

I totally had.

His chest rose and fell sharply.

Mortification overcame me, and words stammered out. "I sh-shouldn't have done that. I don't even know why I did. So let's pretend it never happened? Maybe it didn't? Maybe this is a weird dream, and we'll—"

Luc closed the small distance between us in less than a heartbeat. One arm folded around my waist as his other hand thrust through my hair, tangling up in the strands.

His mouth landed on mine, crashed into mine, and I might've stopped breathing. He pulled me up against him until only the tips of my toes remained on the carpet and all the interesting parts were nearly lined up, chest to chest, hip to hip.

Luc kissed me—kissed me as a deep sound rumbled from the back of his throat. The little shivers of pleasure intensified. My brain completely shut down as my senses were overwhelmed.

He shuddered against me, and my arms swept around him, my fingers digging into his arms and then in his soft, silky hair. The kiss deepened as the tip of his tongue touched mine.

I *sparked*.

His hand traveled down my back, creating a wave of maddening sensations throughout me. Vaguely, I thought the overhead light flipped on and then turned back off, but I wasn't sure and I didn't care. Not when his hands gripped my hips and he lifted me an inch or two and *oh* . . .

Thinking was so overrated.

His kisses were devouring and he kissed as if at any given second we'd be ripped apart and he was making the most of those precious seconds. But then Luc moved, and I didn't even know how we ended up on the bed, but we were falling, topping backward. My back came flush with the bed, and my eyes flew open.

His eyes . . .

They were a beautiful shade of purple, and the pupils were as white and gleaming as freshly fallen snow.

He planted one hand in the bed beside my head and one knee next to my leg, supporting his weight as he hovered over me. "This kiss . . ." he said, voice thick. "This is beautiful too."

My chest squeezed. I knew he was comparing this to our first kiss, the one I didn't remember. The one I would never remember. They were the good memories Luc had. Memories I wouldn't—

"Don't." Luc touched my cheek. "Don't go back there, Peaches. Stay here."

The crushing pressure eased off, replaced by a different sense of urgency. I wanted more than kissing. I wanted—

"What do you want?" he asked, his gaze holding mine.

"You," I whispered, cheeks burning.

"You have me." His thumb dragged along my lower lip. "You've always had me. Always."

My breath caught around a sudden knot in my throat. Raw emotions threatened to rise up and consume me as tears burned the backs of my eyes. I gripped his shirt and pulled. He ducked his head, letting me pull his shirt off. My gaze roamed over his chest, his stomach, and lower.

I reached for him with a shaking hand. My fingers skimmed the dips and hard planes of his stomach, down to the button of his low-riding jeans. Blood thundered.

Catching my hand, Luc pushed it into the mattress, and then he was coming down, his hips settling between my legs and then he was sipping from my lips, kissing me in a way I'd never, ever been kissed before.

His hand left mine, trailing over my arm and then down, under my shirt. Those fingertips brushed over my skin, causing my back to arch. His mouth left mine, blazing a path over the line of my jaw and then down.

He made this deep, throaty sound as the bridge of his nose dragged along the side of my neck. "Peaches."

I shivered.

"God." He nipped at my skin, eliciting a sound from me I'd never made before. "I love peaches."

Things kind of spun and spun from there. My shirt was gone, we were skin to skin, and my legs were wrapped around his moving hips. There was a popping sound in the room and a sudden scent of burnt plastic. Way, way back in my mind, I thought I should be concerned about that, but I was drowning in him, in us, and his skin . . . it was *humming*. I could feel it vibrating under my fingertips, against my own skin, and it was the strangest, most amazing feeling.

There was no room for thinking or feeling beyond this moment. Not when his mouth made its way back to mine, not when I was panting against his swollen lips, and I knew I was on the precipice of something major, something beautifully unknown, and then I was falling over that edge, tumbling and spinning. I was *humming*.

"Luc," I said, gasping.

He suddenly stilled above me, his breath dancing over my lips, and I was waiting—wanting him to do more, want more. He cursed and wrenched away, flipping onto his back, onto the bed.

My eyes went wide, and I was once again staring at the ceiling, my entire body trembling as the pleasant, sultry haze faded. Slowly, I turned my head to look at him.

I sucked in air.

A faint, whitish shimmer surrounded his entire body. One arm was thrown over his face. The other hand was clenched, resting atop his heaving chest. My gaze dipped. His jeans were unbuttoned and shoved down his lean hips. Had I done that?

I so had.

"Luc," I repeated.

"I need a moment." His voice was rough, like sandpaper.

I waited a moment. *"Luc."*

His knuckles looked like they were bleached white. "I can't."

All the liquid heat that had invaded my muscles vanished in an instant. Suddenly cold, I folded my arms over my bare chest and sat up. My hair fell forward, slipping over my shoulders. I shivered for a different reason. "Can't what?"

Luc pulled his arm away from his face. His eyes were squeezed tight. "I can't do this with you."

A sickening sense of dread filled me. "I don't understand. It sure . . . felt like you could. That we . . . that we would."

He made this sound like he was in pain. "Your head is so messed up right now. Doing this feels like I'm taking advantage of you, because come tomorrow, you're going to be pissed at me again," he bit out, jaw clenched.

I hated to even think about it, but he kind of had a point there.

He sat up with startling speed and rose from the bed. He stood before me. His hair was a tumbled mess, his chest and stomach bare, those jeans unbuttoned. "I can't do what I want to do to you, with you, when you don't even know who you are."

30

L uc was right.

And Luc was wrong.

I realized that about fifteen minutes after he walked out of his apartment. Without his shirt.

After flopping onto my back again, I stared up at the exposed beams in the ceiling, wondering what the hell had just happened between Luc and me. I couldn't believe I'd kissed him. I couldn't believe he'd kissed me back. That we ended up where we did, on this bed, and so close to—

Smacking my hands over my face, I groaned. If Luc hadn't stopped, I wouldn't have either. I would've gone as far as we could've. I would've dived headfirst without thinking about any of the many, many consequences.

Like, for example, I didn't have condoms on me, because of my nonexistent sex life. Did he have them? Could I even get pregnant? Get an STD? Like that was exactly what I needed in my life at the moment.

Why in the world was I even thinking about that now, way after the fact?

Because I was dumb.

I dropped my hands to the bed.

My entire body cringed. God knew, with everything going on right now, my head was so not in the right place. I got that. I did. But having him realize that, having him say that was absolutely mortifying and infuriating.

If I was going to make a mistake, I was damn well entitled to make that mistake.

And yeah, that sounded ridiculous, even to me.

Do what I want to do to you, with you . . .

I sucked in a sharp breath as I shivered. What did that even mean? Who was I kidding? I knew exactly what that meant and what that statement was leading to. What did it matter? It didn't. What did was the fact that I was now going to have face him sooner rather than later, knowing he'd seen me shirtless.

Ugh.

I rolled onto my side. The bed smelled like him.

Double ugh.

I had no idea how much time passed as I lay there, my knees drawn up and my skin chilled by the cool air. It had to have been hours, but at some point, I realized there was something else Luc had been right about.

I didn't know who I was. Not at all. I wasn't the Nadia who Luc remembered. And who I thought I was, was a lie. I had to deal with that, because I couldn't spend another day driving around without facing the truth. I was Nadia. I was also Evie. And I had no idea what that meant for me.

But what I did know was that I had to go home in the morning and face *her,* and begin to make sense of who I was.

It was way after midnight by the time I fell into a fitful sleep, waking to a clap of thunder that rattled the entire building. Startled, I flipped onto my side and opened my eyes.

Zoe stood by the bed.

Gasping, I jerked into a sitting position. "Holy crap, Zoe. What the hell?"

"Sorry." She smiled, clasping her hands together. I looked away and then refocused. She was wearing that hot-pink jumper, the one April had said made her look like a toddler. She so did not look like a toddler. "I wasn't standing here watching you. I swear."

"Really?" I pulled my legs up as I blinked rapidly. Gloomy light filtered in through the window, and rain pattered off the glass.

"I actually just came into the room to wake you up, but it

thundered and, well, bad timing." Zoe bit down on her lower lip and then laughed. "But your face was absolutely priceless."

"Ugh." I rubbed at my throbbing temples. "Why are you in here?"

What I didn't ask was where Luc was, because I hadn't seen him since he left and I had no idea if he'd come back after I'd fallen asleep. It was possible.

She knocked a bunch of tight curls out of her face. "I wanted to talk you."

I glanced at the clock. It was too early for this conversation, but I didn't say that to her. I thought about what Luc had said last night. About what Zoe was and how her knowing the truth about me didn't change our friendship.

I so wanted that to be true.

Leaning against the headboard, I exhaled raggedly. "I . . . I don't even know you."

Her expression pinched. "You do know me, Evie. I know it may not seem like that right now, but who I am to you . . . is who I am. That hasn't changed."

"Really?" I cast a quick gaze around Luc's apartment, my attention snagging on the beautiful acoustic guitar by a dresser. A black pick was tucked between strings, as if someone had been playing it recently.

Had Luc returned, and I had no idea? I shook my head. That was so not important. I refocused. "Your uncle?"

She tugged a hair tie off her wrist. "He's not really my uncle."

I'd figured as much. "He's like you?"

"He's an older Luxen. He doesn't want anything to do with what . . . Well, he just wants to live a normal life. So he does."

I pulled my legs up under the comforter. "And your parents? I'm assuming they didn't die in a freak plane accident. You don't know your parents, right? Just like Luc?"

She pulled her tight curls into a low ponytail. "I never knew my parents."

"And Luc—" I shook my head. "How did you know him? You obviously weren't one of those kids."

"No, but I met Luc a few years before the invasion." As she ran her fingers along the top of the dresser, a far-off look crept onto her face. "I was being kept in a facility, along with a handful of other Origin. Luc just showed up one night and he freed us. That's how I met him."

Knots formed in my stomach. "You were kept in a facility?"

Nodding, she picked up what appeared to be a small wooden camel. "Since I was born, up until I was about ten years old."

Despite being irritated with Zoe, with everything, sympathy and horror for her rose inside me. "What was that like?"

She shrugged as she placed the camel back down. "There was schooling and training, classes focused on controlling our abilities and ordinary things, you know—math, language, whatever. All of it was normal to me—to all of us, because we didn't know what was outside the compound. Hell, we didn't even know *where* the compound was. When you grow up in something like that, you don't . . . you don't question things. Things were the way they were because that was how they were. You know? We weren't treated badly. At least that's what we thought."

Zoe moved to the large window that overlooked the street below. "It still amazes me. The whole thing. Like how all the basic human rights can be stripped away, but because you have a bed, a room, and food on your plate, you don't even realize you have no rights. And that was the truth. We were just subjects—experiments. None of us had any rights. We couldn't leave if we wanted to. The older . . . *subjects* couldn't have relationships with one another. Our internet was monitored and restricted. We ate what was provided, even if we didn't like the way it tasted. We woke up when they told us to, and the same when it was time to go to bed."

"God," I whispered.

A winsome smile appeared. "We were property of the United States and didn't even realize it. Not until the entire wall of the west wing blew the hell up."

I jolted. "What?"

"Luc took down the entire wall . . . and nearly all of the staff. Just him, and he was only about eleven years old at the time."

My mouth dropped open as I pictured an eleven-year-old Luc running around, blowing up a building with his magic fingers. "How in the world is that even possible?"

Zoe was staring out the window. "Luc is different."

"Ain't that the truth?" I muttered.

She faced me, her expression serious. "He isn't like the rest of us—like most of us. I've heard . . . Well, I know there were others like him. Those kids? But Luc is—God, I hate saying this out loud, but he is the most powerful of all the Origins."

My eyes widened. Most powerful? That was, well, kind of impressive and kind of scary. Especially since I'd threatened to hit him on multiple occasions.

Actually, I had hit him before.

"Anyway, Luc basically freed us. He helped set us up with Luxen who knew what we were. That's how I met my *uncle*," she said. "And the rest is history."

I had a feeling there were huge parts of that history left out. "So your move to Columbia was coincidental?"

Her head tipped to the side. "Nothing about Luc is coincidental. He wanted me in Columbia, and I owed him a huge favor."

"A lot of people seem to owe him favors."

"A lot of people do, and Luc likes to collect on them." Zoe inched closer. "I owed him my life, though. There was no favor he could've asked for that would've made up for that."

"Seems to me that owing a favor is a lot like having someone owning you."

"You would think that, because you've never been owned."

Flinching, I knew I couldn't argue with that. I didn't know what that felt like.

"I knew you before and I know that's a weird thing for you to hear, but when Luc asked me to come here to keep an eye on you, because he couldn't, I agreed. Not just because I owed him a favor, but because I've always liked you, and I was happy to do so."

I thought about how, when Luc had told me he'd never truly left . . . left me, he hadn't been lying. He'd had Zoe in his place. I still had no idea what to think about that.

"I didn't pretend to be friends with you. I was a friend to you. I am a friend of yours." A moment passed. "I am an Origin, but I'm still Zoe. I'm still the same person who's obsessed with HGTV."

My lips twitched as I glanced over at her. We both said, "Jonathan," at the same time, referencing one of the Scott twins.

A hopeful look filled those odd, beautiful eyes that were so strange to see now. "My favorite food is still chicken tenders—extra crispy. I still think April is totally a test run for having a child who's a constant disappointment."

I laughed, but then I blurted out, "Can you have kids?" Immediately my face turned beet red. "I'm sorry. That's kind of a rude question—"

"It would be if you didn't know me." She sat down next to me on the bed and nudged my foot with hers. "We can have kids . . . if we're with another Origin. I don't think we can with a normal human. At least, no one has as far as I know, but it's not like most Origins have been out in the wild long enough for us to know."

I glanced over at her. Zoe was . . . Well, she was Zoe. She looked the same. "I can't believe I never noticed it. I'm super-unobservant."

"Well . . ."

Rubbing wearily at my arms, I lifted my chin. Honestly, I had no idea what to think about that, about any of this. It was like my brain was short-circuiting, only processing everything that was happening in bits and pieces. I blew out a rough breath as my gaze drifted around the dim room.

"Evie?" she said, and I looked over to her. Zoe's eyes were glossy as they searched mine. "Do you . . . Do you hate me now?"

My breath caught. "I don't hate you." And that was the truth. "I don't think I'm even mad at you. I was. A lot. I'm just . . . I don't know. My head is in a thousand places. I'm irritated one second and just confused the next and—" I cut myself off. "I don't hate you."

Zoe's shoulders relaxed. "Thank God, because I was prepared to, I don't know, make you dinner in order to beg for your forgiveness."

My nose wrinkled. "I don't think that would work. You can't even pop popcorn."

She laughed, the sound a little lighter. "That's true. I would get Luc to cook it."

Surprise flickered through me. "Luc can cook?"

Zoe nodded.

"Is there anything he can't do?"

That faint grin appeared again. "Not many things."

"Wow," I murmured. "Are you going to tell Heidi the truth now?"

She nodded. "I think so. There's no point keeping what I am secret. I don't think we should tell James, though. I mean, we'd have to explain exactly what I am, and as I'm sure Luc has told you, Origins aren't a known thing."

"He did." I didn't think James would care or breathe a word of it, but I trusted Zoe on this. "Does Emery know . . . about me?"

"She does," she told me. "I don't know if she knows all the details, but she knows you're important to Luc."

That statement made me all squirmy, so I looked away.

Zoe was quiet for a moment. "You and Luc doing okay?"

I snorted. "I don't know about that." In the next second, I felt his mouth against mine again, his chest pressing down, his hips . . . Oh God, I needed help, like, therapy-until-I-was-thirty kind of help. "Luc and I aren't anything."

"Huh." Zoe bent over, picking something off the floor. "Then I guess Luc's shirt just got left on the floor via dark magic."

I froze. Sure as hell, she was holding the shirt Luc had been wearing. "I . . ." I blinked. "This is his apartment. He would have clothes lying around."

She widened her eyes and cocked her head to the side. "So he came home last night with his shirt on, stayed in here with you, took his shirt off for *reasons,* and then stormed out of said home last night without a shirt." She waited a moment. "Because, yeah, I saw him shirtless . . . and his pants half unbuttoned, and while I admired the view, it wasn't exactly what I was expecting to see."

"I . . . I don't know what to say about that," I said lamely.

She dropped the shirt on the bed and then crossed one long leg over the other. "I heard you guys last night."

My face burned. I felt it. It was on fire, as if the sun had kissed my cheeks. She *heard* us?

Her brows flew up. "I heard you guys arguing, but I'm assuming you think I heard something else. Something far more interesting than the random bits and pieces I heard *across* the hall. What happened last night?"

I wanted the bed to swallow me whole. "I guess if I said 'nothing,' you wouldn't believe me?"

"Unless nothing involved Luc getting naked."

"Oh my God," I groaned, tipping over onto my side. "Luc wasn't naked. Not completely. He just had his shirt off and I—" I rolled over, face-planting onto the bed. "I had my shirt off . . . and yeah."

Zoe didn't respond for a long moment and then she said, "Did you guys . . . ?"

"Do it?" My voice was muffled and my arms were limp at my sides. "No, we didn't do it. He stopped, saying he couldn't."

"He couldn't . . . ?"

"It sure seemed . . . and felt like he could, but it was a mistake. Seriously." I flopped my limp arms. "I initiated it, because I started to think about everything, and I just . . . I just didn't want to think anymore."

"And making out with Luc comes into play how?"

I flopped again. "Because I wasn't thinking . . ."

"Oh." Zoe went quiet.

"That's bad, isn't it?"

She nudged my dead arm. "Well, I mean, if that was the only reason why you initiated it. No judgment, but if he was . . . um, feeling it more, he probably didn't want to be, you know, used as a distraction."

"Him being used? Me using him?" I lifted my head. "Him feeling it more? He stopped, Zoe. And left—left the room like it was on fire."

"Maybe because he's a good guy?"

I looked at her. "For real?"

Her lips pursed. "Luc is . . . different. He's not someone anyone wants pissed off at them, but he is . . . He is a good guy."

"Ugh." I flopped again.

"You look like a seal," Zoe commented.

"Shut up." My neck started to hurt, so I rolled over onto my back.

"Do you like—"

"Don't ask me that. Please? Because I don't know and I don't have the brain space to even think about that." Or the lady cojones to answer it honestly. "What happened last night, well, it happened. It's not going to happen again. It's done with."

"Huh," she said again.

My gaze slide over to her. "What?"

She lifted a shoulder. "Nothing." There was a pause. "So what are you going to do now?"

I glared at the ceiling. "I'm going to go home."

31

Somehow my car had made its way to Foretoken, and Zoe rode with me to my house Saturday morning. "How will you get home?" I asked as my car sat idling in the driveway. Then it struck me. "You're going to run, aren't you?"

"I can run *really* fast," Zoe replied.

"Not in gym class last year," I pointed out. She always lagged behind when we had to do sprints and other annoying things at a God-awful early time in the morning.

Zoe laughed. "It takes more energy and effort to slow myself down than it does to go at normal speeds for me." She looked over at me, and she had those contacts back in. "Are you ready to go in there?"

"No? Yes?" I glanced at the front of the house and then pried my fingers off the steering wheel. "I don't know what to say to her."

Zoe followed my gaze. "She's probably thinking the same thing."

"And you've . . . you've never talked to her about me?" I knew that Zoe had never been around her, but that didn't mean they hadn't had conversations.

She shook her head. "Sylvia doesn't know what I am. If she did, I'm sure she wouldn't have been supportive of our friendship."

"Because she'd be worried you'd tell me the truth or I'd figure it out?" Anger flashed, brimming to the surface.

"Yes, but I'm sure it's not for malicious reasons, Evie. What happened to you, what's been done, isn't normal."

I snorted. "Oh really?"

She ignored my sarcasm. "Sometimes the truth is hidden as a form of protection."

Even if that was the reason to hide the truth, it didn't make dealing with the fallout any easier, but it wasn't like I could sit out here forever. "I'm going to go in."

"That's good," she agreed. "I'll text you later. Okay? Grayson's going to take over."

My brows lifted. "You mean, watching me?"

She nodded. "That Origin is still out there. We're not taking any chances with you. I would stay, but Luc doesn't think that's a good idea."

"Why?" I frowned.

"Because he's worried that if something were to happen, you would get involved out of fear for me," she explained. "He's not worried about that when it comes to Grayson."

I almost laughed, but dammit, Luc was right. Again. I was really beginning to hate that. "Why isn't Luc watching me?"

"Well, maybe it has to do with the fact that you told him to stay away from you?" she surmised. "Then again, he sure wasn't staying away from you last night, with his shirt—"

"Stop," I whined, shaking my head.

"I think he just knows he needs to give you space. Real space."

"That . . . that would be smart." I sighed. I looked over at Zoe, and then I admitted something important. "I don't . . . I don't hate him, either."

A soft smile curled the corners of her lips. "I know." She glanced at the door. "You'd better get in there."

"Yeah." No more delaying.

"Good luck."

We said good-bye, and it was time for me to get out of the car and face, well, whatever was waiting for me. I slung my bag over my shoulder as I walked to the front door and found it unlocked. Taking a deep breath, I headed inside.

I saw her immediately.

She rose from the couch, her face pale and drawn. I saw then that she wore the contacts. Her eyes were once more like mine.

But that was an illusion. Her eyes had never been like mine.

She'd never been like me.

Her shoulders tensed as her gaze roamed over me like she was checking to make sure I was all in one piece. "I've been worried sick."

If this had happened last week, she'd probably have strangled me for running out of the house and not coming home until a day later. But now? I could tell she was resisting the urge, and maybe that emboldened me not to immediately apologize and beg for forgiveness like I normally would.

So I just stood there, holding on to my bag.

She dragged her gaze away and then slowly sat back down. She leaned forward, picking something up. "I know you saw the pictures."

I glanced at the office door. The glass was cleaned up and the French doors were closed. Inching closer, I dropped my bag on the other side of the couch and then sat down. There were so many questions, but I asked what I felt was the most important one. "Who was she?"

She looked down at the photo, and it was the one that the three of them were in. A long moment passed. "Evelyn was Jason's daughter from a previous relationship."

A ripple of shock made its way through me. Part of me had accepted that all of this was the truth. That my real name was Nadia and that my life was hers . . . but hearing this, that Evelyn Dasher had been someone else, made it feel like I was hearing it for the first time all over again.

"Jason and I could never have biological children. I'm a . . . Luxen and he was human," she continued. "Evelyn's mother had died. Heart disease. Looking back, I can see now that was one of the reasons why Jason became so obsessed with finding treatments for diseases like that and cancer. He was in love with her long after she passed. I didn't realize that at first." She pressed her lips together. "Evelyn died in a car accident three years before the invasion. Jason had been driving. It was a freak accident. He only had minor injuries, but she . . . died at the scene."

I clasped my knees and squeezed tight. "And you all just replaced her with me?"

"That wasn't what we intended." She placed the picture on the ottoman, image down as if that somehow erased it being there. "But I'm not going to lie now. That's what happened. That was all me—"

"Because you killed Jason."

If she was surprised I knew that, she didn't show it. "Luc was honoring our deal. He was leaving, and Jason couldn't allow that. Jason always had to *win*." Her lips thinned. "He pulled out a weapon and was going to shoot Luc in the back. Not with a normal gun. It would've killed him."

"And you decided to kill your husband to protect someone you don't even like?"

Her gaze lifted to mine. "Did Luc talk to you about the Daedalus?"

I nodded.

"Everything he said about the Daedalus is true . . . and there's more, worse than what he even has knowledge of. You may not believe me, but I swear I had no part in the horrific things they were doing."

I wanted to believe her, but how could I?

"I live like a human, but I am a Luxen. I could never knowingly take part in those horrific experiments and the—" She cut herself off, shaking her head. "Our marriage was rocky before Evelyn died, but when I learned about the Origins and hybrids, it was basically over between us." Her gaze hardened. "Killing him was no hardship."

I sucked in a sharp breath. Damn.

"That may sound harsh, but you did not know him."

That hurt more than she intended. I closed my eyes. I had no idea how to respond to that. It took a moment for me to find my voice. "Why did you give me her name?"

"I've asked myself that same question a million times." Her voice was hoarse, and when I opened my eyes again, I saw tears building in hers. "I think . . . I think I just missed her."

I started to stand but found that I couldn't. What was I supposed to think? How should I feel about that?

Was I even real?

I didn't feel real anymore.

"I know this is a lot for you to process. I understand, but there is one thing I need you to know and it's the most important thing." She scooted forward. "Your name is Evie. That is who you are. I can understand the need to find out more about your past, who you were, and I support that. But you are Evie now, and I love you. That is not a lie. None of these past four years has been a lie. You're my daughter. I'm your mother."

Emotion clogged my throat, and it wasn't until that moment I realized how badly I wanted and needed to hear that, but what . . . what did it change? Nothing seemed real anymore.

Words couldn't change that.

Words couldn't make it easier to accept.

But she was the only mom I ever knew.

"I . . ." I cleared my throat. "I don't know what to—"

Glass shattered from somewhere upstairs. I twisted as Mom shot to her feet. "What was that?" I asked.

"I don't know." Her features sharpened. "But get behind me."

I started to do just that, but something—*someone* flew down the steps, a blur of light that slammed into the wall beside the door, rattling the windows. The human-shaped light toppled forward, hitting the floor. The light faded out. Blond hair. Arched cheekbones.

"Grayson," I said with a gasp, starting toward him as he slipped in and out of his true form.

"Evie!" Mom shouted.

I skidded to a halt, but I wasn't quick enough. Terror exploded.

The Origin stood in front of me. A dimple appeared in his right cheek as he smiled. "Hello."

Mom reacted without question.

I saw it out of the corner of my eye. The burst of bright light powered down her right arm. Knowing what she was still hadn't prepared me to actually see it. Static charged the air and the light crackled as it exploded from her palm.

This Origin was fast.

He spun out, and the bolt of energy crashed into the office doors, knocking out several small windows. Twisting around, he threw out his arm. The blast hit Mom in the shoulder, lifting her off her feet and throwing her over the chair.

"Mom!" I shouted, starting toward her.

The Origin appeared in front of me. No sunglasses. *Him*. Brown hair. Handsome features. A stranger. "Mom? Now I know that's impossible."

Stumbling back a step, I cursed under my breath. "Yeah, well. Welcome to my life."

"My world surely beats your world." The ottoman lifted up and flew across the room, slamming into the TV. The screen cracked. "Did you give Luc the message I asked you to?"

I backed up, stepping around the edge of the couch. I bumped into my bag. "Yes."

"And what did he say?" he asked politely.

Anger was like an erupting volcano. "He said you sounded psychotic."

"Liar," he said, and chuckled, taking a step toward me. "I know Luc. That's not what he said. It should've sparked a memory for him. An important one."

It had, but I wasn't telling him that. "I'm so not in the mood for this."

He stopped, his brows flying up. "Not in the mood?"

"Yes." Behind him, I could see Mom's legs. One started moving. I needed to buy time. "My life has imploded. Like, for real. Did you know I'm not even real?"

He blinked. "What?"

"Yeah. My name's not Evie. I'm a dead girl. So I have a lot to deal with, and you're running around killing innocent people."

I'd never seen someone so homicidal before look so confused. "I know who you are. We've met."

A trickle of unease curled its way down my spine. He'd said that before, and I'd forgotten.

"You just don't remember me." He paused. "But I remember you. We briefly met, right after I was freed. You were so sick."

A weird sensation unfurled in the pit of my stomach as I saw Mom draw her leg up.

"You reeked of death." His head tilted. "What did they do to you? I guess we'll find out soon enough."

There was no warning. He moved fast, his arm and hand striking out. The impact of his fist sent me sprawling to the floor. The burst of pain stunned me and the taste of iron filled my mouth.

"I don't like doing that," he said. "I really don't."

I rolled onto my side and spat out a mouthful of blood. My teeth had cut the inside of my cheek. Heart pounding, I lifted my head as my hand dragged over my backpack.

My *backpack*.

The stun gun!

I ripped open the front pocket of my backpack and reached around until my finger slipped over the slim device.

"I would like to say it's not personal." He gripped the back of my shirt and lifted me clear off the floor with one arm. "But it is. He chose you over us—over me."

I didn't even have time to process that. I hit the couch and rolled as I slid the button down, turning the stun gun on. He leaned in as I pushed down on the button. The stun gun spat out electricity, sounding like a thousand little fireworks going off at once. His eyes widened with realization the second before I slammed the business end of the stun gun into his chest.

He dropped like all the bone and muscle had been sucked out of his body. He hit the floor, twitching.

Scrambling from the couch, I stumbled as I made my way to where Mom lay on the floor, moaning. The room tilted weirdly as I dropped to my knees beside her.

"Mom!" I started to grab for her, but the entire shoulder of her blouse was charred and smoking. "Come on, Mom. I need you. Please. Wake up."

Her lashes fluttered, but her eyes didn't open. Oh God, I didn't know what to do. I looked to the front door. Grayson was in his Luxen form and he wasn't moving. I thought he was still alive, because he didn't look like the others had in the club.

With my head throbbing, I leaned forward and peered over the back of the chair. The Origin was still on the floor, but he wasn't twitching anymore.

"Mom!" Tears filled my eyes as I looked around the room. I thought about the gun I'd seen in the office, but I wasn't sure I'd get to it in time. I had no idea how long the stun gun would keep the Origin down. I couldn't remember what Luc had said. Minutes? More? Less?

My hand tightened on the gun. I could use it again. Wouldn't hurt.

I was going to stun gun him into next year if that was what it took. Pushing to my feet, I whimpered as pain arced across my jaw. My stomach dropped.

"Oh shit," I whispered.

The Origin was gone.

Chills rolled down my spine as I took a step back. The fine hair on my arms lifted in startling awareness. I turned slowly.

He was right *there*.

"Now *that* was not nice, *Nadia*."

Surprise knocked me off-balance. He knew my name—my *old* name. Engaging the stun gun, I let out a battle cry that would have made Braveheart proud, and thrust it forward.

Those few seconds cost me.

The Origin caught my wrist and twisted. My fingers spasmed and the stun gun slipped from my grasp. My eyes widened, and he winked at me. "That is not going to happen again."

In the moment, I knew he wasn't just going to break my arm this time. He wouldn't stop there. He'd go through every bone before snuffing my life out. Horror choked me. I didn't want to die. Not like this. Not now.

I didn't even know who I was or who I would become one day. I was just learning about myself—about friends and, oh God, Luc.

And when the Origin finished with me, he'd move on to Mom. There was no way he'd let her live, and Luc . . . he would blame himself. I had no idea where we stood with each other, but I didn't want that for him.

I didn't want that for any of us.

Having no training, I reacted out of the pure instinct to survive. I kicked, catching him in the leg. The move surprised him, and he stepped back. I dipped down and made a desperate reach for the gun.

A fist coiled into my hair, wrenching my head back. I cried out. The Origin dragged me toward the kitchen. Razor-sharp pain radiated down my neck as my feet slipped over the hardwood floor.

He dragged me to my feet and then let go off my hair. The moment of reprieve was over before it had started. A hand curled around my throat. I was off the floor, dangling in air.

It was the last breath I took. Just gone like that. Every cell was shocked and screamed out as precious oxygen was suddenly cut off. My heart stuttered in my chest and the panic made everything worse.

"Let go of my daughter."

The Origin tilted his head just as my vision started to darken. "I can do that."

Flying. I was suddenly flying backward and breathing again. The breathing didn't help, though. Just as soon as I got any amount of oxygen in my lungs, my lower back slammed into the dining table. The impact jarred me all the way down to the tips of my toes. My head smacked into the hanging light fixture, knocking it back. I fell forward, my knees cracking off the floor. Doubling over, I struggled to breathe through the waves of pain.

A scream of pure rage erupted from Mom as blood trickled down the side of my head. I lifted my chin and saw her go full Luxen. She was swathed in intense, beautiful white light.

The air crackled with power. I could feel it in my bones and tissue. She let loose, striking out—

He was too fast.

Shooting forward, he lashed out, swinging his arm. He caught her in the shoulder, and the bolt of pure energy smacked into the wall. Dust plumed, and Mom slammed into the couch, knocking it up into the air.

I cried out as she went down, the couch flipping and landing on her. God, that couldn't be good. I had to get up. I had to—

He was there, his hand curling around my throat again. He lifted my head, forcing my gaze to his. This was it. This was—

"No, I'm not going to kill you." The ever-present, charming smile appeared. "But unfortunately, I am going to hurt you."

32

Shivering in the cooler air, I forced my eyes to stay open. I couldn't let them close. He got . . . impatient when I closed them. He'd think I wasn't paying attention, and he . . . had problems with that. Issues.

This guy had a lot of . . . issues.

He was sitting on the grass a few feet from me, cross-legged, and I was where he'd deposited me, against a tree. He'd dragged me out of the house, and it had been a blur because he moved so incredibly fast, but I didn't think we went that far. I was sure we were in the woods that surrounded the subdivision.

I'd lost my shoes somewhere. I think on the road outside my house. One entire pant leg had been torn off all the way to my upper thigh, having snagged on a branch. Some of my skin had snagged too. That hadn't stopped him. Neither did the moment the edge of my shirt got caught. My trembling hands held the shredded material together.

I was trying not to think of my mom and what kind of condition she was in, because if I did, I'd lose whatever precious control I had, and I couldn't afford that right now if I wanted to survive this.

"He really has no idea who I am?" he asked, nose pinched. "At all?"

"No," I whispered, wincing. Talking made my face throb.

The Origin exhaled loudly. "Well, that's a blow to the ego. I shouldn't be surprised, though." He tilted his head back and stared up at the stars peeking through the bare branches. "He forgot about us more than once, but he won't forget again."

My head had taken a few knocks. Probably a few too many, because sometimes it felt like the ground was swaying under me, but I was starting to put things together.

"Why . . . why are you doing this?" I ignored the lancing pain along my jaw. "Why did you kill those people?"

"I already told you why."

"But that family . . . and Andy—"

He frowned. "I didn't kill them. I'm kind of offended that you think I run around aimlessly killing people."

I opened my mouth, but I was unsure of how to respond to that, but why would he lie? He'd easily admitted to Colleen's and Amanda's murders.

"By the way, what should I call you? Evie? Nadia? Evelyn?" He paused, and I saw the pupils of his eyes burn white. "Peaches?"

I swallowed hard and croaked out, "Evie."

"Hmm. Interesting."

A tremor coursed down my arms. "You met me when I was—"

"When you were a young girl, dying of a disease? Yes. I met you very briefly. You came into the room I was placed in—we all were placed in—and you read to us."

"I don't—"

"Remember? I see." He leaned forward, and I tensed. He could be soft-spoken and friendly, charming, even, but he was like a cobra striking. "I'll remember for the both of us. You read *Where the Wild Things Are* after the world began to fall apart. We liked you."

"It . . . it doesn't make sense."

His placed one hand on the ground by my foot. "What doesn't, Evie?"

"You're . . . one of them. One of those kids—" I gasped as his hand shot out and wrapped around my ankle.

"So, he did talk about us?" Interest filled his voice. He squeezed hard. "Evie?"

"Yes," I said breathlessly, hands spasming around the ragged material of my shirt.

His hand slid up, fingers digging into the raw skin of my calf. "Tell me what he said?"

"It's not possible," I repeated, trembling as the pain arced up my leg. "You can't be one of them."

"Why? Because he killed us all?" He laughed. "Or because I don't look like you'd expect a ten-year-old to look?"

I stared at him.

That smile didn't fade. "We were all dark stars, but Luc . . . he was the darkest. Do you know what I mean?"

I didn't.

But then he looked to the side. His lips parted. "Finally." His gaze swung back to me. "Told you he'd find us. After all, eventually that blond Luxen wouldn't check in, and Luc . . . Well, he's not stupid."

Slowly, he lifted his hand from my leg and then rose with a fluid grace that was shockingly familiar. He turned, standing in front of me.

There was a weird part of me that knew when Luc drew close. I have no idea how I knew, but I did. There was relief. There was also stark terror.

I saw Luc prowl through the cluster of trees, catching a glimpse of him before the Origin in front of me shifted, blocking my view. My heart stuttered in my chest as I glanced around for a weapon of some sort. There were rocks. They wouldn't do much, but they would be something.

The Origin's hands moved to his sides, and I swore he trembled.

"Let me see her," Luc demanded, his voice barely recognizable. It was coldly furious.

The Origin stiffened as if steel had been poured down his spine. "It's always, always been about her. Some things never change. Fine." He stepped aside. "Whatever. She's still alive."

I saw him, and I couldn't explain the raw emotion expanding in my chest. There'd been many, many moments I thought I'd never see him again. Or my mother. Or my friends, but he stood there, shoulders straight and legs spread wide as if he were some kind of avenging angel about to lay waste to a world of sinners and saints.

Luc's gaze flickered over me, from my dirt-caked feet to the mess that was my face. There was a tightening to his jaw, a hardening to his churning eyes. He took a step toward me.

"Don't," the Origin said. "Don't make me do something you'll regret."

Luc halted, but he didn't take his eyes off me. "I already regret so much." The black shirt he wore strained at the shoulders. "I should've known."

"You know?" the Origin asked, turning sideways. Open wonder, as well as a measure of satisfaction, filled the Origin's face.

"Part of me did, I think. I just couldn't believe it." Luc's gaze held mine. "The Daedalus obviously didn't give you the same serum they gave me. You're not aging well. What did they give you?"

"What didn't they give us? Maybe if you stayed around long enough, you would've noticed that we were different than you—than Archer and the rest. That what they gave us was aging us rapidly," the Origin explained. "A souped-up version that included more than a dash of growth hormones. After all, if we aged more quickly, we would've been more useful, wouldn't we? Imagine going through years of puberty in months. It'll make you slightly moody."

"And really psychotic? Is that your excuse? Is that why every last one of you turned into miniature serial killers in training?"

"It definitely had something to do with it, I imagine. You freed us and then you left us." He looked over his shoulder. "For her. Then you came back and you gave up on us."

Luc flinched. "I didn't give up on you. I let you go. I let you escape, because I thought I was doing the right thing."

"You killed all of them and you did let me go." The Origin stepped away from me, his attention fully on Luc. "You didn't look for me. You didn't even take a second to find me. You rushed back here for her."

Luc said nothing for a long moment as he stared at me. "I did look for you. You were gone."

"Did you? You must think that. Just like you think you destroyed the Daedalus."

The breath I took got stuck.

"Where do you think I've been this whole time?" he asked, and Luc didn't show a single reaction to the suggestion the Daedalus was still operational. "Took me long enough to get here, but you don't know that. You've had other, more important priorities. But I've been here. Shadowing you. Watching. I've been so close, trying to figure out how you could just"—he looked up to the sky and shrugged—"let me go. But then I saw her at the club and I knew."

"I let you escape, because I was operating under the false belief that you weren't a sociopath. That out of all those little creeps, you were the one who was going to make it. Obviously I was wrong. You're just as psychotic."

My eyes widened slightly.

"So, what's the point of all of this? You came and you found me, then you waited, and now what? We're here. You and me. That's what you wanted," Luc continued. "Let her go, and then you and I can work this out."

"If I let her go, I don't think she'll make it very far," he replied. "And I'm not talking about what I did to her. I'm talking about what you had them do to her."

I jolted.

Luc turned his head just the slightest. "What does that mean?"

"I've seen some things. Learned things," he said, and I could hear the taunt in his voice. "You have no idea what's coming. I do."

Luc raised a single brow. "Well, that's incredibly vague."

"It's really not." He paused. "By the way, looked into her thoughts. She thinks I killed that family and that guy at some party. That wasn't me."

"And I'm supposed to believe that? Because you're obviously a trusting and sane individual."

"Perhaps I would be trusting and sane if you just paid attention. If you tried with me like you—"

"You're right." Regret tightened the lines of Luc's face. "Maybe if I had done things differently, you would've turned out differently."

"Maybe," the Origin agreed, but then he dipped his chin and smiled. "Then again, I was always smarter than the rest, wasn't I?

I *hid* it better. Even from you, the great and powerful Luc. The most powerful Origin ever created. The prize and ultimate disappointment of the Daedalus."

"You're starting to sound like a fan," Luc replied, his tone bored.

"But I know the truth." He circled Luc, coming to his back, and Luc still didn't take his eyes off me. "There was one fatal flaw the Daedalus didn't engineer out of you."

"Is that so?" Luc murmured, his gaze dropping to my hands.

"Humanity," he answered. "They didn't eradicate that from you. That's why you let me escape."

Luc fell quiet as the Origin made it to his side, standing only a few feet from him.

"I want you to say it." The Origin cocked his head, solely focused on Luc. "Say my name."

I let go of one side of my shirt and reached over, placing my hand in the loose, rocky soil. I dug until I found a decent-sized rock.

"Your name no longer matters." Then Luc looked at the Origin. "And you're wrong about the humanity thing. It comes and goes. *I* just hide it better."

I gasped as Luc struck.

Luc spun, grabbing the Origin by the collar of his shirt. For a second they were eye to eye, and then the Origin was flying backward. He slammed into the tree, the impact sending several branches to the ground. The Origin fell, shaking the ground.

Within an instant Luc was in front of me, his fingers splaying around my cheeks. "Peaches. God." He tilted my head back as I clutched the rock. Warmth radiated from his fingers, easing the throbbing in my jaw.

He was healing me.

"I need you to get up and get out of here," he said as the warmth poured down my spine. "It's going to hurt. It's going to be hard, but I need you to run as fast as you can—"

Luc shifted suddenly, covering my entire body with his, shielding me as something bright and hot hit him in the back. His entire body shuddered as the smell of burnt clothes and flesh stung my eyes. Pain tightened the lines of his striking face. I dropped the rock.

"Luc," I whispered, realizing he'd been hit—hit with something bad. Panic blossomed in my chest as I reached out, grasping the front of his shirt.

He let out a roar of rage that would've sent anyone running, and he spun around, throwing his arms up. A terrible rumble shook the ground, knocking me onto my side. Tiny pieces of rock and clumps of dirt lifted up in the air. Trees all around us rattled as what was left of their leaves floated to the ground. A loud crack reverberated through the trees.

The Origin was standing several feet in front of Luc. "There it is. The great and powerful Origin known as Luc. I'm so scared."

When Luc spoke, his voice was deep and booming, shaking my rib cage. "Oh, you should be."

I slid backward off the ground without being touched.

He stalked toward him, skidding to a stop as the trees trembled with fury. Several of them snapped and lifted, their gnarly roots dripping clumps of soil as the rich scent of earth filled the air.

My God . . .

I made it to my knees just as one of the trees whipped out. I couldn't see the Origin. I had no idea if the tree had hit him or not, but another one flew out. Several kept coming, piling on top of one another, shaking the ground every time they landed.

Luc lowered his arms and started to twist at his waist.

Trees exploded, sending rock and bark shooting in every direction. I didn't even see Luc move. I was suddenly flat on my back and his body was over the top mine as the jagged, sharp pieces rained down. He jerked, and his hands slipped from my shoulders as he fell to the side.

"Luc. Luc!" Confusion gave way to horror as I could see the dark stains spreading all along the front of his shirt at a rapid clip. "No. No!"

His eyes were closed and he wasn't moving. Under my hands, his chest felt still—too still. Bitter panic exploded. "Luc!"

"Oh, I think I might have broken him." The Origin laughed softly. "Just a little."

With my hands shaking, I cupped Luc's cheeks. Blood trickled out of the corner of his lips. "Please. No. God, no." Acute horror choked me. "No. No. *Please*."

"I don't think God is listening." He was closer. The air heated around me. "I think God stopped listening a long time ago."

Luc's skin warmed under my palms. Faint white lines appeared, a soft glow in the darkness, and I cried out, remembering what the Luxen had looked like as they died. Was it the same for an Origin? I didn't know.

Hatred rose from deep inside me, as fierce and bright as the brightest star in the night sky as I stared down into Luc's face. *No.* This wasn't right. This wasn't fair. He saved me years ago, and now he would die because I couldn't fight back. He was going to die trying to protect me—dying and taking all the memories of us with him. Memories I suddenly, desperately knew I needed to learn, to know if those good memories he'd talked about had included me.

"This would've happened eventually," the Origin said. "You'll see."

My cheeks felt damp. Tears coursed down them. My hands slipped off Luc's chest and hit the ground. Under my palms were several thick pieces of bark. Sharp pieces. The same that had impaled Luc over and over, possibly killing him. My fingers curled around one of them.

"I didn't want to do any of this." The Origin's voice sounded like lightning. "Not really."

I never thought I could kill someone.

Maybe who I was before could've. I didn't know, but it was something I never thought I was capable of purposefully doing.

Not until that moment.

I twisted and lifted my gaze. The Origin stood there, this thing that was some kind of creation that had gone horribly wrong. "You didn't have to do any of this."

He tilted his head to the side and frowned. "What do you know? You remember nothing."

He was right. I remembered nothing, but I knew enough.

I didn't give myself time to think about what I was doing. I launched to my feet, cocking my arm back. Surprise flickered across his face, and then that was all I let my brain register as I brought my arm forward with every ounce of strength I had in me, jabbing the piece of bark deep into his eye.

His scream was cut off as I jerked my arm back and slammed the bark into his other eye, ignoring the sound and feel. He went down on his knees, and I followed him as I started to pull the bark out, but it snapped off, embedded deep.

He shifted under me, a solid, heated mass. Bright light surrounded me and then went *through* me. Throwing my head back, I screamed as a deep, intense throbbing pain lit up the center of my chest. I couldn't breathe. I couldn't think. The pain and light swallowed me.

And then I was flying—spinning through the air. I caught brief glimpses of the sky and trees. When I hit the ground, it jolted every bone, but I barely . . . I barely felt it.

I tried to sit up, but I couldn't move more than turning my head, and when that happened, it sort of just flopped to the side.

Something . . . something felt wet *inside* me, like I was drowning from the inside.

The sky erupted in a bright, intense light, and I thought I heard the Origin screaming. The air crackled and spat fire. Shapes took form and blurred as I blinked, trying to clear my vision, but there was a whiteness clinging to the corners. Day turned to night. A roaring sound deafened me as the entire world seemed to bend to the power charging every square inch. The light flared and pulsed. The air . . . The air smelled weird.

Then I saw Luc.

He slammed the Origin into the ground, through it. Dirt spewed into the air, a thick, musty-smelling cloud. Luc lifted him once more before driving the Origin deeper into the hard soil.

"Why?" Luc demanded, clutching the Origin's throat as he lifted him out of the pit his body had made. Arms flopped limp and useless at his sides. "Why all of this, Micah?"

The name. I remembered Luc mentioning his name when he told me about the kids.

Micah coughed out a broken, bloody-sounding laugh. "Because I knew I couldn't beat you. You'd do what I couldn't."

A horrifying moment ticked by and then Luc dropped him as if he were burned. "What?"

Half disappearing into the ground, Micah let out a groan. "You have no idea what is coming. Everything is over. Everything. I'm not going to be here for that. There'll come a time when you're . . ." His voice dropped, and I couldn't hear what he said until his voice rose once more. "They're already here."

I saw Luc's response.

He stared down at Micah, aghast. A heartbeat passed and then half his arm disappeared into the ground Micah had fallen into. There was a flash of intense light, and I knew . . . I knew Micah was no more.

Relief . . . bittersweet relief swept through me, and I closed my eyes. My heart felt sluggish, and there was a bone-deep cold settling into me.

"Peaches. Open your eyes." Hands cupped my cheeks. Strong hands. Warm and alive. My eyes fluttered open again.

"How . . . how are you still alive after that?" I'd seen him— seen all the blood. How was he kneeling above me? "How?"

"Wasn't my time." His gaze roamed over me as he gathered me into his arms, pulling me to his chest. "Peaches, what did you do? Look at you."

"I . . . I jabbed his eyeballs out."

A choked sound left him as he folded one arm around my waist. "I saw that. Not going to forget that for a long time."

My mouth felt weird, like my tongue was swollen. "I don't . . . I don't feel right."

Luc lowered his forehead to mine as his hand slipped from my cheek, down to the center of my chest. "I'm going to make you feel better, okay?"

I thought I said okay. I wasn't sure. The world was a whirling kaleidoscope of pain and heat . . . and Luc. There was a distinct impression of being here before, of him holding me as my body gave out, but then that fragment faded.

"I told you to run." His voice was hoarse as heat flared from his palm, washing over me. I recognized the feeling, welcoming it as it beat back the coldness. The heat spread, working its way through tissue and bone. "Why didn't you run? Peaches? Talk to me."

It took a lot to focus on him. "I thought . . . I thought you were dying. I couldn't let that happen. I wanted . . ."

Something wet danced off my cheek, and I didn't know if they were my tears or his. "You wanted what?"

My head was heavy. "I wanted to know if . . . if I was part of . . . your good memories."

Luc shuddered as he bent, curling his body around mine. His warmth was everywhere, filling every cell and part of me. "Yes," he said, his lips moving against mine as he spoke. "You were all my good memories."

33

As I lay in my bed late Sunday morning, I sent a text back to Heidi, letting her know that I wouldn't be joining her and Emery later. I just wasn't feeling up to peopling at the moment, especially since I knew Heidi had a lot of questions.

Not that I could blame her, but I wasn't sure I was ready to talk about everything.

I didn't have clear memories of returning home last night. I knew Luc had healed me out in the woods, repairing whatever damage Micah had delivered, and I had a vague memory of Luc carrying me back home and finding the house full of . . . well, aliens and people who weren't quite people. There'd been brief glimpses of Mom sitting up, with Zoe beside her. I saw Daemon and I thought I'd seen Archer with a pale, quiet Grayson.

However, I clearly remembered waking up in the middle of the night and finding Luc lying next to me, resting on his side, facing me, and asleep. He'd been holding my hand. Or I'd been holding his. I wasn't sure.

I had no idea if Mom knew he'd been in there, but he'd been gone when I woke this morning, feeling out of it.

But I worried. No matter how awesome he said he was, I knew he'd been in bad shape last night. Luc was powerful—possibly the most powerful creature I'd ever seen, but Micah had done a lot of damage to him.

He'd almost killed him.

He'd almost killed me.

There were still some sore spots—like if I twisted too quickly, there was a flare of pain—but the heavy exhaustion I'd felt since waking was finally lifting. I felt like I'd just recovered from the flu. I had no idea why it felt that way for me after being healed. Luc claimed that humans usually recovered quickly, feeling better than before after being healed.

I wondered if it had something to do with what I'd been given before . . . I was Evie. If that somehow effected how I felt after being healed and if it would prevent me from mutating, because I'd been really hurt last night.

So, I had a lot of questions.

Glancing over at my closed bedroom door, I wondered what . . . Mom was doing. Other than Mom checking in on me this morning, she was giving me space. I knew she'd already called someone to take care of the window Grayson had literally been thrown through. It had been the upstairs hallway window. Work needed to be done downstairs, too.

A soft tapping drew my attention to the bedroom window, and my heart did a weird little jump. There was only one person who would be tapping on my bedroom window.

But in broad daylight?

Thinking I'd better get him off the roof before any neighbors noticed, I rose from the bed and went to the window. Excitement bubbled inside me and so did something . . . something far more sharp, more powerful. I drew the curtains back and saw him perched there, rocking those silver aviator sunglasses.

Luc was holding a Coke.

Fighting the urge to grin, I unlocked the window and pushed it open. "Why didn't you just come to the front door?"

He lifted a shoulder. "I like knocking on windows better."

"Uh-huh." I stepped aside, giving him room. He landed in front of me. Closing the window behind him, I ignored the flutter of anticipation low in my stomach.

He took off his sunglasses, placing them on the dresser, and then he handed me the Coke.

"Thanks." It was nicely chilled. I put it on the dresser. I started to say something, but my gaze met his, and the ability to speak dive-bombed out the window he'd just climbed through.

It was the way he was staring at me, his features stark and gaze intense. Like he was seeing right into me.

Luc stepped toward me and then stopped. His voice came out raspy when he said, "Can I? Can I just touch you?"

My breath hitched, and I nodded.

He moved, careful and slow, touching my face with just the tips of his fingers first. His hands flattened and slipped down the sides of my neck, sending an acute shiver through me. Those hands made their way to my shoulders as he stepped in even closer, his thigh brushing mine. Breathing in his scent, I closed my eyes as one hand slid to my back. Luc curled his other arm around my shoulders, tugging me toward him. His warm breath danced over my temple as we stood chest to chest, my hands touching his sides. We were so close that I felt it when he shuddered. Neither of us moved or spoke for several long moments. We just held each other, and then I felt his lips press against my temple before he pulled away.

"How are you feeling?" he asked, stepping back and shoving his hands into the pockets of his jeans.

"Okay." I cleared my throat, feeling a little unbalanced. "How about you?"

He looked away, and I got hung up in staring at his profile, at the way the muscle flexed when his jaw clenched. "A hundred percent."

I still couldn't believe that he was standing here, that he was okay. I pressed my lips together, wondering why he'd left this morning without saying anything. It felt like after what had happened, he would've stayed.

His gaze found mine. "All you have to do is ask, Peaches."

My eyes narrowed. "Stop reading my thoughts."

"You're making it hard."

I moved backward and sat on the bed. Warmth invaded my cheeks. "I thought . . . I was just wondering if you were okay."

"Were you worried?"

I started to lie but stopped. "Yes."

"You don't need to worry about me." He sat beside me. "I left because I didn't know if you'd want me to be here."

My stomach churned. Couldn't blame him for thinking that. We hadn't had a chance to talk after . . . well, what had gone down between us.

"Is that not what you want?" he asked.

There were moments where I had no idea what I wanted when it came to Luc, but I'd be lying to myself if I said I didn't want to see him.

Looking over at him, my gaze met his. "I . . . I don't need space," I whispered, feeling my cheeks heat. "From you."

His gaze searched mine in that intense way of his, and then one side of his lips kicked up. "That's good."

"Yeah?"

"Yeah."

Shifting, I clasped my hands and looked away.

"Thank you," he said quietly.

"Why?" My gaze flew back to his. "Why are you thanking me?"

His head tilted to the side. "If it weren't for you, I most likely wouldn't be sitting here, Peaches. If you had run, like I'd told you, I think . . . I think this would've had a very different outcome. When you went after him, you bought me the time I needed to heal." He paused. "You saved my life."

At a lost for words, I struggled to find what to say. "I guess I owed you, didn't I?"

A faint smile crept along his lips. "I guess I'm glad you didn't listen to me."

"You're welcome." Our gazes snagged, and a long moment passed. A shiver curled along the nape of my neck. "So, um, we really didn't get a chance to talk afterward, but Micah . . . ? It was him—one of those kids. I'm . . . I'm so sorry. I can't imagine what you must be—"

"Thinking?" he cut in. "I don't know what I'm thinking, but I know I've tried to . . . forget about them. About Micah. That's wrong, isn't it?"

My brows knitted and I shook my head. "I don't think so."

"Really?" He sounded surprised.

"Yeah."

Luc sighed heavily. "I can't . . . I don't even know what to say about that—about him. There was part of me that had thought of him when you told me what he'd said to you in the school parking lot, but I didn't know about the growth hormones. Now some things make sense. You know, how violent and out-there their moods were. I don't know if knowing that they truly weren't at fault for how dangerous they were would've changed anything or not."

"I don't understand why he did this," I admitted quietly. "What he said didn't make any sense. It's, like, why go through all of this and then for what? To challenge you? Taunt you? Get you to pay attention to him? Did you understand any of this?"

"Yes. No." He flopped onto his back and stretched his arms out. The hem of his shirt rose, and a sliver of taut skin appeared. "I mean, I don't even know if he knew what he was doing. Like a damn sociopath. Do they really know why they are the way they are? Obviously, he had—"

"Issues? Lots of issues?"

Luc grinned, but his smile faded quickly. "I did let him escape, because, I told you—I thought he was okay. That out of all of them, he was going to make it. I was wrong. I got played. Looking back, I wonder if he was always behind the others, you know, manipulating them? I don't know." He paused. "But I did look for him, Peaches. Afterward. It wasn't like I forgot about him."

"I know," I whispered, thinking about what Micah had accused him of. "I wouldn't think that you hadn't."

He was quiet as he closed his eyes. "Did you hear him? At the end? He said he knew he wouldn't win a fight with me. It was like he . . ." He lifted his hands and then dragged his palms down his face. "Jesus."

I thought about what Micah had said to me about Luc. That he needed Luc to do something for him. Did he really want Luc to kill him? If so, why fight Luc and not just let him kill him? None of it made sense.

But I didn't need to be able to read minds to see that this was eating away at Luc. Heart squeezing, I reached over and lightly touched his arm. There was a snap of static, transferring from his skin to mine. His eyes opened again and he looked over at me. "Whatever his motivations were, none of it was your fault, Luc."

"Yeah," he murmured.

"I'm serious. You did everything—"

"Did I, though?" He laughed, but the sound was harsh. "What I should've done was made sure he never left that facility."

"Luc—"

"If I had, those girls would be alive. That family—"

"He said he didn't kill that family, or Andy."

His brows knitted. "And you believe him?"

"Why would he lie? I mean, he was pretty open about everything else he did." I couldn't stop the memories from roaring to the forefront of my mind. I started to pull away.

Luc caught my hand. "I'm so damn sorry this happened to you," he said. His voice roughened. "When I saw you sitting against that tree—saw what he'd done to you? I wanted to—Well, I ultimately did what I wanted to do. I never, ever want you to experience anything like that again."

I squeezed my eyes shut once more as I flinched. The fear and pain, I could almost taste them. From the moment I woke up this morning, the terror was a haunting shadow. Even with Luc, who had been there and seen the aftermath, I wasn't ready to talk about any of that.

"I know you don't want to talk about that," he said quietly, squeezing my hand. "But I'm here when you're ready."

Drawing in a shaky breath, I opened my eyes again. Luc threaded his fingers through mine. I pushed those memories aside to dwell on later, because I knew I would the moment I was alone. "What did Micah say to you? He whispered something, but I couldn't hear him."

His gaze dropped to our joined hands, and a moment passed. "Just more insanity, Peaches. That is all."

Just more insanity? I didn't believe it. I'd seen the way Luc had reacted. Micah had said something to him. I pulled my hand free.

Luc sat up. "Peaches . . . ?"

My fingers curled around my knees. "What do we do now?"

His eyes found mine. "I think there's a Godfather marathon on TV right now. We can watch that."

"That's not what I'm talking about."

"I know." He leaned toward me. "But there's nothing we can do other than live with the promise of tomorrow while knowing it may not come. That's the best you can do. Best we can do."

I stared at him. "Sometimes you sound . . . wise."

"What did I tell you? I'm omniscient."

"And then you ruin it."

He laughed. "We do whatever we normally do. This stuff that happened? It cannot rule your life, controlling every waking second. If you let that happen, then what's the point?"

I stared at him. He was right. Again. Dammit.

That now familiar half grin appeared. "It won't be easy, but I have a lot of practice when it comes to multitasking the stupid, the inane, and the important."

"Okay," I said, and then I nodded. A lot of things were up in the air, but it was going to have to be a day-by-day thing.

"I've been thinking about everything," he said after a moment.

I tensed. "That's a loaded statement."

"It is." There was a pause. "Have you?"

I knew what he was talking about. Who I really was. What I may have meant to him. What I *still* possibly meant to him. Friday night. Him. Me. Half naked.

"I have," I admitted.

Luc placed his hand on the bed beside me and leaned in. "There's something I want to make clear between us. Okay?"

"Okay."

"I know you're Evie now. I knew that the moment you walked into Foretoken. You looked like Nadia, you sounded like her, but I always knew you weren't her. Not anymore," he said quietly, his gaze latching on to mine and staying there. "Nadia was who you were. Evie is who you are now."

I swallowed hard. "Do you know who the real Evie was? She

did exist, Luc. I was given her name. She was Jason's daughter. She died in a car accident. I'm not—"

"You're not that Evie. You are *you*." He lifted his other hand and caught a piece of my hair that came loose. He tucked it back behind my ear. His fingers lingered there for the briefest moment. "And you know yourself as Evie. That's all that matters."

My lower lip trembled as I closed my eyes against the sudden rush of tears. "Is it really that simple?"

"It can be."

But it wasn't, because making it that simple meant pretending like everything was normal. I opened my eyes again. "I can't take back what I already know and I . . ." This was a big thing that was hard to admit. "I want to know more about myself—about who I used to be."

His eyes widened only slightly. "Are you sure about that?"

I nodded. "I am."

"Then we can do that," his said, his voice just as soft as mine. "You. Me. Zoe. The three of us can do that, but I want you to know that you are real."

The knot returned to my throat as raw emotion pinged around inside me, and I nodded again. Moving suddenly, I wrapped my arms around Luc. The action obviously surprised him, because he froze. That lasted only for about a second before his arms swept around me, holding me tight to him.

My face was planted against his chest. "Thank you."

"For what, Peaches?"

I let out a hoarse laugh. "I feel like there's a long list."

His hand smoothed my back, curling around the nape of my neck. "There's nothing you need to thank me for."

There was so much, probably too much based on the way the back of my throat burned.

Luc pulled away, seeming to sense that I needed physical space at the moment, and I did. The truth to who I used to be was still a messy ball of emotion. One that would be unraveled with a little bit of time, but maybe never completely.

There was a knock on the door, and a second later it opened. Mom stuck her head in, and I tensed, waiting for her to whip out a gun. Her gaze moved from me to him. "You know, Luc. You could've just used the front door."

"I could have," he replied smoothly. "But where's the fun in that?"

"Hmm." She took a deep breath and seemed to prepare herself for what she said next. "Why don't you guys come downstairs? I'm making lunch."

My eyes practically popped out of my face. Mom was making lunch, and that invite included Luc? What in the hell?

Interest filled Luc's face. "Does that lunch include grilled cheese sandwiches?"

"Actually, it does."

My mouth dropped open.

He scooted to the edge of the bed. "And tomato soup?"

"Luc," she said, and sighed.

"Does it? Because if you say yes, we're going to be new best friends, and yeah, that would be weird, with the age difference and all, but we'll get past that. I know it."

Her lips twitched. "I just put the soup on the stove."

"Hot damn," Luc murmured.

Mom looked over me. "Five minutes."

Sort of shocked, I nodded. "We'll be down in a few."

She left, leaving the door cracked open, and for some reason that made me want to laugh. It was such a mom thing to do.

And it made sense.

Because she is my mom.

My chest felt a little lighter, a little less tight.

I glanced at Luc, not at all surprised to see him watching me closely. "I think she's starting to like you."

"How could she not?" he replied. "I'm irresistible."

"I wouldn't go that far."

"Oh, I bet you would."

My lips turned down at the corners.

"You know what else I know?"

Figuring this was going to be a doozy, I sighed. "What?"

Those beautiful, downright tempting amethyst eyes met mine. "I think you're starting to like me."

Thinking back to what had happened between us on Friday night, the whole starting-to-like-him thing was pretty obvious.

Granted, I'd been overly emotional and had kissed him for all the wrong reasons, but there was no denying the attraction there or the *wanting* . . . or the blossoming curiosity when it came to him, to us.

I didn't know what lay in store for us, if anything did. Luc knew Nadia. Had even loved her. He didn't really know me, but somehow we were here again, and when I saw the half grin appear, my chest swelled and my insides knotted in delicious and scary ways.

His lips kicked up.

"Are you reading my mind?" I demanded.

"Never, Peaches."

My cheeks heated. "Okay. Two things you need to start doing. Stop calling me Peaches and stay out of my head."

Luc's lashes lowered and then swept up. "You want to head downstairs?"

"Sure." I scooted to the edge of the bed. "Wouldn't want you to miss out on your grilled cheese sandwich."

"Or tomato soup. Don't forget that."

"The horror."

Luc rose swiftly, turning to me as he extended a hand. My gaze dropped to it. He wiggled his fingers. I didn't need to take his hand. I could stand on my own, but I took it anyway, somewhat welcoming the charge of electricity that pulsed between us.

A tumble of bronze waves fell over his forehead as his fingers curled around mine. He smiled, and it reached those eyes of his and it reached something in me. Luc turned away.

I let myself smile then, when he couldn't see, and it was huge and wide, reflecting all the weird, messy, exciting, and unknown feelings banging around inside me. I smiled like I hadn't in days. Maybe weeks.

"Knew it," he murmured.

Yanking my hand free, I smacked his back and I smacked it *hard*. "Dammit, Luc!"

He laughed.

"Stay out of my head."

Luc looked over his shoulder at me. His lips curled into a teasing grin as those stunning violet eyes met mine. "Anything you wish, Peaches. Anything."

ABOUT THE AUTHOR

JENNIFER L. ARMENTROUT is the #1 *New York Times, USA Today,* Amazon, iBooks, and international bestselling author of the Lux series and other books for teens and adults. She is a #1 bestseller in Germany and Italy, and a top seller in markets around the world.

Her young adult novels have sold over a million copies since 2011 in the United States alone, and have been finalists for the Goodreads Choice Awards, a winner of the 2017 RITA award, and many others.

Jennifer lives in West Virginia with her husband and dogs.